Moving In

A.J. WOODS

First edition

ISBN: 979-8-9914136-2-6

Cover art by Spellcast Books

This book was professionally typeset on Reedsy.
Find out more at reedsy.com

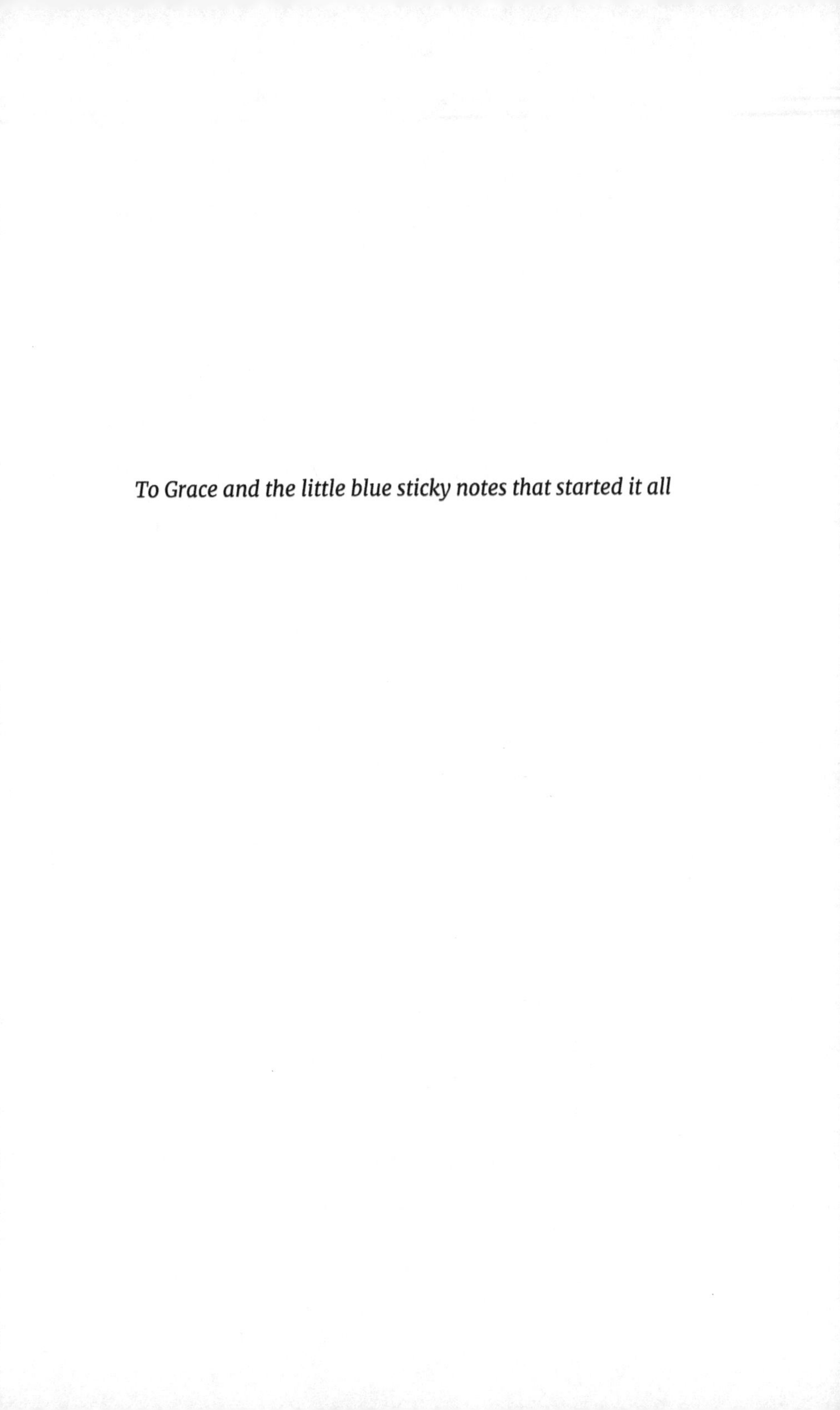

To Grace and the little blue sticky notes that started it all

JANUARY

Chapter 1

Shiloh Brooks is running seriously late. It's not necessarily his fault, seeing as how his 1995 Honda Accord decided that today, of all days, was going to be the day the duct tape and spare parts finally gave out. Today was to be the day that the car that had gotten him through pretty much every major life event since he was sixteen, was finally going to let go. The irony was not lost on him, though. It had served him well for the past ten years, despite the numerous hours he spent on getting it just to run properly and pass inspection. Today, it finally died. It finally said, *no more of this.* No more mourning the past. No more wishing things had gone differently. It was fitting, really, seeing as how today is the day he's finally getting up off his ass and making a change. Although, he wasn't sure how moving in with two strangers was going to help him. It at least was getting him off his best friend's couch which had been his home for the last few months.

Shiloh checks his watch anxiously. He's over thirty minutes late. There's no way they would still be waiting for him. He royally fucked this up. He was going to be stuck on Drew's couch for even longer now unless his best friend decided to dump him under a bridge. Shiloh thinks he deserves that right about now.

As the Uber pulls up to the local coffee shop *Brewed*, Shiloh takes a deep breath. He hopes and prays the two girls that are supposed to be waiting for him inside are still there. He thanks the driver, gives him as much of a tip as he can afford, and swings open the front door. The heater is blasting as he steps inside, and his skin instantly warms. He hears the girls before he sees them.

"Listen, all I'm saying is there must be some sort of correlation between serial killers and being late for very important meetings."

"Let's give him a chance, Ash. I'm sure he's got a good reason for being late."

"What did Brooke even say about this guy?"

"Nothing, really. He's Jordan's coworker's best friend or something like that."

Shiloh turns toward the two women sitting side by side on a blue, vinyl couch. The one with copper hair scowls at her phone while the one with brown hair stares dreamily at a man behind the counter. Neither have seen him enter as they continue their conversation. He's about seventy percent sure these are the women he's supposed to be meeting.

He takes this moment to fix his hair and straighten his flannel. Slowly, he starts toward them and clears his throat. Both women snap their eyes to him in synchrony.

"Uh, hi, are you..." he pauses, suddenly forgetting the names Jordan told him. He takes a deep breath and a chance. "Sorry I'm late. I'm Shiloh."

"Well, well, well, look who decided to finally grace us with his presence," the copper haired girl replies, arms crossed and eyes narrowed. Their coffees look mostly empty and shame floods through Shiloh. He should have been on time, and he should have remembered their names. He's pretty sure they start with the same letter, but he's drawing a blank. A complete and utter blank. He blinks at them, hoping one of them will supply their names before he has to awkwardly ask.

"Be nice," the brown-haired one says, nudging her friend. Her eyes aren't narrowed at him, and it makes Shiloh feel slightly more relaxed. "I'm Ava. It's nice to meet you." She stretches her hand out, and Shiloh takes it. Her smile is soft and as she takes her hand back, her gaze inadvertently goes back to the man behind the counter. She blushes as the man catches her gaze and smiles back.

Shiloh turns his attention to the other woman and sticks out his hand. She takes it, much more roughly than Ava, no smile to be found. "Ashtyn," she says.

Shiloh smiles and sighs, "It's good to meet you both. Again, I'm really sorry about being so late. My car, she's ancient, and she decided today was the day to finally kick the bucket. I had to take an Uber, and it wasn't necessarily in the rush that I was." He pauses as both women settle their gazes on him, sizing him up. "I, uh, would have called, but nobody gave me your numbers." It's a lame excuse but it's the truth.

It's silly, really, the idea that these two beautiful women would consider letting a perfect stranger move in with them. But then again, Shiloh is desperate and he has a sneaking suspicion that they are too. So desperate, they let their best friend's fiancée's coworker, Shiloh's best friend Drew — *Jesus that was hard to follow* — arrange a meeting between the three of them so they could see if this crazy idea could work.

An awkward silence settles over them as they stare at each other, no one knowing where to start.

"So—"

"What's your deal?" Ashtyn interrupts him. Ava sighs, taking a sip of her coffee. Shiloh swallows against his dry throat, wishing he had ordered his own drink. *This is what I get for being late*, he thinks.

"Um, so, I've been crashing on my best friend's couch for the past six months, and I think it's about time I get out of his hair."

"Why?" Ashtyn asks, eyes still narrowed.

"Well, the couch isn't the most comfortable—"

"No," she interrupts him again. "Why have you been crashing on his couch for the past six months?"

Shiloh sucks in a breath. He feels the familiar ache of his broken heart and suppresses it. He was really hoping they weren't going to ask this question. This very specific question that he cannot— no, will not— answer. He cannot bring the words to his lips: *Divorce.*

Even thinking the word sends anxiety filled goosebumps down his arms, and his throat tightens. Shame slithers its way down his spine and settles into his gut. He feels his hands clench into fists, and he has to count to three before he can even begin to think clearly again. The ring hanging on a chain around his neck burns against his chest, an ever-present reminder of his fuckups.

"Personal reasons," he says, knowing Ashtyn isn't going to like the answer. He's right, because her eyes narrow even more to where he can barely see her pupils. He knows she doesn't want this bullshit answer. He knows he should tell them the truth, but he can't. He can't, because he can't even tell himself the truth. He can't admit to himself that the one thing he was supposed to hold onto for the rest of his life slipped right through his fingers.

"If you're planning on living with us, then I expect you to be honest," Ashtyn says. Ava puts a hand on her friend's shoulder.

"Ash," she starts, but it's Shiloh's turn to interrupt.

"I'm just looking for a fresh start. I'm not a criminal or anything. I just-I need to start over and let my best friend have his living room back." Ava offers him a small smile, and Shiloh feels it loosen his anxiety, ever so slightly. Even Ashtyn relaxes a little.

"So, why do you need roommates? You can't afford something on your own?" Ava asks.

"Pretty much everything decent is a little too out of my price range," Shiloh admits honestly. "I know having roommates at twenty-six isn't exactly normal, but..."

"What do you do?" Ashtyn asks. It seems like she doesn't have time for his rambling.

"I'm a bartender. I mostly work nights, so I really won't be around during the day all that much to get in your way." The girls share a glance that conveys more than Shiloh can interpret.

"That would work out well," Ashtyn says, taking a sip of coffee. "We're both teachers. So, our paths really wouldn't cross all that much."

"Not that it would be bad if they did," Ava says, blushing slightly. "Just, that, you know, since we don't really know each other very well."

"That's perfect," Shiloh replies. "I'm pretty low-key, anyway."

"Tell us about yourself, then," Ashtyn says, her features much softer now. She's no longer scowling or glaring. "Where are you from?"

"I was born in Washington state. Lived up there until middle school and then we moved down here because of my dad's work. I've been in Texas ever since. Went to school about twenty minutes from here." The girls look at him as if to continue. "What else do you want to know?"

"I don't know. Hobbies, interests, things we should know. Girl-friend?" Ashtyn asks.

"Partner," Ava corrects her friend.

Shiloh feels the ache again and pushes it as far down as it'll go. "No, no girlfriend. I'm not really the dating type. Other than that, I don't know, I like to run, tinker with things, read-"

"You like to read?" It's Ava's turn to interrupt, her gaze fully on him for the first time since he's sat down. Her brown eyes stare at him, curiously, as if his answer is the most important thing she'll hear all day.

"Yes," he replies, easily. "I've always been a sucker for Hemingway."

Ava smiles widely at his response. "I'm a high school English teacher.

I teach *The Old Man and the Sea* every year."

Shiloh feels himself smile. "A great choice."

"Do not get her started in lecture mode," Ashtyn teases, nudging her friend and Ava lets out a laugh.

"What about you two? Shouldn't I get to know you as well?"

"I'm a kindergarten teacher, because kids make way more sense than adults," Ashtyn says, crossing her arms. "I hate sports, I love watching movies, and if you wake me up before noon on the weekends, I might actually kill you."

"She's joking!" Ava says, laughing nervously. "But she does take her sleep very seriously."

"Noted," Shiloh replies, smiling. He turns his attention toward Ava, waiting for her to speak and she blushes, as if she doesn't like talking about herself much.

"Um, besides what I already told you, I like to play soccer. I'm not very good though. I just play with some other teachers from my school in an after-school league for adults. We don't really take it seriously. Um, I also like watching movies..." She pauses like she doesn't know what else to say.

"I used to play soccer too," Shiloh supplies, and it makes Ava smile. "I played varsity for my high school."

"Oh my gosh, no way! What position did you play?"

"Midfield."

"Wow, I would have thought you were defense since you're so tall-" Ashtyn clears her throat, steering Ava back to the topic at hand. "Anyway, that's all about me. I'm pretty boring."

For some reason, Shiloh doesn't believe this. "So, why exactly do you two need a roommate anyway?"

Neither of them say anything for a moment. Ava bites her lip before beginning to speak. "Our best friend since college just moved out to live with her fiancée. The one your friend works with. And we can't afford the rent on the house without three people because this country doesn't know how to pay their fucking teachers a proper wage—" She stops herself and takes a deep breath. "Look, we've been in this house all throughout college and now past that. Yeah, we could just move to a smaller place but we're comfortable where we're at, and we just need *someone*. You'll have your own room. We won't bother you. You won't bother us."

"You haven't been able to find anyone else?" Shiloh asks. What he really means to ask is, have they not found another girl to move in with them?

"Not exactly," Ashtyn replies, finishing off her coffee. "We had a friend of a friend of a friend, kind of like you, consider it but she didn't work out."

"Are you serious about this?" Ava asks. That gaze settles on him again, and he feels himself shiver. When she's not focused on the barista behind the counter, her stare is intense. And Shiloh thought Ashtyn's glare was bad.

"I am," he says, sincerity lacing his voice. "Like I said before, I'm looking for a fresh start. I won't be a nuisance. I'll keep to myself."

"And you're not a serial killer?" Ashtyn asks. She's joking, but there's a slight tone of seriousness tinging her voice.

Shiloh feels a laugh bubble up in his throat. "I can promise you that I am not a serial killer."

The girls convey something with a silent exchange again, and Ashtyn pulls out a folder from her bag. "Here's a mock-up of how we split everything. Expenses, lease, everything's in there." She hands Shiloh the papers, and he looks through them. Everything looks perfectly in budget for what he was looking for. For the first time since he sat down, he relaxes.

"Got a pen?" he asks.

"You don't want to see the house before signing?" Ava asks, brows furrowing.

"Nah, I trust you. Besides, anything will be better than that godforsaken couch." Shiloh smiles, earning a reciprocation from both women in front of him.

Ashtyn hands him a pen, and he signs.

* * *

"Thank fuck you're leaving," Drew says, flopping next to Shiloh on the couch, toeing off his work shoes, beer in hand.

"Thanks man, love you too," Shiloh replies, zipping up his duffel bag. Looking around, he's surprised at how little he actually owns. "I'm going to have to buy bed sheets, aren't I?"

"Yes, yes you are bud," Drew says, patting his shoulder. "Look man, you know I love you, but this is going to be good for you. You're going to have your own bed again."

"Maybe it'll fix my fucked up back."

Drew laughs softly. "You know it's going to be okay, right? Jordan said these girls are great. He's known them ever since he started dating their best friend, Brooke. They're good people."

"Yeah, I'm not worried about them." A silence hangs in the air. The ring is burning against his chest again. He resists the urge to hold it in his hand.

"Were they...you know...good looking?" Drew asks suggestively, breaking the silence.

Shiloh glares at him. "Shut the fuck up, please."

"Oh, come on Shiloh, you haven't even looked at a woman since–"

"And I'm not going to start with the two women that are letting me live in the same house as them," he says angrily. He really fucking hates when Drew brings this up. "I'm done talking about this with you. And if you bring it up again, I'm not letting you help me move this weekend."

"Oh, God, no, who's going to help you move your duffel bag and two cardboard boxes?" Drew asks sarcastically, gesturing to said boxes.

Shiloh scowls. "I have stuff."

"You mean all the shit you shoved in my storage unit and haven't looked at the past six months?'

"Yes." Shiloh knows Drew is right. He has basically nothing to his name. A box of books here, a bag full of clothes there. Knickknacks and shit shoved into the small storage unit his friend was willing to help pay for. He could have taken more in the separation. Logically, he knows this, but there was no way he was going to leave her with nothing. He couldn't do it. He *wouldn't* do it. Even after all the pain...

Shiloh shakes his head forcefully, shoving the memories deep down until the pain eases.

"I'm not trying to be an ass," Drew says, lightly. "You know you could have stayed here longer...if you needed to."

"No, I need to go. I need to start moving on." The words surprise him as they leave his mouth. When he signed the lease, he felt something shift within himself. It was subtle, but it was there: *hope*. A tiny glimmer of hope that maybe he was going to be okay. Maybe this was the start he needed to get his life back on track, however slow that might be, but a start nonetheless.

"There's that relentless Shiloh Brooks optimism I used to know!" Drew exclaims, clapping Shiloh on the back. "Now, tell me about your new roomies."

* * *

Shiloh's fist pauses as he holds it up to the front door. He should knock, right? He can't just go barging in, even if his name is now on the lease. His knuckles rap the front door in three successive knocks. He tightens his jacket as the wind whips cold January air around him and Drew standing on the doorstep. Texas winters were becoming a lot colder than they had ever expected. It almost reminds him of Washington. *Almost.* Either way, he hates the cold.

Just as he's about to knock again, the door whips open, and Ava greets them with a smile, a strand of Christmas lights hanging from her shoulders. They're in the shape of red chili peppers. "Hey! Come on in, it's freezing out there," she says, ushering them inside. The warmth envelops their bones as they step over the threshold. "Excuse the mess. We're still taking down Christmas decorations." She steps over a box bursting to the brim with garlands, wreaths, and other knickknacks.

"Ash would keep them up all year round if I don't take them down now," she says, laughing softly as she untangles the strand of lights from her shoulders. She places them gently in a box.

Shiloh looks around, taking in the house. There's a kitchen to his left, a living room to his right, and stairs straight ahead. It's small but homey, a feeling that makes something like peace run through him. He tries not to think about the house he left behind.

"So, uh, do you want to see your room before you lug everything inside?" Ava asks. "Make sure it looks good?"

"Yeah, sure," he replies. "Oh, and this is Drew. My best friend."

"Ah, the owner of the infamous couch," Ava says, sticking her hand out. "Ava. Nice to meet you."

Drew takes her hand, smiling, and says, "My couch isn't the only thing that's infamous."

A deep blush overtakes Ava's cheeks as she takes back her hand. "Noted," she says, heading upstairs.

"Knock it off," Shiloh mutters under his breath to his friend. "Go get my shit from the car."

Drew takes the hint and heads back outside, leaving Shiloh to head upstairs and follow Ava. He arrives to a spacious second floor.

"This is your room," Ava says, opening the second door on the left. "We, uh, have to share the downstairs bathroom. Ashtyn won the rock, paper, scissors battle to win the master after Brooke left. Sorry."

"It's not a problem," Shiloh says. "I mean, I'm sure it'll be better than sharing one with Drew." This makes Ava laugh and he smiles in response. "Honestly, this is great." He takes in the rest of the room. There's a full-sized bed, a small desk and chair, and a bookshelf. He has to stop himself from flopping onto the bed.

"Brooke decided to leave most of her furniture," Ava says. "Thought maybe it might help sway a potential roommate."

"Well, that saves me a trip to Rooms 2 Go," Shiloh replies. "Tell her I appreciate it." There's a silence between them before Shiloh fills it. "So, how long have you and Ashtyn been friends?"

"Since elementary school," Ava says, smiling. "We pretty much grew up together. Our moms are best friends and we just clicked. We picked a college together, and we've been inseparable ever since."

Shiloh is about to reply when a thump and a shout from the front foyer interrupt him. They both start toward the front of the house when they hear Ashtyn's voice.

"Watch where you're dropping shit, you blonde fucker!" she exclaims at Drew as she hobbles on one foot.

"Hey, I'll have you know I fuck people of all hair colors," Drew says, smugly.

"Who the hell are you, and what are you doing in my house!?"

"He's with me!" Shiloh says, bounding down the stairs, Ava close on his heels.

Drew puts down the boxes he's carrying and turns his full attention to Ashtyn. "Very sorry about your foot. This blonde fucker does apologize." He sticks out his hand. "I'm Drew."

Ashtyn sizes him up, arms staying crossed in front of her chest. She doesn't say anything.

"Uh, this is Ashtyn," Ava supplies, and Shiloh catches Ashtyn's furious glare toward her friend.

"Ashtyn," Drew says, testing out her name on his lips. Shiloh watches the exchange, instantly recognizing the look that crosses his friend's face. He clears his throat, and Drew's eyes slide to him.

"You done?" Shiloh asks, jerking his thumb toward the front door.

"Just one bag left," he replies. He clears his throat. "Ladies, it was lovely to meet you. Hopefully this is not the last time."

Shiloh's out the front door, not waiting to see if the girls reply, Drew right behind him. When they get to the truck, Shiloh turns on his friend. "What the fuck was that?"

"Why, Shiloh, whatever do you mean?"

"Don't play dumb with me, Drew. I know you too well."

"I was just being polite."

"I would not call that polite."

"What, you got dibs or something?"

"They're my fucking roommates, dude. You fuck this up for me and it's your couch I'm back to crashing on."

Drew lets out a groan and scrubs his face with his hands. "Fine. Fine. I will take my...interests elsewhere."

"Appreciated," Shiloh says through gritted teeth. He grabs his last duffel bag out of the bed of the truck and slings it over his shoulder.

"I mean it, man. I won't. I won't even look at her," Drew says. Shiloh lets out a breath and grabs his friend in for a brief hug.

"Thanks, man. For, uh, everything."

"Anytime, dude. No matter what. You know that." Shiloh does, and he appreciates his friend more than he can ever express.

"I'll swing by the bar next week, okay?"

"Yeah, sounds good," Shiloh replies, releasing his friend. Drew gives him one last smack on the back before getting in the truck. He watches

Drew turn the corner and fade from view. Letting out a breath, Shiloh turns back toward the house and lets himself in.

His boxes of belongings aren't sitting in the foyer where he left them. He drops his duffel and turns right into the living room. The girls are taking ornaments off their dying Christmas tree. Behind them, taking up the entire back wall, floor to ceiling media shelves filled with...DVDs. There must be hundreds, if not thousands, of DVDs filling the shelves. They're organized alphabetically, and as Shiloh steps closer, he can see every genre of movie is present and accounted for. Drama, horror, romantic comedy, musicals, every type of movie one could ever want.

"You a big movie fan?" Ava asks, eyeing him.

"I mean, I thought I was. But this..."

"Is the best thing you've ever seen?" Ashtyn supplies.

Shiloh laughs. "Yeah, something like that."

"It's our combined collection," Ava says. "We started it in college and it's kind of spiraled out of control ever since."

"Why DVDs?" he asks.

"Nostalgia, I guess," Ava replies. "Ash and I didn't have a streaming service we could mooch off of in college, so we'd go to the DVD bargain bin at Walmart and pick as many as we could afford. Then we'd play it on my little portable DVD player in our dorm and see how long we could stay up."

"I always lost," Ashtyn says, laughing.

"Every single time."

Shiloh smiles at the two women who are now his roommates. He's about to turn and head up to his room when Ava's voice stops him.

"We have movie night every Sunday. If you're interested, you're more than welcome to join. If you're not working, that is. You don't have to if you don't want to—"

"That sounds like fun," Shiloh says, interrupting her. And he means it.

Ava bites her lip and smiles at him. "Cool. And, please, make yourself at home. This is, uh, your home now too."

"And if you can fix the garbage disposal, you'll be my new favorite person," Ashtyn says, closing up the ornament box. "Stupid landlord always takes his sweet time with maintenance here."

"Yeah, sure. I'll look at it tomorrow," he says. "I'm just gonna go get settled."

He takes the stairs two at a time and finds his boxes stacked neatly in his room. The girls must have put them in there when he was outside with Drew. This makes him smile. Then, he does what he's been wanting to do since he arrived: he flops onto the bed.

The feeling of his back pressed into an actual bed, instead of a couch, is luxurious. It's quiet in the neighborhood, too. Drew's apartment was always so noisy with downtown traffic that it made it hard for Shiloh to fall asleep most nights. He lies on the bed, letting the silence envelop him. He's alone with his thoughts, something he's been actively trying to avoid for a long time now. He will not let thoughts of Scarlett invade his new space. No, this was *his* space. His space to be alone and start over.

A laugh from downstairs carries up into his room, and he feels himself smile. Yeah, this is going to be good for him.

Chapter 2

Ava Marshall has a headache. It's not unusual for her students to give her a headache, but they're being unreasonably unruly today since they've been off school the last few weeks for Christmas break. It's her last class of the day, and she's counting down the minutes, much like her students tend to do.

She's finishing up her lecture when someone's hand shoots up from the back of the classroom.

"Do we really need to read *The Great Gatsby*, Ms. Marshall?" A blonde-haired student asks, not waiting to be called on. "I've already seen the movie."

Ava sighs. "Yes, Bailey, we do. Movies are not the same as reading the book." The students groan, making her smile. "Oh, quit your groaning. I guarantee most of you are going to love it."

"You just love to torture us," Lucas, a scrawny freshman replies.

"No, I love educating you. Sometimes it might feel like torture, but I promise you, you'll thank me one day for reading *The Great Gatsby*."

The kids groan again, but she catches a few of them smiling, slowly flipping through the pages of the book. For the past few years, she's noticed that most students end up really liking this part of the course, even if they moan and groan about it. She always tries to choose lessons that are appealing to teenagers, along with reading material that doesn't make them want to tear their hair out. It's been a process the last few years.

The final bell of the day rings, and the students jump out of their seats, hurrying out the door. A few shout their goodbyes and Ava shows her appreciation to each of them. She wants her classroom to be a place where everyone can feel seen and heard, no matter what.

"We start reading tomorrow!" Ava yells to their retreating backs. "Do not forget your books. I have extra if you need them."

Once the final student meanders out, Ava lets out a deep breath and sinks into her chair, massaging her temples. She hasn't been sleeping well. This isn't unusual for the first week back to school, but it's especially hard knowing there is a new person in the house, sleeping in the room right next door to her. The walls are thin, and sometimes she can hear Shiloh on the other side, moving around the room, listening to music softly, or talking on the phone. He's mostly kept out of their way, his presence only known by a coffee cup in the sink or a pair of shoes by the door.

The day she met Shiloh Brooks, Ava knew she might be in trouble. Even though he was over thirty minutes late, when he walked into the coffee shop with his faded flannel and dark, windswept hair, he'd made Ava tear her gaze away from Brad, the gorgeous barista behind the counter that always knew exactly what she wanted to order. Her heart skipped a tiny beat when she saw Shiloh, but she'd immediately shut down that feeling. Under no circumstances would Ava develop feelings for the guy that was to become her and Ashtyn's new roommate. Even if he is incredibly handsome, likes to read, and always seems to give her his full attention when she's speaking...

"What are y'all reading?" A man's voice makes Ava jump and goosebumps emerge on her skin. She opens her eyes to find him standing in the doorway of her classroom. He's wearing a dark blue tie dotted with tiny snowmen. It makes Ava smile.

"Hey, Derek."

"Hey, Ava. Sorry, I didn't mean to scare you."

"It's fine. I didn't see you come in."

"So, what book are the kids groaning about this semester?"

Ava barks out a laugh. "*The Great Gatsby.*"

Derek whistles as he walks into her room and sits on the edge of her desk. "Such a *torturous* book," he teases. Ava laughs again, blushing at the proximity of the high school guidance counselor. So close she can smell his cologne. It's a good distraction from the thoughts she was exploring about Shiloh. No, Shiloh is strictly off limits, and Ava's uncanny ability to develop a crush on every single person she meets will absolutely not happen with him. It will *not* happen.

"Did you hear Coach McCormack is finally retiring?" Derek asks, snapping Ava's attention back to him.

"I did," Ava replies, sadly. "I'll miss him. But, maybe now the girls' soccer team can finally win some games." She says this with some guilt. She loves Coach Mack, but he's never had much luck coaching the girls to victory.

"You wanna take over his position?"

"Yeah, I'll shout Shakespearean insults at them while I make them run laps," she jokes, making Derek chuckle. "That will definitely help them win."

"I know you're good, Ava. I've seen you play with the after-school league."

"I *used* to be good," Ava clarifies. "Now I'm just an old lady that can barely run half the length of the field without getting tired."

"Yes, turning twenty-seven really classifies you as an old lady," Derek teases. Ava blushes again. She knows she's not technically old, but damn do those kids make her *feel* old sometimes. So does playing the sport she grew up with, her body barely able to keep up with gameplay these days. In high school and college, Ava could fly down the length of the field, ninety minutes of high intensity running, and she felt the rush. Now, her body feels like dying every time she runs for five minutes. She's grateful the after-school league is just a group of teachers that used to play in college. It's informal, and no one judges her for her running speed.

Derek clears his throat, breaking her away from her thoughts. "So, did you figure out your roommate situation?"

"Oh, yeah!" she says, straightening in her chair. "Ash and I found someone."

"That's great! So, I'll meet them this weekend? At your birthday dinner?"

"I actually haven't told him about that yet," Ava admits, ignoring the way Derek's eyebrows raise at the pronoun. "He just moved in, and we haven't really spent much time with him yet." She does not mention the amount of time she's spent *thinking* about him.

"I see," Derek says, standing from the desk. His cologne wafts through the air, and it makes Ava wants to throw her arms around her coworker and take a deep breath. It's something she could never do but still secretly wishes for nonetheless.

She's known Derek Martin for the last year and a half, having bumped into him on his first official day as Lakeview High's guidance counselor. He'd been wearing an orange tie covered in tropical parrots and there was no way she couldn't *not* compliment him. When she did, he returned the favor by complimenting her "Shakespeare is lit" shirt. They'd spent their entire lunch break together in the conference room, getting to know each other. They'd been friends ever since. Ava harbored a tiny, secret crush on her friend, but he didn't need to know that. That was just for her to know. That was *always* something just for her to know.

"He'll probably be working," Ava says, not sure who she's trying to reassure in this situation. "It'll most likely just be the usual group." There's a tiny part of her that wants Shiloh to be there, just to see Derek's reaction. Not that she *wants* Derek to be jealous of a completely platonic male roommate, but it wouldn't necessarily hurt either. Sometimes Ava wishes her life was like a romantic comedy. She can picture it now: Derek arriving and seeing Shiloh. A surge of jealousy would run through him, and he'd realize how much he cares for Ava. He'd take her in his arms and kiss her senselessly...

"Well, either way, I can't wait," Derek says, putting his hand on Ava's arm, snapping her attention away from her daydream. She feels blood rush to her cheeks, hating the way her body betrays her every time Derek is around. She should *not* be harboring secret feelings for her coworker. She should not be fantasizing about it either.

"I'll see you Saturday," he says, giving her arm one last squeeze before heading out of the room.

"Yeah, see you," she replies to his retreating back. She sits in her empty classroom until her heart stops racing.

* * *

By the time Ava gets home, her headache has subsided slightly. *Slightly*, is the key word.

She drops her purse on the table in the entryway and kicks off her shoes. The house is quiet except for the sound of the shower running. Ashtyn's car isn't in the garage, so Ava assumes it must be Shiloh in the shower. To avoid running into him, she runs up to her room and closes the door behind her.

It's not that she's *avoiding* him, but she definitely needs to make sure she doesn't run into him right after a shower. She won't even let herself imagine what he looks like in a towel. Strictly off limits, even in her imagination. She knows she should probably make that a rule for Derek too...

Her phone buzzing snaps her out of her thoughts. It's a text from Ashtyn: *Hey, I'm gonna be a little late. Can you start on dinner? I know it's my night to cook but I'm stuck here finishing up a shit ton of lesson plans. I looooove being a procrastinator!!!*

Ava outwardly groans but still smiles at Ashtyn's sarcasm. She texts her back that she'll do it and then throws the phone down on her bed. She can't hear the shower anymore, so she thinks it's safe to head back downstairs. She leaves her room, turning immediately down the stairs when she runs straight into a wet, bare, heavily muscled chest.

They both reach out to steady each other on instinct, Ava's hand going to Shiloh's bare bicep, and Shiloh's hands going to Ava's waist.

"Oh my god—"

"Shit, I'm sorry—"

They both speak at the same time, hands still on each other. Ava's gaze travels over Shiloh's torso as if in slow motion. She blushes, and they both step away from each other, one down a stair and one up.

Shiloh has a towel wrapped around his waist, water falling off his wet hair. "Sorry, I didn't know anyone was home."

"No, it's okay! I just got home. Don't worry about it." She can't bring herself to look at him. At his bare chest and the water glistening on his muscles. A chain around his neck catches her attention, though. A gold ring hangs from it. It winks in the light as they begin to pass each other on the stairs, trying not to touch one another.

"I'm about to start cooking if you want to join us for dinner," Ava says, shyly. Shiloh's at the top of the stairs now, looking down at her. She's not looking at him. She's not looking at the ring hanging from his neck.

"I'm actually about to head into work. My Uber should be here any minute," he says.

"Oh, okay. Um, have a good day," Ava says, escaping into the kitchen so she can't look at his bare chest or the ring anymore.

She hears Shiloh mutter a "thank you" before closing the door to his room.

"He's just a guy," she whispers to herself. "He's just your roommate. That's it." But she can't stop thinking about the ring. He'd told them he wasn't the dating type, but that had looked suspiciously like a wedding ring... No, it couldn't be. He would have told them if he was married.

Ava rifles through the fridge, looking for something to cook to keep her mind occupied and away from thoughts of Shiloh. She's stirring her Alfredo sauce when Shiloh heads out the front door, getting into the Uber without even a "goodbye." A few moments later, Ashtyn walks through the door.

"Honey, I'm home!" she shouts from the foyer.

"Good, dinner's almost ready."

"Thank you, you're a Godsend," she replies. She heads into the kitchen and takes a deep breath. "I'm starving."

They catch each other up on their respective days as Ava drains the pasta and separates it into bowls. "So, uh, I kind of ran into Shiloh today," she says, settling into the dining table.

Ashtyn sits across from her. "I mean, he does live here."

"I mean, I kind of ran into him after he got out of the shower."

Ashtyn nearly chokes on her pasta. "Was he naked!?"

"No! I mean, yes. But he had a towel on. I only saw his chest."

"And how was it?"

"Ashtyn!" Ava blushes. "I was mortified." She doesn't mention the ring. It feels too intimate to mention.

"Well, we all live together now. I'm sure you'll see him shirtless again."

"Absolutely not!" Ava exclaims. "Not if I can help it."

"Ave, don't be a prude. We all live together. It's bound to happen,"

Ashtyn says nonchalantly.

"But...he's so good looking." She knows she shouldn't be admitting this to Ashtyn, but she can't help herself. It just slips out.

"So am I!" Ash exclaims. "So are you. So are most people on this planet. Doesn't mean you have to lose your mind every time you have to interact with them."

Ava sighs, rolling her eyes. "You know what I mean, Ash."

"I do. But I also know how much you get inside your own head. So, get out of it before you mess up the best roommate we've had since Brooke." Ava knows Ashtyn isn't being mean. She's just direct.

"Have you even talked to him since he moved in?" Ava asks.

"A few times. But that's why I like him. He keeps to himself and doesn't bother me. And he fixed the garbage disposal."

"Yeah, well, you haven't had to run into him while he's dripping wet and shirtless."

"Ava, I swear to God if you make a big deal out of this..."

"I won't! I swear."

Ashtyn looks at her skeptically. If there is one person on this earth that knows Ava better than she knows herself, it's Ashtyn. "Ava, I say this with the utmost love, but please do not add him to your never-ending list of crushes."

The words, even though Ashtyn says them gently, hit their mark right in Ava's heart. They settle there, making themselves at home so she'll always remember them when she's at her worst. They sit amongst the other things she constantly tells herself: She's "boy crazy." She's always looking for love in the wrong place. She'll date "anyone." Don't smile at Ava or she'll fall in love with you.

Shame floods her and her cheeks heat. Her mom always says Ava's been looking for love since she came out of the womb. She can't help it that she's always been drawn toward the idea of it. Her parents have been married for almost thirty years and are totally in love with each other. She grew up watching romantic comedies and reading epic love stories. She couldn't help but fall in love with love, and she's been chasing it ever since. However, bad boyfriend after bad boyfriend has tainted her view of love the past few years. And yes, she does tend to have a lot of crushes on different people in her life, but it's never serious. Sure, she thinks Brad the barista is swoon worthy, but there's no way she'll ever talk to him outside of getting her morning coffee. And Derek? He's her coworker and friend. There's no way it'll ever get past that. Finally, Shiloh? Never, ever, ever would she think of him as anything other than a friend. So that takes her crush list down to zero. An all-time low for her.

"For your information, my crush list, as you like to call it, is completely empty at the moment and I intend to keep it that way," Ava says matter-of-factly.

Ashtyn looks at her skeptically. "So, when Derek comes over this weekend for your birthday party, you're not going to look at him longingly like you always do?"

Ava flings a piece of spaghetti at her friend. "No, I will not."

"I'm going to hold you to that," Ashtyn says, the flung piece of spaghetti still dangling from her face. Ava can't help but laugh with her best friend.

Chapter 3

Taylor Swift is playing through the speakers. It is a universal truth acknowledged by every twenty something year old that Taylor Swift must be playing if there is a party. At least, with Ava and Ashtyn it is. So, her entire discography is on a continuous loop throughout the house. Taylor's Version only.

The front door opens and Shiloh breezes in, shutting the door behind him as quickly as possible to avoid letting any cold air in.

"Hey," he says, entering the kitchen. His cheeks are flushed and he shrugs off his jacket, hanging it in the coat closet.

"Hi," Ava replies, surprised to see him. It's been a few days since the towel incident and neither have said a word about it. Best to pretend it never happened, for both their sakes. It's barely seven, and all her friends will be here at any moment. She didn't expect him to be here. "Everything okay?"

"Yeah, sorry, Jeff mixed up the work schedule and sent me home. I'm just...gonna go hang out in my room. I'll stay out of y'alls way." He turns to go upstairs, but Ava stops him.

"No, please stay. It's not a big group, and we always have so much leftover food."

Shiloh pauses at the foot of the stairs, looking uncertain. "Are you sure? It's your birthday, and you still barely know me." Ava avoids his gaze, definitely not thinking about him in a towel.

"I'm sure," she says, "All roommates are invited to birthday parties. It's the best way to get to know each other. You can even call Drew if you want. You know, in case you hate all my friends."

Shiloh laughs. "I'm not going to hate your friends. But, uh, are you sure I should call Drew? Ashtyn doesn't really seem to like him."

"It's my party, and she can get over it," Ava says. "Call him." Shiloh smiles and heads upstairs, phone in hand.

Ava stands over the kitchen sink, watching out the window as a car pulls up to the side of the street. It's Derek, which she suspected. Derek is always the first one to any of their hangouts. The moment the doorbell rings, Ashtyn bounds down the stairs and answers it.

"Hey, Derek!" she exclaims, letting him inside. Ava knows Ashtyn will be watching her all night, seeing if she can spot her lusting over her coworker, just to prove a point.

Ava had a good long talk with herself this morning. She is going to shut down this stupid crush on her completely platonic coworker. Nothing good could come of it. The daydreams will stop. The fantasizing will stop. She can do this. She can absolutely get over this stupid, little crush.

Ava can see them from her spot in the kitchen, and she can't help but notice the way Derek's gaze settles on Ashtyn. She's gorgeous, long, copper hair twisted into a French braid that falls down her back. Her dark green jumpsuit that hugs her body is the exact shade of her eyes. Ava knows her best friend is beautiful. It's just a fact of life, but it still stings a little when Derek looks at her like he knows it too. She squashes the sting deep, deep down into her subconscious where it will ruminate.

Ava enters the foyer, and Derek tears his gaze away from Ashtyn.

"There's the birthday girl!" he exclaims, hugging her. Ava does her best not to lean too heavily into the hug. "Happy birthday," he whispers in her ear, causing goosebumps to pop up on her arms. Stupid, traitorous brain.

"Thanks," she replies, hiding her blush in his shoulder. The doorbell rings, pulling them apart, and Ashtyn goes to answer it, eyes narrowed toward Ava in suspicion.

Ava already knows it's Brooke and Jordan. They always arrive right after Derek. After that it will be Daisy, Ashtyn's coworker and mutual friend of the girls. Next, Parker and his husband Damien, both fellow teachers at Ava's school and teammates on the soccer league. Ava feels lucky to have made such good friends with her coworkers. Making friends after college is a lot harder than she thought it would be, hence why it took so long to find a new roommate.

As everyone slowly arrives at their respective times, Ava greets them all with a smile and a hug. It isn't until she hears Shiloh's voice that she realizes he's finally come downstairs. He's put on another one of his flannels and combed through his dark hair. He shakes Derek's hand, and Ava has to look away. She doesn't care how Derek feels about Shiloh. She *won't* care.

"I see you," Ashtyn whispers behind her, breath tickling her ear.

"I know. So, you can see that I don't have a crush on Derek," Ava replies, voice low.

"Sure." Another voice makes her jump.

"Jesus Christ, Brooke," Ava says, turning to her other best friend.

Brooke hands her a glass of wine as an apology and smiles. "Sorry. Just wanted to know what you two were whispering about over here. Turns out it's old news." Just as Ava is about to interject, the doorbell rings again.

"I thought everyone was here?" Ashtyn questions, starting toward the door. Before Ava can warn her who it is, Ashtyn flings open the door and stands face to face with Drew. She stops abruptly.

"Who invited *him*?" she asks icily, a frown taking over her face.

"Nice to see you again too, Red," Drew says, an ever-present charming smile on his face. He breezes past her and into the foyer. "Ava, happy birthday. I'm sorry I wasn't informed of this sooner, so this was all I could find on short notice." He produces a bottle of white wine from a paper bag. "I hope it will suffice."

"Thank you, Drew," Ava replies, taking the bottle from him. "I'm glad you could make it." As Drew claps hands with Shiloh and Jordan, Ashtyn takes Ava's arm and drags her into the kitchen.

"What the hell is *he* doing here?" she hisses.

"Shiloh came home early, and I didn't want him to not know anyone here," Ava says, placing the wine on the counter. "I told him he could invite Drew. You know, to make him more comfortable."

"He knows Jordan," she shoots back.

"Barely, and you know it," Ava replies.

"I can't stand that smug bastard."

"Ash, you barely know him. Will you just please be nice? It's my birthday, after all."

Ashtyn sighs, and her face softens. "Fine, but only because it's your birthday."

"Besides, Jordan works with him, and I've never heard him say anything bad about him."

"That's because Jordan is too nice for his own good," Ashtyn mutters, pouring her own glass of wine.

"Did I hear my fiancée's name?" Brooke asks, rejoining the girls.

"Just that we're very grateful he was able to help us find a room-mate," Ava says.

"Oh, yeah, I've been meaning to ask y'all how Shiloh's been doing here. He looks a lot better."

"Better?" Ashtyn questions.

"Yeah, he's been really torn up ever since his divorce and—"

Both girls freeze at Brooke's words. "Divorce?" They ask at the same time. Ava's mind immediately goes to the ring on a chain around his neck.

"Oh shit, did he not tell you?" Brooke asks, her face falling. "Shit, I thought it would have come up by now. Although, now that I think about it, he's never been one to really tell people his life story. I mean, I don't even know him *that* well, just what Jordan's told me. And that information really only comes from Drew, so I should have realized..." Brooke's babbling now, unable to stop the spew of words coming from her mouth.

It isn't until Ava sees Shiloh entering the kitchen that she shoves a homemade mozzarella stick into Brooke's mouth, silencing her. Ashtyn gulps her wine hurriedly, and Ava follows suit.

"Hey, uh, just looking for a drink," Shiloh says. If he notices the awkward silence, he doesn't say anything. It's silent for a moment longer, Taylor Swift's voice the only thing anyone can hear, while Ava and Ashtyn swallow their wine, composing their faces to say that they definitely do not know anything about any divorce. Or any ring on a chain.

Ava grabs the bottle of wine Drew brought and hands it to Shiloh. "Sorry, all we have is wine." She turns to grab a glass out of the cabinet for Shiloh, but it slips from her fingers. Before it can crash to the floor, Shiloh reaches out and catches it.

"Bartender reflexes," he says, smiling softly. None of the girls say anything as he pours himself a glass and heads into the dining room where everyone else has gathered.

"Forget I said anything," Brooke whispers before making her way toward her fiancée.

Ava and Ashtyn share a look and know exactly what the other is thinking: Do not bring up the divorce.

It bothers Ava only a little that Shiloh didn't tell them. It makes sense though, if it's still a sore subject for him, that he doesn't want to share that information with strangers. Still, Ava wishes he had told them. It's not that it changes the way she feels about him, but it definitely puts things into perspective on why he needed a place to live. And also why he has a ring around his neck. Ava wouldn't have pegged him as divorced. When he'd said he wasn't the dating type, she had made the assumption that he was more of the sleeping around type. Shame floods through her. She's made a lot of assumptions about her new roommate the last few weeks without even really talking to him. It was incredibly unfair to Shiloh, and Ava knows it. Tonight, she is going to change that.

Everyone is gathered around the dining table that is covered with an elaborate charcuterie board, various snacks, and so many of Ava's favorite desserts.

"Oh my God, Parker, I can't believe you made *this* many different kinds of cookies," Ava says, sampling one. Besides being a freshman English teacher, Parker is the designated baker of the group and always brings the goods to their get-togethers.

"I couldn't decide which one to make, so I just made all your favorites," Parker replies, smiling. "Hey, you gonna introduce me to your handsome new roommate?"

Ava blushes and smacks him on the arm. "Watch it," she warns. "Uh, hey, Shiloh!" she calls and beckons him over. He makes his way over, glass of wine in hand, lazy smile on his face. He's at ease, and it makes Ava feel slightly better. "Hey, I wanted to introduce you to my friend and colleague, Parker."

Shiloh extends his hand. "Nice to meet you, man. You two work at the same school?"

Parker takes Shiloh's hand easily. "Yeah, we're in the same department. And this is my husband, Damien."

"Nice to meet you," Damien booms, his voice always the loudest in the room. "I'm at the school too. Choir teacher, if you couldn't tell by my lovely baritone."

"Wow, I didn't realize how many coworkers actually like each other," Shiloh jokes. "Derek told me he's at the school as well."

"Yeah, we got really lucky," Parker says, smiling lovingly at his spouse.

"Do you not like your coworkers?" Ava asks, trying to pry any personal details out of this mystery of a man.

"No, I do. I'm just...not close with them outside of work. We don't hang out." Ava has a sneaking suspicion that Shiloh doesn't really hang out with anyone other than Drew. The thought saddens her.

"Well, we're a close bunch, but we're glad you're here," Parker says, clapping him on the back.

"Honestly, I think we're just all relieved the girls finally found a roommate," Damien replies.

"Well, I'm glad I could help," Shiloh says, smiling at Ava. She feels a familiar tingle shoot down her stomach which she tries to ignore. She excuses herself and heads back into the kitchen to pour herself another glass of wine.

Ashtyn, Brooke, and Jordan are huddled around the island, chatting idly. "What are y'all talking about?" Ava asks, sidling up to her friends.

"Nothing," Brooke says, avoiding eye contact. Ava narrows her eyes at her friends.

"Hey, it seems like things worked out with Shiloh," Jordan says, changing the subject.

Ava chooses to take his cue. "Yeah, he's nice."

"His friend on the other hand," Ashtyn mutters, staring daggers at Drew from across the room.

"Drew's a good guy, Ashtyn," Jordan says. "I wouldn't have suggested his friend for your roommate if I didn't trust him. Besides, you're probably going to have to get used to him, because he's going to be one of my groomsmen at the wedding."

"What!?" Ashtyn exclaims loudly, causing everyone to turn her way. She lowers her voice. "You're good enough friends with that fucker that he's going to be in the wedding?"

"Well, you know how many bridesmaids Brooke has. She's got y'all plus her three sisters, and I was one man short. I figured Drew would be a good fit cause we get on really well at work."

Ashtyn groans loudly and smacks her forehead. "You didn't invite Brandon, did you?" Ava is shocked to hear Ashtyn's ex's name come out of her mouth. She never talks about Brandon. Ever.

"No, of course not," Jordan says, serious. "Don't be ridiculous."

"Well, thank God for that," she mutters as she stalks toward the living room and out of earshot. She purposely throws Drew a death glare, and he returns it with a smile and a wink.

"Those two are either going to kill each other or fuck each other," Jordan says, earning a smack on his shoulder by his fiancée.

Ava laughs. "My bet is both."

"Alright, who's ready for Blockbuster?" Ashtyn yells from the living room, holding up the game box. Everyone cheers and heads toward the living room, except for Shiloh and Drew who just look at each other confused.

"Blockbuster as in the extinct movie chain?" Drew asks.

"It's not extinct," Ashtyn replies matter-of-factly. "There's one left in Oregon that's still open. And you better watch it, because I will not allow any Blockbuster slander in my house."

"Okay, okay," Drew says, raising his hands. "How do you play this game anyway?"

"Everyone splits into teams," Ava says, taking charge. Board game rules are her forte. "Then, you have to try and get your partner to guess three different movies in three different ways. The first way is with only one word to describe the movie. The second is a quote from the movie or one that describes it, and the last way is charades."

"Seems easy enough," Shiloh says.

"You ready to kick some ass, Ava?" Derek asks, sidling up to her. Every time they play this game they have the same teams. Ava and Derek, Brooke and Jordan, Ashtyn and Daisy, and Parker and Damien. They've never included new people before.

"Actually, why don't I team up with Shiloh?" Ava suggests. "Since he's never played before, it'll be easier if we're on a team. Ash, you can be on Drew's team. And Derek you can play with Daisy."

The entire room freezes. Ashtyn is shooting daggers in Ava's direction. Derek doesn't seem to know what to say. Everyone else is looking down into their drinks. They never switch up the teams. It's always been the same, every time they're together. Ava's shaken up tradition.

"Hey, that sounds good to me!" Drew exclaims, breaking the tension.

Ashtyn grimaces. "Ava, can you help me with something in the kitchen please?" she asks through gritted teeth. Ava sighs but follows her best friend anyway.

Once they're alone, Ashtyn whirls on her. "Okay, I know what you're doing in trying to distance yourself from Derek, but why do I have to suffer by playing with Drew? Why don't you play with him?"

"Because it's my birthday and I chose Shiloh. Deal with it."

Ashtyn narrows her eyes. "If Shiloh becomes a Derek situation, I swear to God..."

"Ashtyn," Ava warns, feeling her patience wearing thin. "He's our roommate. I am just trying to get to know him better, so we can all be friends. Can you relax?"

Ashtyn doesn't relax but says, "Fine, since it's your birthday. But just know, I am not happy about being paired with Drew, and I am watching you like a hawk."

"Whatever makes you happy." The girls head back into the living room and join their respective partners.

Turns out, Derek and Daisy make excellent partners. Better than Ava and Derek ever had. They are crushing everyone else. Ava knew they got along, everyone here gets along, but she never knew how much Derek and Daisy truly had in common. Had she been hogging Derek all to herself this whole time, because she had a stupid crush? Maybe he'd wanted to be partners with Daisy, and he'd never gotten the chance because it was expected that he was Ava's... She feels her cheeks burn as Derek and Daisy high-five, having won all their points.

Next up is Ashtyn and Drew. Ashtyn groans loudly. "These are way too hard! He's never going to get them."

"Hey, have a little faith in me," Drew says, clutching his hand to his heart.

Ashtyn rolls her eyes but starts the timer. "Okay, one word: Neo."

"Easy! *The Matrix*."

"That was the only easy one. Okay, quote it: 'I'm like the longest religious movie in existence.'"

Drew frowns for a moment, "That's not a quote from a movie."

"It doesn't have to be a direct quote," Ashtyn snaps. "It can be a quote describing the movie." She repeats her quote.

Drew pauses, considering his options. "*Ben-hur*?"

Ashtyn seems stunned. "How the fuck did you get that?" she asks, a smile cracking onto her face.

"Because I'm a fucking genius! Hurry, do the charades!!"

Ashtyn looks at her card one last time and starts doing her charades. She acts out some kind of shootout that has Drew stunned. Ava's pretty sure she knows what Ash is trying to convey, but it's extremely difficult.

"Oh my god, this could be any fucking action or western movie on the planet," Drew complains, eyes furrowed in confusion. Ashtyn's acting becomes more and more frantic.

Drew guesses wrong a few times, only seconds left on the clock. "Fuck, I don't know! *Butch Cassidy and The Sun*—" He doesn't get to finish, because Ashtyn is screaming "YES!" and throwing herself at him, enveloping him in a bone crushing hug. Ava's mouth drops open in surprise, and she shares a glance of disbelief with Shiloh.

As soon as Ashtyn realizes what she's doing, she releases Drew and steps back a fair amount. She clears her throat awkwardly. "Uh, good job. We, uh, get all the points."

Drew has a slightly dazed look on his face, pink tinging his cheeks. "Yeah, good teamwork," he says.

"Okay, our turn!" Ava interrupts before Ashtyn can even think about what she just did. Ava and Shiloh make an okay team but not great. Turns out, Shiloh is severely lacking in his movie knowledge.

"What do you mean you've never seen *The Silence of the Lambs*!?" she exclaims. "It's like, the one horror movie everyone and their mother has seen."

"Sorry, horror movies aren't really my thing," Shiloh responds.

"Oh, we're going to change that," Ava teases, putting the cards back in the stack.

Derek and Daisy ultimately win the game, putting everyone else to shame.

"Man, we should have been partners sooner!" Daisy says, smiling. Ava can't help but silently agree, even though it pains her.

"Hey, I was a perfectly good partner," Ashtyn interjects.

"Yes, but you're also way more competitive than I am."

"Says the winner," Ashtyn grumbles.

It's getting late, and everyone starts gathering coats and leftovers to take home. Ava says goodbye to each of her friends individually, thanking them for coming. Derek kisses her on the cheek, something he does to everyone, and she tries her absolute hardest not to blush. She doesn't miss the way he walks Daisy to her car. Once everyone is gone and the dishes are stacked in the dishwasher, Ava relaxes.

Shiloh enters the kitchen, looking comfortable and right at home. "Hey, thanks for letting me crash," he says. "I had a good time. Your friends are a lot of fun."

Ava smiles. "Good, I'm glad you had a fun time."

Shiloh hesitates for a moment before stepping closer and holding his arms out for a hug. Surprised, Ava steps in, accepting. It's awkward, at first, and then it feels natural.

"Happy birthday," he whispers.

"Thanks, Shiloh," she replies, not wanting to let go. When he does, she steps back and watches him head up the stairs.

"Well, that was fun," Ashtyn says, startling Ava out of her thoughts.

"Oh, it definitely looked like *you* had fun," she teases her friend.

Ashtyn blushes but frowns. "Do not mention what happened ever again," she says. "I cannot be held accountable for my lapse in judgment during games."

"Okay, okay," Ava says, holding her hands up in surrender. "Maybe you'll be nicer to him now, though?"

"I will never be nice to a blonde man," Ashtyn replies, heading up the stairs for bed. Ava sighs but smiles. Baby steps.

MARCH

Chapter 4

It's been about six weeks since Shiloh moved in with the girls, and he can honestly say he's feeling better than he has since the divorce. He isn't healed by any means, but it's easier not to think about when he's busy working and trying not to run into Ava while in a towel.

It happened so long ago, but it still comes back to Shiloh on occasion. The way her eyes traveled up his body and her lips pursed into a perfect "o." Her pupils dilated, a blush splayed across her freckled cheeks, her fingers gripping his bicep, his on her waist as they steadied themselves. He could tell she was embarrassed. So embarrassed that she'd missed the way his cock had hardened under his towel. At least, he hoped she missed that. Just a look and a brief touch from her had aroused him. It's been so long since he last had sex. It's just been him and his hand for the past year, and even that was starting to leave him unsatisfied. He hadn't thought about another woman since Scarlett. He barely looks at anyone, even the ones that flirt with him at work. It's been unbearable to think of anyone other than Scar...

Shiloh shakes his head and clears his thoughts, focusing on the work in front of him. The bar is packed for trivia night and he's swamped, making drinks as fast as he possibly can. He keeps looking toward the entrance to see when Ava and Ashtyn arrive.

They've been slowly starting to feel more comfortable around each other, especially after Ava's birthday party. So, he decided to invite them to the bar's trivia night, and they happily accepted. Their Spring Break started today, and they were itching to get out of the house, ready to forget about teenagers and kids for the rest of the week.

The MC is setting up at the stage, and the music is blaring. Shiloh can already feel a headache forming behind his temples. Normally, the music doesn't bother him, but for some reason he's feeling the pressure tonight to impress his roommates. He doesn't want them to think he works in a dump or to not have a good time. Ever since he moved in, he's felt the need to prove himself as a good roommate. They've eaten a few dinners together and had a few movie nights that made Shiloh feel almost normal for the first time in a long time. When he's with the girls, he's not thinking about Scarlett or his divorce or anything else terrible in his life. He's just existing as himself, and that's all he can hope for right now.

Shiloh sees Drew cross the room and head toward him. "Hey, man, you here for trivia?"

"Yeah, sure, that's why I'm here," Drew replies, eyeing the front door. It's at that moment, as Shiloh turns toward the entrance, that Ava and Ashtyn walk in with Brooke and Jordan.

"What does she drink?" Drew asks, his eyes never leaving Ashtyn. She's wearing a floral romper that shows off her legs, an asset that Drew is very much appreciating at the moment. Her red hair is piled up high on her head in a bun. Ava is wearing jeans and a black blouse, her brown hair cascading down her back.

"I have no idea," Shiloh replies, shrugging.

"What do you mean you don't know?" he asks, annoyed. "Shouldn't you know this by now?"

"They've never been here, man. I don't know what she drinks."

"Okay, just get me two martinis then."

"Martinis? Seriously?"

"Fuck, man, I don't know! I'm drowning over here. She's giving me nothing." Drew's still watching the girls as they approach, or more accurately, watching Ashtyn. He's been down bad ever since Ava's birthday party when Ashtyn crushed him into a hug after they won their round in Blockbuster. Shiloh reminded Drew that he promised he wasn't even going to look at her, but Drew had retorted that Shiloh hadn't felt that hug.

Shiloh rolls his eyes but grabs the correct glasses. "Okay, two martinis coming up." He catches the girls' eyes and gives them a smile and a wave. Ashtyn smiles and then sees Drew. The smile immediately turns into a scowl.

"Hi, Drew," Ava says, politely. Jordan and Drew clap hands, and Brooke gives him a hug. Ashtyn, however, is leaning on the bar and ignoring him.

"I got you a drink," he says, trying to catch Ashtyn's gaze.

She's not playing into his game. She looks around the bar, everywhere but at Drew. "Oh, really?"

"Wasn't sure what you like so I guessed."

Shiloh places the martini in front of Ashtyn and gives her a small smile. "Made with love."

Ashtyn eyes it for a moment, nothing on her face giving away how she's feeling. Suddenly, she's leaving and heading toward a table without saying a single word. The drink sits on the bar untouched. An awkward silence hangs over the group, music blaring in the background.

"Well, I for one, love martinis," Ava says, taking the glass. She goes to follow her best friend and pats Drew on the arm. "It's too strong, buddy. Take it down a notch."

Shiloh can see Drew's jaw working. He's not used to trying this hard to get someone to notice him. Shiloh sets the second martini down in front of his friend. "Go join their trivia team and woo her with your infinite knowledge of mathematical equations."

"Fuck off," Drew says, downing the drink in a few gulps. He does take Shiloh's advice though and joins their trivia table. Shiloh shakes his head, but he smiles and turns his attention toward the group of women flagging him down at the end of the bar.

Trivia night always gets him a really good paycheck. He knows he can put on his Shiloh Brooks charm and flirt with countless women to better his chances of getting tips. Tonight, though, he feels something weird settle in his stomach. Does he not want the girls to see him shamelessly flirt for money or is it something more? He still hasn't told them about the divorce, and there's a tiny bit of guilt that lives in him as a result. The ring under his shirt burns. He's not sure if Ava saw it when she ran into him that day. He had been much too preoccupied in keeping his hard on from showing. He's been thinking of taking the ring off for a while now, but every time he goes to grab it, his heart squeezes and a wave of nausea rolls through his stomach. He's never been able to get the chain over his head. His hand just stills, and he drops it hopelessly. So, for now, the ring lives around his neck and that's where it'll stay. He tries to squash his feelings and takes the drink orders from the women at the end of the bar.

He's polite, but he tones down his usual charm. He makes the drinks quickly but skillfully. He hands them to the women with a smile but doesn't stay to chat. It's then that he sees Ava coming up toward the bar. His coworker, Josh, makes his way toward her, but Shiloh stops him.

"I got it, man," he says, stepping in front of him. Josh just raises his hands in defeat and turns to take a different order. Shiloh turns toward Ava and gives her a smile. "Hey."

"Hi," she says. She has her empty martini glass in her hand. "It was really good.”

“I told Ashtyn it was made with love, but I guess she didn’t believe me.”

Ava laughs and looks over her shoulder at her friends. “If he’s trying to impress her, try a gin and tonic next time.”

“Noted,” Shiloh says, taking her empty glass. “You want another one?”

“Uh, yeah, sure.” She takes out her credit card and starts to hand it to him.

“First one’s on me,” he says, ignoring her card and starts to make her drink.

“You don’t have to do that!” she protests, trying to give him the card again.

“Ava, what’s the point in having a bartender roommate if you can’t at least get one free drink?”

“Technically, I’ve had two since I’m assuming Drew paid for the first one.”

“Touché. Doesn’t matter though. I’m not letting you pay for this drink.” He sets the martini in front of her and pushes the card back.

“Fine,” Ava says and rolls her eyes. She takes a sip of the drink and sighs. “God, this is good.”

Shiloh can sense the other patrons of the bar looking at them. He knows he shouldn’t linger. He shouldn’t be giving her special attention, even if she is his roommate. Even if they’re starting to become friends.

“You’re pretty popular here, aren’t you?” Ava asks, gesturing discreetly to the group of women at the end of the bar watching them. One lady actually wiggles her eyebrows at him when she catches his gaze.

Shiloh shrugs. “I guess.”

“Don’t be modest,” she says, taking another sip of her drink. “They’re ogling you.”

Shiloh turns his head toward the women and they wave, smiling sweetly and batting their eyes at him. It gives him an uneasy feeling. "They just want free drinks."

"And does it ever work?"

Shiloh shakes his head. "Nope."

"I got one, though."

"You're different."

Ava blushes and takes another sip of her drink. Shiloh knows he should be taking other orders, but he can't tear himself away from his roommate.

"They're still staring at you," Ava whispers, her voice barely carrying over the MC speaking into the microphone. She's watching the women out of the corner of her eye.

"I don't care," Shiloh replies. Ava's about to say something when Ashtyn comes bounding up the bar.

"Hey!" she exclaims. "They're about to start trivia."

"Sorry, I got distracted," Ava replies. She takes her drink and heads back to the table without a second glance toward Shiloh.

"Want a drink before it starts?" Shiloh asks Ashtyn. Her personality is so different than Ava's that sometimes he wonders how they ever became friends.

"God, yes please."

"What would you like? First one's on me, but you're on your own if you want anymore."

"Oh, I'm sure I can find some ole sap's tab to put the rest of my drinks on," Ashtyn says, narrowing her eyes toward Drew mischievously. "I'll take a gin and tonic."

"Be nice to him," Shiloh says as he starts to make her drink. "I know he made a bad first impression, but he's a good guy."

Ashtyn holds up her hands. "You can save your breath. I've already gotten the whole spiel from Jordan."

"Yeah, but I know Drew better than Jordan. He's been my best friend since middle school."

"Shiloh, I don't care how long you've known him. I'm not going to change my mind about Drew."

Shiloh sighs and sets her drink in front of her. "Fine, but you could at least be civil."

"No promises," Ashtyn replies, taking a sip. "Fuck, that's good. Now, go talk to those ladies over there before they drool all over the bar."

Ashtyn spins away toward her friends, and Shiloh sighs deeply. He turns toward the group and turns on his most charming smile. "Ladies! What can I get for you this evening?"

* * *

Team *Tequila Mockingbird* is losing spectacularly. It's actually comical how badly they're losing. The MC just announced the rankings before the last round and they are dead last. Although, it really doesn't seem fair since Shiloh told them it was supposed to be general trivial. All night, the questions have mostly focused on historical events and *Star Wars.*

"Come on, where's the pop culture trivia!?" Ashtyn exclaims. They're all a little tipsy and grumpy about losing. "At least throw some Taylor Swift knowledge in there!"

"This game is rigged for history nerds and...just nerds in general," Jordan says, finishing off his bourbon.

Ava scowls. "What are we in high school? Who calls someone a nerd anymore? Besides, you're a math nerd."

Jordan raises his hands in surrender. "Okay, fair point."

"If this trivia was about books, you'd all be worshiping the nerd ground I walk on."

"Yes, we would!" Ashtyn replies, smacking a kiss to her friend's cheek. "Okay, I'm going to go close out our tab before this last round."

Drew stands, taking out his wallet. "I'll get it."

Ashtyn narrows her eyes, and then it's a race between them to the bar, both holding out their cards toward Shiloh. Ava laughs, feeling all the alcohol she's consumed warming her insides.

"I have never seen Drew this down bad," Jordan says, getting out his own wallet and making his way over to the bar.

"Really?" Ava asks, turning toward Brooke.

"I don't know him as well as Jordan does," she starts, "but it's true. Drew's never been one to really...chase. Most of the time people just flock toward him."

Ava rolls her eyes. "Well, Ash isn't the type to flock."

"I think we all know that, Ave," Brooke says, patting her on the arm. Sometimes she misses having Brooke live with them, but she's ultimately happy that she found her soulmate. And Shiloh's been a good addition to the group.

They finish their last round of trivia, and even with two correct answers, they still end up dead last. As they gather up their coats and head toward the exit, they stop by the bar to bid Shiloh goodbye.

"Hey, you tell those trivia moderators to add some goddamn litera-ture next time," Ava says, making Shiloh laugh.

"I'll let Jeff know. Be safe getting home. I'll be there late."

As they leave the bar, the cold welcomes them. It's March, and while the days are becoming warmer, the nights are still brisk. Ava silently wishes for summer. They bid goodbye to their friends and wait patiently for their Uber.

"I told you we should have ordered it while we were still in there," Ashtyn grumbles, holding her arms against her chest.

"And I told you we should have just shared one with Brooke and Jordan," Ava retorts.

Ashtyn shudders. "Ugh, they always get so touchy-feely with each other when they're tipsy. They're all in love and shit."

"You know..." Ava can't even finish her thought before Ashtyn is glaring at her.

"Do not even finish that sentence."

"You don't even know what I was going to say!"

"I know exactly what you were going to say, and I don't want to hear it."

"I'm just saying Drew is attractive—"

"LA LA LA LA!" Ashtyn screams, covering her ears and taking off down the street away from Ava.

"Ash!" Ava exclaims, running after her friend. Her heeled boots are absolutely not made to be run in.

"I'm not listening to you!" Ashtyn keeps running until she's in the neighboring alleyway.

"Ash, we gotta wait for the Uber—" She's about to continue when she turns the corner and sees Ashtyn crouched in the alley. There's a tiny, white fluffball sitting at her feet, meowing pitifully.

"Ava! Look!" Ava crouches down next to her friend and stares at the little ball of fur. It's a small, white kitten with a patch of brown on the top of its head. The kitten can't be more than, well, she's not actually sure how old the thing is. She's not sure how to age a kitten, but it is so small. It shivers in the cold air, crust covering its eyes. It meows again and Ava's heart shatters into a million pieces.

"Oh my god, Ash, we have to help it." Ashtyn gingerly picks up the tiny kitten, and it doesn't even put up a fight. She tucks it against her chest, wrapping her jacket around it to protect it from the cold.

Ava's phone buzzes, letting her know the Uber is arriving. "What are we going to do?"

"Well, we have to bring it home," Ashtyn says. "I'll just hide it in my jacket during the ride home."

"What are we going to do with it once we're home?" Ava asks, feeling her anxiety spike. They don't have anything at home for a cat. What if Shiloh is allergic? What if it destroys their home? The landlord would definitely have something to say about that. Questions and concerns start to spin in her drunken head.

"I don't know! But we can't leave it here!" Ashtyn objects.

"Okay, fine, you're right. We'll figure it out once we're home."

The girls leave the alleyway with the kitten tucked safely in Ashtyn's jacket, and they make their way to the Uber. Luckily, the kitten is silent the entire ride and the driver is none the wiser. They thank him as they get out and head toward the front door of the house. It's then that the kitten starts fussing and crying.

"Is it hungry? Do we need to get like food or something?" Ava asks, opening the door and bustling them all inside.

"I don't know! I don't know how old it is. And we don't have anything cat related here."

"We gotta go get stuff, Ash!"

"Ave, we're both tipsy. We can't drive anywhere right now."

"Right...wait!" Ava exclaims and then she's pulling out her phone and dialing their sober roommate. He doesn't answer right away, so Ava calls him again and again and again. It's on the fifth call that Shiloh finally picks up. "What's wrong? Are you okay? Did you and Ashtyn make it home safely?"

"What? Of course we made it home safely."

"Ava, you've called me five times while I'm at work. If this isn't an emergency..." His voice is tinged with worry and Ava immediately feels bad for making him stress.

"No, we're both okay. Sorry, I just—" The alcohol is making Ava forget her train of thought. "We found a baby kitten out in the alley near the bar, and we brought it home. Can you stop by somewhere that's still open on your way home and get some cat stuff?"

"Cat stuff?"

"Yeah, she's really tiny so she'll probably need like kitten formula or something. And she'll need a bed if she's staying here overnight. And maybe some toys. And litter. You know, cat stuff." Ashtyn is nodding furiously from where she's cuddling the kitten on the couch.

Shiloh sighs deeply. "I don't know what's going to be open at this time that sells cat things."

"Maybe a gas station?"

"I'll figure it out. So, we have a cat now?"

"Well, I don't know. But we've got to help her out at least for tonight before we can get her to a vet in the morning. You're not allergic, are you?"

"No, I'm not allergic." Shiloh sighs again. "Okay, I'll grab what I can. I get off at two so it'll be a little while until I can get home. Who knows how long I'll have to wait for an Uber."

Ava feels guilty that neither of them can pick him up. "Sorry. We'll stay up with her until you get here."

It isn't until four in the morning that Shiloh walks through the front door with an array of plastic bags hanging from his arms. Both girls jolt awake from where they fell asleep on the couch. The kitten is still curled up on Ashtyn's chest.

"Jesus, what time is it?" Ashtyn mutters, squinting against the harsh lights they forgot to turn off.

"A little past four," Shiloh replies, dumping the bags on the floor. The kitten startles and starts meowing. "Geez, you were right. It's tiny."

"Her name is Jess," Ava says sleepily.

"Jess?"

Ava points to the TV that's currently playing *New Girl*. Shiloh huffs a laugh, and then inspects the tiny kitten that's currently trying to get down from the couch. He catches her in his large hands before she can faceplant onto the carpet.

"Jess," he says again, this time softer and with a smile on his face. He's holding this tiny creature like he'll never drop her. "Well, I got what I could, but there wasn't much of a selection at two AM." He cradles Jess against his chest and brings her over to where he dropped all the bags. He takes out at least five different types of wet foods and a small box that's supposed to be a litter box, along with the world's tiniest bag of litter. "This was all I could find."

"Geez, you'd think we're keeping her or something," Ashtyn replies. Ava looks at Ashtyn pointedly. There was no question on whether or not they were keeping the kitten anymore. No matter what the vet said tomorrow, Jess was theirs. She'd already squirmed her way into their hearts.

Shiloh hands Ava a thing of wet food. "Here, can you get this ready for her? I'm going to try and clean her eyes off."

"We tried to do that earlier. She kept squirming and trying to scratch me," Ashtyn says.

Shiloh doesn't say anything as he takes Jess into the kitchen and runs warm water into a bowl. He sets her on the counter and she sits politely, her eyes squinting up at him. He wets a dish towel with warm water and goes to work on cleaning her crusty eyes. She doesn't squirm once or try to scratch him.

"Geez, okay kitten whisperer," Ashtyn mutters. Ava's in the kitchen mixing the food with some water and her heart sputters at the way Shiloh is handling Jess. He's so gentle, his fingers expertly wiping away the gunk coating her eyes. When he's done, she meows up at him and the way he smiles at her is almost Ava's undoing. She knows she can't blame the alcohol for what's happening to her right now.

"Here," she says, pushing the bowl of food toward them. "It's ready."

Jess bolts across the counter and slides all the way over to the bowl, shoving her face into the food so fast she gets it everywhere. She laps it up as if she hasn't eaten in a long time.

"You said you found her in the alley behind the bar?" Shiloh asks, never taking his eyes off Jess. His arm is against the counter, making sure she doesn't slip off.

Ava can't answer. She's staring too intently at the cat and also Shiloh's forearm. Ashtyn speaks up. "Yeah, I was...messing with Ava and ran toward the alley. That's when I heard a tiny meow and saw her just sitting there. It was cold, so I picked her up to make sure she didn't freeze."

"She definitely looks too young to be away from her mother."

"That's what we thought but there's no vet office open in the middle of the night. We figured we'd just keep her here until we could get in to see one."

"That sounds like a good idea." Jess laps up more of the food until she's satisfied. Once she's done, she goes right back into Shiloh's arms.

"I saved you and this is how you repay me," Ashtyn jokes, a smile on the edge of her lips.

"She knows I'm the one that bought the food," Shiloh replies, smiling.

Ashtyn laughs. "Little traitor."

Shiloh scoops up Jess and takes her to the couch. *New Girl* is still playing on the TV. "You know, I've never actually seen this."

"What!?" Both girls exclaim, staring at Shiloh like he's crazy.

"Should I have?"

"Oh, we're forcing you to watch it now. You have to know how Jess got her name." The girls squeeze onto the couch and go back to episode one. Jess curls up on Shiloh's chest, her belly full.

"Okay, now pay attention. If you fall asleep, we'll just have to rewatch it."

They get only two episodes in before all three of them are asleep, the TV still playing in the background, Jess the kitten sleeping peacefully and purring away.

Chapter 5

Shiloh wakes on the couch with a crick in his neck. Ava and Ashtyn are still sound asleep next to him. Ava's head is on Ashtyn's lap, her feet are tucked up against Shiloh's thigh. Jess is suspiciously absent.

"Guys," he says, sleep coating his voice. He clears his throat, then says louder, "Guys!"

The girls startle awake. "What!? What's going on?" Ava asks, her brown hair a tangled mess.

"I don't know where Jess is."

"Did you look for her?" Ashtyn asks grumpily.

"Uh, no, I just woke up, and she's not on the couch with us anymore."

In that moment, Ava seems to realize they fell asleep next to each other. She snaps her feet back to her side of the couch and sits up straighter, trying to flatten her crazy hair. There's mascara staining her under eyes, and Shiloh has the urge to wipe it away. He starts to lift his hand when he feels his ring press against his chest. His hand immediately drops back to his side.

"Did y'all hear that?" Ashtyn asks, furrowing her brow. Everyone goes silent, and that's when Shiloh hears it. A tiny meow and something like scratching.

"Jess?" Shiloh calls out, getting up from the couch. He heads into the kitchen, the girls close on his heels. He comes up short, and Ava and Ashtyn bump into him. Jess is squatting over the makeshift litter box they set up last night.

"Oh my gosh, she's using the litter box!" Ava exclaims, squeezing Shiloh's bicep. He's not sure if she notices what she's holding onto as she stares at Jess. The last time she'd grabbed his arm, he'd been nearly naked. He tries not to think about it.

The moment is interrupted by the doorbell ringing. Ava jumps back, letting go of Shiloh's arm. There are little nail indents from where she held on too tight.

"Who the fuck is here at…" Ashtyn checks her phone. "Nine in the morning?" They all look at each other dumbly.

"Well, go get it," Ava says, pushing Shiloh toward the door.

"Why me?"

"So you can protect us if it's a murderer!"

"Why would a murderer ring the doorbell?"

"I don't know! To catch us by surprise?"

"Jesus, Ava," Ashtyn says. "You need to stop watching true crime before bed. I'm going back to sleep. Let me know if it really is a murderer."

Ava huffs, and Shiloh heads to the door to see who it is. He's still in his work clothes from last night and he's sure he smells ripe. He's in no shape to be answering the front door. He stifles a groan as the bell rings a second time, impatiently. Sleep and exhaustion tug at his bones.

"I'm coming," he mumbles, heading toward the foyer. He pulls open the door, and his heart plummets at the man standing there. "Dad?"

"Hi, son," Mr. Brooks says. Shiloh's body tenses, blood turning to ice. Anxiety spikes, replacing his exhaustion, and he feels like he's going to be sick. His father is dressed in his normal, charcoal gray suit, tie perfectly aligned, not a hair out of place.

"Hi, Dad," Shiloh says, carefully. His voice barely comes out. He swallows, his throat dry, and it's like an avalanche of rocks tumbling down his esophagus. Everything in him is screaming to run, hide, bolt, get the *fuck* out of here but, he can't. He's rooted to the spot. Everything that makes Shiloh his own, individual person shrivels up and dies when he faces his father.

"Shiloh, if it's those goddamn solicitors again, tell them we're not interested!" Ashtyn shouts from upstairs.

Mr. Brooks frowns and readjusts his cuffs. "May I come in?"

"Of course you can come in," Shiloh says quietly. He feels himself shrink. He should have never told his family his new address.

Mr. Brooks tentatively steps into the foyer. It feels as though he's stepping into Shiloh's own private oasis, something he's tried to avoid ever since he was a child. It's not that he *hates* his father, but he makes Shiloh feel small. Unlike himself. He's always inadequate, especially in comparison to his brother Matthew, even though he loves the bastard more than himself most days.

"The house is...quaint," Mr. Brooks says as if he's struggling to find the right words. Shiloh can hear the girls trying to be quiet upstairs. He doesn't say anything, and his father looks at him expectantly.

"Are you going to introduce me to your roommates? Or just let them scurry around upstairs?"

Shiloh's hands clench into fists. He doesn't want to introduce the girls to his father, but he knows he cannot disobey him either. "Uh, hey, Ava? Ashtyn? Can you come down here for a sec? I want you to meet my dad." He almost chokes on the word "dad." Mr. Brooks takes off his coat and hands it to Shiloh.

Ava and Ashtyn carefully tiptoe down the stairs and into the foyer, suspicion on Ashtyn's face and horror on Ava's. Both are still in their outfits from last night, hair wild, makeup smeared across their eyes.

"Hi, sorry, we thought you were the Bible salespeople again," Ashtyn says, straightening her shirt and sticking her hand out. "Nice to meet you, Mr. Brooks."

Shiloh's father returns the handshake, barely an expression on his face. He turns toward Ava, and she physically shrinks into herself, much like Shiloh tends to do around him.

"Hi," she squeaks, and Shiloh's heart constricts. She sticks out her hand, and Mr. Brooks takes it. He stares at both girls as if they just crawled out of the sewer.

"I apologize if I am intruding," Mr. Brooks says, voice tight. "I can see you were...preoccupied."

Ashtyn stiffens at Mr. Brooks's words while Ava looks embarrassed. Shiloh's skin crawls. Jess decides now is the perfect moment to mosey into the foyer and meow. His father's attention turns toward the tiny creature, and he frowns. Shiloh tries not to look at anyone too closely. He needs to keep a neutral expression at all times in his father's presence.

Jess winds her way through his father's legs, and Mr. Brooks looks at her with disgust. She makes her way toward Shiloh, and he ignores her. She sits and meows pitifully up at him. Again, he does nothing. Any sudden movements could set his father off and on the warpath. Ashtyn scoops Jess up and holds her protectively against her chest. "Sorry, Mr. Brooks. We'd love to stay and chat, but we need to get ready to take our cat to the vet." Her words break the tension in the room.

"Not a problem," he replies. "I'd like to talk to my son privately, anyway."

Ava looks like she's trying to catch Shiloh's eye but, he avoids her gaze. The girls scurry up the steps with Jess in tow and disappear. Then, it's just Shiloh and his father.

"You look like shit," his father says matter-of-factly.

Shiloh sighs heavily. "Thanks, Dad."

"Have you gained weight?"

"I—I'm not sure."

"So is this what you do now that you've thrown your life away? Drink all night and never go to bed?"

The words pierce Shiloh's heart. "No. No, it's not."

Mr. Brooks huffs. "Go get yourself presentable, so I can take you to brunch."

There's no asking. It's an order, and Shiloh will follow it. "Make yourself comfortable," he says, and then heads upstairs.

* * *

"What the fuck, Shiloh!?" Ashtyn exclaims, bursting into his room without knocking. His shirt is halfway over his head, and everyone freezes.

"Uh, sorry?" he supplies weakly.

"Did you know he was coming today?" Ava asks, her eyes avoiding his exposed stomach as he finishes putting on his clean shirt.

"No, I had no idea. And I don't want to talk about this right now."

"Talk about what? The way you turned into a completely different person the moment your father stepped into our house?"

Shiloh doesn't even have time to warm to the fact that Ashtyn said "our house." He continues getting ready, swiping on deodorant and combing his hair. "I don't have time for this." He knows his tone is sharp, but he doesn't have time to care if he's hurting their feelings. This is what his father does to him. And if he's not down in exactly two minutes, he's going to be in even more trouble than he already is. Yes, he's a twenty-six-old man that's worried about getting in trouble with his father, as if he's still a mess making toddler. Sometimes he thinks that's how his dad still sees him. "I have to go. Let me know how things go at the vet." With that, he's down the stairs and opening the door for his father. They get in his BMW and drive in silence to brunch.

He already knows where they're going before they even get there. It's the same place he takes Shiloh every time Shiloh fucks up or he is "extremely disappointed" in him. Or when he needs to rub in how much of a failure his son is. A place where everyone knows his father and no one knows him. When they arrive, his father gets out and gives the keys to Henry, the only valet he lets touch his precious car.

"Good to see you again, Mr. Brooks," Henry says, giving him the world's biggest brown-nosed smile. Shiloh wishes he could smack it off his face, even though Henry's not at fault here. It still stabs him right in the heart when he sees his father smile at someone in a way he's never smiled at Shiloh before.

"Take good care of her, my boy," Mr. Brooks says. Another jab right in the heart but, Shiloh doesn't say a word. The hostess greets them and again, Mr. Brooks smiles at Cheryl like she's his favorite person in the world.

"Your usual table, sir?" she asks, looking between Shiloh and his father.

"Yes, thank you, dear."

Cheryl leads them toward the back where it's slightly more private. She sits them at a table and hands them their menus. "Benny's cooking up some specials today, if you're interested," she says, filling their water glasses.

"Thank you, Cheryl, but I'll just get what I usually get. Same here for my son."

Shiloh doesn't even remember what he normally gets, but it doesn't matter. His father will order for him like he always does. Once Cheryl's gone and Mr. Brooks has taken a sip of water, he begins. "I saw Scarlett the other day."

It's almost the tipping point that sends Shiloh over the edge. The edge that he's been teetering on for months but refuses to fall over. He will hold on to the railing for the rest of his godforsaken life if he has to.

"I don't want to talk about her," Shiloh says weakly. The ring is burning a hole right through his chest. He wants to rip it off, but he can't. All he can do is weakly rub the back of his neck.

"Well, I am her lawyer, and there are things we need to discuss."

Gut punch. Gut punch. Gut punch. Shiloh's so emotionally beaten every time he's reminded of this fact. "I let her take everything. There's nothing to talk about."

"Shiloh, contrary to your beliefs, I'm not here to rub salt in your wound. I'm not here to shame you for your failed marriage."

"You sure about that?" he asks, and it's the first time he cracks in front of his father. To his credit, Tom Brooks doesn't bat a fucking eye. "I wasn't even the one that asked for a divorce."

Mr. Brooks looks at his son for a moment. "I've advised Scarlett to seek an annulment on the grounds that she was underage when you both got married. If the annulment is granted, which I'm fairly certain it will be, we can all put this mess behind us."

Shiloh doesn't move a muscle. The words, each individual one, is a blow to his nervous system. "What the fuck are you talking about?"

"Scarlett was seventeen, and you were eighteen when you got married."

"Yes, I'm aware. Her mom gave us permission. She signed a fucking form."

"And you also know Scarlett's mother tragically passed away a month after your wedding due to cancer. Would it not be plausible that she only signed the form so she could see her only child get married before she died? It would be fairly easy to argue that she wasn't in her right state of mind when she signed, and therefore an annulment could be granted on those grounds."

Shiloh is speechless. It's at this moment that Cheryl comes by and places their food in front of them. Mr. Brooks thanks her and starts in on his meal. Shiloh feels like he's going to throw up. He doesn't even look at his plate.

"Look, I know how hard this divorce has been on you. Well, you're not even technically divorced yet, are you? Since you refuse to sign the paperwork."

"I'm not refusing!"

"Lower your voice, now."

"I'm not refusing," he repeats, voice lowered. "I just haven't gotten around to it." Shiloh hates the way he obeys his father's demands. He's always done what his father has asked of him, but it's never good enough.

"Shiloh, if we go the annulment route instead, you'll never have this tied to you again and neither will we. Our family won't ever have to say one of our children got divorced..." His father's motives are suddenly crystal clear. This is all about him, like it always is. This has nothing to do with Shiloh, other than the shame he's brought to the Brooks name.

Shiloh can barely hear himself say, "No." He shakes his head, eyes on the verge of tears. He cannot let his father see him cry.

"Shiloh, let's think this through. You were young and stupid when you decided to marry that girl." Suddenly, she's "that girl." Not, Scarlett. Not, my client. Not even ex-daughter in law. Just...that girl. And even with all the anger and the hurt and the sadness that is wreaking havoc inside him, Scarlett deserves more than just "that girl." Even if she tore inside him and scraped every single inch of his heart out of his chest. Even if he wasn't the perfect husband, and she wasn't the perfect wife.

Mr. Brooks keeps talking, "I mean, you threw your life away for her. You never even tried to go to college, you've been working dead end job after dead end job, and now you're living with two random girls you barely even know—"

"Don't talk about them like you know them," Shiloh says. He's starting to get angry. Ava and Ashtyn are strictly off limits to his father's wrath. He hadn't been able to protect Scarlett from his father, but he can still protect them.

"And why shouldn't I? It was embarrassing for them to even present themselves to me looking like they'd been up all night, doing God knows what. I mean, if I didn't know any better, I'd think they were whor—"

"Dad?" Mr. Brooks looks up from his food, fork poised halfway to his mouth, surprised that he's being interrupted. Shiloh doesn't think he's ever interrupted his father before, but he cannot let himself hear the word his father was about to utter. "Go fuck yourself."

The world stops. Time slows. Nobody else exists in the world except Shiloh and his father. They stare at each other, wordlessly.

Shiloh's out of his chair and heading toward the exit before he can even comprehend what he's just done. His father could beat him down, spit on him, trash his life decisions, but he could not talk about the girls that way. Shiloh would not allow it.

The fresh air hits him as he exits the restaurant, and he takes a deep breath, feeling the first truly warm day of the season all around him. He has never, ever, spoken to his father like that. He has always just taken whatever his father has thrown at him in silence or agreement. This is the first time he has ever defied him with words. He pulls his phone out of his pocket, and before he can even think about it, he's dialing her number, one he's never deleted.

"Hello?" she answers hesitantly, like she knows it's him, as if she never deleted his number either. Her voice, one he hasn't heard in almost a year, punches right through him. For a moment, he forgets how to speak.

"Shiloh?" Scarlett asks. Her voice, the same it's always been, brings back floods of memories, sensations, feelings that Shiloh has locked up for too long now.

"Do you actually want an annulment?" His voice is hoarse, as though he's been screaming for hours. He has so many things he wants to say to her, but he can't seem to find any other words.

Scarlett sighs, reminding him of when she asked for the divorce. "I told him you weren't ready for this."

"So, it's true?" His voice almost breaks. He feels tears start to slip down his cheeks. He doesn't know when he started crying, just that he can't stop.

"Yes, Shiloh," she says. "I want an annulment. I just think that—"

He doesn't let her finish before hanging up. The tears are unstoppable at this point. He looks behind him to see if his father will leave the restaurant or continue eating until he's done. He knows which one it will be. His feet take him down the sidewalk, hands shaking. He's roughly five blocks away when he stops and takes out his phone again. There's only one person in this world he can talk to about this. One person he loves more than anyone.

His brother answers on the second ring. "Hey, what's up? Make it quick cause I'm about to board a flight to Mexico, baby!"

"Mattie..." The childhood nickname for his baby brother is all Shiloh can manage to say before he chokes on his tears.

"Goddamn it. I'll be there by tonight, buddy. Just hold on."

Chapter 6

The girls are still at the vet when Ava's phone rings. "It's Shiloh," she says, showing Ashtyn her screen.

"Well, go and answer it," Ash replies. "I'll finish up here."

The vet confirmed that Jess is incredibly young and probably shouldn't have been separated from her mother yet. She has a nasty eye infection as well as a couple fleas. They were given kitten formula as well as an antibiotic for her infection. The girls didn't need convincing they were going to adopt the small kitten that had wormed her way into their hearts.

As Ashtyn takes out her wallet to pay, Ava exits the building and answers the phone. "Hey, we're just finishing up at the vet."

"Ava," Shiloh says, and his voice makes her freeze. It sounds off. Not like his normal, everyday voice. It's gruffer, almost gravely, like he's been crying.

"Shiloh, are you okay?" she asks.

"I'm—I just need someone to come pick me up."

"What? I thought—"

"Ava, please. Don't ask questions. Can you just come get me?"

She's silent for a moment, trying to gather her thoughts. Something is definitely wrong. Finally, she sighs, "Of course. Just send me your location." She ignores the fact that he doesn't call his usual Uber. He called *her,* and that's all that matters. She would gladly be there for him.

Her phone dings with Shiloh's location, and she shows it to Ashtyn as they head to the car. "We need to pick up Shiloh."

"And he didn't say why his father couldn't drop him off?"

"No, Ashtyn, he didn't. He told me not to ask questions, and I didn't. You saw the way he was with his dad."

Ashtyn sighs as she ducks into the car. She settles Jess in her brand-new, hot pink carrier. "Fine. Let's go."

As they pull up to the curb ten minutes later, Ava's fears are confirmed. Shiloh's been crying. She feels a pang in her heart as he pulls open the passenger door and gets in without a word. He doesn't even look at Jess.

No one says anything as they drive back to the house. The only sound filling the car is Jess' small meows. When they pull into the driveway, Shiloh gets out, goes up to the front door, and walks in without looking behind him.

"Well, that's not good," Ashtyn says, turning off the car. She gets out and pulls Jess' carrier with her. The little one meows, ready to be inside and fed.

"I'll go ahead and feed her. Maybe you can see what's wrong with him."

"Me?" Ava squeaks. "He told me not to ask questions!"

"Then don't ask questions. Just go and make sure he's okay."

Ava groans but heads inside. Shiloh is nowhere to be seen, and she thinks he's probably hiding in his room. She takes a deep breath and trudges upstairs. Her fist hovers over the door that neighbors her own. She can't hear anything on the other side. After a moment's hesitation, she lowers her fist and backs away. Whatever he's going through, he doesn't want to talk about it with them, and Ava wants to respect that. He'll come to them if and when he's ready. She'll give him his space. She'll wrap up her racing heart and shove it down, deep, deep, deep, so no one will know that it's breaking for her roommate.

* * *

The doorbell rings a little past six as Ava and Ashtyn are cooking dinner. Jess, who is sleeping peacefully in her little cat bed on the floor, perks her head up at the sound. There's no movement upstairs. Shiloh has remained shut in his room, without a peep, for the entirety of the day

"If that's his dad again, I'm going to deck him in the face," Ashtyn says, brandishing a wooden spoon she's been using to stir.

"Maybe I'll answer it," Ava says, setting down her glass of wine. She thinks she might hear Shiloh rustling around upstairs as she opens the door.

The guy standing on their stoop gives her a mega-watt smile that feels oddly familiar. For a crazy second, she thinks it is Shiloh's doppelgänger come to torment him.

"Ashtyn!" he exclaims, as if he cannot possibly be wrong.

"Uh, no," Ava says, frozen to the spot. "She's in the kitchen."

"Well, then you must be Ava! Sorry, fifty-fifty shot. Shiloh's not big into describing."

The guy looks like Shiloh but younger and a bit scragglier. His dark hair is slightly longer and messier, like he just sprang out of bed. Dark stubble lines his jaw, and he's dressed in a bright, yellow shirt with pineapples all over it.

"Do you mind if I come in?" the guy asks. "It's a bit colder here than Mexico is supposed to be right now." Before Ava can even reply or deduce that she's speaking with another member of the Brooks family, Shiloh is at the foot of the stairs.

"Mattie," he says, face lighting up with a smile. The boys meet in the middle of the foyer, their arms going around each other in a tight embrace. Ava catches Ashtyn's gaze as she comes to investigate the reunion. She just shrugs at her friend's confused expression, unsure what is transpiring.

"God, you look like shit," Mattie says, slapping Shiloh on the back. "By the way, I have absolutely nothing with me since all my shit is currently sitting at a baggage claim in Mexico."

"You didn't have to skip your trip for me," Shiloh says.

"I was going with a bunch of assholes, anyway. Don't worry about it. Anyway, are you going to introduce me to your new roomies?"

"Oh, shit, yeah, of course," Shiloh says, as if he's been snapped out of a trance. He seems better than earlier, but still slightly tense. "Ava, Ashtyn, this is my little brother Matthew. Mattie, these are the girls."

"Ava, pleasure to see you again," Mattie jokes and then turns his attention toward Ash. "Ashtyn, wonderful to meet you. Sorry for barging in on what smells like dinner."

"Can someone please explain what the hell is going on," Ashtyn demands, hands on her hips.

"Hey, I'm just as lost as you seem to be," Mattie replies. "All I know is: I get a call from my brother, and I come running, no questions asked. Even if it means I miss my spring break trip to Mexico." Shiloh looks guilty. He avoids meeting anyone's eyes. Jess roams into the foyer as everyone stands in silence.

Mattie's eyes light up. "You didn't tell me you got a cat!"

"We just found her yesterday," Ava says, when Shiloh doesn't say anything. "We took her to the vet today, and, well, I guess we adopted her. Her name is Jess." Jess makes her way, slowly on her little kitten legs, toward Mattie, and he scoops her up.

"What is it with this cat and her love for random men she's never even met?!" Ashtyn exclaims, throwing her arms up. She sighs and turns back toward the kitchen. "Dinner's ready in twenty if you're joining us."

Mattie smiles, "I'm starving."

** * **

Dinner doesn't get a chance to be awkward, because Mattie talks nonstop. Shiloh knows he should say something, but every time he tries to open his mouth, an invisible hand reaches up from his stomach and grips his throat. He owes the girls an explanation, Mattie too, but he just can't bring himself to utter the words. He'll tell Mattie after dinner when they're alone. Mattie might be the only person he's ever really honest with. As for the girls, he will never mention what his father said about them. Never.

"So, Matthew, are you in college?" Ava asks.

"Final year. I'll graduate next May with a BA in Business Finance." He rolls his eyes. "It's riveting stuff. Oh, and you can call me Mattie. Only my parents calls me Matthew. Or Shiloh when he's pissed at me." Shiloh glares at his brother, a smile playing at the edge of his mouth.

"Shiloh, you never told us what you studied in college," Ashtyn says. She's busy looking down at her plate so she doesn't see the flicker of pain that is reflected in his face at her words. Ava catches it, though. She always seems to catch it.

He coughs, then says, "I, uh, never went."

"He was too busy being in love," Mattie says, and Shiloh gives him a death glare. Ava and Ashtyn both stare down at their plates, as if Mattie's words aren't surprising.

"Mattie," he warns.

"What, they don't know?"

"We don't know anything!" Ava exclaims too loudly, not meeting Shiloh's gaze. There it is. Ava can't keep a secret to save her life, something Shiloh has discovered at numerous game nights these past few weeks.

"Who told you?" he asks simply.

"Brooke let it slip that you're getting divorced. That's it. We don't know anything else, and you don't owe us an explanation," Ashtyn says, sincerity lacing her voice. It's the nicest thing she's ever said to him. "Your business is yours alone. We are not entitled to know any piece of you that you don't wish to share." Ava nods along furiously to her friend's words. It's a strange turn from the Ashtyn he met at the coffee shop. The one who demanded to know why he needed a new place to live. Maybe this means Ashtyn has finally warmed up to him.

"Damn, Shi, you've got some good roommates," Mattie says, mouth full of food.

Shiloh takes a deep breath and lets his heart stop hammering for a few seconds before speaking again, "I'm not keeping it a secret from you. I just...don't talk about it. With anyone."

Mattie smiles, "Except me."

Shiloh ignores him and continues, "I've made a lot of shit decisions in my life, but I never thought...I loved her so much." His voice breaks, and he's worried he'll cry again. The girls are silent, letting him continue if he wants to. He decides he wants to. "I got married at eighteen. She was seventeen. I was head over heels in love with my high school sweetheart, and I never thought I'd ever regret a decision like that. Marriage, for me, was meant to be forever, and I was prepared to honor that. I didn't go to college, so I could work right away and support us. She—Scarlett went to school to be a nurse. She was so busy. I hardly ever saw her, because she was studying and interning and doing all the things she ever wanted in life. I wanted to support her, because I loved her. I was so proud of her. Everything I did was for our future..." He pauses. Everyone is staring at him intently, letting him take his time. Mattie knows every detail, but he's still fully invested in his brother's words.

"We'd been married for about six years when I really saw her pull away. She was in her final year of school, and she was working like crazy through it all. There were times she wouldn't come home, and I'd call and call just to make sure she was still alive. She never answered. And then she'd come home the next day like nothing ever happened. I knew, in my heart I knew she was cheating, but I honestly didn't care. I was prepared to forgive her. I knew I wasn't perfect either. I hated my job, and it was taking a toll on me. I would come home drained, just wanting to drink on the couch until I fell into bed. It was no wonder she didn't want to come home. It was no wonder she would fall into an older doctor's bed..." Ava lays a comforting hand on Shiloh's, giving him the courage to continue.

"Last year, we were basically already separated even though we were still living together. We were both checked out of the marriage, even if I didn't want to admit it. I wanted to fight for her, because I truly believed she was the love of my life. I'd known her since I was fifteen years old. I'd only ever been with her. I was scared to admit we'd made a mistake getting married so young. I didn't want to admit that I'd failed her in every way. I couldn't confront her about the cheating, because I couldn't blame her for it. I was emotionally and physically checked out of the relationship even if I couldn't see it. So, when she set divorce papers on the kitchen table one morning, I didn't even fight it. I should have seen it coming. I just didn't expect my father to be her divorce lawyer—"

Shiloh can't even finish his sentence, because both Ava and Ashtyn have screamed "WHAT!?"

Mattie frowns, "Yeah, that one got me too at the time."

"You mean the guy that showed up at our doorstep this morning is not only your father but also your ex-wife's divorce lawyer?" Shiloh doesn't have the heart to correct Ashtyn's use of the word "ex-wife."

"Wait, Dad was here today?" Mattie asks, looking at Shiloh. He can see the pieces falling into place as Mattie realizes something serious must have happened. "What the fuck did he say to you?"

"He told me that Scarlett is wanting to change the divorce to an annulment."

Nobody says anything for a minute. "Can she do that?" Ashtyn asks. "Annulments are pretty hard to come by unless something bad happened."

"He's filing it under the grounds that Scarlett was underage when we got married. We got permission from her mom, but he said her mom's permission can be revoked because she was super sick at the time and 'not in her right mind.'"

"What the actual fuck!?" Ava exclaims, death gripping her fork. Ashtyn shakes her head, and Mattie looks pale.

"That's low, even for Dad."

"It seems pretty on brand for him," Shiloh says simply. He thinks maybe he really does hate his father after all.

"Scarlett's mom was at the wedding," Mattie replies. "She was smiling and kissing your cheek. There are pictures of her! There's no way anyone would believe she wasn't in her right mind to give her daughter permission to marry."

"At this point," Shiloh starts, "I don't even know if I care anymore. If this is what she really wants, then why not just let it go?"

"Why does she even want one? Why is a normal divorce not enough?" Ava asks, the anger still present on her face.

"I haven't exactly signed the papers yet," Shiloh admits. "I've been... ignoring them."

"She probably wants to get married again, and if Shiloh won't sign the papers, well, an annulment would mean she could get married right away instead of having to wait a certain amount of time," Mattie says.

Shiloh doesn't want to admit that Mattie is right. He knows Scarlett moved into the doctor's house the second Shiloh was gone and on Drew's couch. He wouldn't be surprised if she wanted to remarry already. They've both been single a lot longer than they might want to admit.

"I don't fucking care anymore," Shiloh says, sounding harsher than he means to. "If she wants to get remarried then let her."

It's silent again before Ashtyn speaks up, "When we first met, you said you weren't the dating type…"

"I'm not." Shiloh says. "I got my chance at love, and I fucked it up. End of story."

"Shiloh…" Ava starts.

"Trust me, I've tried to tell him," Mattie says as if reading her mind. "He thinks he doesn't *deserve* another chance, or whatever shit he tells himself."

"Don't psychoanalyze me," Shiloh snaps. "I don't owe anyone an explanation."

"You're right, you don't," Ashtyn says. "But that doesn't mean we can't tell you you're full of shit if you think you don't deserve to be happy."

"I am happy," Shiloh says. It's a half truth. Today is definitely not a good example. But, overall? He's happy. He likes his job, his friends, his new roommates and living situation. What more could he want?

"Is this what you want?" Ava asks quietly, her gaze boring into him, as if she could read his mind. He wants to look away, but her brown eyes aren't backing down. He's never noticed how many freckles splash across her cheeks. "You want an annulment?"

Before he can even think about his answer, he says, "No."

"Can I be blunt for a second?" Ashtyn blurts. Shiloh looks at her and nods. "Just sign the fucking papers. The longer you wait, the longer it'll take to heal. I can tell that you're hurting, but you'll never get over this until you're done with her, officially. And unless you want this dragged out into an annulment, just sign the fucking papers."

Shiloh sits a moment, letting her words sink in. He understands now that the annulment is probably just a scare tactic to kick his ass into gear and sign the papers. He hates that it's probably going to work. He says nothing as he gets up from the table, goes upstairs, and comes back down holding the papers. Scarlett's big, loopy signature sits face up for all to see. He hates that she gets to keep his name.

He holds a pen, his hands shaking. Mattie reaches out to steady him. His brother's comforting touch is the only thing keeping him grounded. That, and the girls' gazes. He takes a deep breath and signs. Oddly, he feels good, staring at his signature next to hers. Mattie gives him a reassuring squeeze, and as he looks up, he sees Ava and Ashtyn smiling at him. That's when he realizes his mistake. He actually bursts out laughing. He laughs so hard, everyone looks at him like he's crazy.

"It's not notarized," he gasps. "I fucking signed it without a notary present. It won't be accepted."

Then, Mattie's laughing too, loud and unabashed. They laugh so hard that the girls chime in.

"I'm going to have to call my fucking father." This just makes them all laugh harder, tears streaming down their faces. It's all so absurd, Shiloh has no choice but to laugh or else he'd cry.

"Let's save it all for tomorrow," Mattie says, once he's stopped laughing long enough to speak. "I'll go with you."

"Thanks, brother," Shiloh says.

Later that night, when he's alone in his room, his brother sleeping peacefully downstairs on the couch, Shiloh touches the ring hanging around his neck. He holds it for a moment, letting it sink into his skin one last time. Then, he pulls it up and over his head, placing it in a drawer in his nightstand. He feels naked without it, but he also feels...*free.*

* * *

Ava can't sleep. She keeps tossing and turning in her bed, unable to get the events of the day out of her head. Meeting Mr. Brooks, Mattie, and learning about Shiloh's history felt like surprise after surprise. She never realized just how dramatic the divorce was, and how much it affected Shiloh. And still does. A surge of anger rolls through her again at the way Mr. Brooks treated his son, and she gets out of bed, unable to relax. She heads downstairs, planning to make a cup of tea. She's quiet, careful of Mattie sleeping on the couch. As she enters the kitchen, she stops. Shiloh sits at the dark table, staring at the divorce papers.

"Oh, sorry," Ava says quietly, trying not to startle him. "I didn't know you were here. I'll just go—"

"Stay," he says, and Ava feels the weight of his voice. "You don't have to be quiet. Mattie will sleep through an earthquake."

Ava sits slowly, eyes adjusting to the dark. She wants to turn on a light, but she doesn't want to disturb the energy thrumming in the room. The dark feels safer somehow.

"I'm...sorry about everything," Shiloh says. His voice is pained.

"You don't have anything to be sorry for," she replies, softly. She can't seem to speak above a whisper.

"I know, I just feel like I should have been honest with you from the start. And I wasn't."

"Shiloh," Ava starts, and he reaches out to grasp her hand, surprising her. With the lights out, it feels okay for him to be holding her hand like this. In the dark, it's not so scary to feel the things she smothers during the light of day. "It's okay. Ashtyn and I, we don't see you any differently. We're still glad you made your way to us. We couldn't have asked for a better roommate."

Shiloh tightens his grip on her hand and lets out a breath. "I'm really glad I'm here too."

The silence hangs around them like a curtain, their hands still connected. Ava feels like a lifeline, and she's willing to hold on as long as Shiloh needs her.

"Can I ask you something?" she asks.

"Of course," Shiloh replies.

"Where does your mom fit into all this? Is she...like your dad?"

"My mom is..." he pauses, as if he's not sure where he's going with this, "complicated." Ava squeezes his hand comfortingly, and he continues, "I don't understand how she can be with someone like my father but...I know she loves him. I know she loves me too, even if my father's disappointment can be louder than her love for me." His words break Ava's heart. She can't imagine her father ever being disappointed in her. Even if she went to jail for murder, her parents would defend her to their last dying breath.

"That's not fair," she says. "A parent should never make a child feel like that."

"It's okay. I'm used to it."

"You shouldn't have to be." Her words hang in the air for a moment, and Shiloh takes a deep, shuddering breath.

"Thank you," he whispers.

"For what?" Ava asks.

"For everything."

They sit like that, hands clasped in the darkness of the kitchen, until the sun rises.

Chapter 7

The used car lot is sweltering as Shiloh and his brother make their way through the maze of deserted tires and cars that look far worse than his own. Texas has decided that the middle of March is a good time to start the summer season, though Shiloh doesn't mind much. He prefers the heat to the cold, rainy climate he grew up in. He feels more at peace when he's warm. The cold just reminds him of his father.

Mattie's been staying with them for a few days now, and Shiloh relishes the time they've spent together. He doesn't see his brother as much as he used to. Mattie's always so busy with school and life, and Shiloh is busy...being Shiloh. The girls seem to love him too, which is a plus. They've spent most of the week watching movies, teaching Mattie the rules to Catan, and playing with Jess, who goes crazy for a stray shoelace. Spring Break is over in two days, and they're spending their last full day together shopping for a new car for Shiloh. He would really like to be anywhere other than here, but he's got to stop Ubering to work. It's eating up his paychecks.

But meandering through the car lot is helping to distract him from the way he's felt since agreeing to sign the divorce papers. He knows he'll have to go in and get them notarized when he re-signs them, but it's a step in the right direction. Actually, he knows this is the right decision. It's the only way he can ever truly heal. He hasn't spoken to his father since the incident at brunch. The only contact they've had was a curt email letting Shiloh know about the refiling of the documents. He could sense his father's rage in the words. He's hoping he can soon put all of this behind him and finally move on.

"Alright, play it cool brother," Mattie says. The salesman lumbers toward them, snapping Shiloh out of his thoughts. "Don't make it seem like you can't afford anything."

"I *can't* afford anything," Shiloh says through gritted teeth. It's actually pathetic how much he cannot afford a used car.

"Yeah, but he doesn't need to know that." Mattie throws on his million-dollar smile and extends his hand toward the salesman. "Matthew Brooks. Nice to meet you, sir." The salesman seems impressed with Mattie's forward attitude.

He takes his hand and looks him up and down, a smile forming on his face. "Nice to meet you, Mr. Brooks. I'm Randall. Is there anything in particular you're looking for today?" It's unnerving hearing someone refer to Mattie as Mr. Brooks. That title is reserved only for their father. Shiloh's pretty sure he would prefer his sons refer to him as that instead of "Dad."

"Well, we're trying to get my brother here a new car. His finally died on him, and he's had a hard time letting go. First car and all." Mattie's voice sounds just like Dad's but without the malice and disappointment. It's uncanny, but Mattie's always had the ability to sound like their father. He has that air of confidence without all the heartless attitude. Shiloh loves his brother so much, but he knows what he could become if his father ever sinks his claws into him. It's always been Shiloh's job to protect his little brother, even if it's from their own father. It's why he's so thankful that Mattie moved out of the house when he went to college.

"I'm just looking for something cheap and reliable," Shiloh says, ignoring Mattie's pointed look at him. "And I'd like to get out of here before the sun sets." The salesman seems less impressed with him than he is with Mattie. *Yeah, that tracks*, Shiloh thinks.

"I'm sure we can find you something. What exactly is your budget?"

Shiloh casts his eyes downward, embarrassed at the number he's about to say. He mutters the amount, and the salesman's eyes widen. "Oh," he says simply. "Well, I'm sure there's something in that ballpark."

They wander aimlessly around the lot, not really finding anything reliable within Shiloh's "ballpark." The ones that are seem to be falling apart, similar to his own car. At this point, he considers if a bicycle would be a better option. Just as Shiloh's about to call it quits, Mattie halts in his tracks.

"Holy shit," he breathes, eyes wide. He stares straight ahead toward the back of the lot. There, tucked away behind a large tarp, is what looks to be a...

"Is that a boat?"

"Ah, we just got that clunker in yesterday. Haven't even listed it yet. She's a bit of a fixer upper, to be honest with you. She's missing about half her parts and hasn't run in years." Randall leads them toward it. Shiloh can sense Mattie's enthusiasm before Randall even takes the tarp off.

It's awful. It looks like it's been rusting for the last twenty years, untouched by even a single drop of water. The paint is almost completely peeled off, and the seats are ripped up like a raccoon ran through it.

"She's perfect," Mattie whispers, running his hands along the side of the boat. "How much?"

"Mattie," Shiloh starts, but his brother isn't listening to him anymore. He's fully transfixed on the boat in front of him. Randall tells him a number, and Shiloh almost chokes.

"You can't be serious?" Shiloh says. "That much for a broken piece of shit?" Randall frowns at his choice of words.

"It is kind of a lot," Mattie says, rubbing his fingers over his chin.

"You know, for you, I can probably make you a deal." Randall and Mattie continue to barter until the price gets to a place where Mattie says, "I'll take it." The price is still ridiculously high for what he's getting, but Mattie doesn't seem to mind.

"Excellent!" Randall exclaims. "I'll get the paperwork."

As the salesman leaves, Shiloh turns to his brother. "You do realize we're here to find *me* a car, yes?"

"And did anything tickle your fancy?"

Shiloh scowls. "No, everything was worse than what I already have."

"Okay, well I didn't want to leave empty handed. That would be rude to poor Randall."

"So, you bought a boat to appease Randall?"

"Well, no, not completely. I mean, I've always wanted a boat."

Shiloh can't help but roll his eyes. His brother has always been incredibly lax with money compared to Shiloh. He knows Mattie gets a steep allowance from their father simply because he goes to college. Something Shiloh never got, since he never went. His father has never once offered Shiloh money. Ever. Even if he had, Shiloh would never accept it. He doesn't want to be even more under his father's thumb than he already is. Mattie is different, though. Their father is proud of Mattie, as he should be. Mattie is making a future for himself. He's smart, confident, widely liked. Shiloh knows their father will always be proud of Matthew. Shiloh, on the other hand, will always be the disappointment. Shiloh thinks he can handle that as long as it's not directed toward his little brother.

Mattie turns to Shiloh. "Would you have let me buy you a car today?"

"No, of course not," Shiloh replies. He could never take his brother's money. He is too stubborn for that.

"Okay, then let me have this."

So, he does. Mattie produces his checkbook when Randall reappears, signs the papers, and walks out with a "brand-new boat" that's missing half its parts and doesn't even run.

Shiloh sighs heavily. This is why he doesn't go shopping with his brother.

* * *

"Ta-da!" Mattie exclaims as Ava and Ashtyn wander out of the house. Their faces are a mix of bewilderment and curiosity.

"I thought you were going to get a car," Ava says, her brow furrowed. Ashtyn has an identical expression on her face, although hers feels more extreme. Everything about Ashtyn always feels a little more extreme. Shiloh has a feeling that's why Drew is drawn to her. He won't stop fucking asking about her.

"What the fuck is this?" she asks, gesturing to the boat. It's hitched to the back of Mattie's truck, taking up the entire curb in front of their house.

"It's our new hobby!" Mattie exclaims. Shiloh bites his tongue at the use of the word "our."

"You bought a boat as a hobby?" Ashtyn asks incredulously. "Must be nice to have that much money. Maybe you should have bought your brother a new car."

Mattie doesn't seem to mind the dig. "Look, she called to me. I was supposed to be getting drunk on a boat in Mexico this Spring Break, and since I can't do that anymore, I figured I deserved my own boat. And everyone knows that Shiloh wouldn't accept anything from me. I could buy him a stick of gum, and he'd tell me to return it."

"It looks—" Ava starts, but Shiloh interrupts her.

"Like shit, yeah, we know." As if on cue, something falls and clangs around in the boat. Shiloh exhales, rubbing his hand over his face. "It doesn't even run."

"And where do you plan on leaving this boat that doesn't run?" Ashtyn asks, crossing her arms. "Because I'm pretty sure it's too big to leave in your dorm room."

"Well, I was thinking I could just leave it here for Shiloh to fix."

"Me!?" Shiloh exclaims, looking at his brother skeptically. "You've got to be joking me." This is *not* what he thought would happen when his brother bought the damn thing.

"Hey, it'll give you something to do other than sulk around all day."

Shiloh ignores the comment. "Matthew, I have a job. I don't have time to fix up a boat."

"I know, I know! I don't expect you to fix it overnight. I figured we could do it together, you know, over the summer."

This makes Shiloh pause. "Are you telling me you'll be here for the summer?

"Dad wants me to intern for him. Can't say no, obviously." Mattie doesn't let his emotions show, but Shiloh knows what this means for him. All summer, trapped in the house with Dad. He'll go crazy. He'll need an escape. This creeps into Shiloh's heart, and he feels it squeeze.

He sighs heavily. "Fine. I'll help you with your stupid fucking boat, but you're paying for all the parts." *That* he could absolutely let Mattie pay for. It's his boat, after all.

Mattie smiles, slapping his brother on the back. "Deal." Shiloh knows he would do anything to make sure his brother never stops smiling.

Ashtyn groans and throws her hands up. "Fucking boys." She turns on her heel and goes back into the house without another word.

"You know," Ava starts. "You can borrow my car to drive to work if you need to. If you can't find a new one yet."

The offer surprises him. "I couldn't do that, Ava," he replies. He feels guilt creeping up his throat. He hates relying on anyone other than himself. He could barely stand it in Drew's apartment. There's no way he could inconvenience her like that.

"You could. Especially if you let me help you with this boat project." Her eyes are cast downward as if she's embarrassed at the suggestion.

"You want to help?" The boat creaks ominously as Mattie jumps up into it. Shiloh hates the way he's itching to get started already. But that's just what he does: he fixes things. Other than himself, that is.

"I mean, if you'd like the help. I've always wanted to be a boat person," Ava says.

Shiloh stares at her for a moment. She's looking at him, brown eyes wide and a soft smile on her face. There's no pity, no judgment, no anger at him for not telling them about the divorce. She's just...Ava. He remembers their night in the kitchen, her hand in his and how good it felt. How good it felt to just sit with her and not speak. Her presence was enough to calm him down.

He clears his throat. "Do you know anything about boats?"

"I know absolutely nothing. But I'm willing to learn!"

"Well, looks like this worked out!" Mattie says, smiling. "With any luck, I'll be taking this baby out by July."

"And you'll be bored with it by August," Shiloh retorts.

"And then you'll inherit it. Quit complaining." This makes Shiloh laugh as he assesses the damage inside. He'll need to open the engine and take a look at all the parts. He's excited at the prospect.

"So, does this mean I'm part of the team?" Ava asks, eyeing the boat's interior. There's a sparkle in her eye.

"Yes, you're part of the team," Shiloh replies. Ava lets out a cheer. He hates the way his heart squeezes when he sees her smile and jump into the boat.

"Be careful," he says as if on instinct. "It's a death trap inside there."

"Relax, brother," Mattie says. "She's not a baby." His brother is looking at him curiously. There's no way Mattie knows about that night in the kitchen. He was snoring like an elephant in the next room. And Shiloh doesn't wear his emotions on his sleeve. There's no way his brother can interpret what's been going on in his mind since that night.

"Just don't want anyone getting tetanus," he says nonchalantly. Mattie gives him a mischievous grin, and he knows his brother doesn't believe him.

"Right," he replies, winking. Shiloh scowls at him.

"Going back to Ashtyn's earlier question: where exactly are we keeping this monstrosity?" Ava asks, inspecting the interior. She runs her hands along the ripped seats. "Because we already have one monstrosity sitting in the driveway." She looks pointedly at Shiloh's broken-down car. He hasn't had the heart to get rid of it just yet. It's been sitting there, staring at him sadly, begging to be put out of its misery. It reminds him of his marriage. Shiloh's always been terrible at letting things go.

"Here's what I propose," Mattie says, legs swinging over the edge of the boat. "How about I tow your piece of shit back to school with me and see if I can pawn it off on some idiot. Or, I can sell it for parts and send you whatever money they'll give me. Then, you can leave the boat in the driveway here and work on it when you can. I'll come and help whenever I have time."

"And where are we supposed to park our cars?" Ava asks, hands on her hips.

"Hey, she's not that big. You can still squeeze one car in the garage and the other right next to her."

Ava slaps her forehead, and it makes Shiloh laugh. "Welcome to my world," he says.

He takes Mattie up on his deal to tow the car back to school. Even if he ends up dumping it in a lake somewhere, Shiloh doesn't care anymore. He knows he could never get rid of the car himself. His brother taking it for him is like a weight off his chest.

"Can y'all get your asses in here and tell me what kind of pizza you want? I'm starving!" Ashtyn yells from the front door.

"Coming!" Ava exclaims and goes to jump over the side of the boat. Shiloh immediately holds out his hand to her, offering to help her down. She takes it, and Mattie wiggles his eyebrows. Shiloh flips him off behind Ava's back which causes Mattie to burst out laughing.

"What?" Ava asks, turning around once she's safely on the ground. "Did I do it wrong?" She's still holding his hand. He hates how natural it feels. It brings him back to the kitchen. He lets go, trying to forget the feeling.

"No, Mattie's just an asshole," Shiloh retorts.

"A perceptive asshole," he responds. Ava just shakes her head and heads toward the house and a very impatient Ashtyn.

"We'll be in in a minute," Shiloh shouts over to them, and Ashtyn taps her invisible watch impatiently. "Yeah, yeah."

Once the front door shuts behind them, Shiloh turns toward his brother. "Can you please not do that?"

"Do what?" Mattie asks innocently.

"Make assumptions."

"I'd say it's more of an observation."

"What, that I'm polite to my roommates?"

"You say roommates plural as though you don't treat them differently."

This pulls Shiloh up short. "You're saying I treat them differently?"

"Very differently."

"How so?"

"I've seen the way you look at her." Mattie doesn't have to specify, and Shiloh hates that he knows who he's talking about.

"I look at them the same. They're both my friends."

"You look at Ashtyn like a friend. You look at Ava..." He pauses and sucks in a breath. "You look at her like she'll break if someone loves her too much."

His words send a shiver through Shiloh. "That's ridiculous. I just didn't want her to hurt herself getting off the boat."

"And you would have done the same with Ashtyn?"

"Yes." He's not exactly lying, because he knows Ashtyn would never get in a death trap like that. The opportunity to offer her his hand would never have come up. But he absolutely would if she ever needed it. Maybe it wouldn't have been as automatic as it had felt with Ava but...surely he would still do it. Yes, he absolutely treats them the same. No question about it.

"You know it's not a crime to want to move on, don't you?"

"Okay, that's enough of this conversation. I'm not moving on with my roommates," Shiloh snaps.

"Why not? They're both attractive."

"Watch it, Matthew."

Mattie holds up his hands in surrender. "Okay, okay! Geez." He pauses a moment then says, "Just remember this, brother. They're not going to leave you, because you love them. You're allowed to love them. They're not her."

His brother's words nestle their way into Shiloh's heart, and he feels them settle. "I don't-I don't love them like that."

"I know, it's a different kind of love. But still, the point remains: they're not Scarlett."

Shiloh inhales shakily. "I know," he whispers. "I know." He takes a deep breath before saying, "Dad almost got to them."

"What do you mean?"

"I mean, Dad met them after we'd been up all night with Jess and he...he said something I won't ever tell them about. He-I don't want them to ever have to see him again. He's not worthy of getting to know them."

Mattie touches his arm, and then they're hugging. "Understood," he says, softly, knowing what their father is capable of. "Come on. Let's go before they order the pizza without us."

Shiloh nods and releases his brother. "Thank you for coming when I needed you."

"Fix up my boat, and we'll call it even."

"Deal," Shiloh says and smiles.

APRIL

Chapter 8

"Don't forget to have your rough drafts ready to go tomorrow!" Ava yells to her students as they bustle out of the classroom. She gets a chorus of "yeah yeahs," and she sighs. Just a couple more months until school is out for the summer, and she can pretend she doesn't have to work for a living. It's going to be glorious. Not to mention the prospect of working on the boat with Shiloh. She's not sure what prompted her to offer up her help. She knows next to nothing about fixing boats, but when she saw it sitting there so pathetically in the street, she couldn't help herself. She *had* to volunteer.

Part of her feels like she should repay Shiloh for his honesty in speaking about his divorce. She could tell how difficult it was for him to tell them something so personal. He's not the most forthcoming with his emotions, so seeing him so defeated and sad was a shock to the girls. Ava felt like she needed to do something to say, *I see you. Thank you for trusting me with this information.* Hence the boat.

She tries not to think too much about that night in the kitchen, their hands touching so intimately. She was just there to provide a comforting presence, that was it. Nothing more. No secret hearts racing, blood pumping, head spinning with crazy ideas. None of that.

Be fucking normal for once, Ava, she thinks to herself. She's about to start packing up her things when Derek breezes into her room.

"Hey!" he exclaims. His face is brightly animated by his enormous smile. Ava doesn't think she's ever seen him so excited.

"Hey, Derek," she says, returning his smile. She pretends not to notice how her heart doesn't skip a beat. Instead, it stays its steady, normal rhythm. Something very un-Ava like.

"So, um, I kind of wanted to tell you something."

Now Ava's heart *does* skip a beat. "Uh, okay. What's up?"

"So, you know how Daisy and I got on so well during Blockbuster at your birthday?"

"Yeah, I can't believe y'all never teamed up before then."

"Well, I think we might be teaming up more permanently now," Derek says, barely able to contain his smile. Ava blinks, his words not fully sinking in.

"Are you...and Daisy..."

"We're dating. I mean, we always got along when we hung out with y'all, but we didn't realize how much we enjoyed each other's company until I asked her out to coffee. So, I guess I just wanted to say thanks. You know, for teaming us up."

Derek and Daisy. Together. As a couple.

"Oh my god, Derek," Ava says, trying to hide her shock. "I'm so happy for you!" She envelops him in a hug, and he squeezes her back.

"I hope this doesn't make anything awkward," he says, blushing. Ava tenses. He's not aware of her crush, right?

"Of course not! I'm sure everyone will be thrilled."

Derek smiles. "Thanks, Ava. Hey, maybe you and Shiloh can be a team now."

"What!?" she exclaims, looking at him incredulously.

"You know, next time we have game night?"

"Oh, right," Ava says, heat rising to her face. She lets out a nervous laugh. "I'll probably have to be Ashtyn's partner, though. She's going to give you hell for stealing hers."

Derek laughs. "I think it'll be worth it."

She can't miss the way Derek's face morphs into one of complete and utter happiness, like he's just won the lottery.

"Oh! Before I forget," Derek says. "They're seriously looking for a replacement for Coach McCormack. Try asking around and see if anyone is interested. Otherwise, I'm going to suggest they ask you." He's teasing, but Ava knows Principal Jameson will absolutely ask her if they can't find anyone else.

"Yeah, yeah, I'll look around," Ava replies, absentmindedly.

"Alright, well, I'll see you on Monday. Have a good weekend!" And with that, Derek is out of her room, and she's reeling. So many emotions are running through her mind, she can hardly think straight. There's only one thing that will help her make sense of all this.

She texts Ashtyn and Brooke: *Girls night tonight. MANDATORY!!!*

* * *

The girls have a variety of snacks between them, Jess snuggled on the couch, and *He's Just Not That Into You* playing on the TV in the background.

"So, does this girls night have anything to do with what Daisy told me about at work?" Ashtyn asks, munching on a Red Vine.

Brooke looks between them, expectantly. "What did Daisy tell you at work?"

"That Derek and her are dating."

Brooke shrieks, spilling popcorn everywhere and scaring Jess awake. "Sorry, baby," she says, petting Jess in apology. Ava doesn't look at either of them.

"You know, I've always thought they'd make a cute couple," Brooke continues. She catches the way Ava's face falls slightly and says, "Sorry, Ave."

"No, it's okay. I'm happy for them."

"Are you actually?" Ashtyn asks, skeptically.

Ava sighs, heavily. "Yes, I am. Just because I used to have a crush on him doesn't mean I can't be happy for him now."

"Used to?"

"Yes, used to."

"Since when did the crush disappear?" Brooke asks.

"I don't know. I guess since my birthday. I saw how good he and Daisy worked together as a team. Everyone saw it."

"You sure it doesn't have anything to do with your cute new roommate?" Brooke wags her eyebrows at Ava, making her gasp.

"Brooke!"

"Oh, we already had this conversation," Ashtyn says. "Roommates are strictly off-limits."

Ava's cheeks go warm. "I don't have a crush on Shiloh."

"Okay, okay," Brooke says, hands raised. "What about Brad the barista?"

"Oh my god, can we stop talking about this please," Ava says, turning the volume up on the TV.

"Hey, you're the one that called this girls night meeting," Ashtyn laughs.

"Yeah, because I thought you were going to be nice to me!"

"Ave, babe, we're just teasing you," Brooke says, lightly touching her arm. "Besides, who knows, maybe this cute barista will write his number on your cup, and you'll fall madly in love. Happily ever after secured."

Ava sighs. "That only happens in the movies." She stares dreamily at the TV. Justin Long is about to utter "You are my exception" to Ginnifer Goodwin, and Ava is about to swoon. Deep in her heart, she aches to be in love with someone and to have someone love her back. She yearns for romance. She craves it so badly that she consumes it in all her media: books, movies, music.

"You know you'll have that one day, right?" Brooke asks, giving Ava a small smile.

Ava rolls her eyes playfully, trying to lighten the mood. "Yeah, I know. Just waiting to trip into the arms of my dream man." She catches Ashtyn's eye from across the couch. She looks at Ava like she can read her mind, and she's pretty sure she can.

"Oh, hey," Brooke says. "I meant to ask you. Why the hell is there a boat in your driveway?"

Ashtyn groans. "You'll have to ask Shiloh about that one."

"It's his brothers," Ava supplies. "He's helping him fix it up."

"And Ava so nicely offered to help with it."

Brooke laughs. "You offered to help fix up a boat?"

"That was my reaction," Ashtyn says.

Jess crawls into Ava's lap, and she pets her absentmindedly. She feels weirdly unsettled by their comments. "I don't know why y'all are making it out to be weird."

"You're not exactly one to sport a tool belt."

Ava frowns. "I just thought it'd be a nice thing to do, okay? Especially after he told us all about his divorce." Ashtyn sighs, and Brooke's eyebrows raise.

"So that's what this is all about?"

"No!" Ava protests. "I just..."

"Just because he told us about his trauma doesn't mean we have to treat him any differently," Ashtyn says. "I don't think he'd want us to."

"I'm not treating him differently," she says, voice hard. "I would have offered my help whether we knew about the divorce or not. I'm just trying to be fucking nice. And God forbid I like boats."

Ashtyn softens her voice when she says, "I just don't want you to get too attached."

"What the fuck is that supposed to mean?" Ava explodes. "You act like I'm fucking in love with him or something, when I'm just trying to get to know him and be friends. We live together! If we want him to stick around for a while, so we can stay in this house, then we need to be welcoming and nice. Maybe you could try it sometime."

Everyone freezes. Ashtyn's face hardens, and Ava knows she's struck a nerve. She regretted the words as soon as they were out of her mouth, but she can't take them back. Brooke sits between them, mouth pressed in a thin line. She's always been the middle man when Ava and Ashtyn have fought in the past, which isn't often.

"I am nice to him," Ashtyn says evenly. "Hell, I even like him. That doesn't mean I'm going to go out of my way to make sure he stays. He'll stay if he wants to. If he doesn't, we'll survive."

"He's not Brandon, Ash." The words are out before she can stop them. Ashtyn, to her credit, doesn't give anything away on her face. They never, *ever*, talk about Brandon. Ava knows what it does to Ashtyn.

"I really can't believe you just said that to me."

"Ashtyn, I'm sorry!" But Ashtyn doesn't let her finish. She just gets off the couch and heads upstairs toward her room. She doesn't slam the door. She doesn't scream. She just calmly walks away.

Tears well in Ava's eyes before she can even think of what to do. She knows she'll need to let Ash cool off. They haven't fought in so long that Ava almost forgot how awful it feels to fight with her best friend.

"Come here," Brooke says, holding her arms open. Ava crawls into her friend's embrace, and they sit like that as the movie's credits roll. Girls night is officially over.

* * *

It's midnight when Ava knocks lightly on Ashtyn's door. Brooke went home a few hours ago, telling Ava that Ash would talk to her when she's ready. She thanked her and gave her a tight hug before she left. Now, she stands outside Ashtyn's door, holding Jess to her chest in support.

"Come in." Ava opens the door and finds Ashtyn curled up in her bed, lights out, only the glow of the TV illuminating the room. "Get your ass in here."

Ava goes over to the bed and sets Jess on the blankets before burying herself into them. Ashtyn holds her arms out, letting Ava sidle into her best friend's embrace.

"I'm sorry," she whispers. "I didn't mean to upset you."

"I know," Ashtyn sighs. "I shouldn't have gotten so upset."

"No, you had every right to."

"I just get so mad when I think of him."

"I should have never brought him into this," Ava says. "That was fucked up."

"I know that Shiloh isn't...him." Ashtyn lets out a breath. "I do like Shiloh. He's probably the best roommate we could have gotten after Brooke, and I don't take that for granted. I just don't want either of us to get too reliant on him, you know?"

"Yeah, I know," Ava says, laying her head on her friend's shoulder. "But it's not a crime to be reliant on your friends."

"No, but I know you, Ava," Ashtyn replies, nudging her with her shoulder. "You love people so deeply. And I don't ever want anyone to take advantage of that. Even if you offered your help on a stupid boat."

Ava laughs softly. "I do genuinely like boats."

It's Ashtyn's turn to laugh. "You know you're my best friend, right?"

"Of course. It's me and you against the world." She feels Ashtyn tighten her grip.

"Are you actually okay? With all the Derek stuff?"

"Yes," Ava answers honestly. "I mean, it hurt a little at first. But honestly, I really am happy for him. I can't ever be mad at someone for finding love."

"Eh, who knows? Maybe they'll break up in a month," Ashtyn replies, her flippant attitude back in action.

"Nah, I think they'll make it. Besides, this just means we can demolish everyone in game night, since we obviously make the best team."

Ashtyn holds up her pinkie, something they used to do as kids. "You and me, no matter what?"

Ava hooks her pinky with Ashtyn's. "You and me, forever."

Chapter 9

Shiloh is sitting on his bed, Jess in his lap, watching *New Girl* when there's a knock on his door.

"Come in," he says, pausing the show. Ashtyn peeks her copper-haired head inside.

"Hey," she says, surprising him. He wasn't expecting her.

"Hey," he replies.

"You, uh, you busy?"

"No. Just watching *New Girl* with Jess."

"Do you mind if I come in?" She looks nervous, standing in his doorway. Shiloh doesn't think he's ever seen Ashtyn nervous before. She's always been so confident and self-assured.

"Be my guest." She enters and sits awkwardly on the edge of the bed. "Is everything okay?"

"Of course. Everything's fine."

"Okay, then what's with the surprise visit?"

"What, can't a roommate check on another roommate?"

Shiloh looks at her dubiously. "Seriously?"

"Okay, fine, I wanted to talk to you," she says, rolling her eyes. "It's about Ava."

Shiloh raises his eyebrows. He isn't sure what he was expecting, but it isn't this. "Ava." Her name feels heavy on his tongue, like he shouldn't be saying it when she's not around.

"Yes, Ava. You know, the cute brunette that shares a wall with you?"

"I'm aware," Shiloh says, slowly. "Is she...okay?" Something tightens in his chest at the thought of Ava not being okay. She had seemed completely fine this morning as they chatted over a morning cup of coffee. She'd asked him about when they might start work on the boat, to which Shiloh had replied that he was just waiting on the last of the parts to come in. He'd given Mattie an extensive list of everything he'd need in order to get the boat out on the water. It was going to be a much bigger project than any of them had expected. Even though Shiloh probably should have figured that out just by the look of it. Ava had smiled and said she couldn't wait to get started.

"Yeah, she's fine," Ashtyn says, flippantly, picking at her cuticles.

"Okay, then, is this about me borrowing her car? Because I've been giving her gas money every time I use it." Shiloh hates that he's had to borrow Ava's car, but he also can't ignore the fact that he's been saving money by not Ubering anymore. Budgeting for a monthly gas payment is much more manageable than Uber.

"It's not *exactly* about that," Ashtyn says quickly. "I just...worry about her, you know? She's the best person in the world. She is the epitome of kindness, and she's always doing so much for everyone else that sometimes she doesn't speak up for herself when she needs help. And I just don't want anyone to take advantage of her kindness, you know?"

Shiloh's blinks, stunned. "Ashtyn, I would never. I'm sorry if it came off that I'm taking advantage of her by using her car—"

"No, sorry, I'm not accusing you. It's just, ever since you told us about the divorce, and we've all gotten so much closer, she's gotten a soft spot for you. I'm overprotective, and I just don't want to see her disappointed if, you know, you plan on leaving or whatever. She really likes you."

Shiloh feels a thrill run through him at Ashtyn's words followed quickly by anxiety. "Well, I wasn't planning on leaving. Not for a while anyway. I kind of like it here."

Ashtyn gives him a small smile. "Yeah, we like having you here, too. I just never want to see her disappointed. So, if you don't actually plan on letting her help with the boat..." Her words dangle.

"Ashtyn, I wouldn't have said yes if I didn't mean it. I enjoy spending time with her. You too. I know that when I first moved in, we kind of agreed to stay out of each other's way, but I kind of feel like we're all friends now." He's trying to be vulnerable with her. He wants her to know that he cares for them.

She lets out a deep breath that messes up her bangs. "Yeah, I guess you're alright. I mean, you did fix the garbage disposal for me."

Shiloh grins. "I'm serious. I'm not going anywhere. And I'm not going to hurt Ava. Or you."

They stare at each other, Ashtyn's unwavering gaze never leaving his. Shiloh thinks this might be the most intimate moment he's ever shared with Ashtyn and probably ever will. He tries to convey in his expression that he means every word he's said. That he always will.

"Okay, okay, geez. I didn't mean for us to get all sentimental and shit," she says. There's the Ashtyn that Shiloh knows and cares for. He smiles and opens his arms out for a hug.

"You hug me, and I'll punch you," she says, a playful smile tugging at her lips.

"You hug Ava all the time!" he protests.

"Yeah, and she's the only person I willingly do it for besides my mother!"

Shiloh huffs and brings Jess up to his chest. "Fine, I'll just hug Jess instead."

Jess meows and licks his face. "Traitor," Ashtyn says, sticking her tongue out at the tiny kitten. "I rescue you, and this is how you treat me."

Jess, as if she understands the words, struggles out of Shiloh's arms and toddles toward Ashtyn. She scoops her up and holds her close. "That's better."

"Do you want to watch the rest of this episode with me?" Shiloh asks, unpausing the show. Ashtyn looks like she's about to say no, but then, settles into his bed with Jess on her lap, like a friend would.

"I guess I could stay for one episode."

* * *

By the time Ava gets home a few hours later, they're still sitting on Shiloh's bed watching *New Girl.*

"Hello?" she calls out. Her voice seems to echo throughout the still house.

"We're in here!" Ashtyn yells, not bothering to get up from her spot. Jess lies between them, sleeping peacefully and undisturbed. Shiloh hears Ava come up the stairs, and his pulse quickens. Guilt crawls around in his stomach. He feels bad that they were talking about her behind her back.

"What the hell? Are y'all watching *New Girl* without me?" Ava asks as she comes into the room and notices the TV. Ashtyn extends her arm, inviting Ava into their party. She flings herself onto Shiloh's bed and nestles into Ashtyn, her perfume filling the space.

"Since when did this become the official hang out space?" she asks.

"Since this little traitor," Ashtyn points at Jess, "decided this was her favorite place in the world."

Shiloh decides this might be his new favorite place in the world, too. That idea shatters when his phone buzzes with a text from his boss. He groans, and the girls look at him. "Someone called in sick to work. I gotta go in." It was supposed to be his day off, which is why he'd stayed in bed and watched TV all day. Normally he'd want to be out doing something on his off days, but work has been running him ragged lately.

"Have you thought about getting a new job?" Ashtyn asks, as if he hasn't thought about it every day of his life. It's not that he hates being a bartender. He's actually pretty good at it, if he's being honest. He can make good tips if it's busy, and it's a relatively easy job for him. He just hates the hours. He also hates how unfulfilled it makes him feel. He didn't necessarily plan on being a bartender for the rest of his life, but he has no idea what else he would even be good at.

"Not much I can really do without a college degree," he says simply. It's something his father would say to him.

"Of course there is!" Ava exclaims. "There are a ton of jobs that don't require a degree. You have experience." Her unabashed confidence in him astounds him.

"Yeah, but it probably won't pay as well as the tips I make now."

"And those tips will go down the drain if you have to go to the hospital without health insurance," she counters, and Shiloh doesn't have a reply. She's right, of course. There's no benefits with bartending. He can't remember the last time he even had health insurance.

"Can you stop making sense and get out of here. I need to change."

The girls humph and start to leave. Ashtyn scoops Jess up with her. Ava stops just as she's in his doorway. She looks like she's thinking about something intensely, chewing her bottom lip. Shiloh is about to say something when she looks up at him.

"Hey, you played soccer, right?" she asks.

"Yeah, in high school."

"But, like, you know how it's played? You understand the game, right?"

"Of course," Shiloh replies.

"I...might have a crazy idea," she says, looking at him with a twinkle in her eye.

"Ava, I'm flattered you think I could be a professional—"

"Oh, shut up," she laughs. "I'm serious."

"Okay, what is your crazy idea?"

"Our head girls soccer coach is retiring, and they're looking for a replacement. Would you be interested?"

A high school girls soccer coach? He never would have considered it, but the way Ava's looking at him, like he'd be a perfect fit, lets him contemplate it for a moment.

"I don't have a teaching certificate," he says lamely.

Ava just waves her hand. "Who cares. If I recommend you, they'd probably look past that. Not every coach has to teach a subject. You could just do coaching."

"This isn't like...a pity offer, is it?"

"Of course not! Derek asked me to be on the lookout for someone. Looks like I found someone."

Shiloh thinks back on his conversation with Ashtyn just a few hours ago. *Do not take advantage of her kindness.*

"I'll...think about it," he says, sincerely.

Ava smiles, that same twinkle still in her eye. "Great, I'll tell Principal Jameson to be expecting your application." She leaves, only the scent of her perfume lingering.

How could he ever deny her?

Chapter 10

The next couple of weeks fly by in a blur of game nights, movie hangouts, working late shifts at the bar, and relying way too heavily on Ava's borrowed car. Shiloh thinks back to his conversation with Ashtyn constantly. It nags at the back of his mind every time he slips into Ava's front seat. Her smell lingers, and the car is covered in remnants of her. A small book key chain hangs from her rear view mirror and stray straw wrappers litter the floor. He cleans out her side compartments every time he uses the car, but they're always full again the next time he uses it. It's all very much Ava.

He's scoured the internet for any cheap used car he can find, but he comes up short each time. Either it's ridiculously overpriced and the seller won't barter, or the car is in worse shape than his was. He knows he'll find something eventually, but for now, Ava's car will have to do. He always pays for gas and thanks her profusely, but she doesn't seem to think it's as big of a deal as he does. Again, he thinks about his talk with Ashtyn, and he knows that Ava is nicer than anyone else he's ever met. He feels so lucky to have found them both.

The end of the school year is fast approaching. Shiloh knows Ava and Ashtyn will have the whole summer off, and he'll be seeing them even more than he already is. He's grown comfortable being around them. He considers them friends, not just roommates. He no longer feels awkward sitting next to them on the couch, sharing a bowl of popcorn as they watch whatever movie they pick. He never objects, even if he knows he'll hate it. He's learned so much just by what the girls like to watch. He knows nothing scares Ashtyn. *Nothing.* He knows Ava has tears in her eyes every time there's a love confession in a rom-com. He knows Ashtyn's sense of humor is hilariously similar to Drew's, even though he'll never tell her. He knows Ava loves action movies. The girls have also discovered that he'll cry at any movie that features a dog, even if it doesn't die.

The longer he stays with the girls, the longer he feels like he wants them as friends for life. He's never really had that feeling before, except with Drew. He had some friends growing up, but moving to a new place so young, it was hard to keep in touch. Drew is the only person he's stayed friends with outside of high school. And Scarlett...well Scarlett was supposed to be forever. But with Ava and Ashtyn, he can feel himself becoming reliant on them. He feels himself wanting to be in their presence, wanting to watch movies with them and make fun of each other effortlessly. He looks forward to game nights with their mutual friends or coming home from work and seeing that they're still awake, waiting to share a glass of wine with him. He feels social for the first time in his life, and he likes it. He even enjoys the feeling of Jess sleeping on his chest at night. She's taken to sleeping only in his room, and the girls are extremely jealous. She's already gotten bigger and looks so much better than when the girls found her abandoned in the alleyway. She's mischievous, always stealing the girls' hair ties and Shiloh's toothpaste caps. Shiloh loves the little kitten, and he's secretly happy that she chooses to sleep with him. He also can't stop watching *New Girl.*

Despite all of the good things he's feeling, the divorce paper signing is looming over his head. His father has refused to call him since the incident, choosing to email anything he has to stay to his son. Shiloh received an email this morning with a date set for the papers to be signed, notarized, and filed. He'd been right when he clocked that the annulment was a scare tactic. He hates that it worked, but he's also grateful. He's finally getting all of this over with. It also helps to have Ava and Ashtyn waiting for him at home. They've already planned to throw him a "divorce party" afterwards. What that entails, he has no idea, but he's excited nonetheless. Really, he just wants an excuse to get drunk.

"So, I got you an interview," Ava says, snapping Shiloh out of his thoughts. They're gathered around the dining table, eating dinner. He freezes, fork poised halfway between his plate and his mouth.

"Already?" he asks, surprised. He barely put in his application a few days ago. He'd been debating it for a while now and finally decided to just go for it. He doesn't have any experience in coaching, but he was a varsity athlete in high school and that's got to count for something, right? He doesn't have much hope of getting the job, but when Ava looked at him with her signature Ava look, he knew he couldn't say no.

"Yeah, I told Principal Jameson I highly recommend you. He seemed intrigued."

"You only recommended him so they wouldn't make you do it," Ashtyn retorts, taking a big bite of food and chewing loudly.

"Did not!" Ava exclaims. "Okay, maybe a little, but I really do think you'd be a great fit, Shiloh."

He doesn't want to admit it, but he feels a sense of excitement at the opportunity. The prospect of not working at the bar anymore sounds more and more appealing every day. As does the prospect of health insurance. "When's the interview?"

"Friday."

"As in, two days from now?" Shiloh almost chokes.

"Yes."

"That's the day of my divorce signing." The room goes quiet. The girls knew it was coming, but Shiloh didn't tell them the exact day.

"Oh, shit, I'm so sorry!" Ava exclaims. "Ugh, this is what I get for doing everything last minute."

"No, it's okay," he replies, putting his hand on hers effortlessly. "What time is it supposed to be?"

"Noon, but I can totally talk to Rick and tell him I'm an idiot—"

"Ava," Shiloh says, silencing her. "It's okay. The signing's at nine. I can make both."

She lets out a breath of air and squeezes his hand. "Okay."

"I am screwed though, because I don't own any interview clothes."

"Doesn't Drew have something you can wear?" Ashtyn asks. "He's always wearing some stupid tie."

"Ashtyn," Ava scolds.

Ash just shrugs her shoulders. "What? It's true!"

"Drew's taller than me," Shiloh says. "His stuff wouldn't fit me."

"I'm sure I could ask Derek," Ava says. "Y'all are about the same height, right?"

"I can also just go find something at the mall."

"Ooh, we could go after school tomorrow!"

"Ave, have you ever been shopping with a man? It's not as fun as you might think it is," Ashtyn says. Shiloh suddenly realizes that he doesn't know anything about Ashtyn or Ava's past relationships. They know about his, but he doesn't know a single thing about theirs. Not that he's entitled to that information, he's just naturally curious.

"You've been shopping with a lot of men, then?" he probes.

Ashtyn glares at him. "Wouldn't you like to know."

"You know all about my past," he says simply, shrugging.

Ashtyn doesn't say anything. She just continues eating with a scowl on her face. Ava shoots him a look and very slowly, shakes her head.

Okay, so that's an off-limits topic with Ashtyn. Noted.

"Ashtyn almost fought my last boyfriend," Ava supplies, filling the silence. She says it flippantly, as if it's not a big deal.

"Seriously?"

"He called her ugly, so I said I'd show him ugly," Ashtyn says with venom in her voice.

There's a loud clatter, and Shiloh realizes he dropped his fork. Both girls startle at the noise. He doesn't know what his face is portraying, but they're looking intently at him.

"He didn't really say ugly," Ava says, a flush on her cheeks. "He just wasn't very good with words."

Shiloh feels his blood rushing in his ears. He shouldn't have brought any of this up. He's such an idiot.

"Ave, we both know what he said to you. You don't need to make excuses for a piece of shit like that," Ashtyn says. Her voice is hard, and Shiloh understands now why she came to talk to him that day. Ashtyn will protect Ava with everything she has.

"No one should ever say something like that to you," Shiloh says, his voice thick. "To anyone."

"Don't worry, I took care of him," Ashtyn says, punching her fist against her palm. There's a mischievous smile on her face that makes Ava giggle, and it breaks the tension. "Any man that wants to get with you has to go through me first."

"And none of my boyfriends ever have," Ava says.

"Because they've all been terrible! I refuse to let you settle for someone mediocre. Whoever marries you is going to have to be an actual Prince Charming."

Shiloh can't help but agree with Ashtyn. Ava deserves to be with someone who is above and beyond the best type of person. She doesn't need someone damaged; someone like him. He knows he could never hope to be with someone as pure as Ava.

"Geez, you act like I'm some kind of saint," Ava says. "I'm just a normal girl looking for a normal guy."

"I'll let you know when you find one," Ashtyn teases, making her friend burst out laughing. Her laughter is infectious, causing them all to join in.

It's in moments like these, where they're all laughing together, that Shiloh feels his heart start to heal. Slowly, ever so slowly, these girls have started to stitch him back together again. He'll never be able to properly thank them, but he's damn sure going to try.

Chapter 11

Shiloh is dressed in a dress shirt for the first time since he got married. It seems fitting that he's wearing one again on the day of his divorce. He tugs at the collar, feeling like he's being suffocated. He can't tell if he's terrified or excited at the prospect of seeing Scarlett again.

Ava dragged him out shopping the night before in order to find the dress shirt, and he'd admitted to her that he didn't know how to feel about seeing Scarlett again. He feels like he can admit a lot of things to Ava. She never judges him, only offering a comforting smile and a shoulder squeeze to let him know she's there if he needs her.

Yesterday, she'd just looked at him and said, "You'll know once you do."

As he reaches for the handle of the office door, his heart start to race. Scarlett is down this hallway. His feet move him forward, sweat starting to form on his palms. He wipes them on his pants, hoping to dry them off before he has to shake anyone's hands. He arrives outside the office, the door shut, his father's voiced muffled. She's just behind this door.

He takes a deep breath, steadies himself, then opens the door. It takes him a moment to realize that the room is empty aside from his father and another man, most likely the notary. He's only ten minutes early. Surely Scarlett should be here already. She is perpetually early for everything. Maybe now she's perpetually late to everything. Who knows what could be different in the span of a year.

"Am I early?" he asks, fully entering the room and taking a seat in front of his father. The table stretches the entirety of the room, making it seem endless. Shiloh feels small.

"No, you're right on time," Mr. Brooks says, coolly. He slides the paperwork out in front of him, and that's when Shiloh sees her signature: Scarlett Brooks. Her last name still irrevocably tied to him.

"Did she..."

His father doesn't let him flounder for long. "She thought it best to leave before you got here." And that's all the explanation he gets. He feels like he's been punched in the stomach. She doesn't want to see him.

"So, I just need your signature here," the notary says, pointing at the paperwork. He sits on the other side of the table with Mr. Brooks, and Shiloh feels utterly alone.

He grips the pen in his sweaty hand. Her signature is staring at him, taunting him. *You fucking idiot*, it hisses. *You really thought you were going to get to see her again? You lost that chance ages ago. Just sign the paper and get it over with.* His hand shakes as he brings the pen down to the paper. He almost falters, but then he's signing, his signature materializing next to Scarlett's.

Something like shame or guilt settles deep in his stomach. But then, as he really looks at the papers, the matching signatures sitting side by side, where they'll forever be immortalized, he feels the weight of the past ten years of his life lift slightly off his shoulders. It's like he can fully breathe again. His hands still shake and he suddenly wishes Ava was here to hold him steady.

The notary takes the papers, stamps them, then stands with a satisfied smile. "Alright, we'll get this filed." This is an everyday occurrence for him, unlike Shiloh, who feels like his life is forever changed.

"Son," Mr. Brooks says, holding his hand out. Shiloh takes it tentatively. He hates how tightly his father grips his hand. "This is the start of your new life. Look, I know tempers flared at brunch, but maybe I can pull some strings and get you an internship position with your brother this summer. I think it'd be good for you—"

"I have a job interview today," Shiloh interrupts him.

His father lifts an eyebrow, annoyance flashing across his face. "Where?"

"At Lakeview High. I'm interviewing for the head soccer coach position."

Mr. Brooks lowers the eyebrow. "Oh. Well, I guess it's better than bartending. Although, that's really not hard to accomplish." While his father hasn't brought up what Shiloh said at brunch, he knows he's still punishing Shiloh for it. He probably always will. "I still think an internship would be a much better direction for you."

Shiloh sighs heavily. "I need to go."

Mr. Brooks steadies his gaze and brings out the big guns. "Your mother wants you to come by for dinner sometime."

It hits Shiloh right where it needs to, but he doesn't let it show on his face. "I'll think about it," he says, but he knows he won't. He doesn't want to step foot back in that old house, with its haunting memories. Even if he tries to love his mother, it hurts to see her with his father. He can't bear it, especially without his brother with him.

"You know, you really should be thanking me," his father says. "I just saved you a lot of legal fees. Things could have gotten ugly."

It takes everything in Shiloh not to scream. Instead, he swallows his instincts, looks his father dead in the eye and says, "Thank you, father."

This seems to do the trick, because Mr. Brooks smiles. "Anytime, son. Don't be a stranger!" He gathers up his briefcase and walks out of the room without a backward glance at his son.

Finally, Shiloh's left alone in the room with only the ghost of his ex-wife haunting him.

* * *

Shiloh stands outside Ava's classroom, fist poised to knock. He's just finished his interview with Principal Jameson, and he thinks it went well. He'd been slightly frazzled and emotional when they started, but as it went along, Shiloh felt himself start to relax. Ava must have really talked him up to the principal.

He feels a tiny flicker of hope in his chest at the possibility of getting the job. He thinks he actually *wants* it. It sounds like something he could excel at, but he doesn't dare stoke that flicker. He can't afford to be disappointed. Really, he hates the idea of disappointing Ava more than anything.

He's not sure why, but he feels the need to see her after his interview. His interaction with his father, and Scarlett's absence this morning, had really thrown him for a loop. School is still in session, and as he peers through the window in her door, he sees her at her desk, scribbling on papers. He knocks lightly, and she looks up. When she sees him, a smile crosses her face. He can't help the way his heart skips a beat at her smile. She waves him in, and he opens the door, suddenly facing the stares of twenty high school students. Maybe he didn't think this all the way through.

"Uh, hey," he says, awkwardly.

"Come in! Come in! How did it go?" she asks excitedly. He makes his way across the room and takes a seat next to her desk, still very aware of the students' eyes on him.

114

"Good, I think," he replies. His hands are suddenly sweating again.

Ava notices the students staring at them, and she glares. "I give you all free time, and you're using it to stare at me instead of studying for your exam?" The students go back to their papers, some chattering amongst themselves, some blatantly on their phones, although it doesn't look like Ava cares much.

This is the first time he's really seen the inside of her classroom. There are bookshelves everywhere, filled to the brim with every genre of book imaginable. She's got a comfy reading nook in the corner with big plush bean bags and pretty art framed on the walls. It looks more like a library than a classroom. There's even a Banned Book section.

"Your classroom is nice," he says. Her desk is littered with framed pictures of her and her friends.

"Thanks," she replies, smiling. "I try to make it as inviting as possible. I let kids come in here and read during lunch if they want."

"I wish I'd had a teacher like you," he says. "Maybe then I would have liked school."

"That's the idea," she says fondly and warmth spreads in his chest. "So, how did this morning go?"

"Um," Shiloh starts, feeling very aware of the number of students in her classroom. "She wasn't there. Just my dad and the notary. I signed the papers, and then I was done."

Ava's face falls, slightly. "Are you okay?"

Shiloh swallows. He's definitely not okay, but he's not sure how to communicate what he's feeling. "I'm...fine. Maybe it's for the best that I didn't see her." Ava puts a comforting hand on his shoulder.

"Ms. Marshall, is that your boyfriend!?" someone yells from across the room. Shiloh chokes on a cough while Ava pulls her hand back.

"No, Michael, this is just a friend of mine."

"Everyone knows Ms. Marshall and Mr. Martin are secretly dating," someone whispers loud enough for everyone to hear.

"Can y'all stop gossiping about my love life and study for your exams, please?" Ava asks sternly but with fondness in her voice. The students grumble, but go back to their studies.

"They think you and Derek are dating?" Shiloh whispers, so only she can hear him. He doesn't miss the blush that flushes across her cheeks.

"Anytime two teachers are friends, students think they're dating," she says dismissively.

"Do you like him?" he asks, surprising himself. He knows he shouldn't be prying, but he can't help himself. This morning has been nothing like what he expected. Ava's blush deepens, showcasing the freckles on her cheeks.

"I mean, I used to," she admits. "But he's dating Daisy now. They make an incredibly cute couple." He's surprised at her honesty.

The bell rings, keeping Shiloh from saying anything else. Ava says goodbye to her students as they gather up their things and leave.

"So, you think you got the job?" she asks, her eyes sparkling.

"Uh, honestly, I have no idea," he replies. "The position doesn't need to be filled until August, so who knows how long it'll take for them to call me."

"Well, if I have a say, you'll be my first choice."

"Thanks," he says, feeling his cheeks flush. Her praise is intoxicating. "I, uh, should probably get going. My Uber should be here soon."

"You know you could just wait around here, right? There's only one more class until the end of the day. I can give you a ride home when school is over."

"You don't have to do that," Shiloh says.

"Come on, stay. I can show you the teacher's lounge and introduce you to some of your potential new coworkers. I can even show you the soccer field."

Shiloh hates that he wants to stay. He hates that he's getting his hopes up. He hates how comfortable he feels in Ava's classroom.

"Okay." The word is out before he can stop himself. The smile she gives him is worth it all.

MAY

Chapter 12

Shiloh's divorce party is in full swing. Music blasts, alcohol flows, and people chat aimlessly amongst themselves. The only person Shiloh requested to invite was Drew. Mattie had finals coming up and couldn't make the trip down. So, Ava and Ashtyn invited the usual crew to help celebrate. Derek and Daisy are currently chatting with Jordan and Brooke.

Probably already planning a wedding, Ava thinks, hating herself for it.

Seeing them together as a couple is definitely weird, but also kind of cute. She can't deny they look good together. Meanwhile, Ashtyn is trying very hard to ignore Drew's presence next to her while she talks with Parker and Damien. Shiloh, it seems, hasn't joined the rest of the festivities yet.

Ava sees him leaning against the wall, beer in hand, face unreadable. He doesn't look sad, just lonely in a room full of people.

"Hey," she says, sidling up next to him and bumping her shoulder to his. "How do you feel?"

He sighs. "I don't know, exactly. Different?" He asks it like a question.

"Different?" Ava repeats.

"Yeah, different. I thought I'd feel sadder. I mean, I do feel sad. It's all I've felt for the past few years, but when I finally signed those papers...I felt free." He rubs a hand down his face and breathes out a bitter laugh. "I didn't realize how fucking free I'd feel."

Ava doesn't say anything. She just stands with him, letting him know she's there.

"I'm actually a little scared," he admits after a moment.

"It's okay to feel scared. It's a big life change."

"Yeah, but I never thought I'd move on from this. I still feel like I don't deserve to."

"Shiloh, don't say that," she says, placing a hand on his arm. "You are allowed to move on."

"I don't know, maybe I'll stay single forever and become a crazy old cat man."

Ava laughs, and then says bravely, "Or you'll find the perfect girl tomorrow, and she'll make you believe in love again."

This time, it's Shiloh who laughs. "God, I wish I had your optimism, Ave."

Hearing him shorten her name sends shivers through her body. "Well, I'm always optimistic about love."

"Is that because you've never had your heart broken?" He says it quietly, almost like he's afraid to ask. She has to pause for a moment.

"I mean, I've been hurt," she says. She's had boyfriends. She's had situationships. She's had people she cares about. But has she ever really had her heart broken? No, she hasn't. She's never been in love the way she sees in movies. Maybe she's pretended, but she's never, truly felt it. "No, I guess I haven't. I don't think I've ever actually been in love." She's not sure why she admits this to Shiloh of all people. But he asked, and she feels like she should be honest with him.

"Well, let me tell you, it fucking sucks," he says gruffly. She hates the way he says it, with so much sincerity. So much certainty.

"What is it Tennyson wrote? 'Tis better to have loved and lost than never to have loved at all.'"

Shiloh turns to fully face her, and she's aware of just how close he is. "Did you just quote poetry to me?" There's a hint of a smile on his face, even though he's trying to hide it.

"Yes, yes I did," she says, chin held high. "What's an English degree good for if not to quote poetry to prove a point?"

"Oh, so you're proving a point?" He takes another sip of beer.

Ava sighs. "I don't know. I just can't imagine a world where I don't trust in love."

"Yeah, neither did I."

It hurts Ava to hear him say it, but she also understands why. "I'm sorry," she says, quietly.

"For what?"

"I'm just sorry you had to go through all of this, you know? But, I'm also going to be selfish for a moment and say that I'm glad we have you now." She looks up at him bravely.

His face softens, and he finally smiles. "Come here," he says, slinging an arm around her shoulders and pulling her into him. She wraps her arms around his waist, and she feels his cheek pressed against the top of her head. She holds him to her, hoping that with one single hug she can fix all his broken pieces. She knows she can't, but she can hope. She can always hope.

"I'm glad I have you two as well," he says into her hair.

Ava sighs deeply, letting this moment sink into her skin. She knows it'll end too soon.

"Shiloh!!!" Ashtyn yells, her voice echoing throughout the house. "Get your ass into the kitchen!"

"I think that's your cue," Ava whispers, untangling herself from him. Her body is begging her to keep hugging him.

"God, do I even want to know what's in there?" he asks.

"Depends on how you feel about cake."

Shiloh smiles. "I love cake."

They make their way into the kitchen where everyone is gathered around the table. A cake with sparklers sits in the middle. CONGRATS ON YOUR DIVORCE!!! spelled out in blue frosting. When Shiloh sees it, he lets out the loudest laugh Ava has ever heard come from him.

"Welcome back to single life, brother," Drew says, clapping Shiloh on the back. He's smiling, but Ava can tell there's a tiny hint of pain lingering underneath it. She knows he's happy to finally have the papers signed, but he's also terrified of what this means for him. She wishes she could take his pain and hold onto it for him, until he's ready to let it go. But she can't. So instead, she catches his gaze from across the sparkles and gives him an encouraging smile. A smile that says, *it's going to be okay.*

* * *

Shiloh is very drunk. He doesn't remember the last time he's been this drunk, but he thinks getting divorced is as good an excuse as any.

Taylor Swift plays on the speakers, and he dances harder than he's ever danced before. Normally, he'd never be caught dead dancing in a club, but this isn't a club. He's in his own home, with his own friends and his girls, and he feels free. Free to dance like a drunk idiot.

"Shake that ass!" Ashtyn yells from across the living room. She's also very drunk. Actually, he's pretty sure everyone is drunk, and he's glad he's not the only one. Being the only one drunk at a party is never the move.

The music changes to a slower song, and Shiloh sighs, catching his breath. He feels euphoric. The rush of the alcohol, the music in his ears, the feel of other people in the room with him. He doesn't think he's ever been happier. He never thought he'd be able to say that again.

He never thought he'd be able to survive leaving Scarlett. She was supposed to be his whole world, and then she was gone, leaving him with a broken heart and a self-hatred so strong it almost consumed him.

He lets out a shaky laugh, feeling unsteady on his feet as the alcohol makes his brain fuzzy.

"Woah, careful there," Ashtyn says, steadying him. She may be drunk, but she's definitely not as bad as Shiloh. She wraps an arm around his waist, and he puts his arm on her shoulders.

He spots Ava across the room, swaying slowly to the music with Parker and Damien. She looks...*beautiful.* Her eyes are closed, and she's singing along to the music. Shiloh can't help but feel the need to take her in his arms and spin her around the room.

"Don't look at her like that," Ashtyn murmurs, her voice so low he almost doesn't hear it.

Shiloh turns to look at her, tearing his eyes away from Ava. "What? Why?"

"Because you'll break her heart."

The words hit their mark, deep in Shiloh's heart. He feels like he can't move, can't think, can't do anything. *You'll break her heart.*

He's about to try and say something, anything, when the song changes again, and Daisy drags Ashtyn out of his embrace, forcing her to dance. He feels cold without her presence, and he makes his way to the kitchen, away from the noise and feelings thundering through his chest.

He fills a glass of water from the fridge and downs it in few a gulps. His head swirls, and he steadies himself against the counter.

"Hey," someone says, and Shiloh turns to find his best friend standing in the kitchen.

"Hey," he says, trying to keep his voice neutral.

"You okay?" Drew asks.

"Yeah, just wore myself out. Haven't drank this much since...God, I can't even remember the last time."

"Probably my twenty-third birthday," Drew says with a laugh. He's right. They'd gotten so drunk that night they were kicked out of a karaoke bar for being too rowdy.

Shiloh laughs at the memory. "God, I used to be fun."

"Yeah, you also used to be a pain in my ass."

Shiloh laughs again, knowing Drew doesn't mean it seriously. They sit in silence for a moment.

"I'm not going to ask you how you're doing, because I'm pretty sure you're tired of everyone asking you," Drew says. "But, I am proud of you."

"All I did was sign some papers," Shiloh says. He refills his glass again and continues chugging water.

"It's more than that, and you know it."

He's about to reply when Ava comes breezing into the kitchen. Her presence is like a shockwave to his system.

"Hey, kids!" she exclaims when she sees them. Her eyes are bright, her body relaxed by alcohol. Her smile lights up the entire room. Shiloh thinks about what Ashtyn said earlier, and shame heats his cheeks. He wasn't looking at her any differently than he normally does. He was just happy to see her happy. Just noticing that she's pretty. *Ashtyn has no idea what she's talking about*, he thinks.

"Hey, Ava," Drew says, matching her smile. He offers her a beer from the fridge, and she takes it.

"You good with another?" Shiloh asks, and he immediately fucking hates what he just said. He's a bartender. His entire job is to supply people with alcohol, and now he's checking on Ava, making sure she's not drinking too much, like he needs to look after her or something. *Idiot.*

Ava's brow furrows. "Yeah, I think I'm fine."

Drew looks at him curiously, and Shiloh can't make himself meet his gaze. He wants to sink into the floor and disappear completely.

"Oh, hey, I meant to ask you how your interview went," Drew says.

Shiloh's grateful for the lifeline. "Oh, yeah, it was okay."

"He fucking killed it," Ava says. She takes a long sip of her beer. "He's too modest for his own good."

"I doubt I killed it," Shiloh mumbles. "Besides, you talked me up so much, there's no way I lived up to the expectations."

Ava rolls her eyes. "Shiloh, take the fucking compliment. I really hate that you don't see how incredible you are."

"Shiloh Brooks, the ultimate self-saboteur."

"Fuck off, Drew."

"Ah, my favorite phrase in the English language," Ashtyn says, joining the conversation as she saunters into the kitchen.

"My personal favorite is 'fuck me'," Drew says, winking.

Ashtyn scowls at him, but Ava laughs and says, "Can you two just kiss already?"

Ashtyn's eyes go wide, and Drew nearly chokes on his beer. Ava's words have obviously done their job in surprising the two of them, and she smiles to herself.

"You're on thin ice, Ava Marshall," Ashtyn says, raising a finger up to her in warning. She has a hint of a smile on her face as Ava stares her down.

"Oooh, scary," Ava teases. Shiloh doesn't know if he's ever seen Ava this brazen and unfiltered before.

"Ladies, please, there's enough of me to go around," Drew says, inserting himself into the teasing match.

Ava giggles and wraps her arm around Drew's waist. He leans down and whispers something in her ear that makes her smile wider. The tiniest twinge of jealousy runs through Shiloh, and he tries very, very, very hard to ignore it.

Ava stands on tiptoes and whispers something back in Drew's ear. He's smiling, looking over at Ashtyn, arm still encircling Ava's waist. A blush tinges his cheeks, and he laughs.

"Thanks, Ava," he says. "You always know how to cheer a guy up."

Ashtyn just rolls her eyes and leaves the kitchen without a glance behind her. Drew looks at Ava, and she shoos him out as if he's supposed to follow Ashtyn. He does.

"What did you say to him?" Shiloh asks, trying to keep his voice steady.

"Wouldn't you like to know?" Ava says, mischievously. She's got a twinkle in her eye as she finishes off her beer. Yes, he really would like to know.

Instead, he says, "Fine, keep your secrets." He takes another beer from the fridge and pops the top. It's crisp going down his throat.

"I just gave him a little friendly advice," Ava shrugs. Shiloh doesn't pry, and she doesn't supply more of an answer.

They stare at each other over their beers, gazes unwavering. He's daring her to say something, and she's daring him to ask. Neither gives in.

JUNE

Chapter 13

Summer is finally here, and Ava is free. Free to sleep in as long as she wants. Free to spend her days doing absolutely nothing. Free to help Shiloh with the boat, which she's sort of doing right now. In reality, she's laying across the ripped seats reading a book while Shiloh clangs around at the back of the boat.

"You good down there?" she shouts.

"Just peachy," he replies, gruffly.

With the way things seem to be going, this might be her only chance to actually ride in a boat this summer. She's not exactly sure what's going on, but she does know Shiloh keeps muttering to himself about how Mattie's an idiot, and *he* should be out here in the heat doing all this work. Ava knows Shiloh doesn't mean it. He could easily dump the boat off with Mattie, but he won't. He likes the work too much.

"Need my help yet?" she asks.

"Yeah, you got a flux capacitor lying around anywhere?"

Ava laughs. "I still can't believe you'd never seen that movie before."

"Yeah, well, my father wasn't a big movie person." He doesn't say it sadly, just as a fact.

It's silent except for the clanging of Shiloh's tools. Then, he's standing up and leaning against the boat, looking at her. Ava sits up and sets her book aside, giving him her full attention. Her sweaty legs are sticky against the ripped vinyl. The sun beats down on their heads, unrelenting. Ava loves the heat. She loves the feeling of the sun kissing her skin. During the summer months, she tends to drive with her windows all rolled down, music blasting, letting the wind whip through her hair and the heat envelop her. She loves summer so much.

"You really want to help me with this thing?" he asks, squinting against the sun.

"Uh, yeah, I'm here, aren't I?"

"Okay, then get down here and hold this light for me."

Ava jumps down and holds up the small flashlight into the motor at the back of the boat. "How did you learn to fix things?"

"It was Drew's dad that actually got me into it," Shiloh says. "I needed a job when I graduated, and Sam took a chance on me. He has his own mechanic shop, and I worked there for quite a few years. I was always interested in fixing things since I never seemed to know how to fix things at home."

"Why aren't you working there now?"

Shiloh continues tinkering with the motor. "Scarlett hated it. She said I'd come home smelling like grease and gasoline. So, I quit. Really fucked over Sam with that one. I started bartending, because I couldn't find anything else. Now, I've just been stuck doing it. I thought about going back to Sam and asking him for a job, but I've never been able to bring myself to do it. Plus, fixing things has become more of a hobby to me than an actual job. I don't think I'd like doing it for money anymore."

Ava blinks, surprised at how much he just divulged. "Wow," she says. "You're a man of many trades."

Shiloh laughs. "And yet, I can't seem to find anything that really fulfills me."

"You think coaching could do that?"

"I don't know," he says. "Maybe. What about you? What made you want to be a teacher?"

"Well, I've always been a huge reader, so I knew I wanted to major in English in college. There aren't really too many jobs that I could have done with that, so I got my teaching certificate. Turns out, I love teaching. I love my kids, which is ironic since I don't think I could ever see myself as a mom. But when I see their faces discover a new favorite book, or they get the message I'm trying to teach, it's just so satisfying. Plus, I try to be a positive influence in their lives. Life is hard enough as a teenager, and if I can help ease that difficulty, even for just one kid, then I think I've done my job."

Shiloh stops what he's doing to look up at her. "I loved your classroom," he says. "It felt cozy."

This makes Ava smile. "Thanks. I always wished I'd had a sanctuary of sorts when I was in high school. You know, someplace to escape all the horrors of teenagedom."

"Did you have a tough time in school?"

"No, not nearly as bad as some people. I was just a very overly emotional and dramatic teenager. You know, the world was ending if the boy I liked didn't like me back."

Shiloh continues doing whatever he's doing with the engine, and Ava continues holding the light. "When did you...start dating Scarlett?" she asks. It feels weird to say her name out loud. Like it's not allowed, some off-limits topic between them.

Shiloh, to his credit, doesn't even flinch. "I met her freshman year, and we started dating sophomore year. By senior year, I knew I wanted to spend the rest of my life with her, so I asked her to marry me. I didn't even have a ring. I just asked her, and she said yes. Everyone thought we were crazy, which now I know we definitely were." He takes a deep breath. "She'd skipped a year in elementary school, so that's why she was seventeen when we graduated and eventually got married. Her mom was dying of cancer, and her dad had never been around, so I felt like I needed to take care of her, you know? I was pretty much all she had left, and I hated my parents enough to want to start my own family with her. And, well, we all know how that turned out."

Ava shivers despite the heat. "Do you think you'll ever get married again?" She's not sure why her heart is racing in anticipation of his answer.

"I honestly don't know," Shiloh says. His face is scrunched in concentration. "My gut tells me no."

Ava is about to say something when the alarm on her phone goes off, startling her, and she drops the flashlight. "Jesus Christ," she mutters. She pulls it out and shuts it off. "Sorry, I've got to go and start getting ready." Her heart is still racing, and she tries to shake Shiloh's words out of her head.

"Ready for what?" he asks, confused.

She mentally smacks her forehead. She completely forgot to tell him. "We're playing a friendly game tonight against the students to celebrate the end of the school year, and to send off Coach McCormack. You should come. Maybe you'll get a little glimpse into your future."

Shiloh lets out a small laugh as he gets up and wipes his hands on his shirt. "I guess I could come see what all the fuss is about."

* * *

Shiloh can't take his eyes off Ava as she flies down the field. She's incredible. Her hair, tied back in a ponytail, whips behind her as she takes off, ball at her feet. There's a smile on her face as she does a trick move around one of the students. She gets around her, and then passes the ball to Parker, who shoots it right into the back corner of the net, scoring their first goal of the match. Ava screams and envelops

Parker in a hug while the rest of their team rushes over to them in celebration. They're still losing spectacularly, but they don't care. They celebrate like they've just won the World Cup. The students smile, congratulating them, genuine happiness on their faces.

"Hey, that could be you next year," Derek says. He points toward Coach McCormack, who's laughing and high-fiving the teachers. "They do this every year even though they never win."

"Who, the teachers?"

"Yeah, they lose every year, but they still always agree to it."

"Why?" Shiloh asks.

"Because they love it. And it helps the team feel better if they had a bad season or, you know, their coach is retiring. Ava's actually the one that started it when she first got here."

"She tried to wrangle me into joining," Ashtyn grumbles, but there's a smile on her face.

"Me too," Derek laughs. "I told her my asthma would make it impossible to run more than ten minutes. She didn't believe me until she saw for herself."

Daisy laughs and wraps an arm around Derek, snuggling into his side. "I still think you could have made a good goalie."

Derek smiles at her and presses a kiss to her lips. Ashtyn makes a gagging face behind them that makes Shiloh laugh.

The referee whistles for halftime, and Ava heads toward them, sweaty and chugging a water bottle. Parker and Damien, right on her heels, joining the rest of the group.

Shiloh's about to get up and head to the restroom when Ava plops down next to him.

"Hi," she says

"Hi," he replies.

"So, what do you think?" She stares straight ahead, stray, sweaty hairs plastered to her forehead.

"I think you play incredibly," he says. "You know you're amazing, right?"

Ava scoffs. "I didn't mean what you thought of me. Besides, I can barely run down the field and back without almost throwing up."

"That doesn't mean you don't play well," Shiloh counters. "Everything you do is deliberate. It's like you can see five moves ahead of everyone."

Ava doesn't reply as she grabs his hand and hauls him up. She's dragging him across the field before he even has a chance to protest. Her hand is warm and sweaty in his, but he doesn't mind. It brings him back to that night in the kitchen. A night he tries not to think about.

"Where are we going?" he asks.

Ava still doesn't say anything until they're across the field and heading straight toward Coach McCormack. "Hey, Coach Mack," she says. "I want to introduce you to your replacement." Her words make Shiloh stop in his tracks. He hasn't received a call from anyone informing him he got the job.

"Ah, you must be Shiloh," Coach McCormack says, holding out his hand. Shiloh takes it, and they shake.

"Yes, sir," he replies.

"Ava's told me all about you. Anyone that has her stamp of approval has mine." Ava blushes at the coach's words, and Shiloh stares back at them, dumbly.

"Sorry, I wasn't aware I had received the position," he says.

"Ah, I'm sure they'll call you eventually," Coach Mack says, smacking him on the shoulder. For an older man, he's got a hell of a grip. "I told Jameson to pick whoever Ava gave him. Really, I wanted her to do it, but she kept refusing."

"I teach enough as it is," Ava says, holding up her hands. "Besides, I knew a guy that would be really good at it."

At her words, Shiloh's heart soars, and he knows he can't let her down. He can't let anyone down, now.

The referee returns and indicates the second half is about to start.

"Hey, why don't you stay on this side, and I'll show you some of the plays I like to use. Get you a little prepared," Coach Mack says.

"That sounds great," Shiloh replies, and before he can even turn to thank Ava, she's already running to her place on the field, high-fiving Parker.

The teachers do, in fact, lose spectacularly. However, every one of them has a smile on their face as they high five each of the students, congratulating them on their win. Ava seems to know the name of every single player. Shiloh can't help but think that might be him next year.

As he stood on the sidelines, watching Coach Mack run his team one last time, he felt excitement stir in the depths of his stomach. He's excited to get this job; to meet the team and start coaching.

"Well, Shiloh," Coach Mack says, "I'm handing the baton over to you. Take care of my team." He hands him a binder full of plays and statistics from previous years. It's thick, full of history, and Shiloh can't wait to open it.

"I will, sir," Shiloh says, a smile on his face.

"Oh, and take care of her too," Coach says, pointing toward Ava. "She's the best of the best." Shiloh just nods, trying not to let a blush creep into his cheeks.

"Dang, you got the binder and everything," Ashtyn says, coming up to him, arms crossed, smiling slightly. "You excited?"

"I am," Shiloh says honestly. "It feels right."

"Well, that's something."

"Yeah, I guess it is."

Ashtyn is about continue when Ava runs up to them, throwing her sweaty arms around her friend.

"Ew!!" Ashtyn exclaims, struggling out of Ava's embrace. "Ava, you stink!"

"Aww, you don't like the smell of me?" She rubs her sweaty forehead against Ashtyn's neck, making her squeal.

Oh, you are dead!" Ashtyn yells, finally escaping from Ava's grip. She grabs a stray soccer ball and chucks it at Ava, hitting her right in the head.

"Hey!" Ava exclaims and lunges for Ashtyn, but Shiloh is wedged between them, Ashtyn's hands on his arms as she uses him as her human shield.

"Hey! I'm not involved!" he yells, laughing as Ava and Ashtyn dance around him, trying to get to each other.

"Oh, you're involved," Ashtyn says, still hiding behind him. "All roommate disputes are handled together."

"Well, in that case," Shiloh says and picks Ashtyn up over his shoulder. She shrieks, but a laugh escapes her as Shiloh takes off running away from Ava.

"No fair!" she yells, chasing after them. And then Ava's jumping onto his back, making them all tumble to the turf in a heap of laughs. Shiloh takes the brunt of the fall, so he doesn't hurt either of the girls, but they're both laughing hysterically, tears streaming down their faces. It's here, on the ground in the summer heat, with Ava and Ashtyn next to him, smiles on their faces and their laughs in his ears, that Shiloh, for the first time in a long time, feels excited at the idea of moving forward. Especially if he has the girls by his side.

Chapter 14

The sound of Mattie and Ava's laughter causes Shiloh to stop what he's doing and peek out from behind the boat. They both have badminton rackets in their hands, tossing a birdie back and forth. Even Ashtyn is out with them, sitting on the porch in the shade, her face buried in her Switch. It was the only way she would agree to come outside. He understands why she hides away from the sun's harsh rays. With her pale skin and copper hair, she'd burn to a crisp in five minutes flat.

"So y'all get to play badminton all day while I work my ass off over this boat?" Shiloh asks, teasing Mattie and Ava.

"Hey," Drew says from right next to him. "What am I, chopped liver?" Shiloh's pretty sure the only reason Drew agreed to come over and help is because he wanted to see Ashtyn, even though she's been ignoring him ever since he got here.

"Hey, I offered to help, and you told me to fuck off," Mattie says, shrugging.

"Because you kept giving me the wrong tools!" Shiloh counters but laughs. He doesn't mind if Mattie doesn't help. He's just glad he's here.

Mattie's been in town ever since school got out. Even though

Shiloh doesn't see him much, because Dad keeps him so busy with his internship, he still sees him more than normal. He comes over at least once a week for dinner, and the girls seem to enjoy his company which makes Shiloh's heart swell. The only friction that still lasts is between Ashtyn and Drew. Nothing anyone does can thaw her icy expression every time he's over, which isn't much. Shiloh feels guilty that he doesn't see Drew as much as he used to. He feels like he's abandoned his best friend. So, he invited him over today to help with the boat. Thank God for that, because it seems like Ava and Mattie are having more fun playing games together than actually helping.

"Come take a break and play with us!" Ava exclaims, hitting the birdie toward Shiloh. It hits him in the forehead, making her giggle.

"If we want any chance of taking this thing out before summer ends then I don't have time for games." He throws the birdie back. He's joking, but the sentiment remains true. He's already so behind on his scheduled repairs. Ava sticks her tongue out at him before resuming her game with Mattie.

"I think this starter motor is completely useless," Drew says, looking into said motor. "I can probably ask my dad if he can order one. Mattie's paying?"

"Drew," Shiloh starts, but Drew gives him a look.

"You know he doesn't hold a grudge," Drew replies. "He knows what you've gone through."

Shiloh still feels guilty. He hasn't been able to face Drew's father since he skipped out on him all those years ago. Another lost father figure in his life.

"Yeah, I know," Shiloh says, sighing. "I still feel like a shithead, though."

"Oh, he's used to that," Drew says, giving him a smile. "You know how my sister is. The ultimate shithead."

"Okay, fine, call him and see if he has one in stock."

Drew gets up and heads toward the shade of the porch as he calls his father. The sun beats down on Shiloh's shoulders, and he steps toward the edge of the driveway, in the shade of a large oak tree.

"Hey! That's out of bounds!" Ava exclaims, her voice carrying across the yard.

"The boat is the edge of the line! If it's inside the boat then I think that counts as my point," Mattie counters.

Ava groans and tosses down her racket. "Fine, I'll get it."

Shiloh's phone buzzes with a message, causing him to look away from Ava and Mattie's argument. Scarlett's name flashes across the screen, and a rush of adrenaline courses through his system. He feels like he might pass out. The boat groans ominously as Ava jumps into it to retrieve the birdie.

"Be careful!" Shiloh calls out absentmindedly. He can't take his eyes off the phone screen.

"Yeah, yeah" Ava mutters. "Got it!" She holds the birdie up triumphantly and tosses it back to Mattie.

Shiloh glances up at her. "Don't you dare jump off the side, Ava. Use the steps at the back," he says.

"Good God, I'm not a child," she replies, rolling her eyes. However, she complies, making her way to the back of the boat where she can step off onto the steps.

Shiloh's phone buzzes again with another message from Scarlett. He stares at it in his hand like it might explode. He swipes to open the message. As soon as the message from Scarlett opens onto his screen, he hears Ava shriek in surprise. His head snaps up immediately, and he turns to see her tumble forward out of the boat, head first. Everything seems to happen in slow motion.

Shiloh drops his phone and lurches forward, arms outstretched toward Ava but he's so far away, at least ten steps. Her foot catches on the lip of the boat as she tries to step off onto the steps. Her body catapults forward, her entire front half careening toward the pavement. Her arms pinwheel out in front of her as her forehead makes contact with the blades of the propeller attached to the motor. It slices open her skin, blood spurting onto the concrete. And then Shiloh's there, faster than he can even comprehend, catching her body in his before it hits the driveway. He lets out a gasp as the wind is knocked out of him by her body landing on top of his. He can already feel a bruise forming on his tailbone, but he doesn't even care. He cradles Ava's body against his own, trying to make sure she's okay. But he knows she isn't. Blood gushes from her head wound all over his shirt and drips onto the ground.

Ashtyn jumps up from her spot on the porch and runs faster than Shiloh has ever seen her move. She kneels in front of Ava, eyes wide. "Oh my god, Ava!"

"I'm fine! I'm fine! Shiloh caught me," Ava says, but her voice is anything but calm. She's shaking uncontrollably, and Shiloh holds her to him, trying to keep her steady.

"Someone get me something to put against this!" Ashtyn commands, cradling Ava's head in her hands. Mattie and Drew have both run over, expressions of concern on their faces.

"Shirt, Matthew! Give it to me!" Ashtyn exclaims. Mattie doesn't even think twice before pulling his shirt over his head and passing it to Ashtyn. She balls it up and presses it against Ava's forehead, making her wince in pain. It breaks Shiloh's heart into a million pieces. He should have been there to offer her his hand. He should have helped her off the boat. This wouldn't have happened if he hadn't been distracted by his stupid fucking phone. It sits cracked and abandoned on the pavement.

"Okay, this is going to need stitches," Ashtyn says. "Ava, are you dizzy? Can you stand?"

"I think so," she says, her voice wobbly. Tears are welling in her eyes. "It just really fucking hurts."

"Here, I can carry you," Shiloh says, scooping her up into his arms. He holds her securely to his chest so as not to drop her.

"Look at me," Ashtyn says. "Follow my finger." She holds up her finger and moves it back and forth in front of her face. Ava's eyes follow it exactly. "Okay, I don't think you have a concussion. Thank God Shiloh caught you before you smacked your head on the pavement."

"She still has a gushing head wound," Shiloh says roughly, frowning. "We need to get her to the ER."

"Shi, I'm fine. I can walk."

"Like hell you can," he says, carrying her toward Drew's truck. He wrenches the door open and places her in the backseat gently. He gets in next to her and buckles the seat belt for her. His hands are shaking, but it doesn't hinder him from securing Ava safely in the car.

"Let's go!" he calls to the others. They're there immediately, piling into the truck. Drew drives cautiously but urgently toward the ER.

"Is this a bad time to say that I really hate hospitals?" Ava says, her face paling.

"Don't worry, I'll hold your hand the whole time," Ashtyn says, still pressing Mattie's shirt to Ava's forehead. The blood is starting to seep through the cloth. He didn't realize how much a head wound can bleed. There's blood all down the side of his shirt, and he feels sick. Not because of the blood, but because it's Ava's blood, and it shouldn't be profusely leaking out of her body.

They arrive at the ER in record time, thanks to Drew. Shiloh's about to take Ava in his arms again, so he can carry her through the doors, when she puts a hand against his chest. "I can walk, I promise. Just give me a shoulder to lean on."

Shiloh obliges even though everything in him is screaming to hold her. Nothing can hurt her if he's holding her. She wouldn't have fallen out of the boat if he'd been there to hold her hand. He helps her out of the car and snakes an arm around her waist. She presses against his side, holding the shirt to her forehead. Ashtyn has already charged ahead inside. It makes Shiloh feel good that she trusts him to take care of Ava, to get her safely inside.

They gather in the air-conditioned lobby where Ashtyn's already at the front desk filling out forms for Ava. The nurse looks up at them and doesn't even seem surprised.

"Sir, you can't come in here without a shirt," she says in a monotone voice, eyes going to Mattie.

"Well, ma'am, my shirt is currently being pressed against this young woman's gushing head wound. So, I think I'd like to keep it there."

The nurse doesn't look amused. She just holds up a few towels. "Use these. That shirt isn't soaking up much of anything anymore."

Shiloh takes the towels from the nurse gratefully. He turns toward Ava and slowly, ever so slowly, removes Mattie's shirt from her forehead. The wound isn't super deep, but it's still spurting blood. Ava closes her eyes as it runs down her face. Shiloh hurriedly throws the shirt toward Mattie and replaces it with a clean towel. He holds it firmly against her wound, making her face scrunch up. He hates that he's causing her pain, but he knows it needs to be pressed tightly against the wound. Mattie puts the blood-soaked t-shirt back on and shivers.

"Sorry," Ava says weakly as she squints at Mattie. "I ruined your t-shirt."

"Ava, I promise you, I hated this shirt anyway."

This makes Ava laugh, and Shiloh's grateful to hear the sound come from her lips. He uses the other towel to try and wipe away the blood on her face. It's thick and sticky and not coming off easily.

"Let's go to the bathroom," he says. "I need to wash off your face with water."

He knows he should let Ashtyn handle this, but she's busy filling out all of Ava's paperwork. He probably doesn't even know the answer to any of the questions on those forms. He decides he'll let Ashtyn handle that, and he'll handle this. They make their way toward the bathrooms and find a single one unoccupied. He ushers her inside then shuts the door and locks it.

"Okay, up you go," he says, hoisting her up onto the counter. He starts the sink's stream and waits for it to warm up. He can't seem to look at her. If he does, it might break his heart.

"I'm not dying," Ava says, her legs swinging aimlessly off the edge of the counter. "It's just a little cut."

Shiloh sighs as he runs the towel under the warm water. He brings it up to her face and starts to wipe away the blood. He's standing between her legs. "I should have been there to help you," he says. Her eyes are closed as he wipes the towel gently against her face.

"I'm not a child, Shiloh," she says. "I just tripped. It could have happened to anyone."

"Yeah, but I was distracted. I shouldn't have been distracted when it comes to something like this."

"Something like what?"

"Something like you." She shivers underneath his touch. As the blood comes off her face, Shiloh can see the array of freckles that dot her cheeks and across the bridge of her nose. They're painted on her cheeks almost perfectly, as if someone placed them there deliberately. He realizes this is the closest to her face he's ever been. He could easily lean in and kiss her. Shame floods through him at the thought. Here she is, in pain with blood pouring down her face, and he's thinking about kissing her. *You're so fucking selfish*, he thinks.

Her eyelashes are stuck together, and he wipes them with his thumbs. They come apart underneath his touch, and she's able to open her eyes. Their gazes hold for a moment until a banging against the door startles them.

"Hey, they're ready for her!" Mattie says from the other side of the door.

"Wow, that was quick," Ava says, hopping down from the counter. Shiloh instinctively shoots out his hands to steady her. She grabs onto his bicep tightly, her face contorting with pain.

"You okay?" he asks.

"Yeah, I'm good," she says, not taking her hand away. "Just a little light headed." Shiloh wraps his arm around her waist again and leads her out of the bathroom. Ashtyn is waiting next to a nurse by the doors. Shiloh leads Ava over toward them but doesn't release his grip. Ashtyn reaches out for her.

"It's okay, I've got her," she says. Shiloh reluctantly lets Ava go and watches as they walk her into an area he cannot go.

"Come on," Drew says, hand coming up to grip Shiloh's shoulder. "Let's get you cleaned up."

It's then that Shiloh looks down at his stained hands. They're covered in Ava's blood, and they're shaking. His shirt is also stained, but he doesn't really care. It's nothing compared to Mattie's.

Drew steers him toward the bathroom they just vacated, and Shiloh can see the mess they left behind. Wet paper towels covered in blood litter the floor. The counter is smeared with it. Shiloh feels sick and vomits into the toilet.

"Geez, you okay, dude?" Drew asks. He starts to clean up the mess on the counter. Shiloh heaves again, but there's nothing left to come up. He spits, trying to clean out his mouth, and rests against the edge of the toilet seat. He tries not to think about how gross it is.

"Shiloh?" Drew says, concern lacing his voice.

"I'm fine," he replies. He can start to feel his adrenaline wearing off and his back screams from the impact of the pavement. He knows he's going to bruise.

"She's going to be okay," Drew says. "You probably saved her from a much worse injury by catching her. I don't know how the fuck you got over there so fast."

"Yeah, me either," Shiloh mutters, his voice edged with worry and panic that won't subside. He leans against the wall and winces from the pain.

"You sure you're okay? You took a lot of that impact."

"I'm fine," Shiloh snaps. "Ava's the one we're supposed to be worried about."

Drew frowns, but doesn't say anything else. He resumes cleaning up the counter while Shiloh tries to steady his breathing and calm himself down. Ava's going to be okay. They're going to stitch her up, and she will heal. He repeats that to himself until his hands stop shaking long enough for him to scrub the blood off.

Chapter 15

Ava winces as the doctor staples her forehead wound shut. It doesn't hurt, she got a nice dose of lidocaine injected, but the noise makes her flinch. It's so loud in the small room.

"Be still," the doctor commands. Ava hates the firmness in his voice, like he has no empathy. Ashtyn squeezes her hand comfortingly and gives her a reassuring smile.

He's done within a few minutes and places a large bandage over the staples. It surprises Ava how quickly everything gets done. He gives her a sheet on how to care for the staples, and when she should come back to get them removed. She thanks him, and he leaves without a reply. *Five-star bedside etiquette,* she thinks.

"How do I look?" Ava asks, turning toward her friend.

"Like a badass," Ashtyn says, smiling at her. She still hasn't let go of her hand.

Ava can't believe she tripped out of the boat. It's so ridiculous, actually. She had been staring at Shiloh when her sandal caught on the lip of the boat, and she'd gone tumbling forward. She wasn't sure how on earth Shiloh was able to make it to her before her body hit the pavement. She braced herself for an impact and instead, she'd just felt Shiloh's soft body against hers. She's so grateful he was there to catch her. And then, help clean up her face while Ashtyn took care of the paperwork. His face had been so close to hers, his breath against her skin. His fingers gently rubbing against her eyelashes, giving her a moment's reprieve from the pain.

She shakes her head, a stab of pain reminding her of what's there now. She can't be thinking like this about her roommate. He would have done the same thing for Ashtyn, if she had tripped instead.

"You ready?" Ashtyn asks, snapping Ava out of her thoughts.

"Yeah. I'm starving."

They make their way toward the lobby where the boys are waiting for them. Mattie's shirt, which was once green, is now almost completely dark brown. Shiloh's white shirt is also stained with her blood, and she knows he'll never be able to get it out. Once they notice Ava and Ashtyn, Shiloh jumps out of his chair and runs his hands over her arms, eyes roaming her face.

"Are you okay?" He's looking at her with concern in his eyes.

"Yeah, I'm fine," she says. "Just embarrassed."

Shiloh's brow furrows. "Ava, you don't have anything to be embarrassed about." He wraps his arms around her in a hug, careful about her injury. Ava's suddenly self-conscious as everyone stares at them. She clears her throat awkwardly and pulls away. Shiloh's arms drop to his side.

"Well, I'm famished," she says, breaking the awkward tension in the room. "I feel like I deserve something greasy." There's a chorus of agreement, and they head back toward Drew's truck. Ava tries not to look at the stains on his backseat. She definitely needs to offer to help pay for him to get it cleaned.

They go through the drive through at Whataburger and grab dinner to bring back to the house. Ava feels the lidocaine start to fade, and her head begins to throb. Ashtyn rubs a comforting hand on her back as if she can tell Ava's starting to feel the pain again. Her best friend has always been so perceptive to Ava and her emotions.

As they pull up to the house, food secured, Ava sees more blood staining the concrete through the window. She thinks the black motor probably has blood all over it too, and Shiloh will have to clean it. She'll offer her help, of course. She also sees Shiloh's phone lying abandoned in the driveway. He never picked it up after he dropped it. He must have been too concerned with Ava to go back for it. The thought warms her heart. He doesn't even glance at the phone as he helps her out of the truck. It's Mattie that picks it up and stashes it in his pocket.

"Come on, let's get you settled," Shiloh says, his hand warm in hers.

Jess welcomes them home with meows. She seems to sense something is amiss, because she winds herself through Ava's legs instead of Shiloh's. She always greets Shiloh first.

"Hey, stinker," Ava says, scooping up the kitten. Jess meows and licks her face.

"Careful," Ashtyn warns, and Ava is about to roll her eyes when Ashtyn continues. "She'll get a taste for blood."

This makes Ava laugh loudly, scaring Jess out of her arms. She plops to the floor and toddles toward the kitchen in search of food. Tears leak out of Ava's eyes, her laughter echoing throughout the house. Ashtyn joins in, grabbing her arm and leading her toward the couch.

"Sit," she says, and Ava settles onto the couch. She melts into the cushions, her adrenaline finally dying down. She finally relaxes, and the smell of hamburger grease makes her mouth water. Ashtyn lays a blanket over Ava's lap and hands her the food.

"Wow, maybe I should cut my head open more often if I'm going to get this type of treatment," Ava quips, taking a big bite of her burger.

"Don't push it," Ashtyn says, but there's a smile on her face as she sits next to her friend. They put on *New Girl,* and the laughter it elicits from everyone makes Ava feel immensely better.

* * *

Much later, there's a soft knock on Ava's door. She's cuddled up with Jess in her bed, trying to finish the last chapter of her book. She took some painkillers for her head, and it's feeling much better. The staples feel itchy, though, causing her some discomfort.

"Come in," she says. Jess peeks her head up at the guest. It's Shiloh.

"Hey, you mind if I come in for a minute?" he asks, lingering in the doorway. Jess meows loudly.

"You heard her, get your ass in here."

Shiloh smiles, and Ava thinks it might be the first one she's seen since this afternoon. He perches himself on the edge of her bed delicately. Jess immediately gets up and settles herself into his lap.

"God, she's obsessed with you," Ava teases. Shiloh doesn't say anything as he scratches behind Jess' ears. She purrs happily.

"I, uh," Shiloh clears his throat. "Just wanted to check and make sure you're doing okay."

Ava sighs. "I'm okay, Shiloh. I promise."

Shiloh squeezes his eyes shut and rubs a hand across his forehead. "I know you say that. I just—I should have been there for you. Instead, I was too busy freaking out at my stupid fucking phone and—"

"Why were you freaking out at your phone?" she asks, interrupting him.

Shiloh pauses and looks up at her. He takes it out of his pocket and hands it over. The screen is completely cracked and a message thread is pulled up. Ava sucks in a breath as she sees Scarlett's name at the top. There are two messages from her. The first one reads: *Hi, Shiloh. Just wanted to say thank you for signing the paperwork. I know I should have sent this message a while ago but I've just been so busy with work and everything. I hope you're doing well and I wish you nothing but the best.*

The second text is simply a red heart emoji.

"Oh," Ava says, simply. "Well, I can see why you would have been freaking out."

Shiloh sighs heavily. "I didn't even read it at first. I just saw her name flash up and then you fell. I—I'm sorry."

"Shiloh," she says, putting her hand on his shoulder. He winces so hard, Jess jumps out of his lap. Ava's brow furrows and, then she pulls up his t-shirt without even thinking about it. He doesn't protest.

Ava gasps as she sees the ginormous purple bruise starting to form on his shoulder that extends entirely down his ribs and toward his hip. It's taking up half of his entire back.

"Shiloh!" she exclaims. "Why the hell are you so worried about me when you're hurt too?"

"I'm fine," he says gruffly, shrugging his shirt back into place.

"You are not! Your entire back is purple. Did I—did I do that?"

"It was not your fault," Shiloh says, looking into her eyes and gripping her hand. "I would do it all again if it meant my body was the one that bruised instead of yours. If you had hit that pavement..." He closes his eyes and sighs deeply.

Ava doesn't want to think about what would have happened if Shiloh hadn't thrown his body in-between her and the concrete. Her head wound could have been fatal. She would probably have broken a bone or a few ribs. Instead, because of Shiloh, she came away with just a couple of staples in her head. She feels herself overcome with emotion and tears start to streak down her face.

"Thank you," she says, realizing she hasn't said those words to him yet. "Thank you for saving me."

Shiloh reaches his hand up to her face and wipes away her tears with his thumb. "You know I always will."

Ava smiles, sniffling. "Is now a bad time to ask how you feel about that text?"

"I don't know," he says. "I haven't really had any time to process it. Part of me just wants to delete it and forget it ever happened."

"Why?"

"Because then I wouldn't have to think about it. I wouldn't have to figure out how I feel."

"Well, avoiding your emotions isn't necessarily the best way to go about things," Ava says, eliciting a small laugh from him. He's still holding her hand.

"I was raised by Tom Brooks. That's the first thing you learn when you're born." The way he says it makes Ava's heart break.

"How did you grow up to be the man that you are today if you were raised by someone like that?"

"What do you mean?"

"I mean, Shiloh Brooks, that you are an incredible person that is capable of feeling deep emotions for other people. How did you turn out that way if your dad is the complete opposite?"

Shiloh thinks for a moment before answering. "Well, for starters, my brother. When he was born, I just knew I had to protect him from my father. I knew I didn't want to be like my dad, maybe because I intrinsically knew it was wrong to be so cruel. And then, after, I think it was also Scarlett. The love I felt for her...it made me want to be a better person. It made me want to be emotionally vulnerable with another person."

"And now?"

"And now I feel confused. Confused, because I no longer love the person I promised to love forever." His hand rubs his neck.

It's at this moment that Ava realizes she didn't feel the ring hanging from his neck when his body was pressed against hers. He must have taken it off sometime between when she saw him shirtless outside the shower and now. She's not sure if he's aware that she knows about the ring, but she thinks probably not. He never mentioned it to either of them. Sitting so close to him now, she can see it's really not there anymore.

"Ava!" Ashtyn's voice startles them. Her face pops into the doorway. "You need anything before I go to bed?" She notices Shiloh, but doesn't say anything.

"No, I'm okay. Thanks, though."

"Okay. Goodnight." She doesn't shut the door behind her.

"I should probably get to bed too," Shiloh says, standing.

"You sure you're okay? Those bruises look pretty bad."

"Yeah, I'll be fine. You?"

"I'm good."

"Okay. Goodnight, Ava."

"Goodnight, Shiloh."

He shuts the door behind him, finalizing their interaction for the night. Jess is gone, too, having followed Shiloh to his room.

Ava shivers and feels her head start to throb. She sighs and snuggles deeper into her bed, letting the covers envelop her. She abandons her book on the nightstand and clicks off the lamp. She has a feeling she won't be getting much sleep tonight.

Chapter 16

Shiloh has troubling sleeping for the next couple of weeks. His body feels like it got hit by a truck. His bruises are so tender, it's unbearable to sleep on his back, so he has to lay on his stomach in order to get even a few hours of sleep. He's running on coffee and energy drinks alone these days.

He's been ignoring the messages from Scarlett. He thinks about his conversation with Ava, but he doesn't want to engage with those feelings. He doesn't know how he's supposed to feel about Scarlett's words. Because, at the end of the day, that's all they are: words. She couldn't even face him that day they signed the papers. All she could manage was a text, weeks later. He deletes the thread, blocking out any lingering feelings that arose when he saw her name flash on his screen. He's done.

A few days after the incident, Drew helped him power wash Ava's blood stains from the driveway. He didn't want her to be reminded of it every time she walked outside. Although, she probably would never be rid of the incident, since she now has a pretty permanent scar on her forehead. She got her staples out a few days ago, after having them for a couple of weeks. He's pretty sure his bruises have lasted longer than her staples did, but he doesn't mind. He would do it over and over and over again if he had to. He's just thankful he's the one in pain now, instead of her. He couldn't bear it if her body had been bruised like this. It was unimaginable.

The boat stares at him menacingly now, taunting him. He thought of calling Mattie and telling him to get rid of it forever, but Ava convinced him otherwise. Even after it had destroyed her forehead, she still wanted to work on it with him. He was weary of continuing, but Ava agreed she wouldn't get in the boat again until it was water ready, and she'd let Shiloh do most of the work. He reluctantly agreed. It was so hard to say no to her.

"Hey, what are we doing for your birthday?" Drew asks, and Shiloh can see Ava's ears perk up at the mention of a birthday.

"I don't know. I haven't really thought about it."

"When is it?" Ava asks. She's sitting in a lawn chair, flipping through a catalog of boat furniture. Shiloh told her she could design the inside of the boat since they were going to have to rip out all the old seats.

"July third," Drew says. "We always do something Fourth of July related."

"No, *you* always do something Fourth of July related," Shiloh counters.

"Shiloh, that's literally in a few days! Why haven't you planned anything?"

"I didn't realize I was supposed to." He's also been incredibly focused on other things.

"Birthdays are a big deal in the Marhsall-King household," Ava says. "Well, I guess it's now the Marshall-King-Brooks household. Anyway, you get to pick whatever you want for your birthday, and we all have to go along with it."

"Anything?" Shiloh asks, dubiously.

"Anything," Ava nods. "I once dragged Ashtyn to a Houston

Dynamos game, because they were playing on my birthday."

"Wow," Drew whistles. "I bet she was thrilled."

"Oh, she hated it. But she was a good sport about it, because it was my birthday. So, Shiloh, make your choice."

Shiloh has to think about it for a moment. The last few years, he hasn't really done anything fun for his birthday. He normally just went out to dinner and caught a movie with Scarlett, or went to someone's Fourth of July party. He hasn't had a true birthday celebration in years. He thinks of celebrating with the girls this year, and he likes the idea.

"I want to go camping," he says. He's not sure why he chooses camping of all things, but the idea excites him. He hasn't been camping in years. He used to go with Mattie all the time when they were younger. The idea of sleeping under the stars, eating off a grill, fishing in a lake, all make him feel peaceful. And if there's one thing he needs right now, it's some goddamn peace.

Ava's eyebrows raise. "Okay, camping. That might be a harder idea to pitch to Ash, but I can make it work."

"God, I can't even remember the last time I've been camping," Drew says.

"I used to go with Mattie a bunch in Washington before we moved. I don't think I've gone in Texas."

"I think I know a good place," Ava says, smiling. "There's this little campground in mine and Ash's hometown that's cute."

"How far away is it?" Shiloh asks.

"Only about an hour."

Shiloh didn't realize the girls grew up only an hour away from here. "What about Jess? We can't just leave her alone for a weekend."

"I can ask Brooke to check in on her," Ava says. "Oh my gosh, this is so exciting! I've never been camping."

"I thought you were the one that knew about this campground," Drew says.

"Well, yeah, but I've never actually camped there. It used to be a hangout for high school kids to go and get drunk underage. You know, things I definitely never participated in."

Drew laughs, and Shiloh feels himself smiling. "Somehow, I don't believe you," Drew replies.

Ava giggles and gets up from her chair. "No one tell Ash. It'll go better if it comes from me."

* * *

"Camping!?" Ashtyn screeches, whirling around to stare at Ava incredulously. "No, no, no, no. Absolutely no way am I going camping, in July, of all months! It will be a million degrees."

Ava sighs heavily. "Come on, Ash! It's Shiloh's birthday, and this is what he wants to do."

"And let me guess, fucking Drew is going to be there, isn't he?" Ava doesn't have to say anything. Ashtyn already knows. "No," she says firmly.

"Well, you can't say no."

"And why the hell not?"

"Because we don't say no to birthdays! That's the rule."

"Yeah, well, no one has ever wanted to do something this ridiculous," Ashtyn fires back.

"Oh, really? Because I remember you being less than thrilled about going to a soccer game with for me for my birthday."

Ashtyn glares at her, but doesn't say anything. Ava knows she needs to try harder to convince her friend. "This is Shiloh's first birthday with us. We can't just say no to what he wants to do."

"Oh, I can absolutely say no. He's been here, what, six months? I don't even tell a guy I love him in six months."

"Ashtyn Marie."

"Ava Danielle."

Ava huffs and crosses her arms against her chest. "I already told him you said yes." She's lying, but Ashtyn doesn't need to know that.

"What!?"

"I already told him you're coming. So, if you don't go, you're going to ruin all the plans he's already made." They literally haven't made any plans yet. Again, she doesn't tell Ashtyn this.

"Ava, I swear to God."

"If this was my birthday, and I wanted to go camping, you'd go, no questions asked."

"You would never want to go camping for your birthday," Ashtyn counters.

"No, I wouldn't. But if I did, you'd go and you know it."

Ashtyn sighs. "I hate that you're right."

"I know," Ava says, smiling. "Besides, we're going to the camp-grounds near home. Maybe you can stop by and see your mom. I was thinking of seeing my parents too."

"Maybe I can sneak away and sleep there, instead of in a stuffy tent."

"You wouldn't dare."

"I would if it meant I could escape being near Drew."

"You know, he's not nearly as bad as you make him out to be."

Ashtyn narrows her eyes at her friend. "Don't tell me you've been charmed by his wicked ways."

This makes Ava laugh. "No, Ashtyn, I haven't been charmed by him. I just like him. And he's Shiloh's best friend, and we like Shiloh."

"I like Shiloh. Doesn't mean I need to like his friends."

Ava rolls her eyes, knowing she won't win this argument. "Okay, well, we're going camping, and you're not going to complain."

"Oh, if I'm going camping then I'm allowed to complain."

"Fine, just don't let Shiloh hear you."

Ashtyn rolls her eyes, but a smile tugs at her lips. "How you liking the new addition?" she asks, gesturing toward Ava's new scar.

"I don't know. I kind of think it makes me look tough." She flexes her nonexistent arm muscles. She honestly doesn't mind the scar too much. If she wears her hair down, it's mostly hidden anyway.

"Okay, Scarface," Ashtyn says, making Ava's jaw drop. She grabs Jess as she walks past and holds her up like a gun.

"Say hello to my little friend!" she says in her best Al Pacino voice.

The boys walk in at that exact moment, Jess poised in Ava's hands, and Ashtyn laughing so hard she's crying. Their faces are a mix of bewilderment and intrigue.

"Do I even want to know what's going on here?" Shiloh asks, shutting the front door behind him.

"Ashtyn agreed to go camping!" she exclaims, and then immediately claps a hand over her mouth, realizing her mistake. Ashtyn narrows her eyes at Ava.

"I thought you said you'd already told him I was going."

"She did," Shiloh says, easily. "She was telling Drew."

"You are all horrible liars, and I hate you for making me go camping."

"We love you!" Ava exclaims to Ashtyn's retreating back as she stomps up the stairs. She turns to face the boys and smiles. "I told you it'd be better coming from me."

JULY

Chapter 17

Ava is home. Every time she returns to her hometown, a sense of peace washes over her. She loves living near the city, because there's always so much more to do, but she can't help feeling a little restless sometimes. She likes the stability home gives her. She knows where everything is, and she feels grounded. Plus, her parents are here, and she misses them. Even though they're only an hour away, sometimes it feels like a continent away with their busy schedules. Both of her parents are still working, and between that and her own hectic schedule, she normally only gets a Facetime once a week or so. She's debated moving back home eventually, but she knows Ashtyn probably wouldn't go for it. She's too happy where she is, and Ava feels like she would be abandoning her best friend if she moved away. They've never lived in different places.

She knows she shouldn't try to base her entire life around her best friend but...she's her best friend. They've been through so much together. She can't imagine her life without Ashtyn by her side, or at least in the same city as her. Maybe that's crazy, but she wouldn't have it any other way, and she knows Ashtyn feels the same.

As they pull up to the campsite, one Ava's very familiar with, she feels herself relax. Selfishly, she picked this campsite because she wanted to be in her hometown and near her parents for the holiday. She also knew this one would be less crowded than the ones near the city. She and Ashtyn used to come down here on the weekends with their friends in high school and screw around. It's the place Ava had her first kiss with Garrett Smith. A terrible first kiss that tasted like stale beer and bad breath, but it was still her first. Ashtyn also had her first kiss here that very same night with Brandon. Although, she had described hers as magical. Ava was jealous, so jealous that Ashtyn's had been so perfect, whereas hers had been terrible. She'd convinced herself she actually liked it and dated Garrett for a few months before he eventually broke up with her. She was devastated. She was so, so, so sad. At least, that's what she'd told herself at the time, even if she didn't necessarily feel it. She thinks back to her conversation with Shiloh about being in love. Had she ever really been in love, even if she'd said so? No, she doesn't think she has. The thought depresses her.

The July heat is relentless, and Ava is sweating before she even gets out of the car. Drew's truck containing him, Shiloh, and Mattie pulls up behind them. As she looks in the rear view mirror, her new scar smiles back at her. It's still not fully healed, but it's slowly starting to fade into her skin color. She touches it gingerly. Maybe it really does make her look tough.

"If Drew pisses me off even once, I'm going to my mom's and sleeping there," Ashtyn says grumpily, snapping Ava's attention toward her friend.

"You will do no such thing," she admonishes. "We are here for Shiloh's birthday, and you are going to behave. My parents will be here later tonight to grill for us. You can invite your mom too."

"Are you kidding me? I'm not subjecting my mother to Drew! Oh, he'd love to meet her and charm her and make her love him, and then she'll tell me, 'Oh, Ash, why don't you like him? He's such a charming young man.'" Ashtyn's imitation of her mother makes Ava chuckle, but she doesn't love the way she's talking about Drew. She doesn't understand what rubs Ash the wrong way when it comes to Drew. Sure, he's a little crass sometimes, but he's always been so nice to Ava. She remembers what he said to her the night of Shiloh's divorce party, all those months ago, and she smiles to herself. Maybe, just maybe, she'll tell Ashtyn one day.

"Just, please, try to be nice. For Shiloh. For me." Ava bats her eyelashes at her friend.

Ashtyn glares at her, but then her expression softens. "Fine, just for you, my love." She smacks a kiss on Ava's cheek, and then gets out of the car, groaning at the heat. Ava can tell it will take all of Ashtyn's willpower not to complain this weekend.

The boys begin unpacking their supplies, and Ava counts her lucky stars she won't have to set up their tent by herself. The campground isn't packed, but there are definitely other people neighboring their campsite. The patrons seem friendly, waving and greeting everyone that comes by.

The boys get the tents set up, and by the time they're done, everyone is drenched in sweat. Even Ava, who didn't have to lift a finger.

"Let the birthday festivities begin!" Drew exclaims, handing every-one a beer from the cooler. The boys, in synchronicity, tap their beers and shotgun them, spilling liquid all over the ground.

"Woo!" Shiloh yells, finishing his first, and Ava thinks this might be the most relaxed she's ever seen him. His face is illuminated by an enormous smile.

"Alright, I'm gonna need to go into town and spend as much money as humanly possible on fireworks," Mattie says, crushing his can and letting out a burp. Ava pops the top on her own beer and takes a sip. It's ice cold going down her throat.

"We passed a stand on our way into town," Drew says.

"We can go tomorrow," Shiloh replies.

"Good, that'll give us time to go see Ash's mom tomorrow," Ava says.

Drew frowns. "She's not coming with your parents tonight, Ava?"

"No, she's not allowed anywhere near you," Ashtyn says, eyes narrowed at him.

"What the hell?"

"Carol, like Ashtyn, isn't much of an outdoorsy person," Ava says, trying to diffuse the situation.

Drew just rolls his eyes and pops open another beer. "Whatever you say."

Ashtyn's about to snap back, but Ava stops her with a look. She's about to tell her to knock it off when a loud voice yells from across the campsite. "Ava!?"

She almost drops her beer as her blood runs cold and anxiety spikes through her system. *You've got to be kidding,* she thinks to herself. She thought about him for two seconds and now he's here, summoned by the embarrassment of her past to torture her.

"Ava Marshall! Holy shit!" Garrett Smith yells. He lumbers over to them, beer in hand and trucker hat on his head. He's wearing an American flag tank-top that she's pretty sure is from high school. Ava feels a wave of shame wash over her at the sight of him. What did she ever see in a guy like that?

"Hey, oh my gosh, Garrett! Wow, it's nice to see you," she lies. He pulls her into a bone crushing hug that she meekly returns. He still smells like stale beer and bad breath. Suddenly, she's sixteen again, insecure and awkward.

"God, what's it been? Like ten years?"

"Nine," she corrects.

"And Ashy! What up, girl?" he exclaims, going in for a hug.

Ashtyn dodges him expertly. "Hi, Garrett," she mumbles, pretending to be engrossed with her phone.

"What brings y'all back home?" he asks, taking a long glug of beer.

"Oh, um, just came camping for the holiday," Ava says. She feels like she wants to crawl in her tent and never come out.

"Dang, you got a new decoration on your face," he says, gesturing to her forehead. Garrett suddenly seems to realize they aren't alone and turns his attention to the boys. "Oh, hey, I'm sorry! I didn't see y'all. I'm Garrett. Ava and I go way back." He shakes the boys' hands as they introduce themselves.

"Hey, man," Shiloh says, his eyes skating between Garrett and Ava. She really wishes she could be anywhere but here.

"I'm over at campsite twelve if y'all need any beer or fireworks. We're stocked for the weekend. Just give me a holler," Garrett says, oblivious to the way Ava wants this conversation to end immediately.

"Thanks, Garrett. We'll see you around," Ava says, giving him a wave and heading in the direction of the bathrooms. Ashtyn goes with her, and they quicken their pace until they reach their destination. Inside the restrooms, it smells like urine, and Ava wrinkles her nose. But, she'd rather be here than with Garrett Smith. She slumps against the wall and touches her forehead self-consciously. She hadn't been embarrassed about the scar until now. She's still gripping her can of beer, but the smell of it makes her sick. She chucks it into the trash.

"Jesus Christ, remind me to never book this campsite again," she says, rubbing her fingers along her temples.

"I don't want to say 'I told you so' but...I told you so," Ashtyn says, trying to hold back a laugh and failing.

Ava smacks her arm playfully. "Is he still over there?"

Ashtyn stands on her tiptoes and peeks out the tiny, dirty window. "Yes, he's still talking with them."

"Ugh, he's probably embarrassing me!"

"I'm pretty sure he's embarrassing himself. There's not much he could say about you that would be embarrassing."

"Besides the fact that he was my first kiss, and then I dated him for four months."

"That was high school, Ave. Everyone has embarrassing high school memories they wish they could forget."

"Yeah, but not everyone has them walk up to you in present day in front of your friends."

Ashtyn peeks out the window again. "Wow."

"What? What is it?" Ava asks, trying to look out the window, knocking her shoulder against Ashtyn's.

"Ow," Ashtyn grumbles. "I was just going to say, it looks like Drew is taking one for the team and walking with him back to his campsite. The coast is clear."

Ava sighs gratefully and makes a mental note to thank Drew later. Before they leave the bathroom, Ashtyn grabs her by the arm. "Hey, don't let a reminder of a stupid ass time in high school ruin your weekend. We're here to have a good time, remember? And your 'decoration'," she puts air quotes around the word, "is actually badass, and you look stunning as always."

"Look who has a positive attitude, now," Ava replies, smiling, feeling grateful for her friend's words.

"Yeah, well, I don't like seeing you upset. And I really don't like seeing people from high school. Especially idiots." This makes Ava laugh, and she loops her arm through Ashtyn's as they head back to the campsite.

"Ah, they return!" Mattie exclaims as they rejoin the group.

"Shh!" Ava shushes him. "Don't be too loud. You might bring him back."

"Don't worry. Drew's taking care of it."

"Taking care of it?" Ashtyn asks, skeptically.

"Yeah, they're talking trucks. Drew pretended to be interested, so Garrett would take him and show him his new F-150 or some shit. I don't know, he just wanted to get him away, so y'all could come back."

"Oh," Ashtyn says, simply. Ava doesn't miss the surprise that crosses her friend's face. *Good* surprise.

"You sure know how to pick 'em, Ava," Mattie teases.

"Mattie," Shiloh warns, and Ava sees that his relaxed attitude is gone. He's tense, his hands balled into fists, and she feels responsible for ruining his mood.

"What did he say after we left?" Ava asks, sensing that something is off.

"Nothing," Shiloh replies.

Mattie seems to get the hint and holds up his hands. "Just got the sense that he's a tool."

"Yeah, something like that," Ava chuckles nervously. "He's harmless. Just annoying."

Drew eventually saunters back, sans Garrett, and Ava gives him an appreciative hug. She whispers, "thank you" in his ear, and he gives her a reassuring squeeze back as if to say, *you got it.* She doesn't miss the way Ashtyn's gaze lingers on Drew. Her usual coldness towards him seems to have slightly melted. *Slightly.*

It's a little after five o'clock when Ava's parents pull up to the campsite. She's barreling into them for a hug before they even get out of the car.

"Hi, monkey!" Her dad says, crushing her in a hug. His nickname for her as a child, because she used to climb up on every available surface, has stuck. Even at twenty-seven, he still thinks of her as his little girl. Her mother hugs her next and kisses her forehead, right on her scar. She called them the day after the accident, so they wouldn't freak out too much about not coming to the hospital with her. Being an only child, Ava's always felt very connected to her parents. They were her best friends before Ashtyn. She believes in happily ever afters because of them.

"Look at you," her dad says. "Our battle-scarred daughter."

Ava laughs. "Yeah, because tripping off a boat like a clumsy idiot is really battle worthy."

"Well, I think it suits you," her mom says, wrapping her arm around her daughter's shoulders.

"Come on, come meet everyone," she says, leading them over to the group. "Mom, Dad, this is Shiloh, our roommate. Shiloh, this is Bill and Evelyn, my parents."

"Oh my goodness, he's so handsome!" her mom whispers in her ear, and Ava blushes, shushing her.

"It's nice to meet you, Mr. and Mrs. Marshall," Shiloh says, respectfully, shaking their hands. Ava knows he's nervous about meeting her parents. She can't help but think it's because of his relationship with his own parents.

"Please, son, just Bill," her dad says, giving him a pat on the shoulder. Ava sees the way Shiloh relaxes, smiling softly. She's glad her father can make him feel welcome and at ease.

"Bill, this is my brother, Matthew, and my best friend, Drew."

Ava's father shakes their hands, and her mom gives them all hugs. "We're a hugging family!" she exclaims. She wraps Ashtyn into a hug, and Shiloh raises his eyebrows.

"Ava, my mom, and her," she says, as she's wrapped in Evelyn's embrace. "That's it."

Drew whispers something to Shiloh that makes him laugh, and Ashtyn flips them off behind Evelyn's back.

"I felt that," Evelyn says, pinching Ashtyn's cheek lightly, making her blush.

"Sorry, Evie. It's these damn boys. They push my buttons."

"Everyone pushes your buttons, dear."

This makes Drew and Shiloh howl with laughter, and Ashtyn's blush deepens to the shade of her hair. Ava has to bite back the giggle that's forming in her throat, so her best friend's wrath isn't directed at her.

"Come on boys, help me unload these steaks," her dad says, making his way over to the trunk of the car.

The boys and Ava's father take over the grill, talking meat and cars and drinking beer. It's all so stereotypical. Ava, her mom, and Ashtyn sit at the picnic table, sipping on Chardonnay that Evelyn brought with her. Ava's grateful she has something other than beer to drink.

"Alright, which one do you like?" Evelyn asks, directing the question at her daughter.

"Mom!" Ava exclaims, nearly choking on her wine. "I don't like any of them. I mean, I like them all as friends, but I don't *like* like any of them." She tries to hide her blush in her wine glass.

Her mother looks over to Ashtyn for confirmation, and Ash just holds up her hands. "Hey, I don't know of any current crushes. She's at an all-time low."

"Oh, honey, what about Derek? He's so nice."

"He's actually dating Daisy now," Ava says, weakly. "They hit it off at a game night. My birthday, actually."

"Oh, how wonderful! I love Daisy. She's so cute."

"She won't shut up about how happy she is," Ashtyn says, finishing off her wine. "It's sickening."

"Oh, honey, you'll find someone," Evelyn says, patting Ashtyn on the back.

"Nah, I think I'll swear off men for the rest of my life."

Evelyn scoffs and refills their wine glasses. "You say that now, but when you meet the right person, you'll change your tune."

"Evie, no disrespect, but you haven't seen the dating scene these days. It's torture out here."

"I'll drink to that," Ava replies.

"Don't tell me my fairy-tale believing romance lover is turning into a cynic," Evelyn says, putting her arm around Ava.

"No," Ava sighs. "It's just getting a little harder to believe is all. It also doesn't help when you run into your first ever boyfriend and realize you have no idea what you were thinking back then."

"Garrett?"

"Yes, Mom, Garrett."

"Oh, honey, I asked your father every day what you were thinking when you were dating him."

"Mom!" Ava exclaims, a laugh escaping her lips.

"He was kind of a stinker," she says, wine flushing her cheeks.

"Literally and metaphorically," Ashtyn replies. This makes them all giggle hysterically.

"Mind if I crash?" Mattie asks, coming up to the table and plopping down next to Ashtyn.

"Be my guest," she replies, setting a glass in front of him and filling it with Chardonnay. "But this is a wine only zone."

"Fine with me," Mattie says, taking the glass. "I needed a break from the car and boat talk."

"Says the guy that bought a boat," Ava teases.

"Hey, I did that for my brother."

Ava looks at him quizzically. "I thought it was for you."

"Please, I only told him that so he wouldn't think I was giving him something to do. Which is exactly what I *was* doing." The girls just stare at him. "He needs something to do, you know? He needs purpose."

"You think he doesn't have purpose?" Ava asks. She's curious about Mattie's insight into Shiloh.

"He does, but sometimes he doesn't see it. So, I needed to push him to get out and do something, instead of moping around the house all day like he did at Drew's. The boat was just a starting point. You did the rest, Ava."

She laughs. "You mean cut my head open on said boat?"

"No, not that" Mattie says, rolling his eyes but smiling. "You got him the job at the school."

"I mean, I didn't get him the job. I just recommended him. I thought he'd be good at it. He did the rest himself."

"And you have no idea how much that pushed him. To have someone he cares about believe in him? To push him to do something better? That shit's life changing."

Ava's stunned at his words. "He-he told you this?"

"No, of course not," Mattie laughs. "But he's my brother. I know him better than anyone. I can read him like a book. Plus, you've seen our father in action. There's a reason Shiloh isn't always forthcoming with his emotions."

"Yeah," Ava says, quietly.

"I'm going to go check on your father," Evelyn says, noting the privacy of this conversation. She gives Ava a kiss on the cheek and leaves the table. There's a silence that hangs around them for a minute.

Mattie clears his throat. "I, uh, wanted to thank y'all. For, you know, taking a chance on my brother. Ever since he moved in with y'all, he seems better. Happier. And that means everything to me."

"Mattie," Ava starts, but Mattie continues.

"I shouldn't be saying this, but when things ended with Scarlett, I thought I'd lost my brother forever. He lost everything he thought was important to him, and he just became this shell of a person. He was fucking miserable, and having a dad like ours didn't help. I thought I'd never see him happy again, you know? So, to see him today, here, smiling and drinking and relaxing...that's everything."

Tears prick Ava's eyes. She's about to say something, when Ashtyn crushes Mattie to her in a hug. His eyes widen, but then he wraps his arms around her in reciprocation.

"What the shit!?" someone yells from across the campsite. Ava turns and sees Shiloh with his hands in the air. "Ava, your mom, and Ava's mom! That's who you said gets your hugs, and now you hug my brother! Before me!? What the hell, Ashtyn?"

"You gotta earn it, Brooks!" Ashtyn yells, not letting go of Mattie. "He earned it."

"Oh, I'm gonna earn it," Shiloh says and starts running toward them. Ashtyn shrieks and lets go of Mattie before scrambling away from the table and Shiloh barreling toward her. "Get your ass over here!"

Ashtyn squeals, running in circles as Shiloh tries to pull her into a hug. Ava can't stop smiling at them and their ridiculous antics. She turns back to Mattie and grabs his hand. "We love him, you know that, right?"

"I know," he says, squeezing her hand. "He loves you too." Shiloh and Ashtyn's laughter echo around them, warming Ava's heart.

* * *

Later that night, after they've stuffed their bellies with steak and a surprise cake for Shiloh, they sit around the fire, roasting marshmallows. Ava's parents left after dinner, giving kisses and hugs and parting waves. She misses them already, but she's comforted by the presence of her friends.

"Alright, I'm fucking beat," Ashtyn says, getting up from her chair after she finishes devouring her third s'more. "I'm exhausted from being chased around by a lunatic!" She flicks Shiloh on the head as she passes him. He just smiles. Mattie and Drew also retire to their tent, and then it's just Shiloh and Ava, sitting across from each other as the fire dwindles down to embers.

"I liked your parents," Shiloh says, softly.

"Yeah, they're the best," Ava replies, smiling. She's warm from the fire and the booze in her system. "Oh, hey, I got you a birthday present." She rushes into the tent and comes back with a wrapped gift.

"You didn't have to get me anything, Ave," he says.

She plops into the chair next to him and hands him the present. "I know, but I figured this is your first birthday with us, and I should get you a present."

Shiloh takes the gift and Ava's heart races. She'd been utterly clueless as to what to get him. So, she'd thought back to the day they'd met, when he mentioned how much he liked Hemingway.

"It's not much, and if you don't like it, I can return it," she babbles. But as soon as Shiloh unwraps the Hemingway collected works box-set and smiles, she knows she won't have to return it.

"Ava," he says. He seems to grapple with his words for a moment before saying, "Thank you."

"I noticed you didn't actually have any Hemingway on your shelves, and you'd mentioned that you liked him when we first met so—" She's cut off as he pulls her into a hug. He smells like campfire as she buries her nose into his shirt. Her body begs him to hold her tighter. After a moment, though, he lets go, still smiling.

"Thank you," he says. "Seriously, I love it."

Ava lets out a breath. "Good. I'm glad."

Shiloh holds the books in his hands, running his fingers over the spines. She finishes off the last of her beer, then says, "Hey, sorry about Garrett earlier."

Shiloh looks up, frowning. "Ava, you have nothing to be sorry for."

"Yeah, but—"

"No. No, buts." His gaze is intense, and she has to look away.

"What did he say after I left?"

"Nothing."

"You're lying."

Shiloh doesn't refute the statement. He just continues sipping the last of his beer, avoiding her eyes. He holds the books tightly on his lap.

"Come on, Shi, what did he say?" Ava feels bold, the booze urging her forward.

"I'm not telling you," he says, his voice also thick with alcohol.

"I'm sure I could guess."

"Ava…" His voice is pleading, but she continues.

"Did he tell you he was my first kiss? Right down there by the creek." She points over Shiloh's shoulder toward the slope that leads down to the water. "It was the worst kiss of my life."

Shiloh doesn't react. He just stares at her, gripping his can, flames reflecting in his eyes.

"Did he tell you he was my first official boyfriend? We dated for a few months before he dumped me for Ashley Mason. I was devastated."

Something in Ava's voice makes Shiloh raise his eyebrows. "Were you really?"

Ava chuckles throatily. "No. I told everyone I was, but I was actually relieved. I hated him."

"Then why—"

"Did I date him? I don't know. He was the only boy that was giving me any attention. I wanted to be in love so badly that I just ran with the first opportunity presented to me." Shiloh's face contorts into something that resembles pity, and Ava groans. "Please, don't pity me. I was just an idiot teenager with low standards." Ava starts to pick at the tab on her beer can, not meeting Shiloh's gaze. She doesn't want to see that look again.

"I wasn't pitying you," he says.

"Well, it looked like pity."

"It wasn't. I was thinking about how a piece of shit like that didn't deserve to be with someone as incredible as you."

Ava freezes at his words, and her heart starts to race. "I'm—I'm not that great."

"Why do you always do that?"

"Do what?"

"Act like you don't know how amazing you are? When we first met, you talked about yourself like you were the most boring person on the planet, when that couldn't be further from the truth."

"I—" But she doesn't know what to say. Her words lodge in her throat. He doesn't mean that. He's just saying that to make her feel better. He's just being nice. It's something a friend would tell another friend. She feels a nervous laugh bubble up to her lips. "Ha. Good one." There's no humor in her voice, and she stands, not meeting his gaze. "I'm gonna head to bed. "

She starts toward the tent, but Shiloh gently, ever so gently, grabs her wrist as she walks by, halting her in her tracks. "Ava," he says, voice quiet, fingers caressing her wrist, making her shiver. "I meant it. I mean everything I say to you."

She wants to stay there, letting him hold her wrist like that, reveling in his words. Instead, she takes her wrist back and says, "Goodnight." She heads into her and Ashtyn's tent, wriggling into her sleeping bag with a racing heart.

It's much later in the night when Ava wakes with the need to pee. She's sweating, the heat sticking all around her, suffocating. She doesn't want to get up, but she untangles herself from the sleeping bag nevertheless. That's when she notices the tent is empty, and Ashtyn isn't next to her. She probably had to pee as well.

Ava exits the tent and heads toward the bathroom. She does her business, not finding Ashtyn in any of the stalls. As she exits the bathroom, she hears hushed whispers on the other side of the building. She stops in her tracks and pushes her back up against the adjoining wall. She can just make out Drew and Ashtyn's voices. She knows she shouldn't be listening, but she can't get her feet to move.

"I can't get you out of my head," Drew whispers. His voice is thick with either alcohol or sleep, Ava can't tell.

"That sounds like a you problem," Ashtyn retorts, her voice equally low.

"Ash."

"Don't call me that."

"Ashtyn."

There's a palpable silence between the two, and Ava knows she should turn around and forget this happened, but she's frozen to the spot. She can't see them, but she has a pretty good idea of how they might look. Ashtyn, arms crossed, looking up at him defiantly. Drew, lazy smile on his face, gazing down at her adoringly.

"I know what you did for Ava," Ashtyn says after a moment. Her voice isn't as hard as it normally is. There's a softness to it. "I...wanted to say thank you."

"Ah, it was nothing," Drew says nonchalantly. "Any excuse to talk trucks, amiright?"

"Drew," Ashtyn says, and there's no threatening warning, no anger. Instead, she sounds almost pleading. "There's no way you would have willingly talked about trucks with an asshole like that. I know it had to be more than that."

Drew is silent for a moment. "Don't worry about it. I took care of it."

"And I'm thanking you for that," Ashtyn replies. Then, there's silence, and Ava knows she needs to leave. She shouldn't be listening to this.

She silently pushes herself off the wall and heads back to the tent. She gets in the sleeping bag and leaves the opening of the tent the way she found it, so she doesn't reveal she was awake. She falls asleep before Ashtyn gets back, her dreams full of sweat and stale beer breath.

Chapter 18

When Shiloh wakes the next morning, his heart is racing. He can't believe what he said to Ava last night, the way he just grabbed her wrist without thinking. He hates how perfect her skin felt underneath his fingertips, and how he could feel just how fast her heart was beating. It reminded him of when he held her body after she'd been hurt, but his adrenaline had taken over all his senses at that time. And then there was the gift she'd given him. No one had ever gotten him books as a gift before. He loved it. He loved that she remembered what he said about Hemingway when they first met.

Fuck, he never should've grabbed her wrist. He crossed a line. But he couldn't just let her go on thinking she's boring or unremarkable, because she's not. She's exciting, and fascinating, and...remarkably beautiful. The word strikes him in the face and he has to take a deep breath. It doesn't matter if he finds her beautiful or not. She's his roommate. They are strictly just friends, and based on the way she reacted last night, that's exactly how she wants to keep their relationship.

He hates how she spoke about herself. How that asshole Garrett spoke about her behind her back. Shiloh wanted to punch that idiot in the face. He'd asked which one of them was banging her, said that he regretted not "getting it when he could have." And called her scar a "decoration" to her face. He'll forever be grateful to Drew for taking Garrett away and telling him that if he ever showed his face around them again, they'd kick his ass. It was an unspoken agreement they wouldn't tell the girls what happened. Neither of them needed to hear it.

Shiloh puts a hand up to his chest to try and calm down. Drew and Mattie are sleeping next to him, snoring softly, none the wiser to his racing heart. He should get up, start making breakfast, and try to get his mind off Ava.

He unwraps himself from his sleeping bag and heads toward the restroom to brush his teeth and splash his face with water. He makes a mental note to himself not to drink as much as he did last night. He needs to keep a clear head for the rest of the weekend. Especially around Ava.

His dreams were full of her last night. His cheeks flush as he looks at himself in the dirty mirror. It's like she's written all over his face. He's not sure where all these feelings are coming from, but he can't stop them. They're flooding his bloodstream, straight to his heart, bursting their way in without permission. Of all the people in the world he could choose to start liking after his divorce, his stupid heart decided it would be his off-limits roommate. *Way to go, Brooks*, he thinks to himself.

When he's finished freshening up, he heads back to the campsite, prepared to start making breakfast, but he sees his brother has beaten him to it.

"I was going to do that," Shiloh says.

"It's your birthday weekend. You're supposed to be relaxing."

"Geez, Mom, I didn't realize I was still a child."

Mattie flips him off which makes him laugh. The rest of the campsite starts to come alive, people getting ready for the day and setting up their Fourth of July gear.

"Where's Drew?" Shiloh asks, noticing their empty tent.

"He went to go pick up coffee for everyone. He heard Ashtyn's grumpy in the mornings without it, so off he went."

Shiloh laughs. "God, he's got it bad."

"Think she'll ever warm up to him?"

"I don't know," he says truthfully. "But then again, she did hug you yesterday. You gonna tell me what you did to get her to do that?"

"Never," Mattie replies, mischievously. Shiloh rolls his eyes but chuckles. He couldn't believe it when he looked over and saw Ashtyn crushing Mattie in a hug. He'd chased her around for a good twenty minutes before giving up. He'd earn her hug the right way, eventually.

"It wasn't anything romantic," Mattie says, almost embarrassed. "You know I wouldn't do that with any of your friends."

"No, I know. You're good. I was just messing with you." He feels guilty at the thoughts he was exploring about Ava not ten minutes earlier in the bathroom. *Friend*, he has to remind himself.

"Is it bad that I want a beer already?" Mattie asks and another laugh escapes from Shiloh.

"Yes, Matthew, it is. It's nine in the morning."

"Fuck it, I'm on vacation," he says, and pops the top on a can of beer.

By the time breakfast is ready and Drew is back with the coffee, the girls are still not up.

"Alright, who's going to be the one to wake them?" Shiloh asks.

"Not it!" Mattie and Drew yell at the same time, and Shiloh sighs. Of course, the task falls to him. He takes a deep breath and gets up.

"Uh, hey, guys," he says to the zipped-up flap of their tent. "Breakfast is ready. And Drew picked up coffee."

At the mention of coffee, Ashtyn unzips the tent and peeks her head out. "What kind of coffee?"

"Iced caramel macchiato!" Drew yells from the table. "Just like you like it."

Ashtyn scowls. "How does he know that?"

"Beats me," Shiloh shrugs. "Come on."

"Give us a minute to get dressed." And with that she's zipping up the tent again. Shiloh heads back to the table and sips on his own coffee.

"How do you know her coffee order?" he asks Drew.

Drew smiles. "I literally just fucking guessed."

A laugh bursts out of him. "You know, one of these days, she might just kill you."

"And what a glorious day that will be," Drew says, dreamily. Shiloh just rolls his eyes and digs into his breakfast. The girls join them a moment later, taking their coffees gratefully. Ava doesn't seem upset by anything that happened last night. Hopefully, she's decided to just forget about it. Shiloh knows he is sure going to try.

"How did you sleep?" Drew asks, his voice chipper. He's always been a morning person.

Ashtyn holds up a finger to silence him, taking a long sip of coffee. When she's finished, she sighs and says, "It's been so long since I've shared a room with Ava that I forgot she snores like a fucking jackhammer."

Ava gasps, outraged. "I do not!"

Shiloh decides to test the waters. "I share a wall with you, Ave. You snore."

She looks at him, eyes wide, mouth slightly ajar.

"Ha! See! I told you!" Ashtyn exclaims, holding her hand out for a high-five from Shiloh. He gives it to her, and he sees Ava trying to hold back a smile.

"Damn, you snore so loud you can be heard through a wall? That's impressive," Mattie says.

"I hate you all," Ava replies, shoveling eggs into her mouth. She narrows her eyes at them, but she doesn't look menacing at all. She looks cute. *Snap out of it,* he thinks to himself.

They finish breakfast, and then get ready to go swimming and fishing down by the creek. Shiloh can't remember the last time he's been fishing. It was his mom, of all people, that used to take him when he was little. His dad hated it. Thought it was stupid and beneath him. But his mom used to take him every weekend. Taught him how to bait his hook and cast his line. It was their thing, until Shiloh grew up and found other things to care about. Until his mom started caring more about what their father thought than ever before. He stuffs those feelings deep down into his subconscious. He doesn't need to think about that this weekend.

As they get their stuff ready, Shiloh looks over at the girls' tent and immediately has to look away. Ava's wearing cutoff shorts and a pink bikini top. He doesn't know if he'll survive this camping trip, anymore.

"I'm gonna go get us a spot," Shiloh says, heading toward the slope. "I'll meet you down there." He's gone before anyone can protest. He seriously needs to get a grip.

He easily finds a spot a little more secluded from the mass of people out today. There's enough room for them to cast their lines and for the girls to float in their inner tubes. He hopes they'll float away from them so he won't be tempted to look at Ava. He has no idea what's happening to him. Nothing has changed between them. Nothing has happened for him to be feeling like this, right?

Of course she's beautiful, he thinks. That's undeniable. Anyone can see that. Ashtyn is also beautiful. But his heart doesn't race when he sees Ashtyn in a bikini. He doesn't occasionally think about Ashtyn when he's in the shower. He doesn't grab her wrist and tell her that he means everything he says to her. No, he only does that with Ava. He has to stop thinking like this. It's ridiculous. It's also impossible. He shakes his head. Things will go back to normal when they get home and get back to their normal schedules.

He doesn't hear Mattie until he's right next to him. He nearly jumps out of his skin at the sight of him. "Jesus Christ, when did you get there?"

"Like two minutes ago. I was waiting to see when you'd snap out of whatever the hell you were thinking about."

Shiloh turns to tell his brother that he wasn't thinking about anyone when he sees Ava, in her pink bikini, coming down the hill. It's as if time slows, and he has all the time in the world to soak her in. The cutoff shorts are gone, and she's only in her swimsuit.

The freckles.

Holy shit, the freckles. They're everywhere. Across her shoulders, down her arms, all down her long soccer legs. There's a larger one that sits on her hip, right above the line of her bikini bottom. The sun illuminates them, providing a map of her body that Shiloh desperately wants to decipher. Her hair is tied up in a messy bun, a few strands escaping and lying on the nape of her neck. Her scar shines underneath the sun. It suits her, honestly. It looks like it's always been a part of her. She stops and turns to shout something up at Drew, and then he's looking at her butt, and it's almost his undoing. She has tiny stretch marks on the back of her thighs, and he feels his dick harden in his swim trunks.

"Don't make it obvious," Mattie whispers, and it snaps Shiloh out of his Ava trance.

"What?"

"I said, don't make it obvious."

"Make what obvious?" He swallows thickly.

"Jesus fucking Christ, you're dense."

Shiloh just frowns at his brother, turning back to finish setting up his fishing stuff and also conceal his hard on. He can't believe how easy it was for him to get turned on. Just a girl in a swimsuit, and he's done for. No, not just a girl. *Ava*. Ava in a swimsuit.

He has to stop thinking about her in said swimsuit. He closes his eyes and thinks of literally anything else. He lets out a breath, as they finally reach the bottom of the hill and join him. He will just avoid looking at Ava for the rest of the day, and he'll be golden.

He does a relatively good job at doing so. He stays on the far side of the creek, fishing, while she floats with Ashtyn in their tubes. She occasionally gets in his line of sight, but he always moves farther down river whenever she does. He's not sure, but he thinks Drew might be doing the same thing with Ashtyn. He hasn't looked at her in a while. Only Mattie seems to be unfazed.

They barely catch anything, the fish probably disturbed by the high volume of guests in their water. After a couple of hours, Mattie declares, "Alright, I'm fucking bored of this. I'm off to go buy some fireworks."

"Oh, thank God, I'm coming too," Drew says.

"What the hell? This is supposed to be my birthday afternoon activity!"

"Yeah, well, nobody is making you stop. Keep going. We'll be back by the time you're done," Mattie says, and then they're gone. Shiloh just rolls his eyes, casting his line once more.

"I hate to bail, but I gotta go meet my mom," Ashtyn says, making her way out of the water. "Besides, if I stay here any longer I'll burn." And then she's gone too.

It's just him and Ava, again. How does this keep happening?

"You're not going to see Ash's mom?" he asks. Ava makes her way to shore, swimming through the water like she was born in it.

"No," she says, once she's up and out of the water. It drips off her body, and Shiloh has to actively make sure he doesn't turn his head to look at her.

"Oh. I thought you said yesterday you were going."

"Yeah, but Ash doesn't normally get to see her mom so I figured I'd give them some privacy. I can see her another time. Hey, can you spray me? I don't want to burn."

And then she's right next to him, holding out a bottle of spray sunscreen for him to use on her. It takes everything in him not to run away in the other direction like the coward he is. He takes the sunscreen from her, and she turns so her back is facing him. This is when he gets an up-close look at her back, the freckles that lay across her shoulders like constellations. He's captivated by them, mesmerized. His fingers want to trace patterns along her back.

"Any day now, Shi," she says, and it snaps him back to attention. He sprays the sunscreen across her back, coating her skin. He tries not to look too closely at any part of her body as he sprays her down, especially her butt. Then, she turns to face him, holding her arms out and waiting for him to spray her front. He swears she's doing it on purpose to torment him, but by the way her eyes are squinted shut, he doubts it. He sprays her quickly, but efficiently, then gives her back the bottle.

"Thanks," she says.

"Anytime," he replies.

She has no idea how fast his heart is beating.

By the time everyone gets back, it's dinner time. The campsite is alive with people, much busier today than it was yesterday. Kids run around screaming and laughing, tumbling through the dirt. Adults sit around campfires, drinking and playing music. It's a cacophony of different stereos loudly blaring.

Ashtyn seems more relaxed since she came back from seeing her mom. She's sitting next to Ava, legs in her lap, giggling. Mattie and Drew are cooking dinner, and Shiloh is going through the bags and bags of fireworks they brought back.

"How much did you spend on all of this?" he asks, amazed.

"It's better if you don't know," Mattie replies. "It might give you a heart attack."

"We got a little bit of everything," Drew says, flipping over the burgers that are sizzling on the grill. He holds a beer, sipping it.

"Are we even allowed to shoot them off here?"

"No," Ava says, looking up from her spot on the chair. Her cheeks are pink from the sun.

"Why the hell did we spend hundreds of dollars on fireworks if we can't shoot them off, then?" Drew asks. Shiloh ignores the "hundreds of dollars" comment.

"I didn't say you couldn't shoot them off at all," she replies, rolling her eyes. "I just said you couldn't shoot them here."

"And where are we supposed to, then?" Mattie retorts.

Ava shrugs. "Beats me." She's biting back a smile, and Shiloh thinks he likes seeing her like this, relaxed and mischievous. A loud laugh reverberates throughout the campsite, and Shiloh sees Ava's face fall for a fraction of a second. Garrett Smith is across the way, beer in hand, chatting amongst the other guests. He pointedly ignores their group. *Good riddance,* Shiloh thinks. He has no doubt Drew would make good on his promise to teach him a lesson. Drew was always the one picking fights in school, putting bullies in their place. Even though he doesn't make it a habit of fighting anymore, Shiloh knows he could snap back into that mindset in an instant, especially if it was to defend the girls.

Drew must notice Ava's demeanor change, because he grabs a drink out of the cooler and tosses it to her. "Here, catch."

She catches it easily but frowns. "Canned margaritas?"

"Yeah, I picked some up when Mattie and I went into town. I figured you and Ashtyn would be burnt out on shitty beer by now."

This makes Ava laugh, and even Ashtyn smiles. "Aww, Drew, who knew you could be so sweet?"

Drew dramatically stabs his chest with his fist. "You wound me, dear Ava. Have I not been a perfect gentleman since I met you?"

Ava sits up, clears her throat, and in a relatively perfect impression of Drew, says, "My couch isn't the only thing that's infamous."

Everyone howls with laughter as Drew flushes beet red. Shiloh thinks it might be the only time he's ever seen his best friend blush.

"He did not say that to you!" Ashtyn exclaims, laughing hysterically.

"Of course he did!" Ava says, but there's fondness in her voice.

Drew kneels down in front of Ava, head bowed. "Please, accept my sincerest apologies," he says, reaching out and taking her hands in his. "My infamy knows no bounds."

Ava, giggling, leans down and smacks a playful kiss on Drew's cheek. "You're forgiven, sir. But you'll have to try harder with this one." She jerks her thumb toward Ashtyn. Ashtyn gasps, smacking Ava lightly on the shoulder.

"Oh, don't worry," Drew says, winking. "I plan on it."

After the sun goes down, they sneak back down to the river where people have gathered to shoot off fireworks. For one crazy, insane moment, Shiloh wonders if this is where Ava had her first kiss with Garrett. He feels a surge of jealously at the thought of that disgusting piece of shit kissing Ava. He shakes it from his mind and continues setting up the fireworks. He can't keep thinking like this. It'll go back to normal once they're home, he has to remind himself. He puts all his energy into setting up the fireworks and lighting them.

Ava and Ashtyn wave sparklers through the air. The sky is alight with fireworks from all over town, and as Shiloh lights the first one, it ignites and shoots into the sky, bursting into an arrangement of colors. It's intoxicating, hearing the cheers of everyone as the fireworks go off. Their oohs and aahs echoing across the water. He doesn't miss the way Ava's face lights up every time one goes off. He thinks he'll do anything to keep her smiling like that. Her smile is infectious. She has her phone out, snapping pictures of every second as if she's afraid to forget how happy she is in this exact moment. He takes out his own phone, still cracked but functional, and snaps a picture of her, face lit up with a smile and a sparkler in her hand. She's stunning. He snaps some pictures of the others, cementing this moment in time forever in his phone. He doesn't want to forget it either.

And then, of course, Garrett Smith walks down the bank of the river, staring at them intently. His arms are full of his own fireworks. The crowd turns and notices him, curious at the new array of things to blow up.

"I got firecrackers if anyone is interested!" Garrett announces, his voice carrying across the water. Kids flock toward him, grubby hands extended in want of whatever he's giving out.

"Man, that guy does not give up," Mattie mutters, hands in his pockets. Garrett smiles smugly as he hands kids sparklers and firecrackers, as if he went out and bought all of this just to spite them. Drew must have really struck a nerve with him.

"Well, then it's a good thing I got some...unique stock," Drew says, as he casually saunters away and runs back up the hill.

"What the hell is he talking about?" Shiloh asks his brother.

"We, uh, may have, and by we, I mean Drew, may have bribed the guy at the firework stand for some rather large and illegal fireworks."

"Matthew!" Ava exclaims, but there's a smile on her face.

And then Drew is back, running down the hill with even more bags full of fireworks. One holds a ginormous box that Shiloh isn't sure he wants to know what it is.

"We're gonna put on a show," Drew says.

And that's exactly what they do. They set off firework after firework, essentially competing with Garrett for the crowd's attention. Kids throw poppers at each other's feet, sparklers dance in the air, and the booms of explosions echo across the water.

"Alright, last one!" Drew announces, pulling out the largest firework Shiloh's ever seen. *El Diablo* is written on the box.

"Jesus, is that one going to explode in our faces?" Ashtyn asks, eyes wide.

"I guess we'll have to see," Drew says and then lights it.

"Wait!" Ava screams. "We need to take a group picture! Hurry, as it explodes!" She holds her phone up, and everyone crams into frame as quickly as possible. They're all smushed together, a pile of smiles and laughs, as the firework explodes behind them into the largest array of colors of the night, and Ava snaps the picture.

Chapter 19

July slowly comes to a close, and if they want any chance of taking the boat out before the end of summer, they need to seriously get to work. So, that's what Shiloh and Ava are doing. They've been out every day, working to get the boat running and interior restored. Shiloh's been hesitant to let Ava help with much of the heavy lifting, since he doesn't want a repeat of her injury, but she's so goddamn stubborn. She refuses to sit on the sidelines, even though she promised she would.

Shiloh watches as she rubs sunscreen across her face, her fingers running over the splotches of freckles that dot her cheeks. The sun burns the pavement of the driveway, making it feel like a million degrees outside. She gets most of the sunscreen rubbed in but has a white streak on the corner of her mouth.

"You, uh—" Shiloh starts, raising his hand.

"What, did I not get it all?" she asks, rubbing at every spot besides the sunscreen mark.

"Yeah, do you mind?" His hand gets closer to her face but waits for permission.

"Oh, yeah, sure," she says, turning her face up to him, allowing his fingers to run along her skin.

He takes his thumb and rubs the sunscreen into her skin, making the corner of her mouth tug upward by the motion. She's warm to the touch.

"There," he says, his fingers lingering ever so slightly on her skin, her freckles just beneath his whisper of a touch. The freckles that haunt his dreams. His hand extends, cupping her face with his fingers. He lingers for a moment longer before finally taking his hand back. "All good."

"Thanks," she says quietly, her eyes cast downward as if she can't meet his gaze. There's a slight flush to her cheeks that's not from the sun. "So, what do we have left to do?"

Shiloh clears his throat. He tells her everything that's left on his list of repairs, and she nods. They get to work silently, and Shiloh can't help himself from stealing glances at her. Her pale skin has a new glow to it from working in the sun for so long. Her freckles are illuminating, peeking out from the sleeves of her tank top and the tops of her shorts. He wishes, so selfishly, that he knew where every single one lay on her body. He thinks of her in her pink swimsuit, and he has to shake his head to clear his mind.

She turns toward him, and he glances away instantly, embarrassed at the thoughts flowing through his mind. He shouldn't be thinking things like this. "Have you thought about what you're going to name her?"

Shiloh already knows, but he doesn't want to tell her just yet. "No, I haven't thought about it."

"It should be something epic," Ava says. "Like Tempest of the Sea, or something like that."

This makes Shiloh chuckle. "Always with the grand literary references."

"Or The Juliet!"

"You're pushing it," he teases, a smile on his face.

"Hey, this has been a labor of love! It should have a lovely name," She argues but she's smiling too. "It also maimed and marked me forever, so I feel like I should get a say in what the name is."

"I'll think about it."

"Don't name it something stupid."

"So little faith in me." She grins at him, and it smacks Shiloh straight in the heart.

They work in silence for hours, ripping up seats and rotting wood while music floats out of the portable speaker they brought outside. It's not too loud, as to not disturb the neighbors, but it keeps them company while they work. Ava sings along quietly, her head bopping to the beat. Her voice travels through the air and into Shiloh's ears, making him shiver despite the heat.

Around dinner time, Ashtyn comes out of the house to tell them to come eat. Shiloh helps Ava out of the boat, not letting a repeat injury ever happen again. She takes his hand without argument and hops down easily.

"See how easy that was?" he teases her. She smacks him playfully on the chest, and Shiloh's skin sizzles from her touch.

Jess greets him as soon as he's back in the house, winding her way through his legs. He picks her up, and she licks his nose.

"She kept staring out the window at you," Ashtyn says, glaring at them. "She literally cannot be away from you."

"Were you supervising from inside, Jessica?" he asks the kitten. She meows in answer, putting her paw against his chin. She rubs her face against his own and purrs happily.

"I will never understand her fascination with you," Ashtyn says, laughing.

Ava snorts and says quietly, "I get it."

The entire room freezes at her words. Ashtyn's mouth hangs open, and Shiloh's eyes widen. Ava, not seeming to realizing she said that out loud, looks up and sees everyone staring at her. She flushes deeply. "I just–I mean, like, because she knows who bought her all of her stuff! You know? Cats are super intuitive." Her face is so red it matches Ashtyn's hair.

Shiloh takes this moment to tease her and lighten the mood. "No, I get what you're saying. I'm irresistible. People just can't help but fall in love with me. I mean, look at her—" Jess licks his face as if on cue, "—she's obsessed with me. It's okay Ave, I get it."

He's not sure it's possible, but Ava somehow flushes even deeper. "You wish I was obsessed with you," she mutters, crossing her arms in front of her chest. She's daring him to keep going, and he wants to. He wants to poke at her, tease her, elicit a reaction from her that makes her mouth purse into that perfect "o" shape. And then he wants to take her perfect face in his hands, and kiss the look right off her face...

The thought actually makes him drop Jess to the floor. Luckily, she's big enough now to where it barely even phases her, and she toddles off toward her food bowl. Shiloh catches Ashtyn's eyes darting between him and Ava with an intensity he doesn't want directed toward him.

He laughs awkwardly, trying to make his face as neutral as possible. "I, uh, wish for a lot of things, Ava." He lets the words dangle, letting Ava interpret them in whatever way she wants. Hoping, against all odds, that she interprets them in the way he wants, but knowing she probably won't.

Her lips turn up in a smirk, but it doesn't reach her eyes. "Guess you need a genie."

The silence that settles over them is filled with tension. He hates that he steered the conversation in uncharted territory like this, but he knows why. Because he can never have her in the way that he wants, even if he wishes. The universe has made it abundantly clear that Ava Marshall is off limits to Shiloh Brooks. And if it wasn't the universe, then it was definitely Ashtyn. The way she's glaring at him right now makes him squirm.

"I'm, uh, gonna go take a quick shower before dinner," he says, darting off toward the bathroom, where he looks at himself in the mirror and feels the weight of what he just said settle into his bones. He's made his bed, and now, he must lie in it.

* * *

Well, that settles it then. Shiloh Brooks is definitely not interested in Ava Marshall. She knew this, but now it's been confirmed with his own words. This is good, actually, because it can put to rest all the feelings that have been bubbling up inside her ever since they went camping, and he held her wrist like it was the most precious thing in the world. Ava shakes her head, clearing her mind. He does not like her in that way. Case closed. Time to move on.

"Ava," Ashtyn starts, looking up from her dinner.

"I was just kidding!" Ava exclaims defensively.

Ashtyn just blinks at her. "I was going to ask you to pass the salt."

"Oh. Sorry. Here." She passes her friend the salt. They chew in silence, the sound of the running shower in the background. The food feels heavy going down her throat, and her stomach churns.

"Are we going to talk about what just happened?"

"What, two friends teasing each other?"

Ashtyn narrows her eyes at Ava. "You know, I was thinking of using a different word."

"Banter? Friendly jabs? A jolly good time?"

"Flirting."

The word makes Ava roll her eyes. "If that's Shiloh's idea of flirting, then it's no wonder he's still single."

"Ava."

"Ashtyn."

"I was talking about you."

"Oh, please, I was not flirting. I was just messing around. You know, like I do with all my friends. I literally kissed Drew on the cheek when we went camping."

Ashtyn sighs heavily. "Ave, we talked about this—"

"Ashtyn!" Ava slams her hands on the table, making the silverware rattle. "Jesus fucking Christ, I wasn't flirting. If this was a girl, you wouldn't be chastising me like this. Just because it's an attractive guy doesn't mean I was flirting with him! I'm very aware Shiloh is off limits romantically. That doesn't mean I can't be fucking friendly." The words settle over the table, and Ashtyn doesn't say anything. Ava storms away from the table just as Shiloh returns from his shower. She jostles by him, bumping his shoulder on the way, but she ignores him, stomping up the stairs and slamming the door to her room like an angry teenager. A twenty-seven-year-old teenager.

She tells herself she doesn't care if they're talking about her downstairs. She feels tears prick her eyes, and she sniffles, trying to stop them before they can cascade down her cheeks. She really, really, really hates this idea that she flirts with every man she comes across and that, of all people, her best friend thinks it too. It infuriates her, actually.

She slides down against the door, bringing her knees to her chest and wrapping her arms around herself. Anger bubbles inside her, and she clenches her fists, angry tears she cannot control leaking out from the corners of her eyes. Her friendships with men shouldn't be overanalyzed by others, trying to see if there's any romantic subtext hiding in the seams. No one thinks twice about how she interacts with her girlfriends, even when she's overtly affectionate. It's only when she's a little too friendly with a man that everyone gets their panties in a twist.

There's a knock on her door. "Go away," she says, trying not to reveal she's been crying.

"Come on, Ave," Ashtyn says. "I want to apologize."

"Apologize to the door."

Ava hears her friend sigh heavily and lean against the other side of the door. "I'm sorry. I shouldn't treat you like that."

"Like what?" Ava probes.

"Like you fall in love with every man you meet. I know-I know how you feel about that, and I'm sorry that I played into it. I just..." Ashtyn pauses, taking a deep breath. "I just know how close you and Shiloh have gotten. And I can't stand the thought of anything changing—"

Ava's up and opening the door before she can even think about it. Ashtyn, leaning against it, stumbles forward and straight into Ava's arms. She can't stand being mad at her best friend for more than a few hours. They've never had a fight last longer than a day.

"I need you to trust me," she says. Ashtyn nods, a very rare, lone, tear slipping down her cheek. Ashtyn never cries. Ava can remember only one time she saw Ashtyn sob uncontrollably, and it's a day they don't talk about.

"I know, and I do trust you. I just...you know how protective I am of you." Ava knows. She also knows that Ashtyn's protectiveness comes mostly from her own experience, not Ava's. Ava has never felt the crushing weight of the love of her life choosing someone else. Not like Ashtyn has.

Ava squeezes Ashtyn to her tightly. "Listen to me," she says softly. "I love loudly. You know this. Everyone always thinks I'm flirting, even if I'm not, because that's just who I am. I want everyone to know that I love them, romantically, platonically, you name it. And I also know that you are the complete opposite. You love quietly and in private. And I know why you do that. It's completely understandable. But, I'm not you. I'm me. And I want to be able to tease my friends without everyone thinking I'm in love with them. I do love Shiloh. Just like you do. But I'm not in love with him. You have to trust me on that one."

Ashtyn nods, her head buried in Ava's shoulder. She sniffles, her tears soaking into Ava's t-shirt. "I'm sorry," she says.

"I'm sorry, too," Ava replies. "I shouldn't have stormed off like a petulant teenager. I'm too old for that shit."

"No, you had every right to. I need to stop comparing you to me. And I definitely need to stop comparing Shiloh to Brandon. It's not helping anyone."

Ava is surprised to hear Ashtyn actually admit this. She looks her friend dead in the eyes and says, "He does not define you."

Ashtyn stifles a cry and holds on tighter to Ava. Shiloh ascends the stairs and stops when he sees the girls embraced in tears. He looks trapped, like he wants to hurry into his room or go back downstairs. Ava holds one arm out to him, inviting him to join the hug-sesh.

"Come on," she says. "Roommate comfort time."

Shiloh hesitates for a moment, and then comes forward, wrapping both girls up in a hug.

"You tell anyone I cried, and I'll kill you," Ashtyn mutters, making Shiloh laugh.

"Noted," he replies. He leans down to Ava's ear and whispers, "I'm sorry."

Ava shakes her head. "It's not your fault."

"Okay, enough!" Ashtyn exclaims, shrugging out of the hug and wiping her eyes on the back of her hand.

"Is now a bad time to mention that I finally hugged you?" Shiloh asks, smiling.

Ashtyn scowls at him. "That didn't count, because I was hugging Ava. If my arms were not around you then you can't count it."

Shiloh huffs. "Good God, I didn't realize this was going to end up being such a debated topic."

This makes Ashtyn smile, and Ava's heart warms. "You keep hoping, Shiloh. Maybe one day your wish will come true."

Shiloh brings his hands together, like he's praying. "One day," he teases.

Ashtyn heads back downstairs, and Ava is about to follow her when Shiloh grabs her arm lightly. "Hey, we good?"

"Of course," Ava says. She ignores the way her arm is currently on fire at his touch.

"Okay, so bright and early tomorrow for the boat?"

"Count on it."

AUGUST

Chapter 20

The next few weeks fly by in a flurry of boat work. Shiloh and Ava work tirelessly, day in and out, to finish up the boat restoration. They're back to their normal ways, that day in the kitchen nearly forgotten. Shiloh hates that he planted the idea that he doesn't care about Ava in her head, but it's better this way. It's better she doesn't know how much he actually thinks about her. Instead, they're back to their normal, easy conversations, occasional teasing, and overall comfort of being around each other. Just two friends hanging out and restoring a boat together. You know, normal stuff.

They're two weeks into August when Shiloh thinks the boat is finally water ready. The interior has been completely restored, mostly thanks to Ava, while the motor and everything else is thanks to Shiloh. Mattie has been absent the last few weeks due to their father keeping him busy at the firm. This is the first day he's seen his brother since their camping trip.

They're in Mattie's truck, towing the boat toward the marina, where Shiloh reserved a permanent spot. They barely have any time to actually take it out before school starts, and Shiloh starts his new job, but he stills feels proud that they were able to finish it before summer officially ends.

"I can't believe you actually fixed this thing," Mattie says.

"Honestly, if I didn't have Ava's help, I probably wouldn't have finished it."

"I'm surprised you actually let her help, seeing how you almost lost your shit when she got hurt."

Shiloh huffs. "I did not lose my shit."

"You threatened to throw the boat into a wood chipper."

"Only if she wanted me to."

Mattie whistles under his breath and shakes his head. He looks like he wants to say something, but he refrains. Instead, he says, "Well, I'm glad you got it finished. Even if we only have a couple of weeks to enjoy it."

"Says the person that didn't help at all."

Mattie just grins as they pull into the marina. It's not close to the house, but it's as close as they're going to get, which is about thirty minutes away. Mattie expertly backs the boat onto the ramp and lowers it into the water. Shiloh will have to pilot it into the designated spot.

They get out of the truck and unhook the boat from the hitch. It sinks into the water, and Shiloh jumps in, starting the motor.

"I'll meet you at the dock!" he shouts over the noise. Mattie gives him a thumbs up and hops back into the truck.

The boat thrums under Shiloh's hands, and he loves the way it feels. He got his boating license just a few days ago, preparing for this moment. He's just driving it to the dock, he's not actually taking it out on the water for its first drive. He wants to save that moment for Ava. She deserves it after all the work she helped put into the thing.

He pilots it across the water and toward the marina, loving the way the wind whips through his hair. He finds their dock and slows down, parking it in the assigned spot. Mattie's heading down the ramp toward him.

"You finally gonna show me what you named her?" he shouts.

Shiloh turns the boat off, the waves rocking it back and forth. He throws Mattie the rope, and he ties it securely to the pole. The boat is finally home, where it belongs.

Shiloh feels nervous, showing his brother the name. He didn't consult with anyone before painting it. He just did it.

"You don't get a say, because you didn't help fix it," Shiloh says.

Mattie holds up his hands. "Hey, that's fine with me. She's mostly your boat anyway. I just paid for it."

Shiloh rolls his eyes but laughs anyway. "Alright, take a look."

Mattie heads toward the back of the boat where the name is painted. He stops short when he sees it.

"What do you think?"

Mattie's face erupts into a wide grin. "I think she's going to love it."

* * *

The sun beats down on Shiloh and Ava as they make their way down to the boat docks. His hands are over Ava's eyes as he leads them toward their spot.

"Shi, please don't let me fall in the water," she says, giggling.

"I've got you, don't worry," he says from behind her. Nerves shoot through his body as they get closer to the finished boat. What if she hates the name? What if she thinks it's stupid?

"Are we almost there?" she asks, stumbling a little. She grabs onto his arm, and goosebumps pop onto his body even though it's a million degrees outside. She doesn't move her hand, steadying herself.

"We're here," he says, stopping. Ava's body leans into his, and he has to stop himself from devouring her right here and now. He stares at her bare shoulders, freckles dusting every inch of them. They're especially dark because of how much time they've spent in the sun this summer. He thinks about every freckle that's still unknown to him, that he'd like to find.

He clears his throat. "Before I take my hands away from your eyes, I just wanted to tell you how glad I am that you decided to help me this summer. I know it wasn't necessarily glamorous work, especially the whole cutting your head open thing, but having you help me...it made it bearable."

Ava laughs, and Shiloh feels the sound of it reverberate through his whole body. "So, to thank you for that..." He takes his hands away from her eyes and waits. She blinks rapidly, letting her eyes adjust to what is in front of her.

The boat sits in the water, freshly painted, the name emblazoned in a deep blue color on the side: AVA

Ava's hand goes to her mouth, a small gasp emitting from it. "Shiloh," she whispers, tears starting to form in her eyes. "You—you named it after me?"

"Well, yeah, I mean, I figured you helped me work on it, and it's basically as much yours as it is mine—"

He's cut off as Ava whirls around and jumps into his arms, wrapping herself around him. His arms come around her on instinct, holding her to him. She's warm, and he can feel the sweat on the back of her shirt, but he doesn't mind. He just wants to keep holding her like this, pressed against him. He feels faint, but he holds her steady.

"I can't believe it," she whispers, her lips brushing his neck. It sends shivers through Shiloh's entire body. "You could have named it literally anything at all, and you chose...me."

"I didn't even consider any other name," he says. Ava pulls back and looks him in the eyes. Their faces are inches apart. Her breath is warm on his face, but he doesn't pull away. He's daring her to close the gap. Daring her to forget what he said all those weeks ago.

"When I asked you if you had any ideas on what to name her..." She lets her words dangle.

"I already knew."

"Thank you," she breathes, their noses brushing, lips barely a whisper away from each other. Shiloh wants to close the distance between them. Her legs are still wrapped around his waist, barely an inch of space between them.

"Of course," he whispers, and he feels his lips brush hers ever so slightly due to the movement. It's barely a touch, but it's a jolt to both of their systems, and they snap their heads away from each other. Ava unwraps her legs and slides down his body tortuously. She lets out a breath, and steps out of his embrace. She turns and stares at the boat again, hiding her face from him. Shiloh adjusts himself discreetly.

"You, uh, want to take her for a spin?" he asks. His voice feels thick, like someone poured molasses down his throat. He knows it's just what Ava does to him. Their near kiss has ruined him.

Ava doesn't turn around to face him when she says quietly, "Yes."

He grabs her hand, even though it's torture, and guides her carefully into the boat. He climbs in after her, and it rocks in the water underneath their weight. Ava plops onto the newly upholstered seats she picked out. She runs her hands over them gingerly and smiles softly. Her face is red.

"Here," Shiloh says, tossing her a life jacket. "Put this on. You have a habit of falling out of boats."

Ava laughs and snaps the jacket across her chest, securing it tightly. Shiloh does the same with his, then starts up the motor. It purrs to life, and the sound is glorious.

Ava's eyes light up, a slight flush to her cheeks. "I can't believe it's actually running. I can't believe we actually did it!"

Shiloh steers the boat out of its dock and out onto the open water. The boat glides smoothly across the waves, wind whipping the hair out of their faces. Ava has a permanent smile plastered to her mouth as she takes in the feeling of being on a boat. She looks beautiful. Shiloh has to tear his eyes away from her and focus on steering the boat.

"Mattie should be here," she says, turning to look at him. "I mean, it is his boat."

"I don't think Mattie would ever classify it as solely his boat. I think he'd say it's all of ours."

"Did you ask him about the name?" She asks it shyly.

"I did," he replies, a blush coating his cheeks.

"And?"

"And he thought it was perfect."

She bites back a smile. "Well, thank you, again," she says, staring out across the water.

Shiloh slows the boat and cuts off the motor, letting them float in quiet for a moment. The only sound is the water lapping up the sides of the boat from the current. It rocks them gently.

Ava sighs deeply. "Summer's almost over."

"Yeah, sorry, I wanted to get the boat out earlier but—"

"That's not what I meant," she says, interrupting him. "I just meant...we won't have this project to do together anymore. And school is starting again soon, so everyone will be busy, and I'll just miss being able to hang out all the time, you know?"

Shiloh has to swallow before he can say anything. "I mean, we do still live together."

Ava barks out a laugh. She's not looking at him, and Shiloh wishes she would. If she does, maybe he'd get the courage to tell her he's going to miss it too. That, maybe, they could find something else to do together. Shiloh thinks he'd buy fifty more run down boats for them to fix, just to make her happy and spend time together. He's about to tell her that when she turns to him with a mischievous smile on her face. She unbuckles her life vest and before Shiloh has a chance to react, she jumps straight off the boat and into the blue water.

"Ava!" he yells, rushing over to the side of the boat where she disappeared. "Ava!"

There's nothing for several seconds, and then she surfaces, taking in a deep lungful of air. "Come on in!" she exclaims. "The water's perfect!"

"What did I say about falling off of boats?!" Shiloh exclaims, trying not to let panic infuse his voice.

"You said I had a habit of doing it. I'm just proving that to be true." She splashes him, and Shiloh has to hold back a smile. "Join me."

So, he does. He unclips his life jacket, removes his shirt, and jumps straight into the water. It's freezing, and the cold envelops him like a blanket, soaking him to his bones. As he surfaces, he splashes Ava. "I thought you said the water was perfect!"

"Perfectly freezing," she says, teeth chattering slightly. "I figured you'd like to experience it for yourself."

"I would have been fine just watching you," he replies, jokingly.

Ava laughs and splashes him again before swimming away. They swim around for a few minutes until they can't take it anymore.

"Okay, I can't do this," Shiloh announces, hauling himself up onto the boat. He holds his hand out to Ava and pulls her up. Her white tank top is soaked, and he can see her bra peeking through. There are goosebumps on her flesh, and Shiloh throws her his shirt.

"Here, use this to dry off."

"Shi, I can't use your shirt as a towel," she says. She tosses it back to him and takes off her own shirt. His shirt hits him in the face as he's unable to move to catch it. He's just staring at her as she wrings her own shirt out over the side of the boat, trying to get as much water out as possible. She stands there in her soaking wet cutoff shorts and bra, like nothing in the world bothers her. Once she's done, she pulls the shirt back over her head.

"What?" she asks, looking at him. Shiloh stands there, dumbly, shirt in hand, heart racing.

"I didn't say anything," he says, pulling his own shirt on and avoiding her gaze.

He turns the boat back on, and they cruise through the water, back toward the docks, letting the sun warm their freezing skin. Shiloh tries to calm his racing heart and not stare at Ava's shirt hugging every curve on her body. It takes everything in him to focus on driving the boat instead of kissing her senselessly.

* * *

"I don't know about you, but I could go for an afternoon coffee break," Ava says, once they're back in the air conditioning of her car. Her clothes are still damp even after baking under the August sun. She shivers as the AC cools her wet skin, her hair sticking to the back of her neck. It's refreshing and shocking at the same time, kind of like their very near kiss back at the boat dock.

"God, that sounds good," Shiloh replies, resting his face on the vent, letting the cold air cool his sweaty face. His shirt sticks to his chest, outlining his muscles. Ava has to look away.

She really wasn't thinking when she'd jumped into his arms. It was purely an emotional response to him naming the boat after her. Seeing her name painted on their labor of love shot straight through to her heart and filled her with so much emotion. She couldn't help but attack Shiloh with a hug. His skin had been so warm against her own, and she'd felt euphoric at the way his arms wrapped around her perfectly. They've hugged before, but this was different. This was a full body, legs wrapped around his waist, lips on his neck type of hug. It was *not* a hug shared by two roommates.

And then his lips had just barely touched hers, and she felt like she'd been electrocuted. Every single conversation she's had with Ashtyn came shooting back into her mind. *Do not develop a crush on Shiloh Brooks.* It was the number one rule, and now she'd almost kissed him. She wanted to. Had felt her body pulling toward him. But she couldn't. She wouldn't. So, she'd pulled back, let go of him, just like she was supposed to.

Ava pulls out her phone. "I'll set up a mobile order for pick-up. You want your usual?"

"Yes, please."

Ava submits the orders then selects a song for them to listen to. The music blasts through the speakers, enveloping the car and preventing them from speaking. As they pull up to *Brewed*, her phone dings with a notification that the order is ready.

"I'll run in and grab it," she says, and Shiloh just nods. He's been unusually quiet on their drive. Normally they drive with all the windows down, music blasting, singing along. Well, she sings along. Shiloh just hums to himself with a smile on his face. She wonders what he's thinking about. Does he feel weird about their almost kiss, too? She thinks back to what he said that day in the kitchen: how he doesn't wish for her. She'd probably freaked him out by that hug, making him feel awkward and uncomfortable. She'd have to make sure she didn't do it again.

As she enters the coffee shop, she notices Brad the barista behind the counter, and he meets her eyes when she approaches the counter. He gives her a sexy smile that makes her stomach pool with sudden desire. Her clothes are still slightly damp, and she's sure her hair looks insane. Nevertheless, Brad looks at her like he's incredibly interested. It makes her heart skip a beat.

"I left a little something on your cup," he says from across the counter. He's busy making orders, but it doesn't stop him from winking at her. Ava feels a blush creep up her skin as she takes the coffees. That's when she sees it. There's a phone number on the cup with her name on it. She almost drops it as she turns around and looks at Brad again. He's talking into his headset, taking orders from the drive thru, but he smiles at her again and mouths, "Text me." She has no idea what to do, so she just nods dumbly and leaves on shaky legs, her heart racing.

Anxiety, mixed with desire, courses through her veins as she makes her way back to the car. She gets in silently and sits for a minute before startling at Shiloh's words. "You okay?"

She almost forgot he was there. "Yeah," she breathes. She hands him his coffee while death gripping her own. She's not sure if she's trying to hide the number on her cup from Shiloh, but even if she was, he wouldn't be able to see it, because she's holding the cup so tightly. For a moment, she's worried she might have smudged the marker. She's not sure if that would be a good thing or not.

"Geez, you look like you've seen a ghost. You sure you're okay?"

"I—I think I got asked out," she stutters, not looking at him. She unleashes her grip on the cup and turns it to show Shiloh. The marker, miraculously, has not smudged.

"Oh," he says, pausing the sip of coffee he was about to take. "Uh, is that a good thing? Cause you kind of look like you want to throw up."

"I'm just surprised," Ava says honestly. "I never expected something like this to ever happen to me. This is movie type shit." She's itching to text Ashtyn. She needs to talk to her best friend and divulge everything.

"Are you going to text him?" She's surprised by the question. He's not looking at her, staring intently at his own cup, brows furrowed together, in an expression that she can't read.

"I don't know. Do you think I should?" It's out before she can stop herself. She's not sure why she's so curious about his answer.

Shiloh looks up at her. He thinks for a moment, as though he's choosing his words carefully. Then, he smiles, but it doesn't reach his eyes. "Yeah, I mean, why not? Isn't this what you've been waiting for? Movie type shit?" His words are empty, his expression blank. It's like he's trying to put on a face that displays nonchalance.

"Yeah," she says, trying to force a smile. "You're right."

What exactly was she expecting from him? For him to tell her no? That would be ridiculous. She already knows how he feels about her. She thinks about their near kiss at the boat dock once again, and she knows she has to do this. She can't turn down the opportunity of someone interested in her, just because she almost kissed her roommate. Because he named a stupid boat after her.

They ride back to the house, and the only sound filling the car is silence. She forgot to turn on the music.

Chapter 21

"Oh my god! You have to text him!" Ashtyn exclaims. They're in her room, Jess splayed between them on the bed. Shiloh is at his last shift at the bar. After today, he'll officially be done and ready to start work at the school in a couple of weeks.

"You think?" Ava wrings her hands together nervously.

"Oh my god, Ava, you've been lusting after Brad the barista since the day you saw him two years ago. Are you kidding me? Of course you have to text him! This is what you've been waiting for."

She knows Ashtyn's right. Hell, the day they met Shiloh she'd been intently staring at Brad, hoping he'd notice her. So, why does it feel so weird now? If it's everything she's been waiting for, then why does it feel wrong?

"What am I supposed to say?"

"I mean, you just start with 'hey' and see where it goes from there."

"I'm going to throw up."

"Give me your phone," Ashtyn says and snatches it from Ava's hand. Ava doesn't even protest. Ashtyn types away and then shows her. She's always been the mastermind behind Ava's first texts to her crushes. "Here. If you want to send it, go for it."

Ava looks at her phone. Ashtyn has typed out: *Hey! This is Ava from Brewed :) Really glad you gave me your number!*

It's so incredibly simple that she almost laughs. She presses send before she can even think about it.

"Okay, that was easier than I thought," Ashtyn says, curiously. "Normally we have to type out like ten different messages before you're happy with them."

"Yeah, well, maybe that's the problem," Ava says. "I overthink everything anyway."

"Okay, what have you done with my best friend?" Ashtyn asks, pointing an invisible sword at her. "Where is she!?"

Before she can think of a funny reply, she blurts out, "Shiloh named the boat after me."

Ashtyn's arm drops. "What?"

"He fucking named the boat *Ava*. That's me. That's my name!"

"Well, I'm glad you remember your own name," Ashtyn says, blowing out a breath. "Is that like a big deal?" Her tone becomes more serious.

"Of course it's a big deal! Are you kidding me? Of all the names in the world, he picked my name for his fucking boat. And when he showed me, I got so emotional that..." She stops before she says anything else. She can't tell Ashtyn that they'd almost kissed. Not after everything Ava told her about not being in love with Shiloh and to trust her that she wouldn't develop feelings for him. No, she can never know.

"That what?" Ashtyn questions.

"That I just started crying," Ava lies. "It was so embarrassing."

"I mean, he's seen you cry before, Ave. I'm sure it wasn't that big of a deal."

She sighs heavily. "Yeah, you're right.

"Ava," Ashtyn starts, but Ava's phone buzzes, interrupting them. It's Brad.

She pulls up the message and sucks in a breath: *Hey, Ava! Glad you texted! I've been wanting to give you my number for months now and I finally got the courage, haha. Would you want to go out with me next Saturday? There's a new Italian restaurant that just opened down on Main that I've been wanting to try out. Just needed to find the perfect person to share it with :)*

Ava shows the message to Ashtyn. "I should say yes, right?"

Ashtyn looks at her, but she's not as excited as she was earlier. "You should do what feels right, Ave." Her words are sincere, but there's something she's holding back.

Suddenly, nothing feels right. Anxiety shoots through her body, and she feels sick. She knows she should do this. She knows she never stood a chance with Shiloh. That it would ruin everything if she admits she has feelings for him. Because that's what this is, right? Feelings for Shiloh? The one person she is absolutely not allowed to have feelings for. He already told her he doesn't think he ever sees himself getting married again, and isn't that what she wants? She wants epic, romantic, life changing love. She knows Shiloh could never give her that.

She looks back down at her phone. Brad is cute. He's hot, actually. He makes incredible coffee. He left his number on a coffee cup, something she's been dreaming of him doing for forever now. This is the perfect moment. It's movie type shit.

"Okay, I'm going to say yes," she says, replying to the text. Stress courses through her veins. She can't decide if it's anticipation for the date, or if she's pretending to be excited. Either way, she'll find out soon enough.

Chapter 22

There's a knock on the front door as Ava finishes applying her lip gloss. She feels her body thrum with something unknown. Anticipation? Dread? She's not really sure yet, so she just shoves the feeling down and goes to open the door.

Ashtyn's out with Daisy for a girls night, and Shiloh's holed up in his room with the TV blaring. Since school begins soon, they start in-service on Monday, and Ava knows he's excited. He's been studying Coach Mack's binder and watching old matches. The past few days, they've been out on the boat a couple more times, enjoying the last remnants of summer. But she knows something has shifted since their near kiss, and Brad asking her out. She's trying very hard to ignore it and pretend everything is fine, that nothing has changed. If things go well with Brad, maybe they can go back to normal.

Ava opens the door and there's Brad, ever so handsome, in a button down and slacks. He has a bundle of flowers and a smile on his face. No one's ever gotten her flowers before.

"Oh my gosh, Brad, you didn't have to do that," she says, taking the flowers from him and smelling them. They're gorgeous, but the smell is so intense that she has to hold in a sneeze.

"Never show up to someone's house empty handed," he says. "At least, that's what my mom always told me." Ava smiles and invites him in while she puts the flowers in some water and a vase. Jess meanders down from the stairs and starts to twine herself through Brad's legs.

"Are you a cat person?" Ava asks as Brad stares down at Jess with a funny look on his face. She's begging to be pet, but he doesn't do it.

"I'm more of a dog person," he says.

Ava scoops Jess up and nuzzles her goodbye before they head toward the door. Just as they're about to leave, Ava hears Shiloh's door open, and he heads down the stairs. Then he's across from them at the foot of the stairs. An awkward pause settles between them.

"Oh, sorry," Shiloh says, freezing in place. "I thought you were gone already."

"Oh, no, you're good," Ava says, trying not to look anyone directly in the eye. "Um, Brad, this is my roommate, Shiloh. Shiloh, this is Brad."

"Nice to meet you," Brad says, sticking his hand out. Shiloh takes it with a stiff smile on his face.

"You, too," he says. They size each other up for a moment, and Ava has to refrain from rolling her eyes. *Boys,* she thinks. Jess sits next to Shiloh's foot, and he scoops her up.

"Come on, Jessica," he says, holding the cat close to his chest. "Let's go watch *New Girl.*"

"Alright, well, I'll be back later," Ava says to his retreating back. She rolls her eyes, and then takes Brad's hand as she leads him out the door. It's slightly clammy, and she has stop herself from letting go and wiping her own hand on her dress. He opens her car door for her like a gentleman and drives them downtown.

They arrive at the restaurant where Brad pulls her chair out for her and continues to act completely chivalrous. Everything is going exactly as Ava pictured it should. She feels beautiful in her black dress. She feels confident in her flawless makeup. She feels respected and doted on. So, why is she feeling like something just isn't quite right?

"So, what made you want to finally ask me out?" Ava asks, rather boldly for her, as they settle into their table and order drinks.

"I don't know," Brad says, smiling at her. "I saw your mobile order pull up like always, and I just thought, why not?"

Alright, not exactly the romantic answer she was hoping for, but that's okay. Not everything has to be a perfect moment. "Well, I'm glad you did," she replies. "I've been crushing on you for a while now." She takes a sip of her wine to hide her blush.

"Yeah, I kind of figured," Brad says, easily. "A lot of the regulars do."

This makes Ava blush harder, and her stomach sours. She's not even special. She's just like every other girl that comes into the coffee shop, apparently.

"Oh," she says, slightly embarrassed. "Then what made you want to ask me?"

"Because you're beautiful," he says, reaching out to take her hand, as if it's the most obvious answer in the world. This should make Ava feel incredible, but it mostly just makes her feel empty. Her stomach flip flops. The idea of eating right now makes her feel nauseated.

"Thank you," she says meekly.

Brad just smiles at her, like he's been told thank you by countless women before. "So," he says, almost too loudly. "You're a teacher, right?"

"Yeah, I teach English at Lakeview."

"Uh oh, better make sure my grammar is perfect then," he says, laughing at his joke.

Ava has to force herself to smile. "I focus primarily on literature. I only do grammar lessons when they have standardized testing."

"Cool," Brad says, absentmindedly. He flips the menu over and over again.

"Um, do you like to read?"

"Not really. I'm more of a movie person."

This makes Ava perk up. "Oh my gosh, I love movies! My friend Ashtyn and I have a huge DVD collection."

"Why?"

The question throws Ava off. "What do you mean?"

"Why do you still have DVDs? Everything is on streaming services now. DVDs are, like, super outdated."

"Oh. Well, it started when we were in college—"

But Brad doesn't let her finish. Instead, he flags down the waiter and tells them that they're ready to order. Ava has barely glanced at the menu, so she chooses the first thing she sees and hopes she likes it.

"Sorry, what were you saying?" Brad asks once the waiter is gone.

"Oh, nothing," Ava replies, waving her hand in front of her face. "Just that I really like movies too."

"Oh, yeah! Movies are great. Just can't stand romantic comedies. They're always so stupid."

Ava has to bite her lip to keep herself from frowning. "Oh, I love romantic comedies."

"Yeah, I got that vibe from you."

She finishes her glass of wine and asks for another, feeling like she's going to need it to get through this night.

They continue getting to know each other over the course of the evening, and everything she learns about Brad leaves her either bored or annoyed. So, when the check comes and he pays, and he looks up at her from his lashes and asks if she wants to come back to his place, she surprises herself by saying yes.

She's not exactly sure why she says yes. Maybe to prove to herself that she had a good time, and she's appreciative of the interest he's shown in her. Maybe she just wants to feel beautiful and desired by someone for the first time in a long time. Maybe she's just hoping to no longer be bored. Either way, she takes his hand as he leads her back toward his car, and she ignores every red flag he's thrown onto the field tonight.

When they get back to his place, it's perfectly clean and rather empty for a bachelor pad, with only a sparse amount of furniture decorating the place. There are no pictures or art hanging from the walls. It's so incredibly boring, just like him. Brad pours her a glass of wine, and they collapse onto the couch, his fingers running up and down her arm. It sends goosebumps up her skin, but she's not sure if they're the good kind.

"Is this okay?" he whispers, leaning in closer. She nods, trying to get in the mood. She's in front of a handsome man, alone in his apartment, in a sexy dress. He's been a gentleman the entire night. He's paid attention to her. He's told her about himself. He's been...fine. So incredibly fine.

Then he's leaning in and kissing her. For a split second, she's sixteen again, down at the river kissing Garrett Smith with his stale beer breath. Except, now it's wine breath. Then, she remembers she's here and kissing Brad. His lips are so wet, and his hands are gripping her arms too hard. He's all teeth and tongue and nothing else. She pulls away for a moment, but he's back on her, pulling her face to his.

"Wait," she says around his lips. He either doesn't hear her or ignores her. "Stop!" she says, louder.

Brad pulls back, an annoyed look on his face. "What?"

"It's too much," she says, trying to catch her breath. She has to resist the urge to wipe her mouth on the back of her hand.

He rolls his eyes. "You came back to my apartment. What did you expect?"

"I just need a minute," she says, feeling like the wine might come back up at any moment. She can't get the taste of him off her. It's nauseating.

"We just barely started kissing, and it's already too much for you?"

"Yeah, it's just been a while since—"

"Good God, Ava, don't be so fucking boring." His words are like a gut punch, and tears prick her eyes. "If you didn't come to fuck me, then I don't know what you're doing here."

Ava feels herself physically recoil. "Okay, I think I'm going to go," she says, gathering up her purse. She absolutely has to get out of there immediately.

Brad doesn't even look at her. "You'd be a lot prettier if you'd learn to just shut your mouth."

His words are so nasty, Ava actually feels her food come back up her throat. She swallows it down and puts a hand over her mouth as she hurries toward the door. She doesn't look back as she leaves and slams the door behind her. She's out on the curb with no ride, tears streaming down her face, her mouth sour, and her entire body trembling.

She pulls out her phone and calls Ashtyn. It goes straight to voicemail. Of fucking course her phone would be dead the one night Ava is in dire need of her best friend. She tries again, knowing nothing will change. She's right. Straight to voicemail again. She could call an Uber, but she doesn't really want a stranger to see her in her current state. She only has one other option left. She shouldn't. She really, really shouldn't, but her finger presses the button before her brain can catch up. She calls him, and he answers on the first ring. Of course he does.

"Are you okay?" Shiloh asks, immediately.

"Um, not exactly," she replies, her voice coming out gruffer than she meant it. "I mean, I'm fine, I just need a ride home."

"Where are you?" Ava hears him gathering his keys.

"I don't know the exact address," she says. "I'll just pin my location for you."

"Are you safe?"

Ava looks at the darkened street, only a flickering street lamp illuminating the curb. "I'm fine. Just hurry."

"I'll be there as fast as I can."

Ava's not sure how he does it, but he's there in record time. She doesn't even have time to take a step toward her car before Shiloh's out and pulling her into his arms. She sinks into him and feels her eyes fill with tears again. He doesn't ask her what happened. He doesn't say anything. He just holds her and rubs circles on her back as tears fall down her face, soaking his shirt.

"I'm sorry. Ash wouldn't answer, and I didn't know what else to do. I didn't want to call an Uber and have them see me cry."

Again, Shiloh doesn't say anything. He just tightens his grip on her, and she melts into his embrace. "You don't have anything to apologize for," he finally says, quietly. Ava just nods, and they stand there for a moment longer before pulling apart and getting into the car. They don't say anything for the rest of the way home, but Shiloh holds her hand in his. She pulls out a can of mints from her console and eats as many as it will take to get the taste of Brad and bile out of her throat.

When they pull into the driveway, Shiloh turns off the car, and they sit in silence for another moment. Ava wipes away her mascara streaked cheeks with a napkin.

"Do you want to tell me what happened?" His voice is so quiet. Ava feels her throat tighten. "You don't have to, if you don't want to."

"He just wasn't very nice," she says, tightening her grip on Shiloh's hand. The way his fingers feel in hers is a lifeline.

"Did he hurt you?"

"Not physically, no." A pained look crosses Shiloh's face, and he unhooks their hands and gets out of the car. Ava's hand feels cold, but then Shiloh is at her door, holding it open for her and offering her his hand again. She takes it, and they walk into the house together. The front door shuts, and they stand in the foyer, in the dark, not saying anything, tethered together by their joined hands. She knows the flowers are still sitting on the counter, and she doesn't want to look at them.

"No one should make you feel like that, Ava," Shiloh says, his voice tight.

"I haven't told you how I feel."

"No, but I can see it on your face. Whatever happened tonight has upset you."

Ava takes a breath, and tells him what happened. She hates hearing Brad's words come out of her own mouth, but she needs to tell someone. Shiloh is suddenly crushing her into his chest, his arms going around her. "Do not ever listen to what someone like that has to say. He's a fucking piece of shit."

Ava can't seem to say anything as she starts to cry again. She holds onto Shiloh, and she can't imagine ever letting him go.

"You—you are so beautiful" Shiloh says, cradling her head in his hands. He's looking down at her. Her eyes have adjusted slightly to the dark, and she can just barely make out his features. He looks at her intently, their foreheads slightly touching.

Ava shakes her head. "You're just saying that."

"No," he says, fiercely. "I'm not. Every time you walk into a room, I can't tear my eyes away from you. I want to hear everything you have to say. I never want to stop listening."

She blinks up at him. His words have stunned her. They dive into her bloodstream, and give her a feeling she can only imagine drugs give other people. Her body thrums. She carefully puts her hand up against his face, and she feels him shiver. Her thumb caresses his cheek, skimming the edge of his lip. She's never felt so intimate with someone before, even the people she's shared a bed with. It's never been like this.

"Kiss me," she breathes before she can second guess herself. Before she can tell herself it's a mistake. Before she can think of the consequences. Because, right now, this is all she wants.

Shiloh lets out a breath, and then lowers his lips to hers. They stop just as they brush hers, testing if she really wants this. She stands on tip toes and closes the distance between them. He tastes so sweet, she can barely believe it. His lips, so soft and gentle, fit perfectly against her own. She has never kissed this gentle and gingerly before, as if every second their lips are pressed together is the most important moment of their lives. Their kiss deepens ever so slowly as their hands go into each other's hair, exploring. Ava's arms go around Shiloh's neck, and then his hands are slowly traveling down her body and hoisting her up, her legs circling his waist. Warmth spreads throughout her entire body. This is what almost happened at the boat dock. It's so completely different from the kiss that she had not even an hour ago. It's like night and day. She doesn't want to think of anything else other than the kiss that is happening right now.

One arm is holding up her ass, while the other is pressed against her cheek, and yet Shiloh is still kissing her as if she weighs nothing. Ava remembers back at the boat dock, when they were similarly embraced, but neither could go through with the kiss that they obviously both wanted. She's wanted a kiss like this her entire life. Her mouth opens, and Shiloh's tongue meets hers. Their lips move perfectly together. They pull back ever so slightly after a moment, lips still only inches apart, breathing deeply.

"Did you mean it?" Ava asks.

"I mean everything I say to you," he replies, sincerity lacing his voice. They're the same words he told her at the campsite, when he told her she was the complete opposite of boring. His hands have traveled up her dress and are skimming her bare skin. She shivers at his touch and feels herself smile.

They're about to kiss again, when headlights flood into the kitchen.

Ava, as if on instinct, pulls out of Shiloh's embrace, knowing Ashtyn is about to head through the front door. She can't help but notice the look that crosses Shiloh's face.

"Don't tell her," Ava whispers immediately, not able to meet his gaze as she steps away from him. Her lips are begging her to go back to him. Her entire body screams for his embrace, but she knows she can't, not with Ashtyn about to come into the house.

"Okay," Shiloh replies, voice rough. He's up the stairs and in his room without a second glance back, and Ava feels his absence heavily.

Ashtyn enters through the front door a moment later, flipping on the light in the foyer, and jumps when she sees Ava. "Jesus! What are you doing in the dark?" She sets her stuff down, and then sees Ava clearly for the first time. She knows her makeup must be ruined, either from crying or kissing, and Ashtyn gasps. Then, she's holding Ava in her arms. "Ave, what happened? Are you okay?"

Ava doesn't say anything. She notices the stupid fucking flowers in the kitchen over Ashtyn's shoulder.

"I think I'm going to have to get a new barista," is all she manages to get out before bursting into tears.

Chapter 23

Shiloh slumps against his bedroom door, falling slowly to the floor. His heart is racing and breaking simultaneously. He takes a deep breath, feeling the remnants of Ava's kiss on his lips and throughout his body. She's all over him, and he can't get the feeling of her body pressed against him out of his head. He puts his head between his knees, trying to steady his breathing and stop his body from trembling.

He thinks about everything Ava just told him about her date, and he has to keep his rage in check. He wants to go find Brad the barista and pummel him, even though he's never hit another person before in his life. The words he spoke to her makes his blood boil. Seeing her standing on the curb, tears streaming down her face, made him irrational. All he could do was pull her into his arms and make her feel safe. It's all he's ever wanted to do. And then she'd told him to kiss her. And he'd had to obey her, could not deny her.

He can hear Ava and Ashtyn talking softly downstairs. He never should have kissed her, even though he's been wanting to for so long now. He can still feel the words, *don't tell her*, hammering against his skin. It makes his fists clench. He wants to forget she said that. How she jumped away from him, just like at the boat dock, after reality set in. But he understands why. Because Ashtyn would absolutely freak out if she knew they had kissed. She'd already warned him once about Ava, and told him not to get attached. This was pretty fucking attached.

He leans his head back and realizes this is the first girl he's kissed since Scarlett. After the divorce, he never sought the company of another woman. He'd stayed holed up in Drew's apartment, blaming himself for everything that went wrong. He hasn't enjoyed the touch of a woman in so long. Kissing Ava tonight felt like coming alive. The blood is rushing through his veins, and he feels like he might explode from her mere presence. How could one person make him feel so good?

His eyes drift across the room and sees the outfit he picked out for his first day of school, hanging on the door of his closet. He sucks in a breath as he realizes what he's done. He just kissed Ava and now, in a few days, he'll be driving with her to the first day of work, because he still doesn't have a fucking car. He doesn't have a car, because all he could focus on was fixing the boat, because it meant he got to spend time with Ava. How is he supposed to share a space with her after this? How, when all he wants is to take her in his arms and kiss her senseless every time he sees her? Get down on his knees and pledge his loyalty to her. He can't. He wants to barge downstairs and kiss her again, consequences be damned. But she asked him not to tell Ashtyn. He knows that if he kisses her again, he'll never want to kiss anyone else for the rest of his life.

He sleeps fitfully the entire night, unable to calm himself down. Right before dawn, he gets up out of bed and slips out of the house, his old wedding ring snug in his pocket. He knows he shouldn't, but he borrows Ava's car without asking, hoping to be back before either of the girls are even awake. He drives in the early morning dark toward the docks.

When he arrives, it's eerily quiet and completely empty. He makes his way toward the boat and jumps in, starting up the engine. He's not sure why he feels the need to do this, but something in him is screaming. He drives out into the middle of the lake then cuts the engine. The early morning silence welcomes him into its embrace. He pulls the ring out of his pocket and holds it in his upturned palm. The boat rocks softly against the flow of the river as the water laps up the sides. The wind runs through his hair, and he shivers. The irony is not lost on him that he's in a boat named *Ava* while holding a ring that symbolizes his marriage to Scarlett. He's held onto this ring for so long now. It sits in his hand, glaring up at him, reminding him of all his mistakes. He closes his fist around it and sighs deeply.

"Scarlett," he says. He lets the wind carry his voice out into the breeze, where no one can hear. Only the air will hear what he has to say. "I'm sorry."

Tears start to prick his eyes, but he doesn't feel the need to stop them. There's no one here to see him anyway. "I'm sorry I wasn't who you needed me to be. I'm sorry I stopped fighting for you. I'm sorry I let us go. I promised to love you, till death do us part, and I—I broke that promise." His voice starts to crack as the weight of his words ascend out of his mouth and into the universe. "And now I don't know how I'll ever be able to say those words again to someone else. How am I supposed to promise to love someone else if I couldn't even do it right the first time? What the fuck am I supposed to do!?" He's yelling now, letting his tears fall freely. He screams into the wind, releasing his frustrations, his anger, his sadness, all in one long bellow. "I feel like a fucking failure!"

He shudders, but he lets himself feel, for the first time in a long time, every emotion that his body produces. He lets himself feel everything that he's been bottling up since the divorce, since Scarlett set those papers in front of him, and he knew it was over.

He's angry. At Scarlett, at himself, at the world. Angry that she found solace in someone else. Angry that he didn't try harder to make her happy. Angry that he didn't stand up for himself, and just let himself wallow in pity. Angry at his parents, and the way he was raised. Angry at himself for not processing these emotions earlier.

He's sad. Sad that his marriage ended in divorce. Sad that he's let it affect every aspect of his life thus far. Sad that he hasn't figured out if he wants to be in love again. "I don't want to fail her like I failed you," he says, looking down at the ring. He remembers the feeling of putting it on for the first time. A sign of his commitment and love for Scarlett. Now it sits, unworn for so long, loveless in his palm.

He's scared. Scared at the feelings he's beginning to form for Ava. Scared that their kiss has changed them irrevocably. Scared to feel like this again, to hurt like this again. He can't go through this again. He told himself he wouldn't. He wouldn't allow himself to feel this type of pain ever again. But, now, he feels like he's putting his heart out there once more, and it's fucking terrifying. She could break his heart. Or worse, he could break hers. Ashtyn warned him that he would do exactly that.

"She...she makes me feel again," he says, his voice barely above a whisper. He can't believe he's saying it out loud, even though there's no one around to hear him except this inanimate object. "And I'm scared to death."

He's not sure who exactly he's talking to anymore, whether it's Scarlett, the ring, or the universe. He just needs to say things out loud and admit them. He doesn't know what he's going to do when he gets back to the house. Will Ava want to talk to him? Will she avoid him? He doesn't know. He just knows he'll do whatever she wants him to do.

He closes his fist around the ring and brings it up to his mouth. Then he throws it as far as he can into the depths of the water. It sinks, deep down, where it can never haunt him again.

* * *

It's still early when Shiloh quietly slips through the front door. The lights are all off, so he startles when he enters the kitchen and sees Ava sitting at the dining table. She looks up, startled herself, at Shiloh's presence.

"Sorry," he says quietly. "Didn't mean to scare you."

"It's okay," she says, avoiding his eyes. "I couldn't sleep." She doesn't ask him where he's been. She just holds her cup of coffee closer to her. Shiloh can see the flowers Brad got her shoved into the trash can.

"Ave—" he starts.

"I'm sorry," she blurts out, interrupting him.

Shiloh sighs, heavily. "You have nothing to be sorry for."

"Yes, I do. I shouldn't have asked you to kiss me. I was emotional, and I took things too far between us." Her words wound him, but he tries not to let it show on his face. "I think...we should just try and forget about it. For the sake of everyone."

Shiloh doesn't miss the way she says "everyone", as if this has anything to do with anyone other than just the two of them. "Okay," he says, thickly. "Consider it forgotten." As if he could ever forget the way her lips felt against his own. He couldn't even if he tried.

Ava smiles, but it doesn't reach her eyes. She stands, mug in hand. "There's coffee in the pot if you want some," she says. And then she's gone, climbing up the stairs to her room, leaving Shiloh behind. He swallows every word he wants to say, respecting what Ava wants from him: to forget. He pours himself a cup of coffee, sits at the table, and tries to do just that.

Chapter 24

Shiloh stares at himself in the mirror. It's his first day of in-service at school, a whole week of his new job, but without any kids yet. They'll arrive next week. He's excited, but he's also incredibly nervous, especially since Ava will now be not only his roommate, but his coworker too. He's trying to hype himself up to go downstairs and face her. Ever since she asked him to forget about their kiss, they've avoided hanging out one on one. They've both been hiding in their rooms, only coming out when they know Ashtyn is there to be their buffer. He knows he should be acting more mature, but every time he wants to say something, an invisible hand comes and grabs him by the throat, silencing him. He's felt better since getting rid of the ring, though. It's no longer a presence in his life, keeping him weighed down by the past. Now, it's just the kiss he and Ava both refuse to acknowledge.

Shiloh smells the coffee brewing downstairs. Ava hasn't set foot in *Brewed* since her disastrous date with Brad, not that Shiloh blames her. He and Ashtyn have avoided it as well, in solidarity. Therefore, Ava's begun brewing coffee at home, trying to recreate her favorite drink. It's been a process, to say the least. Shiloh wishes he could joke around with her, tease her, flirt with her even, but there's been this intense tension between them ever since that night and the following morning.

He tries, desperately, not to think of their kiss. The kiss that haunts his dreams and waking thoughts. Sometimes, he feels like a teenager again, with this intense burning desire to catch even a glimpse of his crush. He has to prepare himself to go downstairs, because he's so nervous about seeing her. Ava is the whole reason he even got this job, and now he feels like he can't be in the same room as her anymore, let alone share a car ride to work. He tells himself he'll go down in five minutes.

Once his five minutes are up, he takes a deep breath and descends the stairs. As he enters the kitchen, he realizes Ashtyn is already gone, and it's just him and Ava. It makes his heart race.

"Hey," he says, his voice coming out hoarse.

Ava whirls around and stares at him. "Hi," she says, nervously.

"Mind if I steal some coffee?"

"Not at all," she says, lowering her gaze. "I made enough for everyone. Ashtyn already took hers to go."

Shiloh fills his mug up and takes a sip, the coffee burning all the way down his throat. He doesn't even wince. They're silent for a moment, before they both begin speaking at the same time.

"So, uh—"

"I think—"

They both stop, flushing.

"Sorry, you go first," she says, taking a sip of her coffee.

"No, you go," he says, awkwardly. He wants to go back upstairs and hide under the covers.

She seems to consider her words. "I was just going to ask if you're excited."

"Oh. Um, yes, I think I am. A little nervous, honestly."

"I was nervous my first day, too. But this week will all be about getting you situated, meeting all the other teachers, and getting used to a routine. Next week is when the chaos begins." She has a slight glint in her eye, a teasing look on her face. It's almost like before. *Almost.*

"Thanks for the warning," he says, trying to keep his voice light.

She bites her lip, then says, "We should get going."

She heads toward the front door, brushing past him, and he can't help himself. He reaches out and lightly grabs her elbow. "Ava."

She freezes, her body tensing, and Shiloh immediately releases her. She looks up at him from underneath her lashes. She doesn't say anything.

Shiloh clears his throat. "Uh, thanks. For driving me today."

"Of course," she says, looking away. "Let's go. Don't want to be late for your first day."

* * *

Ava holds onto the steering wheel for dear life, knuckles white. She can feel Shiloh's body taking up so much space in her passenger seat. She hasn't been able to get their kiss out of her head. Every time she closes her eyes, she can feel his lips against hers, his hands on her ass. and she feels heat spill through her body. She's been in a constant state of turned on since that moment, and she can't seem to shake it, even though she told him to forget about it. It's been impossible.

She knows he's been avoiding her just as much as she's been avoiding him. Today is the first time they've been alone since that morning in the kitchen, and she had to restrain herself from jumping him. Even now, she has a hard time focusing on the road and not looking over at his muscled thighs. But goddamn, she can't help but stare at him, remembering how his hands were running up and down her body, making her feel things she's never felt before.

Every time she falls asleep, her dreams are full of Shiloh. She can't escape him, even in sleep, and she wakes feeling frustrated and horny. There's only so much a vibrator can help with, especially when her desires sleep in the room next door. As they drive toward the school, Ava presses her thighs together, begging herself to think of anything other than Shiloh.

"So," she starts, trying to make sure her voice doesn't sound too wobbly. "Got any burning questions?" She knows she has some of her own, but she's too much of a coward to ask him.

"Uh," he starts, eyes focused outside the window. "Not that I can think of right now." His leg is bouncing, up and down, and Ava wants to reach her hand out and steady him. She doesn't. She just grips the steering wheel tighter.

"I'm sure you'll be great," she says reassuringly. There's so much more she wants to tell him, but she bites her tongue, remembering what she asked of him. Things are so tense, she could cut the air with a knife. She knows she's the one making it awkward. She basically begged Shiloh to kiss her. What if he only did it because he felt bad about how badly her date went? She was a mess, and maybe he was just trying to make her feel better. Maybe he thought it was bad. Maybe it was only good for her. Telling him to forget about the kiss was a good thing, for both of them, she rationalizes.

Before she can spiral further into herself, they pull up to the school. She already knows she's going to have a busy day, and she doesn't need to be distracted thinking about Shiloh. She parks in her assigned space and takes a deep breath. Shiloh does too.

"If you have lunch at the same time as us, you can join me and Derek in the teacher's lounge. We normally eat together."

Shiloh smiles, but it doesn't reach his eyes. "Yeah, thanks. I'll see how busy I am."

Then, they're out of the car and walking up to the building in silence. Ava goes to her classroom, while Shiloh goes to the gym, and they wish each other a good first day. Once in her room, she plops into her chair and wills herself not to cry. She puts on a smile and tells herself to keep it plastered to her face for the rest of the day.

* * *

Shiloh's day consists of meetings, meetings, and more meetings. It also consists of introductions, more than he can keep track of. There are so many ice breakers; if he has to hear one more "fun fact" about someone, he might explode. By the end of the day, he's more exhausted than a full shift at the bar. He has so much to learn, so many people to meet and impress, and so much to do before the first day of school. He didn't realize how much teachers actually do, even if he's not technically considered a teacher. It's impressive.

This routine goes on for the entire week. It's actually kind of helpful, because he hardly sees Ava except for the rides to and from school. They chitchat aimlessly about their day and other meandrous things, keeping themselves well out of kiss territory. It's nothing like before. He wonders if it'll ever get back to the way it used to be, or if he's ruined it forever.

It's finally the first official day of school, where he'll be coaching a few PE classes as well as the girls' soccer team. He knows he's overdressed. Coaches don't really have much of a dress code, except on game days, but he felt the need to dress up on the first day, in his best clothes. Maybe it's the lesson instilled in him by his father: always dress like you're going to court. He hates thinking that way.

As he heads downstairs, the smell of coffee drifting through the house, he stops himself short when he sees Ava in her first day outfit. It's not like he's never seen her dressed up before, but that was before they kissed. Now, it's like he sees her in a whole new light. It's nothing special really, just a normal, flowy black dress, paired with platform sandals. No, it's the fact that she's sitting at the table, sipping her coffee, looking so beautiful, and he's here, also dressed in his best slacks and tie, and she's set out a cup of coffee for him. He can picture it clearly. He comes down, kisses the top of her head, caressing her shoulder, thanking her for the coffee. It's all so...domestic, and Shiloh suddenly craves it. His body is begging him for it. But he can't give in. She's not his, and he's not hers.

"Hey," he says, making Ava's head snap up from her phone.

"Hi," she replies. "I made you a cup of coffee."

"Thanks."

"You...you look nice," she says, quietly.

"You think?" Shiloh asks. "You don't think it's too much?"

"No, I think it's perfect."

"Well, you look nice too." Even in the dim light of the kitchen, he can see her flush. "You ready?"

"Uh, yeah, just let me finish my coffee."

"No rush," he says, sitting down across from her. He takes a sip from his own mug and frowns, recognizing the flavors. "Did you...make my coffee order for me?"

Ava flushes even deeper, trying to hide her face from him. "Well, I feel bad that you can't get it anymore from *Brewed*, so I tried to recreate it."

Shiloh's heart almost leaps out of his chest. He takes another sip and sighs dramatically. "God, this is so much better than that asshole could ever make it." Ava's biting back a smile, and Shiloh thanks God he's finally able to elicit that type of reaction from her.

"You think so?"

"Oh, yeah" Shiloh says, nodding his head enthusiastically. "Best coffee I've ever had."

Ava giggles. "Shut up."

And there it is. She's back. They're back. Maybe not completely, but it's a start. And it's all Shiloh could ever ask for.

* * *

Ava's on her conference period when there's a knock on the door.

"Come in!" she calls. She's expecting another teacher, maybe even Shiloh, so she's surprised when she sees one of her students from last year lingering in the doorway. "Hey, Bailey."

"Hey, Ms. Marshall. Can I come in and chill for a little bit?"

"Of course. Is everything okay?"

Bailey slumps in a beanbag in the corner of the room near Ava's desk. "Yeah," she sighs. "Just a tiring first day."

"You're not skipping class, are you?" Ava asks, gently. She doesn't want to be too strict, but she also doesn't want to get Bailey in trouble.

"No, it's my lunch period."

"Okay. Well, you're welcome to stay as long as you need to."

Bailey smiles and closes her eyes as she leans against the beanbag. Ava has always prided herself on creating a safe, welcoming space for all her students, past and present. She knows how hard school can be for some kids, and if she can help alleviate some stress or pain by letting kids come into her classroom and relax for a moment, then she'll do that.

"Ms. Marshall?"

"Yes, Bailey?"

"Have you ever been broken up with?" Ava can see Bailey is trying hard not to cry. She's biting her nails, looking at the books lining the shelves on the walls.

"I have," Ava says, honestly. More times than she cares to admit.

"How did you survive it?" Ava knows how Bailey must be feeling, like it's the end of the world, because her partner broke up with her. Feeling such intense emotions as a teenager is exhausting.

"Slowly," Ava says. "I know it feels really bad right now, but—and I know how cliché this sounds—time really does heal all wounds."

Bailey sighs heavily. "It really doesn't feel like it."

"It never does when you're seventeen."

"It's the first day of senior year, and I've already been dumped!" Bailey exclaims, throwing up her hands. "We spent every day together this summer. This fucking sucks." She looks up, guilty at her use of language, but Ava doesn't admonish her.

"I know it doesn't feel like it right now, but I promise you, you will survive this. High school is only a tiny blip in the grand scheme of things. You're going to meet so many people in your life, and I promise you, you will survive this."

"But how?"

"By doing things that you love. By hanging out with your friends and your family and remembering that there is more to life than dating."

Bailey gives her a warbled smile, a tear slipping down her cheek. "Thanks, Ms. Marshall. You've always been my favorite teacher."

This makes Ava smile. "And you, Bailey, are a fantastic student who is going to do amazing things in life."

Bailey sighs. "I should probably go eat something. I have soccer last period, and I don't want to run on an empty stomach."

"You excited about your new coach?" she asks, probing.

"Yeah, all the girls can't shut up about how hot he is." Ava's taking a sip of water when Bailey says this, and she chokes, spitting water all over her desk.

"Are you okay?" Bailey asks, getting up from her beanbag.

"Yeah," she manages to get out, trying to mop up the mess. "Went down the wrong pipe."

"Alright, well, I'll see you later, Ms. Marshall! Thanks for the advice!"

"Anytime, Bailey," Ava replies to her student's retreating back. She has to sit there a moment, trying not to think about Shiloh. Her lunch is next period, and she hasn't heard anything from him all day. She wants to know how his day has been. Is he having fun? Does he like the kids? The other teachers? She shakes her head, emptying her head of these thoughts.

This morning felt like before the kiss. She's hopeful that maybe they can put it behind them and get back to how they used to be, just like she's been wanting. She checks her watch and sees she has enough time to go and check on him. She probably shouldn't, but she just can't help it. She has to. As a friend, of course.

She heads down to the gym, saying hello to various students milling about during their lunch period. As she approaches, she can hear the sound of shoes squeaking on the gym floor, laughter echoing throughout the building.

She's about to head inside when she stops, the glass wall of offices opposite the gym catching her eye. She sees Coach Mack's old desk, now mostly empty except for Shiloh's nameplate and one picture frame. She can't see the picture, so she slips in quietly, making her way over to the desk. She stops short when she sees what's in the frame. It's the picture she took of all five of them during the weekend camping trip, fireworks exploding in the background. She has no idea when he printed it out, but it makes her heart swell. Looking at the photo, she knows she can never let herself feel for him what she wants, because it's not just their relationship at stake, but everyone's. Everyone would be affected if things ended badly between Ava and Shiloh. Ashtyn, Drew, even Mattie.

She hears a whistle blow, and Shiloh's voice booms through the gym. "Okay, five minute water break!"

Anxiety spikes through Ava's bloodstream, and she bolts out of the office before Shiloh can see her. She makes her way swiftly back to her classroom, feeling like this morning's progress shattered the moment she saw that picture on his desk. She takes a deep breath, telling herself that this is it. She will get rid of her feelings for Shiloh Brooks, no matter what.

SEPTEMBER

Chapter 25

"Let's hustle, ladies!" Shiloh shouts at his team. "Bailey, tighten up that pass. Maddie, fix your stance." In a fun turn of events, he loves coaching. He didn't have any doubts that he would like this new job, he just didn't realize he would *love* it.

"Coach B, can I go say hi to Ms. Marshall really quick?" Bailey asks. "Please?"

Shiloh looks up and sees Ava waving from the other side of the field. Soccer season doesn't start until the second semester of school, but he was able to schedule a few friendly scrimmages for this semester to see how his team plays. They're warming up to play a neighboring town's team, and Ava and Ashtyn have both come out to support him and the girls.

"Yes, but make sure you jog over there." Bailey rolls her eyes but complies.

"Coach B, is it true that you and Ms. Marshall live together?" Maddie asks, balancing a soccer ball on her head.

Shiloh sighs. "How on earth does anyone know that?"

"Because you drive together in the same car," she replies simply, as if that's common knowledge to everyone. "Are you dating?"

"No, we're not," he says, knowing they won't stop asking if he doesn't answer. "We're just friends. Now, get back to your warm-up."

Maddie huffs, but does what she's asked. The girls giggle to each other as they continue their warm-up. He's barely been here a few weeks, and they're already gossiping about him. He looks across the field to where Ava is talking to Bailey. Ashtyn, Derek, and Daisy have all joined in. He holds up his hand in a wave, and they all wave back.

He's surprised when he sees Derek make his way over to him from across the field. They're friendly with each other, but Shiloh wouldn't consider himself close friends with the guy.

"Hey man," he says.

"Hey, how's it going?" Derek asks.

"Can't complain."

"That's good." This might be the longest conversation they've ever had just the two of them. He can't help but remember Ava admitting to him that she used to have a crush on Derek. "You liking the job?"

"Yeah, I love it," Shiloh says, ducking as a stray ball comes straight for him. "It feels good to be back on a soccer field, even if I'm not the one playing." Derek nods absentmindedly, as if he's distracted by something. "Did you, uh, want something?"

"Oh, yeah!" Derek says, as if he just remembered why he came over here. "Has Jordan told you about the bachelor party?"

"Uh, no." He definitely has not heard anything about a bachelor party.

Derek sighs. "Of course he didn't. His brother was supposed to be planning it, but he bailed last minute, and now I'm stuck planning it."

"Aren't bachelor parties just for the wedding party?" Shiloh asks, passing a fly ball back to the girls.

"Yeah, but Jordan wanted to invite everyone. That includes you." The ref whistles, signaling everyone to start getting ready. "September fourteenth! Eighties themed! I'll see you there!" Derek exclaims, before heading back to the stands. Shiloh doesn't even have time to process what just happened as his team surrounds him, getting ready for the match. He'll deal with that later.

"Remember," he says, addressing the girls. "This is just a scrimmage. So, we're gonna test out different positions for everyone to see what works and what doesn't. It doesn't matter if we win or lose."

"Don't worry, Coach," Bailey says. "We're used to losing."

By halftime, Shiloh understands why Coach Mack kept losing. He had a lot of the girls playing the wrong positions, and the plays weren't working that way. Shiloh's switched up positions for most of the girls multiple times during the match, and he thinks he might have found a winning situation. The team sits on the bench, guzzling water before they have to get back onto the field.

"Looks like you found your calling." Shiloh whirls around to find Ashtyn on his side of the field. Ava is still seated in the stands with the rest of their friends. Something has shifted, and they're back to being awkward around each other again.

"You think?" he asks.

"I never saw you this happy at the bar," she says, a rare, soft smile on her face.

"Yeah, well, I didn't get to yell at kids at the bar." This makes Ashtyn bark out a laugh, and Shiloh smiles. It feels good to be normal with at least one of his roommates.

"Coach B, is THAT your girlfriend?" one of the girls asks, making the rest of the team erupt into giggles.

"Y'all ask me about a girlfriend one more time, and I'm gonna make you run until you puke." He's teasing, but the girls must think he's serious, because they immediately stop giggling and look away.

"Man, you're good at that," Ashtyn replies. She places a hand on his arm. "Not to get all gross, but I'm proud of you."

Shame floods through Shiloh. She doesn't know about the kiss, and he feels guilty at her praise. He shrugs lamely, "It's not much."

Ashtyn frowns. "No, it is. It's been, what, seven months we've known each other and...you seem good. Really good."

"Took you seven months to finally like me?" he teases.

Ashtyn laughs. "Careful. I can still change my mind." But the smile she gives him lets him know she won't. "Oh!" she says, lowering her voice. "Ava wanted me to tell you to try putting Veronica in as a forward. Said she's like freaky fast or something like that." Shiloh wishes Ava had come over to tell him herself, but he thanks Ashtyn for the advice.

"Hey, have you noticed her being weird at all?" Ashtyn asks, and it takes everything in Shiloh not to confess right then and there.

"Uh, I'm not sure. Maybe she's stressed about the start of the school year?"

Ashtyn bites her lip. "I think Brad really upset her. She hasn't been the same since. God, I want to kill him."

Shiloh blows out a breath. "Yeah, I feel the same way."

Ashtyn smiles. "Thanks for looking out for her. I don't think I ever thanked you for picking her up when I couldn't."

Shiloh's shame intensifies, and he can't look Ashtyn in the eye. "It was no problem. You know I'd do anything for y'all."

For one crazy, insane moment, it looks like Ashtyn might hug him. No, he cannot earn his first hug from her when he's keeping a secret this big. A secret that involves her best friend. Luckily, the referee's whistle signals the end of half time, interrupting them.

"Guess that's my cue," she says. "Hey, maybe if you win, we'll take you out for ice cream after!"

Shiloh lets out a meek laugh and shoos her away playfully. He feels guilt eating away at his insides. He can't think about this right now. He shakes his head and gets back into coaching mode. He decides to take Ava's advice and tries putting Veronica in the forward position.

"But I've never played forward before!" she exclaims, panicked.

"And I have no doubt at all that you'll be amazing," Shiloh replies, encouragingly. "Remember, this is just for fun." Veronica just nods, and goes to her position as the ref signals for the next half to begin.

Turns out, Ava is a genius. Veronica should have been a forward her entire life. She's faster than any of the other girls and has already scored once, tying up the score board. There's two minutes left, and she's got the ball, tearing down the field. She passes the ball beautifully to Bailey, who easily maneuvers around their largest defender. Then, Bailey passes right into the middle of the box as Veronica speeds toward it, launching the ball into the back corner of the net.

The girls erupt into a scream of celebration as the ref whistles for the end of the game. They've won. They actually won their first scrimmage. Shiloh thinks they must not celebrate very often, because they're all screaming, rushing the field and enveloping each other in hugs. Normally, he'd tell them to keep their celebrations minimal in the name of sportsmanship toward the losing team, but because it's just a scrimmage, he allows it.

He catches Ava's eye from across the field. She's standing, jumping up and down on the bleachers like a crazy person, pointing at him like he just won a championship instead of a scrimmage. He wills her to run across the field and launch herself into his arms, but he knows she won't. Instead, they hold each other's gazes, neither saying what they really want to.

Chapter 26

"Holy shit, dude!" Drew exclaims. "You clean up nice."

Shiloh frowns. "I feel ridiculous." He looks down at the pale pink suit jacket he's wearing, then at Drew's matching baby blue one.

"It's eighties themed, dude! You can't skimp out." Drew pushes back his slicked down hair, something Shiloh vehemently declined to do.

"Where did you even find this jacket?" Shiloh asks, checking himself out in the mirror. His white linen pants are freshly ironed—*thank you, Ashtyn*—and he's wearing a pale pink button-down shirt with a matching jacket and bow tie. Why Jordan insisted on an eighties themed bachelor party, he'll never know. He's also still not sure why he was invited, but he doesn't think about it too much. It feels nice to be going out and drinking with friends.

"Thrift store, obviously," Drew replies.

Shiloh just rolls his eyes. He can hear the girls downstairs, chatting amongst themselves, and nerves shoot through him. Brooke's bachelorette party is also tonight, though they're going in separate limos and wouldn't meet up until much later. He knows he can't avoid Ava the whole night.

"I have to tell you something," Shiloh blurts, making Drew freeze. He looks at him in the reflection of the mirror, eyebrows raised. "I kissed Ava."

Drew's eyes go wide. He puts his hands on his hips, frowning. "Remember when you gave me your whole spiel about how they're your roommates, and I can't even try to make a move on Ashtyn?"

"Yeah, I'm aware. Okay, I fucked up."

"You fucked up?"

"Yes, I fucked up."

"Okay, I think we've established you fucked up."

Shiloh glares at his best friend. "I'm serious, dude. She told me to forget about it, and we're actively avoiding each other.

"Avoiding each other as you work at the same place, and she drives your sorry ass to work every day."

"You know what, forget it."

"No, no, I'm sorry. Just trying to figure out the situation," Drew says, hands raised in surrender. "Tell me what happened."

So, Shiloh does. He tells him everything, from when he started having feelings for her during his birthday weekend to when they kissed to now.

"So...do you...you know, like her?" Drew asks, drawing the words out.

"Dude, I don't fucking know! I mean, I love them both. They're my roommates and they've basically become my family. But I don't think about kissing Ashtyn like I do with Ava."

"God, I do," Drew says wistfully, and Shiloh smacks him on the shoulder. "Okay, sorry. Back to you."

"Scarlett fucked me up, man," Shiloh says, scrubbing a hand down his face. "I mean, really fucked me up."

"Yeah, well, that's what happens when you marry the first girl you fall in love with."

Shiloh glares at Drew again. "Seriously? Not helping."

Drew sighs. "Do you maybe think you have a romanticized version of your marriage with Scarlett stuck in your head?"

"Romanticized version?"

"Look, I was there for your entire relationship. I saw more than you probably realize. You were both kind of terrible for each other. When you told me you were getting divorced, I thought you'd be so fucking happy. So, when you were miserable, it kind of threw me for a loop. Until I realized that all you kept thinking about were the happy times you lost, instead of all the miserable times you were finally free from."

Drew's words make Shiloh freeze. Had he been doing that this whole time? Only choosing to remember the good and ignoring the bad? Romanticizing a lost relationship?

"I...never thought about it that way."

"Of course you didn't," Drew replies, gently. "Look, I cannot even begin to fathom what it feels like to be in love. I've never felt that. But, I know what it is to care for someone. Sometimes, you choose to ignore the bad parts. Why? Fuck if I know. I'm not a therapist. Either way, you and Scarlett are over, and that is definitely for the better, whether you realize it now or later."

"I did love her," Shiloh says, quietly.

"I have no doubt that you did. But, now, you're allowed to *not* be in love with her anymore."

The words are so fucking simple, but they hit their mark in Shiloh's brain. It's like the last piece of a puzzle that he thought he'd lost. He can finally see the fully formed picture. "How long have you been wanting to say all that to me?"

"Bro, I've been trying to tell you that for the past year. You just weren't ready to hear it." His best friend is smiling at him.

"What do I do about Ava?"

"Shiloh! Drew! Get your asses down here!" Ashtyn yells from

downstairs. "Your limo is here."

Drew sighs. "One step at a time, brother. For now, let's get fucked up." Drew slings his arm around Shiloh, and he can't help but think that's a great plan.

When they get downstairs, Shiloh has to try and not stare blatantly at Ava. She's wearing a baby pink dress that hugs every curve of her body. Her makeup is flawless as usual, and her hair is curled, something Shiloh has never seen before. It falls down her bare back, and Shiloh swallows nervously.

Ashtyn glances up at them, a smirk on her face. "Good God," she says, staring at Drew and his slicked back hair. "You look…"

"As incredible as you do," he says, fingering the fabric on Ashtyn's blue dress. Shiloh can see now that they're accidentally matching, just like him and Ava. Ashtyn snatches her dress out of Drew's grasp, a scowl on her face. Her hair is tied back in a high ponytail.

"You keep your grubby fingers off my dress," she grumbles, but Shiloh can tell she's relaxed, maybe even teasing. It's shocking to see her like this with Drew. The limo honks outside impatiently.

"You're being summoned," Ava says, peeking out the window.

"And when will we be meeting up with you lovely ladies for the evening?" Drew asks, eyes never leaving Ashtyn. It's like he's already forgotten what Shiloh told him about his predicament with Ava.

"Midnight. At the Blue Velvet bar. Behave yourselves until then," Ashtyn replies, and Drew gives her a mischievous smile.

"I'll be waiting for you," he says, and Ashtyn rolls her eyes in response.

The limo honks again, and then Ashtyn is ushering them out of the house before Shiloh can even tell Ava how nice she looks. Maybe that's for the best. He needs to get his mind off of her tonight.

They cram into the limo where Jordan, Derek, Parker, Damien, and a few other guys Shiloh doesn't know are passing around beers, everyone wearing some sort of eighties themed suit. They seem to be the last ones to be picked up.

"Welcome to the party!" Jordan yells, obviously already a little drunk. Shiloh takes a beer from Derek, gratefully. They're about to head out, when Jordan's phone rings.

He answers it loudly, one finger pressed into his ear, trying to drown out the other voices in the limo. "Hello? Yeah. What? What do you mean they canceled? And there's no one else? Okay. Okay. Okay, we'll come pick you up." He hangs up the phone. "Hey, go tell Ava and Ashtyn to get in here. Brooke's limo canceled. Looks like this party is going co-ed earlier than expected."

Shiloh's anxiety spikes while Drew jumps up immediately and yells, "I'll do it!"

The girls arrive a few minutes later, confused looks on their faces. "Come on!" Jordan exclaims, ushering them in. "I'll explain on the way."

They scooch in, and Shiloh's not sure how they're supposed to fit any more people in the back of this already stuffed limo. Ava ends up next to him, their legs smushed together, and it takes everything in Shiloh not to stare at her.

They pick up Brooke and the rest of the girls, including Daisy and Brooke's three sisters, next. The limo is packed with so many bodies that everyone is touching everyone. Shiloh's sitting so tightly next to Ava, he's surprised she's not sitting on his lap. They don't look at each other. She's talking intently with Ashtyn and Daisy, sipping on champagne, while Shiloh tries to act natural. He takes another drink, hoping the alcohol will settle his nerves.

"So, you're Shiloh?" a blonde woman sitting across from him asks, settling her eyes on him. He didn't notice her come in, he's so focused on Ava's presence next to him.

"Yeah. Sorry, I didn't catch your name."

"Bethany," she says, extending her hand out for him. "Brooke's sister and maid of honor." Shiloh takes her hand and shakes it. He can feel Ava turn to look at him for the first time since she got in the limo.

"Nice to meet you," he says, giving her a smile.

"You moved into Brookie's old room, right?"

"Uh, yeah, I did." Bethany is sizing him up as she sips her drink. She's wearing a white, sequin dress.

"You're wondering why I'm wearing white at my sister's bachelorette party," she says, her voice silky smooth. Shiloh thinks that if things were different, he would find her incredibly attractive. In fact, he does find her attractive, but he is very aware of Ava next to him, and how he wishes it was her talking to him like this instead. But since Ava won't, then he'll take advantage of Bethany's attention.

"A little," he admits, letting alcohol infuse his voice to a slightly lower octave, even though he wasn't thinking that at all. He'd barely noticed what she was wearing.

Bethany giggles. "All the other dresses I could find were too hard to get out of. If I'm going out, then I need a dress I can easily take off." Shiloh chokes on his beer, a deep flush creeping up his neck. Ava turns sharply toward them.

"Hey, Beth," she says, voice sharp. "Can you get me a refill, please?"

"Ask Brooke," Bethany says, smile tight. "She's right next to the cooler."

Ava sucks in a breath, and Shiloh can see her jealousy in the way she turns her back and awkwardly maneuvers her way toward Brooke. He turns back toward Bethany, and she takes the seat Ava just vacated. "So, tell me about yourself."

* * *

Ava is *not* jealous that Shiloh and Bethany are currently laughing together at the bar. Their driver dropped them off at the second bar of the night, and those two have been inseparable ever since they started talking in the limo. Ava tries not to stare daggers at Brooke's sister, since she definitely does not have feelings for Shiloh. He's free to talk with whomever he wants.

"What is your problem?" Ashtyn asks, swaying slightly on her feet. She's always been a bit of a lightweight.

"Nothing," Ava says, nonchalantly. She takes another sip of her drink, not really liking the way it tastes. Shiloh makes better drinks.

"You've been acting weird for weeks."

"I have not!"

"Have to. Ever since your date with Brad."

"Ew, please don't mention him," Ava says, frowning, trying to make it seem like Brad is the reason she's been weird, and not the fact that she wants to jump Shiloh's bones. In truth, she's barely thought about Brad at all. He takes up no space in her brain.

"Sorry," Ashtyn says, wrapping her arm around Ava. "That asshole didn't deserve you."

"Who doesn't deserve Ava?" Drew asks, coming up to their table. He looks ridiculous in his blue suit, but he somehow pulls it off. Much like Shiloh in his pink suit...

"Hi, Drew," Ashtyn purrs, her usual icy demeanor thawed by alcohol.

"Hi, gorgeous," he says, smiling at her.

"Don't flirt with me," she replies.

"But it's my favorite thing to do."

"I've said it once, and I'll say it again, just kiss already," Ava says, the irony not lost on her.

"Oh, Ava, the first time I kiss Ashtyn, we are both going to be sober, so I can remember it for the rest of my life," Drew says, a dreamy expression on his face.

Ashtyn actually laughs, loudly. "You wish."

"Every night before bed."

Ashtyn laughs, again, then takes Drew's hand and drags him out onto the dance floor, where they join the rest of the group, leaving Ava alone at the table. She finishes her drink and takes the glass back to the bar. She notices a very attractive man sitting alone at the bar, making eyes at her. She gives him a tight-lipped smile and tries to flag down the attention of the bartender.

She's about the order another drink when Shiloh sidles up next to her, his cologne going straight to her brain and intoxicating her more than alcohol ever could. She has to avert her eyes from his pink suit. The suit that hugs every curve of his muscles and accentuates every single detail of his flawless physique.

"Hey," he says.

"Hi," she replies. She grips the edge of the bar.

"You having a good time?"

"Sure."

"What's wrong?"

"Nothing, Shiloh," she sighs heavily.

"Ava," he starts.

"Stop," she says, not wanting to cry in public.

"Stop what?"

"Just...don't say whatever you were going to say," she says. She rubs her temple, feeling a headache start to arrive. "Why don't you go find Bethany? You two seem cozy."

"Oh, so you noticed?" Shiloh asks, his eyes laser focused on her. She shifts uncomfortably underneath his gaze.

"Everyone in a hundred-mile radius would have noticed."

Shiloh looks around the bar dramatically. "I don't think anyone else has noticed." He's right. Everyone in their party is on the dance floor, alcohol infusing their bodies, not a care in the world. The only one that gives a shit about Shiloh talking to Bethany is Ava herself. "Ava, are you jealous?"

Ava humphs. "Of course I'm not jealous of Brooke's gorgeous older sister that could have any man she could ever want talking to you, while I struggle to find a single person to even look at me." She's not sure if it's the alcohol that makes her say all that, but she can't look Shiloh in the eyes. She can't help but notice that the attractive man at the bar *is* looking at her. She catches his gaze over Shiloh's shoulder.

"Ava, I'm looking at you." The entire world stops for a moment at Shiloh's words. Then, it resumes, as Bethany sidles up to them and slips her arm around him.

"Come dance with me!" she says.

Ava looks at Shiloh, defiance on her face. It's a look that says, *Go. Dance with her.* She catches the man's gaze again and gives him a flirtatious smile. Shiloh notices and glances behind him. He frowns and takes Bethany's hand, leading her to the dance floor. Ava hates the way jealously floods her system. She makes her way over to the mystery man and gestures to the seat next to him.

"May I?" she asks, bravely. Under normal circumstances, she would never approach a stranger herself.

"Please," the man says, smiling at her. "I'm Alex."

"Ava," she replies.

Alex flags down the bartender. "Whatever she'd like," he says, and Ava orders her signature martini. She's trying desperately not to look at Shiloh and Bethany, but she can't help herself. As they dance together, Bethany's hands roam Shiloh's body like she owns him.

"He your ex or something?" Alex asks, catching Ava staring at Shiloh.

"What? No! He's my...friend."

"Interesting way of looking at a friend."

Ava blushes, embarrassed at Alex's words. "I'm sorry. Things are just weird right now."

"That's okay," Alex says. "You want to make him jealous?"

Ava's head snaps up at his words. "Wha—what?"

"I said, do you want to make him jealous?" Alex leans in closer, his breath hot on her ear. "He's looking."

Ava shivers and has to stop herself from looking over at Shiloh. "Put your hand on my thigh," she says, breathily, before she even has time to think. Alex obliges, and Ava feels goosebumps break out over her skin.

"That definitely got his attention," Alex whispers. "I'm not going to end up with a black eye, am I?"

Ava laughs, loudly, as if he just said the funniest thing in the world. "No, he would never."

"Okay, because he's looking at me like I'm about to breathe my last breath."

Ava can't help herself. She takes a peek at Shiloh, and Alex is right. His gaze is laser focused on them as he dances with Bethany. He couldn't be farther away from her if he was on a different continent.

"Do you want to dance?" she asks, placing her hand on Alex's arm. He runs his fingers up and down her bare thigh, tantalizingly. Under any other circumstances, she would be swooning over Alex. But right now, all she can think about is Shiloh.

Alex stands and offers her his hand. She takes it, and he leads her out onto the dance floor, only a few paces away from Shiloh and Bethany. Ashtyn, along with the rest of their friends, send shocked glances Ava's way as she winds her arms around Alex's neck, and his go around her waist.

"Everyone is looking at us," he whispers, mouth close to Ava's ear. He's right. All of Ava's friends can't seem to believe she's dancing with a stranger.

"I guess I've never really been one to garner the attention of a handsome stranger," she says.

"I don't believe that," Alex replies.

Ava is about to reply when Ashtyn sidles up to them, drink in her hand. She's definitely drunk.

"Who is this?" she asks, eyeing Alex up and down. Alex introduces himself, and she glances at Ava approvingly.

"Well, Alex, take care of her," Ashtyn says, wiggling her eyebrows at them before spinning back into the middle of the dance floor, somehow not spilling even a drop of her drink.

"That was my best friend, Ashtyn," Ava supplies.

"And I'm assuming she doesn't know anything about the guy you're trying to make jealous," Alex says, spinning Ava out and then into his arms.

She's breathless as she says, "Not entirely." She's suddenly aware that Shiloh is gone. Bethany is dancing with Brooke, seemingly unperturbed by Shiloh's absence. She looks everywhere, not finding him.

"Um, I gotta go to the bathroom," Ava says, untangling herself from Alex. "I'll be back in a minute." Alex doesn't say anything, as if he knows she won't be back.

She heads for the front door, letting the cool September air chill her bones as she steps onto the curb. The bass of the music inside can be heard from out on the street, and Ava takes a deep breath, trying to clear her head.

"You done?" a voice asks her from the alleyway. Shiloh steps into the streetlight, hands in his pockets.

Ava turns sharply toward him. "I don't know what you mean."

"You know exactly what I mean, because I was doing the exact same thing you were."

Ava sucks in a breath. "I told you to forget about it."

"Forget about what?"

"You know what."

"And what if I don't want to forget about it?"

"Shiloh, don't be ridiculous. We're roommates. We—we can't."

"Who says? Ashtyn? Because I will happily go in there right now and explain everything to her."

"Explain what exactly?" Ava asks, throwing her arms up. "That I took things too far? That I asked you to kiss me, and I shouldn't have? That I ruined our friendship?"

"Ava, I wanted to kiss you," Shiloh says. "You didn't ruin anything."

She can't help the surprised look that crosses her face. "You...you wanted to kiss me?" She can barely get the words out.

"Yes," Shiloh says. "I've wanted to kiss you for so long now."

"You don't mean that," she says, her voice barely a whisper.

"Ava, what the fuck do you mean, 'I don't mean that?' All I do, every single fucking day, is think about you. I wake up in the morning thinking of you. I go to sleep, and I dream of you. Every time you walk into a room, I think that you are the most beautiful person I have ever seen in my entire goddamn life. I can't get you out of my head. I think of that kiss, and my body begs to know when I get to do it again. I meant what I said tonight. I am looking at you. I didn't give a fuck about anybody else tonight. All I could think about was you, and how I wanted to be the one dancing with you."

Ava stares at him, unable to comprehend what he just said. "You," she starts, her voice barely coming out. She swallows, staring at Shiloh. She can't finish her sentence.

He takes a step toward her. "Kiss me." Ava blinks at him. "This time, it's me asking. Kiss me."

Ava's entire body thrums with wanting. *He* is asking *her* to kiss him. "Please," he begs, and it's Ava's undoing. She launches herself at him and smashes her lips to his. It is not at all like their first kiss. This kiss is hungry and wild, a battle of tongues and teeth and pleasure. Shiloh lets out a grunt as his back hits the wall of the alley, his hands encircling the small of Ava's back. She cups his face in her hands, bringing his face down to her as she kisses him for dear life. She opens her mouth and lets his tongue explore hers, a moan slipping out of her. It is the hottest kiss of her life.

A bartender throws a bag of trash into the dumpster down the alleyway, and the crash of beer bottles startles them apart, both breathing heavily. Ava suddenly feels stone cold sober.

Shiloh sighs and leans his forehead against her own. "Jesus Christ, Ava," he breathes.

The way he says her name sends shivers through her body. She's so incredibly turned on, and she notices she's not the only one. "I...I really like you," she says, embarrassed at the elementary school like admission. She's about to say more, when she hears Ashtyn calling her name.

Shiloh holds onto her tighter, but she steps away, her body cold. "Not yet. She can't know just yet."

Shiloh just nods, "If that's what you want."

"For now," Ava says, and heads toward her best friend's voice.

Chapter 27

It's past two in the morning when the limo drops them off at home. Ashtyn is so drunk she can barely walk. She's draped between Shiloh and Ava as they prop her up and lead her into the house. Getting up the stairs is tricky, but they manage it, and tuck her into bed.

Ashtyn sighs dramatically as she snuggles into the blankets. "You two are so cute," she says. "I love you."

Shiloh can't see Ava's face, but he can guess she's probably blushing. He knows he is. He hasn't been able to stop staring at her since their kiss in the alleyway.

"I love you too. Now, get some sleep, Ash," Ava says. She closes the door to Ashtyn's room, and then they're alone, facing each other.

"So," Shiloh starts. "You like me?" He feels brave in the darkness of the hallway.

Their eyes have slightly adjusted, and he can see Ava bite her lip. "I should have never told you that." She says it like a joke but shyly.

Shiloh steps forward, reaching out to grab her waist and pull her close. This time, she doesn't pull away. "Well, what if I told you that I like you too?"

"Then I would tell you that you could probably do better."

"Don't," he says, fiercely, grabbing her chin lightly, so she has to look up at him. She sucks in a breath as their noses brush. "Don't sell yourself short, Ava Marshall. I could never do better than you, because you are perfect."

"Prove it," she whispers.

So, he does. He closes the distance between them, his hands cupping her jaw, and his mouth finds hers. She gasps, her mouth opening as if on instinct, her hands immediately wrapping around his neck. Shiloh hears a moan slip through his own lips as her hands travel to his hair, nails scraping along his scalp. His hands travel down her body as he wraps them around her waist and pulls her even closer. His mouth moves effortlessly against her, tasting her again. He can't get enough. She's just as sweet as the first time and just as hot as the second. He takes her bottom lip in between his teeth ever so gently, savoring the way it makes her hips nudge into his.

"Shi," she breathes against his lips, and it's almost his undoing. Whispering his name so intimately, just for him to hear. Their tongues meet, touching, tasting, teasing. He doesn't want to come up for air. He wants to drown in her: her scent, her taste, her everything.

Ava pulls away slightly, and Shiloh's mouth makes its way to her neck. She gasps and arches into him, her breasts rubbing against his chest. He kisses her throat, up her jaw, and back to her lips. She eagerly responds. Her hands cup his face, holding him in place, so he can't go anywhere. As if he could ever want to be anywhere else.

Their lips separate for a moment, and she looks at him, her eyes blazing. He returns her gaze, their foreheads touching, as he picks her up. He carries her toward his bedroom, shutting the door behind them.

"You're so fucking beautiful," he breathes against her mouth. She smiles, so softly, and then her feet are back on the ground, and she's running her hands underneath his shirt and over his chest. His jacket tumbles to the floor.

"Ca—can I?" she stutters, holding the edge of his shirt up. He nods and helps her take it off. Her eyes rake over his chest, and he shudders at her gaze. Her hands start at his shoulders and move down over his pecs and across his stomach. She stops right at the waistband of his pants, fingertips grazing his hips. "I think you're beautiful, too." Shiloh doesn't think he's ever been called beautiful by someone before, and he loves the way it feels.

He takes a step backward and lets his knees hit the edge of the bed. He sits and drags Ava on top, so she's straddling him. His hands travel up her back, and he fingers the ties of her dress.

"Undress me," she breathes, eyes fluttering. Shiloh pulls the ties loose, and the dress falls apart in his hands, revealing her body inch by inch. It's tantalizingly slow, until Ava gets up and steps out of the dress. He drinks her in as she comes and settles back on his lap, only in her bra and underwear now. He kisses the tops of her shoulders, knowing her freckles are exposed, but unable to see them in the dark. He prays he'll be able to see them in the morning.

Her hands unclasp her bra, and she tosses it to the floor. He kisses his way down her body and to her breasts, where he teases her nipples with his tongue. She gasps, throwing her head back in pleasure. She rocks against his erection, and his hands cup her ass, reveling in the feeling of her.

Her hands grip the hair at the back of his neck. "Fuck," she whispers. Shiloh takes this moment to spin her, so she's lying back on the mattress, and he's on top of her. He takes her hands and puts them above her head, kissing down her body, teasing her at every opportunity. He travels lower until he gets to her navel. His fingers skim the edge of her panties.

"May I?" Shiloh asks, planting a kiss on her hip.

"Yes," she says, her voice thick with desire. He hooks his fingers in her underwear and pulls them down, slowly. He has to suck in a breath when he sees her fully undressed for the first time. She's so goddamn sexy, and she had the nerve to say he could do better. He touches her, feeling how wet she is. His thumb goes to her clit, and she gasps, grasping the bed sheets tightly.

"Does that feel good?" he asks, kissing the inside of her thigh.

"Yes," she whimpers. "Fuck, Shiloh." Hearing his name on her lips, while she's lying naked in his bed, almost has him coming in his pants. He's so hard and aching for her that he has a hard time not gripping himself. He knows one touch from her, and he might explode.

"Do you want me to taste you?" he asks, thumb still circling her clit.

"Please," she begs, no hesitation in her voice. He loves how confident she sounds. He grabs her thighs and brings his face down to her, his tongue finding the perfect spot. She tastes exquisite. Ava cries out, arching against the bed. Shiloh loves hearing how he makes her feel. She's gasping, moaning, and he has to stop himself from taking his cock in his hand and coming just from the sound of her voice.

"Shiloh, I'm...fuck I'm gonna come," she cries, his tongue continuing to tease her. He inserts a finger inside her, his tongue circling her clit as he feels her orgasm rip through her, her cries echoing in the room. Ava's lying on the bed, spent, as Shiloh makes his way up her body, kissing every inch of her.

"Jesus Christ, Shi," she mutters, breathing hard. He lets out a laugh as he nuzzles against her neck. Her hands travel down his body and palm him over his pants. "I want to make you feel good too," she says, continuing to rub him.

He shudders against her and nods silently. She switches positions with him and begins unbuttoning his pants. "Ava..." he starts, and she stills. "I haven't...I haven't been with anyone since..." He can't bring himself to say her name in a moment that is meant just for him and Ava.

She kisses him, her fingers caressing his face. "Do you want to?"

she asks against his lips.

"Yes," Shiloh shudders. "More than anything. It's just...it's been so long."

"It's okay," she says, taking his pants and boxers off all the way. He's exposed to her now, and she takes his length in her hand.

Shiloh groans, loudly. "Fuck," he says, eyes fluttering at the feeling of his cock in her hand. She takes him in her mouth and licks up his length. He could never have expected this moment to feel better than he imagined. Her mouth is around him, teasing him up and down, her hand cupping his balls. He risks a look at her, and he almost comes just from the sight of his cock in her mouth. He sits up, taking her face in his hands, stopping her from continuing.

"Wait," he says.

"Are you okay?" she asks, worry crossing her features. "Was it not good?"

He silences her with a kiss, deep and intimate. She sighs, and when he pulls back, he's smiling at her. "It was perfect," he says. "But if you keep going, I'm going to finish too soon. I want us to take our time."

Ava smiles at him and gets back on the bed, straddling him. He can feel her wetness rubbing against him, and he groans. He kisses her, his hands traveling up and down her body, memorizing every inch of her.

"Shi," she breathes, and he trembles underneath her. "I want to. I want to feel you inside me." Shiloh nods, flipping Ava to be underneath him. He reaches into his bedside table and pulls out a condom. Ava's eyes are hungry as he puts it on himself.

Once it's on, Shiloh makes his way back up her body. He kisses her deeply, his tongue exploring her mouth. His cock nudges against her entrance. He looks into her eyes, making sure she's okay.

She nods and guides him closer to her. He sinks into her, inch by inch, until he's fully inside her, and they both gasp at the feeling. He pumps into her, reveling in the way they feel together.

He has to slow himself, trying not finish too soon. He fucks her, slowly, sensually, kissing her deep and intimate. Ava sighs deeply while she kisses him and touches herself. He can feel himself building.

Her hips rock into him, her moans settling deep into his bones. "Come for me, Shi," she says in his ear, and that's all it takes for him to finish, feeling her own orgasm wrap around him. He thinks it might be the best feeling of his entire life.

He collapses next to her, breathing deeply. Seeing her next to him, naked and in his bed, makes him shudder in pleasure. He takes her face and kisses her deeply, relishing in the feeling of being able to do that.

"Stay," he says, his voice barely above a whisper. "Stay with me."

Ava just nods, and he wraps his arms around her, securing her body tightly to his. They fall asleep like that, embraced together.

Chapter 28

Ava wakes to the feeling of another body next to her. She peeks out of one eye and sees Shiloh sleeping peacefully. A shiver runs it way through her body, though she's wrapped warmly in his bed. She can't believe what happened last night. It was the stuff of her most intimate dreams. She takes a moment to study him. His skin is still slightly bronzed from how much time they spent in the sun together this summer. His dark hair is mussed from sleep, and he's breathing deeply, his chest rising and falling. His arm is outstretched toward her. She reaches out and barely presses her fingertips to his cheek. There's a light stubble on his jaw that she wants to trace. She takes in the planes of his chest, the light dusting of hair that lines his skin. She can't believe she's allowed to touch him, that he moaned at her touch last night. She remembers how expertly he touched her, and pleasure runs through her body.

Shiloh sighs deeply and presses his face into her hand. "Hi," he says, not opening his eyes.

"Hi," she whispers. She can't bring her voice to a normal level, afraid she might scare him away. His eyes open slowly, and she drinks in the sight of him. He's so beautiful, she can't fully process him. He reaches up and tucks a piece of hair behind her ear.

"You're still here," he says.

"Should I not be?" she asks, suddenly self-conscious.

"You are exactly where I would like you to be," he says, pulling her body close to his. His arms encircle her, and she melts. He's warm from sleep, and she feels like she's being held in a cocoon. They're nose to nose, legs tangled together. Ava's heart races, and Shiloh's hands run their way down her waist.

"I've wanted to know how many freckles are on your body for so long," he whispers, as though he's telling her his most intimate secret.

"Really?" she breathes.

"Yes," he says, his eyes roaming her naked body. Fingers touching, so gently, over her shoulders, her arms, down her stomach and to her hips. "You have one here." He rubs his thumb over her hip, where a lone freckle sits. He leans down and presses the softest kiss to it. "And here." He kisses the top of her shoulder. "And here." A kiss to her cheek. "Here." Her other cheek. "Here." Her nose. His lips hover over her own.

"There's more you still haven't found," she whispers.

A mischievous look crosses his eyes. "Should I go looking for them?"

"Yes." His hands roam her body, and every freckle he finds, he claims with his lips. It makes Ava feel worshiped.

"Can I tell you a secret?" he asks once he's surfaced again, and she can barely nod her head. "You do snore."

A laugh escapes her, and she clasps her hands over her mouth immediately, suddenly aware that Ashtyn is in the house. Shiloh smiles at her, and Ava feels heat pool between her legs just at the sight of him.

She's about to kiss him when Ashtyn yells from the other side of the house, "Shiloh!!!"

Ava's eyes widen, and she feels the automatic reaction to hide under the covers. Shiloh grips her arms, his face calm. "Stay," he says, as if it's the simplest thing in the world.

"I can't," Ava replies. "She'll kill me if she finds me here."

"Why?"

"Because..." Ava doesn't know how to finish her train of thought. Because she's not allowed to have a crush on Shiloh? Because they were both worried Ava would ruin things by having feelings for their new roommate? "I'm just not ready to tell her, yet. Hide me!"

They can hear Ashtyn's footsteps getting closer to Shiloh's room. The doorknob turns, and Ava dive bombs underneath the covers near Shiloh's feet, trying to look like a lump of blankets.

The door opens. "Shiloh! Do you know if Ava came home with us last night? She's not in her room."

"Geez, Ash, can't you knock first?" Shiloh says, sitting up and trying to act casual.

"Oh please, I've seen you shirtless a million times. It's nothing special." Ava can't help but disagree. "Now, have you seen Ava?" Her voice doesn't sound like she was up until 2AM, drunk as a skunk.

"You know, can't say that I have," Shiloh says. "Maybe she got up early and...went for a run." Ava has to stop herself from smacking her forehead.

"A run? Are you serious?" Ashtyn asks, incredulously. "Ava has never gotten up early and gone for a run."

"Then I don't know where she is."

"But she came home with us last night? I can barely remember anything."

Ava squeezes Shiloh's leg, trying to relay a secret message to him.

"Uh, yeah, she helped me get you to bed. But, she might have left after that. I don't know. She hit it off with that guy at the bar." Ava feels horrible that she's making him lie to Ashtyn, but she also feels a tiny thrill at the prospect of hiding in plain sight.

At that moment, the doorbell rings. Ashtyn groans loudly. "I literally haven't even had my coffee yet," she grumbles, her footsteps receding as she goes to answer the door. Ava is about to make a mad dash toward her room when the voice at the door stops her. Shiloh freezes too. It's faint but undeniable: Mr. Brooks.

"Fuck," Shiloh breathes.

"Shiloh!" Ashtyn calls. Ava can hear frantic footsteps up the stairs, and she hides under the covers again. "Uh, hey, your dad is at the door."

"Tell him I'll be down in a minute," Shiloh says, gruffly.

"Okay. I'll start a pot of coffee." Ashtyn shuts the door behind her, and Ava peeks her head out of the blankets. Shiloh's face is blank, but his body is stiff as a board. She lays a hand on his bare shoulder, and he jumps.

"Sorry," she says, softly.

"No, it's fine," he replies, gently caressing her hand. "My dad just unsettles me." There's so much more that she can tell he isn't saying. So many emotions flitting across his face.

"I'll just go back to my room," she says, easing herself off the bed and wrapping a blanket around her. Shiloh gets up as well and pulls on a pair of sweatpants and a t-shirt.

"Here." Shiloh throws her one of his shirts, and she puts it on hurriedly. It smells like him, and she has to stop herself from inhaling it. She peeks out the door, and when the coast is clear, she dashes toward her room, shuts the door behind her, and lets out a sigh. Something uneasy settles in the pit of her stomach, where butterflies had erupted just moments before.

* * *

What the actual fuck is my father doing here, Shiloh thinks to himself. He could not have come at a worse time. First, Ashtyn interrupts his morning with Ava and now this. Things just never seem to go right with the two of them. He feels uneasy.

He'd seen the way Ava's eyes widened when she heard Ashtyn coming into his room, hated the way she'd immediately hid. He didn't want her to hide. He didn't want her to sneak out of his room and back into her own. He wanted her to stay, safely in his arms. But now, he's going downstairs to face his father. He hasn't seen him since signing the divorce papers, and he can't fathom why he's here now. Either way, he knows it isn't good.

The smell of coffee punches him in the face as soon as he enters the kitchen. His father is leaning against the island, mug of coffee in hand, chatting aimlessly with Ashtyn. She looks relieved as Shiloh enters the room.

"Well, that's my cue. I'm gonna go upstairs and..." She pauses, scrambling for an excuse, "...do something." She scurries upstairs, leaving Shiloh alone with his father.

"Well, at least she was presentable this time," Mr. Brooks scoffs. "Even offered me a cup of coffee. How polite."

"What do you want?" Shiloh asks, cutting to the chase. He's on edge, his skin on fire. He doesn't like that his father showed up unannounced, that he's comfortable enough to do so.

"Is that any way to talk to your father? You've really been starting to show your true colors lately, Shiloh."

He has to grit his teeth to stop himself from screaming. He wants to do exactly what he did at the restaurant, all over again, but he doesn't. He composes himself, taking a deep breath. "How can I help you, father?" He drips his voice with as much sarcasm as he dares. Even when he wants to defy his father, something in him resists.

Mr. Brooks just sighs. "Your mother wanted me to talk to you. And since you refuse to answer any of my calls..." He lets the sentence dangle, but Shiloh doesn't rise to the bait. He continues, "I've come to pick you up for breakfast. At the house. With your mother and I."

"I'm assuming I don't get a choice in the matter," Shiloh says. So, this was why his father came over unannounced. To surprise him into attending a family breakfast. It's easy to ignore phone calls, but it's another thing to ignore his father's visits.

"Shiloh, your mother wants to see you. Just get in the car."

He's about to refuse his father, when Ashtyn's voice carries downstairs. "You dirty dog!" He hears Ava shush her friend.

"Am I interrupting something?" his father asks, annoyance lacing his voice.

"No," Shiloh says, not wanting his father anywhere near the girls, especially Ava.

"Where is he?" He hears Ashtyn hiss. "Was it that hot guy from the bar? Is that whose shirt you're wearing?"

"Ashtyn, be quiet!" Ava insists.

Shiloh doesn't miss the way his father's face contorts in disgust, and Shiloh wants to smack the look right off. "Shiloh, I really don't know why you want to be associated with women like that." His voice is loud enough that Shiloh knows the girls can hear him. He's right, because there's a telling silence from upstairs. "I mean, honestly, it's embarrassing."

"Don't—don't talk about them like that," Shiloh says, weakly. He hates how he feels himself start to shrink again.

"How can I not, when they flaunt their exploits for the world to see?"

Before Shiloh can reply, Ava is stomping down the stairs, rage on her face, fists clenched. She's wearing only Shiloh's t-shirt, long legs fully on display. Ashtyn is a few steps behind her. "Good morning, Mr. Brooks," she says, forcing a smile on her face. "Just wondering, was it your sole purpose this morning to come into my house and insult me? Or were you just coming to berate your son?"

It's funny, actually, seeing his own father speechless for possibly the first time in his entire life. To his credit, he hides it well. He stands up straight and looks Ava head on. "Apologies…" he pauses, as if he could not possibly remember her name for the life of him. "I did not mean to insult you."

"Oh, so you're just here to bully your son, then?" she retorts, and Shiloh feels a sense of pride wash over him. Ava's only met his father once before, and she's already standing up to him, something Shiloh hasn't been able to do for twenty-seven years.

"That," his father starts, "is absolutely none of your business, young lady."

"Stop," Shiloh says. "Just, stop. I'll come with you to breakfast. Just, let me go get ready." He can't sit there and listen to his father insult Ava. It's killing him inside. He'll go to breakfast if it means getting him away from the girls.

Mr. Brooks just nods approvingly, not looking at either of the girls. He's only focused on his son. "Hurry."

Shiloh hurries up the stairs, Ava and Ashtyn close on his heels. He looks at them apologetically, but doesn't say anything as he goes to his room and gets dressed as quickly as he can. His bed glares at him, demanding him to get back in, hold Ava close, and ignore his father. But, he can't. His self-hatred settles deep into his bones, holding him down so he obeys his father and gets in the car.

Chapter 29

Mr. Brooks talks nonstop the entire drive to the house as Shiloh sits silently next to him, seething.

"I mean, honestly, I didn't realize I was entering a house full of vipers. Those girls—"

"They have names," Shiloh snaps.

Mr. Brooks just grimaces, ignoring his son's interruption. "I don't really care what their names are. They have no right to speak to me that way."

Shiloh thinks they actually have every right to speak to his father that way. He wishes *he* could, but he bites his tongue and keeps quiet the rest of the ride.

Familiar sights pass them: the park where he taught Mattie to ride a bike, the public pool they would escape to in the summer, and the soccer fields where Shiloh would go to practice his shots. He closes his eyes against all the memories. He doesn't want to remember the before anymore. He just wants to focus on the *now.*

As they round the bend of his old neighborhood, Shiloh feels himself shrink as he sees the house he grew up in. It's been so long since he's come back here, it makes him feel like a child. The home sits, pristine, on the corner of the street. The lawn is perfectly cut, not a blade out of place, and Shiloh remembers how they were never allowed to play in the grass.

He remembers when they first moved into the house, the heat of Texas suffocating him. He fiercely missed the cool air of Washington, and the way his mother took him fishing down at the creek. Everything changed when they moved to Texas. He's not sure what the catalyst was, only that nothing felt the same.

He steps out of the car, and his hands start to tremble. He fears that stepping back into the house will turn him seventeen again, young, dumb, and...hopeful. He can feel himself start to slip into that mindset already.

Mr. Brooks groans, startling his son. "I really should have had you wear something nicer. You know how your mother likes you to dress."

"Sorry," is all Shiloh's able to mumble. He tries not to remember when his mother didn't care what she looked like. When they would go fishing and get covered in mud. It's like it never happened.

"Well, no point now. Let's go in."

The first step inside the house is the hardest, and the smell of Shiloh's childhood slams into him immediately. It's all too sweet, citrus candles flickering in every room, suffocating him. Despite the candles, it's freezing. His skin crawls as he enters into the foyer, where pictures line the wall of people he no longer recognizes. Mattie is in almost every photo, whereas Shiloh's only framed picture of himself is his senior photo. He looks at his smile, so hopeful and excited about his future...with Scarlett. It all seems so long ago.

"Shiloh!" his mother exclaims, rounding the corner and greeting him with a stiff hug. She kisses both of his cheeks fleetingly, and then she's looking at him full on, her blue eyes scanning every inch of his face. Her dark hair is gathered in a low bun at the nape of her neck, and she's wearing a dress that's much too formal for a Sunday morning breakfast with family.

"Hi, Mom," he says, quietly. Her face, barely wrinkled by age, is soft. So different from the stern expression his father always wears.

Gloria Brooks squeezes his arms. "I wish you would have dressed up a little more, but that's okay."

"I tried to tell him," Mr. Brooks says, shrugging off his coat and hanging it in the closet. He gives his wife a knowing look that she reciprocates.

"I'm sorry," Shiloh says. He shouldn't be here. He should be back at his actual house, with Ava and Ashtyn and Jess. He should be *home*. He glances at the door, longingly, knowing he can't leave. Knowing what's waiting for him on the other side.

"Come, breakfast is ready," his mother says, ushering them all into the dining room.

Shiloh sits at the table meant for four. His mother and father settle into the heads of the table, with Shiloh nestled in between them. He feels trapped, their claws sinking deeper and deeper into him.

"So, honey," his mother starts, "tell us about your new job." She forks a piece of fruit and puts it onto her husband's plate. "Have you started, yet?"

Shiloh swallows. "I started at the end of August."

"Oh, how wonderful! And you're, what, coaching football?"

"Soccer."

Mr. Brooks rolls his eyes. "What a ridiculous sport."

"What made you decide to do that? I didn't think you were much into sports," Mrs. Brooks says, continuing to heap food onto her husband's plate before her own.

"I played in high school, Mom."

She pauses, as if he's caught her off guard, then smiles awkwardly. "Oh, of course. I just forgot. I'm sorry."

"It was actually my roommate, Ava, who recommended me for the job." Saying her name at his childhood dining table makes him shiver. He stares at the food, his stomach rolling at the thought of eating.

"Don't even get me started on those girls," Mr. Brooks says, finally digging into his plate, now that his wife has finished putting food on it for him. "They're a piece of work."

Shiloh clenches his fists under the table, but his mother just shakes her head disapprovingly. "Honestly, Shiloh, don't you think it's a little weird to have roommates at twenty-six years old."

He clears his throat. "I'm twenty-seven."

Again, his mother pauses. She's not used to him correcting her like this, but something inside him is stirring. Awakening. "I turned twenty-seven in July, in case you forgot. I didn't get a call from either of you."

"We did not forget," his father says, sternly. "You know July is when we go on our annual cruise. We didn't have service."

Shiloh doesn't even try to argue. He knows it's a bullshit excuse. They either forgot or didn't care enough to wish him a happy birthday. Not that it matters. Everyone he wanted to celebrate with that weekend had been there.

"Either way, the sentiment still stands," his mother continues. "It's unseemly to have roommates at this age. I mean, Matthew is younger than you, and he's already living on his own."

"Speaking of Matthew," Mr. Brooks starts, "he did such a fantastic job at the firm this summer. I really think he should consider law school."

"Oh, he'd make such a fantastic lawyer," Mrs. Brooks gushes. "I think you can convince him with time."

Shiloh tries not to roll his eyes. Mattie has never wanted to be a lawyer. Will *never* want to be a lawyer. But there's no convincing their parents of that.

Mr. Brooks continues, "I'll wear him down eventually." He chuckles like his son's future is inevitable. "I sent him a little extra money this month to try and incentivize him. You know, since it's his final year and all."

Shiloh's parents continue talking about Mattie like Shiloh isn't even here. He's not sure why they invited him here, if all they want to talk about is his brother.

Shiloh clears his throat, "Mattie and I—"

His mother raises a hand to interrupt him. "You know how I feel about that nickname."

Shame heats his cheeks. "Uh, sorry, Matthew and I—"

"He's not a child," Mr. Brooks says. "Just because he's younger than you does not mean you should treat him as such. The least you could do is use the name we chose for him"

The anger finally releases within Shiloh. "Mom used to love it."

It's like a bomb drops onto the table. Mrs. Brooks looks shell shocked, her eyes wide, and her mouth set in a firm line. Mr. Brooks, to Shiloh's surprise, actually looks surprised for all of five seconds. The expression soon passes, shifting to one of neutrality.

"Well, I don't think that's true."

"When he was first born, I called him Mattie. I couldn't say Matthew because of my lisp, which you relentlessly teased me about, so I started saying Mattie. Mom thought it was cute and started saying it, too. You, Dad, berated her until she stopped."

"Shiloh—" Mrs. Brooks starts.

"It's true," Shiloh interrupts.

"Shiloh, do not speak to your mother that way."

"Why? It's true. In fact, Mom used to do a lot of things before you told her they were stupid. We would go fishing. You said to stop. Mom liked—"

"Shiloh!" Mrs. Brooks exclaims.

Mr. Brooks holds up a hand to his wife, silencing her. "Shiloh, I will not have you speaking like this in my own home."

"Oh, but you can come into my home and treat me and my friends the way you did? You treat your wife as if she can't have her own opinion. You hurt everyone you come into contact with." If Ava can stand up to his father, then he can too. It's been a long time coming.

"I am your father. I will speak to you as I see fit."

Shiloh turns to his mother, pleadingly. "Please, Mom. You have to see that this isn't okay." She won't meet his gaze. Her hands sit on the table, shaking.

"You are upsetting her!" Mr. Brooks exclaims, slamming his hands down on the table, making his wife jump. It shatters Shiloh's heart into a million pieces.

A lone tear slips down her cheek, and she hurriedly wipes it away before schooling her face into a blank stare. "Shiloh, if you're going to act like this, then you can leave. I won't have you behaving this way in my house."

He has a decision to make. A choice between the family he was born into, or the family he's found. He knows what he will choose.

"If I leave this house," he starts, "then I'm never coming back."

His mother finally meets his gaze, but her face doesn't give anything away. "So be it."

The words are like nails in a coffin, and Shiloh gets up, leaving the table and his parents behind for good. No one says a single word as he shuts the front door behind him. He feels the finality of that door shutting, rescinding the relationship he has with his parents forever. He knows there's no going back after this. All he has left is his brother. But, he also has Ava. And Ashtyn. And Drew. Maybe he's not as alone as he thinks he is.

Before he can rethink his decision, he runs. He runs as far and as fast as he can, until he's out of breath, and the house is long behind him, where his father can no longer reach him. He is finally free.

Chapter 30

Ava paces her room anxiously when she hears the front door open. She runs down the stairs and throws herself into Shiloh's arms before she can even stop to think. He holds her tightly, the sound of sobs muffled as he presses his face into her neck.

"It's okay," she whispers. "I've got you. I'm here."

They sink to the floor, arms entwined around each other. Ava holds him to her, keeping him as intact as she can. Ashtyn's eyes widen as she enters the room and rushes over to them. She kneels next to them, her hands going to Shiloh's back comfortingly. She catches Ava's eye, worry crossing her face.

"We're here for you," Ashtyn says, sincerity lacing her voice. "We're your family. For as long as you need us."

Shiloh doesn't have to tell them what happened. He just needs to know that they are going to be here for him no matter what. He cries in their embrace and whispers, "Thank you. For everything."

"We're not going anywhere," Ashtyn says, as Ava continues to hold him. "We love you."

The words fill the room, a comforting presence settling over them as Shiloh sniffles and wipes his eyes on the back of his hand.

"Fuck," he says. "That was way worse than I thought it was going to be." He huffs out a bitter laugh and stands.

"Do you want to talk about it?" Ava asks, carefully.

"No," he replies. "Not yet. First, I think I need a drink with my brother."

* * *

It's later in the afternoon when Ashtyn nudges Ava with her foot. "Come on, just tell me if it was good!" she probes. They're sprawled on Ava's bed, Jess between them.

"I already told you, I'm not telling!" Ava exclaims, swatting her friend away playfully. As far as Ashtyn is concerned, Ava had a one-night stand with Alex from the bar, and he left before anyone else was awake. She feels so guilty lying to her best friend, but she also knows Ashtyn will lose her shit if she finds out Ava actually slept with Shiloh last night. Especially after the wholesome moment when he came back from breakfast. Ava's never seen Ashtyn act so loving toward Shiloh before. She also never meant to go toe-to-toe with Mr. Brooks, but her emotions got the better of her. She still doesn't know what transpired after Shiloh left, but she knows he'll tell her if he wants to. Seeing him cry like that had broken something inside her, and her feelings for him had only grown since their morning together.

Ashtyn scowls playfully at Ava, pausing her thoughts about Shiloh. "You've never been one to shy away from explicit details, Ava Marshall. Something is different, here."

Ava's breath hitches. She knows exactly what is different. "The difference is this was a one time thing that will never happen again." Even she doesn't believe that, because there's no way she can keep her hands off Shiloh after last night. She'd already fought the urge to jump back into his bed when Ashtyn took a shower. He'd pulled Ava aside and kissed her deeply, leaving her breathless and incredibly turned on, despite everything that had happened with his parents. "I won't tell her," he'd said. "Whatever you want, I'll do." And that had been the end of it. She isn't exactly sure where that leaves them, only that she's dying for more.

An incoming Facetime from Brooke silences any lingering questions Ashtyn might have had. "Hey, bride to be!" she exclaims. "How are we feeling this afternoon?"

"Like I got hit by a train," Brooke says. Her hair is a tangled mess, and she has mascara stained under her eyes. They hear Jordan snoring next to her.

"Did you just wake up? It's two o'clock, Brooke!"

"Leave me alone. God, I wish I was twenty-two again."

"Don't we all," Ashtyn teases. "Hey, Ava has news."

Ava's eyes widen. "Uh, no, I have no news actually."

"Yes, you do! Tell her!"

"Tell me what?" Brooke asks, trying to rub the sleep from her eyes, but she just smears the mascara further into her skin.

"Ava had a one night stand last night."

Brooke's hand freezes, and her head whips up to the camera. "What!?" This is slowly turning into a mess. "Was it that cute guy from the bar?"

"Yes, I had sex with the cute guy from the bar last night," Ava says. "And that's the end of it!"

"Since when do you have one night stands?"

"That's what I said!" Ashtyn interjects.

"Since I wanted to!" Ava replies. "Can we drop the subject now?"

"No, we need a girls brunch. Now," Brooke says. "I can be ready in twenty minutes."

"It's afternoon, Brooke. It's past lunch."

"Okay, call it whatever you want, just be ready in twenty minutes."

* * *

The very last thing Ava wants to be doing right now is sitting at a very late lunch with her friends, lying through her teeth about the guy she slept with last night. What she really wants is to lay in Shiloh's bed and let him do everything he did to her last night. Instead, she's fending off questions from Brooke and Ashtyn. She's never been a good liar, but she knows she needs to be right now. She picks at her salad absentmindedly.

"Shouldn't we be talking about Brooke's wedding? I feel like that's more important," Ava says, trying desperately to change the subject.

Brooke rolls her eyes. "We've been talking about my wedding for months now. Everything is ready to go. Now, we just wait for October third."

"Okay, but are you nervous? Excited? Tell us things!"

Brooke frowns and narrows her eyes. "Ava, when have you ever *not* wanted to tell us about a guy? What is going on?"

"Nothing! I don't know why you're grilling me about some random guy I'm never going to see again."

Ashtyn and Brooke share a look. "Okay, fine. If you don't want to share, then don't share."

"Thank you."

An awkward silence settles amongst the friends for possibly the first time in their lives. It's unnerving, but it's better than Ava lying through her teeth.

"Oh, did I tell you I was able to add Shiloh to Drew's hotel room? I know he's not part of the wedding party, but I figured he could be y'all's plus one. Unless Ava wants to invite bar hottie," Brooke says, signaling the waiter for another mimosa. Ava narrows her eyes at her friend.

"I'm sure Drew will be thrilled to have company," Ashtyn says sarcastically.

"You know, I was kind of surprised at his lack of flirting at the bach party," Brooke replies, tone light. "Normally, he'd be all over one of my sisters. It looked like Shiloh took up that mantle last night."

Ava chokes on her drink, trying to hide the blush that starts to stain her cheeks. Shiloh may have flirted with Bethany last night, but Ava was the one he took to bed.

"That's because Drew was by my side the entire night," Ashtyn says, rolling her eyes, but her tone lacks her normal annoyance.

Ava takes this opportunity to take the heat off herself. "Yeah, you two seemed cozy last night."

Ashtyn frowns. "Watch it."

"Hey, you always want to talk about me, I figured it's your turn now. What's the deal with you two?"

"There is no deal with me and Drew. He's just fun to mess with."

Brooke sighs, "Ash, I love you, but you can't toy with Drew like that. There's more to him than meets the eye."

"I'm sure there is. Doesn't mean I want to get to know him."

"Even if he's best friends with your *family*?" Ava throws Ashtyn's own words back at her. Ashtyn freezes, thrown off by Ava's reiteration of this morning.

"Don't use my words against me, Ava," Ashtyn admonishes. Ava just shakes her head and rolls her eyes. Nothing she or Brooke say will get Ashtyn to change her mind about Drew. "Or do you want to talk about your night again?"

"Okay, fine, geez," Ava says, holding her hands up in surrender.

"Anyway," Brooke drawls, taking charge of the conversation before the tension can grow. "Like I said, I got Shiloh into Drew's room. You two have your own room, as well. The rest of the wedding party will all be on the same floor, and we'll get ready in my suite. The rehearsal dinner will be at the hotel restaurant. They have a back room reserved for us.”

“Ooh, fancy.”

“Ash, I guess I should let you know now that you and Drew are walking together during the procession.”

“What? Why? Can’t I walk with Derek or someone?”

“No, Ava’s walking with Derek. And I already paired my sisters off, so that leaves you with Drew.”

“You’re doing that on purpose.”

“I am not!” Brooke exclaims, but there’s a small glint in her eye that Ava thinks might be an indication that she’s lying.

Ashtyn actually looks uncomfortable. “You know I hate weddings, and now you do this?”

Brooke’s face softens, and she places a comforting hand on Ashtyn’s arm. “I know. And you don’t know what it means to me that you’re going to be in this wedding for me. I understand how hard that’s going to be.”

Ashtyn huffs, but doesn’t say anything. Ava knows how much convincing it took from Brooke for Ashtyn to agree to be in the wedding. She loves Brooke like her own sister, but they all know what weddings mean to her.

“Fine,” she grumbles. “But I get to step on his foot at least once.”

Brooke erupts in laughter. “Fine. Just don’t injure him before you walk down the aisle.”

“No promises,” Ashtyn says, but there’s a small smile on her face.

* * *

Shiloh’s brother stares at him, face unreadable as he digests the information Shiloh just shared.

“I don’t even know which one to address first,” Mattie says, taking a sip of his beer.

"I know, it's a lot."

"Does this mean I'm going to have to suffer through holidays alone?"

Shiloh sighs and scrubs a hand down his face. "Looks like it."

"I mean, I can't say that I blame you. But...I just worry about Mom.

Shiloh feels a pang in his heart. They never discuss their mother. Their father? Sure, they both hate him. But their mother? That's a different story.

"I-I'm not trying to hurt her. I just have complicated feelings about everything," Shiloh says. He omitted the part of the story where their mother told Shiloh to leave.

"She loves you." Mattie doesn't say it to hurt Shiloh, but it still lands right on his heart.

Shiloh sighs, heavily. "I love her. I do. But, I just don't think she loves me more than she loves Dad."

"I know, it's not fair of me to compare my relationship with Mom to yours. I just wish circumstances were different."

Matthew has always loved their mother. Shiloh also loves her, but after today, he sees things differently. He knows that his parents prefer Mattie, and that's okay. Hell, he prefers Mattie too, but their rejection still stings. Especially on days like his birthday. "I do too, Mattie. I really do."

"I just want you to be happy, brother."

Shiloh gives Mattie a small smile. "I'm trying."

"And if that means cutting them out, then you know I'll support you. I'm not going anywhere."

Shiloh reaches across the table to grasp his brother's hand. "Thank you."

"It's all they're going to talk about for the next year," Mattie groans. "God, if I have to suffer through Thanksgiving alone, then you're going to have to buy me more alcohol."

Shiloh signals to the waiter for another. "Anything you want, brother."

Mattie smiles. "Now, let's talk about Ava."

He groans, but smiles despite everything. Just hearing her name sets his skin ablaze. "I don't even know where to begin with that one."

Mattie laughs loudly. "I mean, I could have told you this was going to happen. You haven't been able to keep your eyes off her since the moment you met her."

Shiloh frowns. "That's not true."

"My dude, you literally threw your body in-between hers and concrete pavement. You named a boat after her. You saw her in a bikini, and your dick almost fell off. I'm surprised you didn't get together sooner."

"We're not...together exactly," Shiloh struggles for the words. "Ashtyn can't know."

"Why?"

"Because Ava doesn't think she'll understand."

"Understand what exactly?" Shiloh doesn't have an answer to this, so he just shrugs. Mattie looks at him curiously. "Do you want more?"

"I don't know. I want to say yes, but Ava's the first girl I've been with since Scarlett, and I'm worried..." He trails off, biting his lip.

"What, that you're falling for the first girl you happened to stumble across after your divorce? That's ridiculous." It's like Mattie took the words right out of his mouth.

"Is it?"

"If this was any other girl, I would say no. But this is Ava. I've seen the two of you together. She's different."

Shiloh can't help but agree. This feels different somehow. With Scarlett, everything felt so rushed. With Ava, he feels like he can take his time, and she won't go anywhere. Like she will wait for him. "I'm afraid that loving her is a death sentence." He says it so quietly, he's afraid Mattie didn't hear him.

"For you or for her?"

"For her."

Mattie looks at him intently. "One failed relationship does not a doomed life make, brother. You are allowed to try again. You are allowed to succeed this time. But more importantly, you are allowed to fail again. In fact, it's a guarantee. No matter who you choose to be with, you are going to have difficulties. You are going to fight and argue and get mad at each other. It's how you deal with those obstacles that will test your relationship. Maybe you and Ava succeed. Maybe you fail. Either way, you will survive. You can't let one bad thing dictate the rest of your entire life."

Shiloh's heart thumps heavily in his chest, and he huffs out a small laugh. "How did you get so wise?"

Mattie shrugs. "I had a really great big brother. Plus, if our parents taught me anything, it's that I don't want what they have."

"You know, you don't have to deal with them if you don't want to."

"Yes, I do. It's the burden of being the favorite."

This makes Shiloh bark out a laugh. "God, you're such a shit sometimes."

"Again, I learned from the best."

"I'll toast to that," Shiloh says, raising his beer. Mattie clinks his bottle against Shiloh's and smiles. If there is one thing in this life that he can count on, it's his little brother.

OCTOBER

Chapter 31

They've been in the car barely an hour when Ashtyn groans out of boredom. "Are we there yet?" she asks, stretching dramatically.

"We've been driving an hour. We still have three more to go," Shiloh says, eyes never leaving the road. Ava's grateful he offered to drive them, because she hates driving for long stretches of time. Of course, Brooke and Jordan chose to get married out of town. Now, Ava has to sit next to Shiloh for four hours and *not* reach out and grab his hand. It's torture. Utter torture.

She knows he's sneaking glances at her, because she's also sneaking glances at him. They've barely even kissed since their night together, afraid of Ashtyn discovering them. But, there's been plenty of discreet looks and caresses of hands as they pass in the hallway. Every day, when they drive to work together, Shiloh holds her hand the entire way and kisses it when they arrive at school. Then, they untangle themselves from each other and walk in discreetly, like they've always done. Ava still doesn't know how she's going to tell Ashtyn. She also doesn't exactly know what she and Shiloh are to each other, because they haven't talked about it. She knows she is totally and completely enamored by him, but does he want more? He's said before he doesn't see himself getting married again, and that's something Ava's always wanted for herself. Is she willing to sacrifice that for him? She doesn't like to think about those things, so she doesn't. Instead, she just lets herself revel in the feeling of his hand in hers. That's all she can hope for right now.

"Can't we do something fun to pass the time?" Ashtyn whines.

"Like what?" Ava asks, setting down her book.

"I'm sure you could count cows for fun," Shiloh says. Ashtyn flips him off from the backseat. "I saw that."

"Eyes on the road, mister," she replies, frowning. Shiloh salutes her sarcastically.

Ava laughs as Ashtyn huffs and crosses her arms. "One," she says, as they pass a field. "Two. Three."

She gets to fifty-five before she's asleep, breathing deeply in the backseat. Shiloh flicks a glance to her before putting his hand on Ava's knee. Goosebumps pop up on her skin immediately. His thumb rubs lazy circles against her jeans, the skin underneath begging to feel it.

"You're making it very difficult to concentrate," Ava whispers, her eyes never leaving the page of her book. Shiloh doesn't say anything as his hand travels slowly upward toward her thigh. A throbbing begins between her legs as his hand caresses her inner thigh. She has to grit her teeth and tighten her grip on the book to stop herself from moving his hand where she really wants it.

Ashtyn stirs in the backseat, and they both jump, Shiloh taking back his hand, and Ava sitting up straighter. Ash adjusts her position, then begins breathing deeply again, signaling that she's back asleep.

Shiloh sighs and flexes his knuckles on the steering wheel. "Just a few more hours," he says. Ava just nods and goes back to her book. They don't touch each other again.

* * *

They arrive at the hotel three hours later, Ashtyn still napping peacefully in the backseat.

"Aww, she tired herself out counting all those cows," Shiloh teases, and Ava has to hold back her laughter as she playfully smacks his shoulder.

"Shh, you'll wake her up!"

"We're at the hotel, she has to wake up anyway. Ashtyn!"

Ava doesn't even have time to warn him before Ashtyn's eyes are open, and she's glaring at him with a gaze so intense, Shiloh has to look away.

"What did I tell you about waking me up?" Ashtyn says, her voice gruff from sleep.

"I tried warning him," Ava says, holding her hands up.

"I thought you'd want to know we made it! You know, since you were complaining the whole time." Ashtyn just glares at him again as she undoes her seat belt and gets out of the car, without another word.

"It's an Ashtyn thing," Ava says. "Don't try to make sense of it."

Shiloh smiles at her and reaches over to squeeze her leg discreetly. She returns his smile, her insides melting.

"Meet me for a drink later tonight?" he asks, almost shyly.

Ava squeezes his hand. "Of course."

It's ten o'clock when Ashtyn is tucked into bed, and Ava is able to sneak down to the bar to meet Shiloh. She spots him immediately, hunched over a drink, ignoring the bartender flirting with him. She sees he's already ordered a martini for her. Her heart swells.

"Hi," she says, touching his shoulder as she sits on the stool next to him. He turns at her touch, and a smile lights up his face.

"Hi," he says, his hand covering hers. "I got you a drink."

"Thank you," she says, shyly. The bartender, seeing them interact, seems to get the hint and makes her way to the other side of the bar.

Ava takes a sip of her drink and sighs contentedly. "Never as good as yours, but it'll do."

Shiloh smiles at her again, and it pierces Ava right in the heart. His hand comes up to her face and tucks a piece of hair behind her ear. His thumb caresses her blushing cheek. Ava's foot slides up and down his leg underneath the bar. She interlaces her fingers with his on top of the counter. It all feels so natural, and yet, so invigorating. Her heart beats a million miles an hour.

"What are we doing?" It's out of her mouth before she can stop herself.

Shiloh sighs. "I don't know. I—I just know I don't want to stop."

"Me either," she says, squeezing his hand. Shiloh pulls her face to his, and then he's kissing her, and she's slipping between his legs and off the stool. He kisses her deeply, sweetly. Ava has to remind herself that she's in public, and she pulls back slightly, their noses brushing.

She sighs. There's so much more she wants to say, but Shiloh's "I don't know" stops her. She doesn't want to rush him into any kind of declaration that he's not ready for. She can wait. She can do that for him. Besides, she isn't in any kind of rush either. She just wants to enjoy this moment.

"Drew isn't coming until tomorrow. I have an empty room tonight," Shiloh says, his hand resting on her hip.

"Is that an invitation?" she asks, coyly, burning with desire for him.

"It is."

"Then let's go."

The door to his room is barely shut before Shiloh's hands are on her, and she's crashing her lips to his. They're hungry, insistent, compared to their first time together. Now, Ava knows how wanted she is by Shiloh, and how much she desires him. Their hands fumble at each other's clothes, their kisses full of teeth and tongue.

Ava gets Shiloh's shirt off, and then she's trailing kisses down his stomach as he groans. His hands make their way into her hair as she kneels, unbuttoning his jeans.

"Ava," he starts.

"I was first last time," she says, pulling down his pants. "Now, it's your turn."

He's about to protest again when she palms him over his boxers, and he lets out a hiss. Her fingers skim his hips, making him shiver under her touch. She smiles, loving the way she makes him feel.

She pulls down his underwear, and his erection springs forward, long and hard. She takes him in her hand as he lets out a moan that makes her instantly wet. She pushes him backward toward the bed, where he falls, and she has a better angle to take him into her mouth. She licks up his length, teasing him, making him beg for her. He whispers her name, and butterflies erupt in her stomach. She works him expertly with her mouth, feeling him deep in the back of her throat. He's breathing heavily, gripping the bed sheets. Ava's belly fills with hot desire at the way she's making Shiloh feel. Seeing him naked in front of her is a privilege.

She pulls back for a moment to rip off her own shirt and straddle him. Her clit rubs against his cock through her jeans, and she has to stifle a gasp. Shiloh's hands grip her waist, and his lips find hers again, kissing her deeply. He unbuttons the top of her jeans and slips his hand down to rub her through her underwear. She throws her head back in ecstasy, his lips chasing her throat. She feels herself start to build already, and she puts a hand on his arm.

"I—I'll finish too soon," she stutters, breathing heavily.

"Ave," Shiloh says, caressing her face. "I want you to come as many times as you want."

The way he says it, so sincerely, has her rocking against him again, eyelids fluttering as her orgasm suddenly washes through her, her body shuddering against his with intense pleasure.

"Well," she says against his lips once she's finished. "That was one."

Shiloh chuckles deep in his throat as he kisses her again, flipping her underneath him. The rest of her clothes vanish so they're skin to skin.

The lamp in the room casts a dim glow over their bodies, and Ava sees Shiloh look her up and down.

"I can finally see them all," he says, his thumb rubbing circles over her hip. Ava looks at him curiously, and he actually blushes. "Your freckles. I told you, I've wanted to know where each one is."

"I've never really given them much thought," Ava says, voice quiet.

"Well, I can tell you, they're all I think about."

"I've never really had the light on before," she replies. "So, I don't think anyone has really ever seen them like this."

"Do you want me to turn it off?"

"No. I like you looking at me."

Shiloh's nose grazes hers as his hands caress her skin. She hooks a leg up over his hip, feeling him hard against her. "Well, I like looking at you too."

Butterflies erupt in her stomach, and a shiver descends down her body. Is this what it's supposed to feel like? Is this how it was always supposed to feel like? Like, just him looking at her makes her feel as if she might explode from the pleasure of it all?

Shiloh's mouth explores her body, expertly, until she feels herself start to build again, as he kisses her where she's most sensitive. Her hands grasp his hair as he teases her with his tongue, and she feels herself tremble at the release she knows is coming. *Again.*

When she's finished, gasping and moaning, she manages to get out, "You're going to spoil me."

Shiloh huffs out a laugh. "Good."

Ava spins so she's on top, straddling him. Shiloh retrieves a condom from his bag and puts it on as Ava watches him hungrily. As soon as it's secure, she sinks down onto him, groaning as he fills her up, deep and full. His hands grip her hips, and she rides him, slow and sensually.

"God, you feel so good," Shiloh whispers, his eyes fluttering closed.

Ava feels time slow as their bodies move together, pleasure building between them, their lips finding each other again and again and again. Every pump inside her has her building, ecstasy rippling through her entire body. His tongue teases her nipples, and her clit rubs against his cock. She has never had sex that feels this good before. As if her entire body is on fire, and every stroke of her partner is a gift, not a burden she must bear.

She moans, loudly, the friction sending her crashing into oblivion. Shiloh finishes soon after, groaning as his orgasm spills out of him. Ava leans down to kiss him, and he caresses her cheeks.

She rolls off of him, and he gets up to go to the bathroom and clean himself up. She leans back against the bed, watching him go. Good God, he is a glorious sight. She hears the shower turn on, and then he peeks his head out at her, a sly smile on his lips.

"You coming?"

* * *

Shiloh wakes to the sound of the hotel room door opening, and his best friend shouting "Rise and shin—" Drew stops as he sees the person accompanying Shiloh in bed.

Shiloh bolts upright, jostling Ava, who groggily opens her eyes to the scene in front of them. When she sees Drew staring at them, mouth slightly agape, she starts, tugging the blanket to cover her naked body.

"Um, am I in the wrong room?" Drew asks.

"No, you're just early," Shiloh grumbles, trying to wipe sleep out of his eyes. They weren't supposed to fall asleep together. Ava was going to go back to her room with Ashtyn, but they just couldn't keep their hands off each other until they fell asleep, exhausted from the night's escapades.

Drew turns discreetly, so Ava can hurriedly put on her clothes from last night. "What time is it?" she asks, panic infusing her voice.

"Eight thirty," Drew replies back to them.

"Thank God," Ava sighs. "Ash should still be asleep."

"Speaking of Ashtyn, does she know about this little thing going on?"

"No!" Shiloh and Ava both exclaim at the same time. She pulls a shirt over her head. "And it's going to stay that way."

"You're asking me to lie to her?"

"No, I'm asking you to not say anything. There's a difference," Ava says. She's fully dressed now and tells Drew he can turn around.

When he does, he's frowning. "Do I even want to know?"

"No, probably not," Ava says, making her way toward the door. She turns around for a moment to look at Shiloh, gives him a small smile, then leaves. Why is it that every morning between them gets interrupted?

"What the actual fuck, man?" Drew asks, as soon as she's gone. Shiloh leans back in bed with a sigh, a hand coming up to rest on his forehead. "Was this the first time?"

"No," Shiloh admits.

"And is there a specific reason you're keeping this from Ashtyn?"

"It's Ava's reason, and I'm respecting it. I think they may have had a conversation about me being off limits. You know, because of the whole roommate thing. She kind of had a similar conversation with me about Ava."

"And you just couldn't stick to that?"

"It's Ava," Shiloh says, his voice coming out strained. "She's...she's Ava."

Drew gives him a small smile as he sits on the edge of the bed. "I know what you mean. Doesn't mean you should be lying to Ashtyn about it, though."

"I know, I know. We will tell her. Once we figure out what the fuck we're doing."

"What do you mean?"

"I mean, we haven't really gotten past the sleeping with each other part."

Drew rolls his eyes. "Well, I can't really help you there. I never get past the sleeping together part."

"Thanks," Shiloh says, dryly. "I'll be sure to take all of your advice from here on out." He sighs and sits up, trying not to mourn the emptiness of the bed too much.

"Well, sorry I interrupted your morning fun," Drew replies. Shiloh tosses a pillow at his head, which he swiftly catches. "Just know that my couch is no longer available to you. You've burnt that bridge."

"I'm not going to be needing your couch, asshole. It's going to be fine." He says it mostly to convince himself.

Chapter 32

Thankfully, Ashtyn is still sound asleep when Ava slips back into their room. She musses up the bed, so it looks like she slept in it, and then hops in the shower, trying to scrub the scent of Shiloh off her. She knows it's useless. He is seared on her skin like a tattoo. She knows she has to tell Ashtyn, and she will, but she will wait until after the wedding. She knows Ashtyn is already on edge, because of said wedding, and Ava doesn't need to make anything worse by telling her best friend that she's sleeping with their roommate. It can wait. She just has to play it cool around Shiloh. Surely, she can do that, right?

She stays in the shower longer than she should, knowing that when she gets out she'll have to lie to her best friend once again. They don't lie to each other. They just don't. But, Ava can't bring herself to say the words. They sit, unattended in her gut, causing misery by the second. She will tell her. Later. She finally turns the water off, feeling the remnants of Shiloh's hands on her. How could one man make her feel so good when no one before him could?

A knock on the door startles her. "Hurry up! I gotta pee!" Ashtyn calls.

"Coming," Ava replies, wrapping herself in a towel and opening the door to her friend. Ashtyn barrels in, not even waiting for Ava to leave before she pulls her pants down and sits on the toilet.

"Gross, Ash," she teases.

"Ava, I have peed in front of you more times than I've cried. Don't act so surprised."

By the time they're both showered, dressed, and downstairs, the breakfast bar has been utterly picked through.

"Oh, look, there's Drew and Shiloh," Ashtyn says, waving. "Maybe I can steal some of Drew's food."

Ava has to calm her racing heart as they make their way over to the two boys sitting in the corner of the breakfast area.

"Good morning, gorgeous," Drew says, as Ashtyn sits down next to him and plucks a piece of toast off his plate. She takes a big bite, smiling sweetly.

"When did you get here?"

"Just this morning. Walked in on quite a sight."

Shiloh chokes on his coffee as Ava looks discreetly away. Ashtyn gasps. "Shiloh! Did you have someone in your room this morning?"

"No, I did not," Shiloh says evenly, looking pointedly at his best friend.

"Oh, don't be shy," Ashtyn teases. "We're all family here."

"I didn't," Shiloh replies. Drew grins at him as he eats another forkful of eggs.

"Okay, keep your secrets."

"Oh, look, there's Brooke and Jordan!" Ava exclaims, diverting everyone's attention. The soon to be newlyweds make their way over to the table, grins on their faces. Jordan slaps Drew on the back. "Glad you made it, buddy."

"Wouldn't miss it for the world."

Brooke looks radiant as she embraces Ava and Ashtyn, her tiny arms squeezing them as hard as she can. "I'm so happy you're here."

"Brookie!" someone shouts from across the room, and Ava sees Brooke's three sisters heading in their direction. Bethany has her sights on Shiloh, and a ripple of jealousy surges through Ava. Brooke greets her sisters with hugs and kisses, oblivious to the way Ava's hands clench into fists under the table. Shiloh's foot nudges hers, and she looks up to see him smile at her. It's a smile meant just for her, to let her know she has nothing to worry about.

"Shiloh," Bethany purrs, plopping herself in the chair next to him. The chair Ava had purposely avoided. "How are you?" If she's upset about him ditching her halfway through the bachelor party, she doesn't show it.

"I'm good, Bethany," he replies, politely, not taking his eyes off his coffee. Ashtyn is looking between them, eyes narrowed. She's probably coming to the wrong conclusion, but Ava isn't going to be the one to correct her.

"Bethany," Ashtyn says. "Did you get here last night?"

"I did," she replies, face neutral. She's never been the biggest fan of Brooke's best friends.

"And did you have a good night?"

"Ashtyn," Shiloh warns.

Bethany smiles coolly. "It was fine. But, I'm hoping to have a better one tonight." Ava doesn't miss the way her gaze slides to Shiloh, and she has to physically grasp the chair to keep herself seated. This is going to be a long day.

* * *

The day is, in fact, long. Every hour feels like some new adventure. Driving to the venue, making sure everyone arrives on time, securing food, hanging up dresses, and ensuring everything runs smoothly for tomorrow. The venue, an old farmhouse that's been updated and modernized, is beautiful. String lights hang over every surface, tables are decorated with flowers, and the arch they are getting married under is exquisite. Ava takes everything in as they run through the procession during rehearsal. It's everything Brooke has ever dreamed of.

"It's incredible," Ava says to her friend. Brooke smiles, holding back tears as she tugs Ava into a crushing hug.

"I can't believe I'm getting married tomorrow," she muses.

"I can," Ashtyn says, sidling up to them. The wedding coordinator is yelling at them to get back to their places, but Brooke waves her away.

"Give me a minute to enjoy this with my friends," she says. The coordinator frowns, but allows it.

"She's going to have an aneurysm if everything isn't perfect tomorrow," Ashtyn teases.

"That's her job," Brooke replies, giggling. "She was highly recommended on all the bridal Facebook groups I joined."

"Well, then we better not disappoint her," Ava says, dragging them back to their designated spots. "We have all of tomorrow to enjoy this."

They run through everything a few times before they're released for dinner. Ava's stomach grumbles as she enters the hotel restaurant. She's barely eaten all day, and she's starving. She makes her way to the banquet table that offers an array of food for her to scarf down. She loads her plate and heads toward a lone table to sit by herself. Brooke and Jordan are making their rounds around the room, thanking people for coming. She's not sure where Ashtyn is. She must have lost her in all the chaos. All she can think about is the food on her plate and shoveling it into her face as fast as possible.

"Mind if I join you?"

Ava looks up at Shiloh, her cheeks full of food, and she swallows. "Please." If it had been anyone else seeing her stuff her face, she'd be embarrassed. But this is Shiloh. He's seen her eat almost every night for the past nine months.

He takes a seat next to her, and she tries not to stare at the way his dress shirt fits his frame perfectly. At the skin underneath that she ran her hands over just last night.

"Is this the first time you've sat down all day?" he asks, smiling at her.

"Pretty much," she admits. "Also the first full meal I've had since breakfast."

"God, wedding weekends are brutal."

Ava stills. "Was–was your wedding like this?"

Shiloh frowns, and she's afraid she might have upset him when he says, "A little. It was definitely smaller than this, but it was essentially the same. A million things to do, so little time. I just wanted to be married, but Scarlett wanted the whole shebang."

"I'm sorry, I shouldn't have asked," she starts, but Shiloh puts a hand on her arm.

"You can ask me anything," he says. "Even the hard stuff."

Ava gives him a small smile. "Is it hard? Being here?"

"I thought it would be," he admits. "Maybe tomorrow it might finally hit me, but it hasn't yet. Right now, I'm just happy to be sitting here with you."

Ava feels those damn butterflies in her stomach again, and she pushes her finished plate away from her. "Want to get out of here?"

"God, yes."

She doesn't see any sign of Ashtyn or her friends, so she takes Shiloh's hand, and they hurry toward the elevator. Once they're secured inside, her hands find his shirt, and she pulls him toward her hungrily. His hands find her hips immediately, and their lips crash together. Ava's back hits the wall of the elevator, as Shiloh's hands travel up her skirt and skim the edge of her panties. Her arms wind their way up and around his neck, pulling him as close to her as possible.

He is already hard against her. They're so lost in each other that they barely register the ding of the elevator as it lands on their floor, the doors open, and someone gasps in shock.

Ava pulls back with a start and sees Ashtyn, mouth open and eyes wide, standing at the entrance of the elevator, stock still.

"What the fuck is going on?" she asks, her face hard. Her eyes flick between Shiloh and Ava wrapped around each other, expression unreadable. The doors go to close, and Shiloh steps in to keep them open, Ava hurrying out onto the landing.

"Nothing," Ava says, stupidly.

"Ash—" Shiloh starts.

"Don't call me that." It's so harsh that Shiloh actually winces, and Ava wants to put her hand out to him, but she doesn't. "This really doesn't look like nothing."

Ava opens her mouth to say something, but nothing comes out. She tries again, but still, nothing happens.

Ashtyn's face contorts into one of anger. "How long?" When neither of them answers, Ashtyn crosses her arms. "I said, how long?"

"The night of the bachelor party," Shiloh says, and Ashtyn sucks in a breath. Ava closes her eyes guiltily. "But we kissed the night Ava came home from her date with..." He doesn't say Brad's name.

"Wow," Ashtyn says. "So, you've been lying to me this entire time, Ava? At lunch, when you told us all about that guy from the bar? Everything was a lie?"

"I—I didn't want to lie," she stutters. "I just didn't know how to tell you! I knew you'd be mad."

"Mad? I think that's an understatement." The tone of her voice conveys the sentiment.

"If you want to be mad at anyone, then be mad at me," Shiloh says. "Don't take it out on Ava."

"I told both of you not to do this. I made it pretty fucking clear."

"Ash," Ava starts, but her friend doesn't let her finish.

"Did either of you think about this? Or could you just not keep it in your pants any longer? What happens when this stops, huh? When you can't stand to be around each other anymore, because it ends badly? Then what? Shiloh moves out, and we're back to square one, not able to afford the rent? We lose the house? I fucking told you not to get attached!" She's shouting now, and it sets Ava's nerves on edge.

She starts to get angry. "And this is why I didn't tell you! Because you can't trust me to make my own decisions."

"Yeah, decisions that could fuck up not only your life but mine too," Ashtyn fires back, and Ava winces. Shiloh reaches out to put a hand on her arm, but she pulls away. Ashtyn continues, "I asked you not to fuck this up."

"So, that's what this is?" Ava asks. "Me fucking things up? Not me trying to be happy? Not me enjoying myself for the first time in a very long time? It's just Ava fucking things up, per usual!"

Ashtyn narrows her eyes. "You can't honestly expect me to believe that you two could be happy together. He doesn't want what you want, Ava!"

"How the fuck do you know what I want?" Shiloh asks, and his voice is harsher than Ava has ever heard it. "How could you, when all you ever do is push people away?"

"Push people away, huh? What is letting you live in our house to you, then? What is calling you my fucking family to you? I have never pushed you away, Shiloh. Just because I'm not jumping up and singing your praises every day, does not mean that I do not care for you. Which is why seeing you two sneaking behind my back really fucking hurts. You've made it abundantly clear that your ex fucked you up, and you don't know if you will ever be able to commit again. So, forgive me if I want to protect my best friend from having her heart broken."

Shiloh looks like he's about to say something when Ava interrupts.

"That's not your decision to make, Ashtyn. That's mine. Mine! I'm not one of your kindergartners that needs help learning how to read. I am a grown ass adult that can make her own decisions, whether they make sense to you or not."

Ashtyn is silent for a moment, staring at the ground, arms crossed against her chest. "Okay. Have your fun. Fuck each other's brains out until you get bored, but don't come crying to me when it falls apart. Until then, I don't want to look at either of you." She marches past them and into the elevator, pressing the button for the ground floor. The doors shut in their faces, leaving Ava and Shiloh alone. Ava's heart hammers in her chest, blood rushing to her ears.

"Ave." His voice is so soft, but she just can't hear it right now.

"I can't," she says, taking a step away from him. "I can't do this right now."

"Ava."

"No, Shiloh, I seriously can't do this right now. I mean, honestly, what the fuck were we thinking?" Tears start to stream down her face as everything crashes down around her.

"We? You were the one that wanted to keep it a secret." His words are like a slap to the face, and he immediately says, "I'm sorry. I didn't mean that."

"No, you're right. I mean, I was crazy to think this could ever work."

"Ava, what are you talking about? I'm–I want to try. I lo–I really like you."

Ava smiles at him sadly, tears blurring her vision. "It'll pass. It does for everyone else, anyway."

Before he can reply, she's running down the hallway and into the stairwell. She takes the stairs down to the bottom floor and flings herself out the back door, where the night sky greets her and her choking sobs.

Chapter 33

It's past midnight by the time Ashtyn returns to their room. Ava's been tossing and turning in bed for hours already, worried about where her friend might be, worried about how angry she truly is. She sits up but, Ashtyn immediately goes into the bathroom and turns on the shower without a word.

Ava knows she truly fucked up this time. Having Ashtyn catch them like that...words can't describe the amount of guilt and shame eating away at Ava right now. She leans back against the bed, listening to the shower run.

When Ashtyn is finished, she gets into her bed without even a glance in Ava's direction. The room is so eerily quiet, and Ava hates the heaviness that hangs between them. She barely sleeps a wink that night, and then her alarm is screaming at her to get up and meet Brooke in her suite. She realizes she must have slept at least a little, because Ashtyn isn't in the room when she sits up and rubs her eyes. Never, ever, has Ashtyn gotten up before Ava for anything. It stings, knowing her best friend doesn't even want to look at or speak to her. But, Ava swallows her feelings. Today is not about her. It's about Brooke, and she will not ruin it, no matter how much she's hurting.

She pads her way down the hall to Brooke's suite, where everyone is awake and bustling about. She's the last to arrive it seems, and Bethany narrows her eyes at her.

"Oh, Ave, thank goodness you're here!" Brooke exclaims. "You're up next for hair."

Ashtyn is in the makeup chair, eyes closed. She doesn't even seem to notice Ava's arrival. Brooke's other sisters, Melissa and Olivia, greet her, and they chat aimlessly amongst themselves. As Ava settles in the hair chair, she tries to put on her best smile. She knows she'll need to wear it for the rest of the day.

* * *

Luckily, the day is busy enough that Ava hardly has time to breathe, let alone think about any of her predicaments. She and Ashtyn smile for pictures, they act the part, they even laugh a few times. But once the camera is gone, Ashtyn is back to her cool demeanor. Ava tries to ignore it, focusing all her energy on Brooke instead and making sure she has the best day ever.

As they line up in their respective places outside the venue, Derek by her side, she sneaks a glance at Ashtyn. Even Drew is trying to cheer her up, but it's not working. She just scowls at him, which would be normal for her, but Ava knows it's not. Not today, anyway.

"Hey," Derek says, nudging her. "You okay?"

Ava turns to look at her friend. "Yeah, sorry, I guess my mind's just preoccupied."

"It feels like forever since we've hung out. I guess I've been preoccupied too."

"It's okay, Derek," she says, squeezing his arm. "You have a pretty good reason for being busy. I don't think I ever told you, but I think you and Daisy are perfect together."

Derek actually blushes. "Sometimes, when I wake up in the middle of the night, and she's right next to me, I have to pinch myself. Like I can't believe someone like her could love me." Ava feels tears well in her eyes. She thinks back to the beginning of the year, of her crush on Derek, how her heart would stutter in his presence. Now, all she can think of is Shiloh. "And I have you to thank for it."

"Me?"

"Yeah, it was you that paired us up together that night at your birthday. You were the push we needed." The night Ava had paired herself up with Shiloh, in order to get rid of her crush on Derek.

She's about to say something when Brooke's wedding coordinator signals that it's time to begin. Ava sighs and interlocks her arm with Derek. "Glad I could be of service," she whispers, and he laughs in response, covering her hand with his.

The doors open, the orchestra begins playing, and the wedding party proceeds down the aisle. Ava tries not to look for Shiloh in the crowd. Instead, she focuses on Jordan, smiling radiantly as he watches everyone walk down the aisle. Once they're all settled, the crowd rises and the music swells, Brooke and her father emerging at the entrance. She's absolutely gorgeous, and Jordan's smile warbles as a tear slips down his cheek. Brooke also has tears in her eyes.

Ava keeps her gaze trained on Brooke and Jordan as they join hands, looking deeply into each other's eyes, utterly in love. As they say their vows, promising to love each other forever, Ava feels a tear slip down her own cheek, and she risks a glance toward the crowd. Of course, she finds Shiloh immediately. As if he can sense her gaze, his eyes shift to her, and their eyes meet. She sucks in a breath at his beauty. Their gaze holds, as Brooke and Jordan kiss, and they are declared husband and wife.

* * *

Ava sits on the edge of the sink in the bathroom, trying desperately not to cry. This is Brooke's day. She should be out there celebrating her friend, and instead, she's hiding, feeling miserable for herself. She hates it.

The reception is in full swing, and the music pounds throughout the venue. Ava's head throbs, and she rubs her temples, trying not to think about going back out there.

A beautiful, blonde woman in a blood red dress enters, and Ava looks away, trying to hide her tear-stained face. It doesn't seem to work, because the woman stops, her eyes going to Ava. "Oh, sorry," she says. "I didn't mean to intrude."

"No, you're good," Ava replies, keeping her voice steady. "Just needed to get away from it all."

"Yeah, I understand that," she says, going to the sink to fix her makeup. She gives Ava a small smile. "You all looked beautiful in your bridesmaid dresses."

"Oh, thank you. Are you friends with the bride or groom?" Ava asks, dabbing at her eyes so she doesn't ruin her makeup. She doesn't recognize the woman.

"Oh, uh, neither really, if I'm honest. My fiancée, he's old friends with the groom's family. I'm just here as his plus one." That's when Ava notices the ginormous rock on her finger.

"Wow, that's a beautiful ring."

"Isn't it?" The woman gushes, examining the ring intimately. "My first marriage, it wasn't very special, so I'm very lucky to have found someone that did such a good job with the proposal."

Ava's not sure why, but she asks, "Was it romantic? The proposal, I mean."

"Oh, so romantic! It was the day I finally signed my divorce papers from my first husband. Joshua surprised me with a candlelit dinner on the terrace of our favorite restaurant, roses everywhere, and then popped the question with dessert. It was straight out of a movie."

Ava smiles politely. "That sounds perfect." But she doesn't really mean it. She's sure the proposal was perfect for this woman, but Ava finds herself thinking that if it was a movie, she probably wouldn't want to watch it.

"What about you?" The woman asks. "Anyone special in your life?"

Ava feels a pang of loneliness as she thinks of Shiloh. "Um, it's complicated. Hence the hiding in the bathroom."

The woman smiles at her sadly. "I'm sorry. I didn't mean to pry."

"No, it's okay. I just..." Ava pauses. "I think I messed a lot of shit up."

"Mind if I offer some advice?"

"Please."

"I speak from experience when I say I know about messing up a relationship. I didn't fight for my first marriage. I kind of just let it implode. I did a lot of things I regret. I know I can't complain now, because I've found someone new that I love very much, but I do regret how much I didn't do for my first relationship. If this is something you want, you have to fight for it. You can't just let it slip by you while you watch."

"It's just so complicated," Ava says, quietly.

"Is it? Or are you making it complicated?"

Ava huffs out a laugh. "Can it be both?"

The woman smiles. "It can. Do you love this person?"

Ava sucks in a breath. "I don't know. I—I think so. But I'm scared to admit it." She's never felt this feeling before. Everyone she's ever been with... it's never felt like love. Not until Shiloh. She's loved him, the moment they met, but is she *in* love with him? She thinks she might be.

"Aren't we all? But you know what's scarier than admitting it? Not admitting it, and missing out on something that could be the best thing in your life."

Ava feels a sprig of hope bloom in her chest at the woman's words. "Wow, who knew you could get such good advice from a stranger in a bathroom."

"Women's bathrooms are the best places to get advice," the woman laughs.

"I'm Ava, by the way," she says, sticking out her hand.

The woman takes it with a smile. "Scarlett."

Ava's smile slips from her face, as if on instinct, and her hand goes limp. There's no way. There's absolutely no way. 'Wha—what did you say?"

"My name's Scarlett. Scarlett Brooks, but soon to be Samuels."

She drops Scarlett's hand and takes a step away, feeling the air in the room start to constrict. "I—I have to go," she manages to get out before stumbling for the door. She runs out of the bathroom and straight into a chest she's all too familiar with.

"Hey," Shiloh starts, his hands going up to steady her. Ava hears Scarlett calling her name as she hurries after her. Her voice, it's like a beacon, because Shiloh's head snaps up immediately, and he stills. Ava feels his grip on her arms falter. Time freezes. She turns to see Scarlett stare at her, and then at Shiloh, his arms steadying her. Something clicks in her eyes and they go wide, her face turning to one of recognition. Ava retreats, stepping out of Shiloh's embrace and leaving them both far, far behind as she runs. Runs anywhere but here.

* * *

Scarlett. She's right in front of him. And Ava...Ava's gone. She's no longer in his grasp. Scarlett is looking at him curiously, as if she knows something he doesn't.

"Oh my god," she says as recognition crosses her face. "It's you.

The person she was talking about was you."

"Wha—what are you doing here?" Shiloh manages to get out. He feels unable to breath. He hasn't seen her in so long, and her presence is like an elephant standing on his chest. The last time he saw her was when he left their house for the final time. She hadn't even looked out the window to watch him go.

"I'm Joshua's plus one," she says, gently, and he vaguely recognizes the doctor's name. "I went to the bathroom to freshen up and struck up a conversation with Ava."

Hearing her name on Scarlett's lips is like a bucket of ice water dumped straight on his head. "What did you say to her? Why is she upset?"

"I'm assuming because she realized who I was about two seconds ago. And if you are the person she was telling me about, then I understand her reaction. I can only imagine what she's heard of me."

"I don't know what you're talking about."

"She—" Scarlett stops, assessing her words. She was always so careful with her words. "She's fond of you. And judging by your... demeanor, I'm assuming you share the sentiment."

"You don't know anything," Shiloh says, anger building in his chest. "You don't know anything about her, and you don't know anything about me. Not anymore." He wants to run after Ava, but his feet are planted to the floor, unable to move.

"Shiloh," she starts, and he's about to interrupt her when she says, "I'm sorry."

He stops and stares at her. She looks almost the same as she did when she was seventeen. Her long blonde hair cascades down her back, her blue eyes soft and full of wisdom. He notices the diamond on her left hand, glinting under the lights, so very different from the one she wore for him. It should hurt, but for some reason it leaves him feeling nothing. He thinks of his own ring at the bottom of the river.

"I'm sorry," Scarlett says again. "For everything. For how it ended between us. For how I acted. For scaring you with an annulment. For not facing you at the signing. I should have said this to you sooner, I know that now. I'm—I'm sorry. I'm so sorry."

It's the first time she's said sorry about what happened between them. He knows it won't fully heal the scar that he will forever wear on his heart, but it does feel like a start.

"Scarlett," he says, his throat constricting, tears pricking his eyes. He swallows, trying to compose himself. "Thank you. I'm sorry, too."

She takes a small step forward and grasps his hand in hers. It's jarring, but he doesn't pull away, because it's also so familiar. "She's beautiful."

Shiloh knew, from the first day he met her, that Ava is beautiful. But he also knows she is smart and kind and silly and incredible in so many ways. He thinks of the way she sets up her classroom, inviting to all kids no matter what. How she cares for her friends. How she struck up a friendship with a stranger in a bathroom. How he loves her. How he has always loved her.

Words falter on his tongue. He thought he'd have so much to say if he ever saw Scarlett again, but it's all died out, now. There's nothing left to say.

"Go," Scarlett says, as if she understands. "Go get her." She squeezes his hand one last time, and then she's walking back to the reception without a backward glance. Shiloh knows this is the last time he will ever see Scarlett, and he doesn't feel sad anymore. He feels hopeful.

He rushes in the direction that Ava went, hoping to find her. He makes his way outside, the cool October air chilling his bones. The parking lot is empty of people, and he slumps against the wall, slowly lowering himself to the floor. His heart races, and he tries to steady his breathing, taking big gulps of cold air into his lungs.

"Sorry, this hiding place is already taken." He jumps at Ashtyn's voice. She's hidden by the evening darkness, sitting on the curb next to him, knees up to her chest. She looks just like he feels at this moment.

"Ashtyn," he starts.

"Just leave me alone, Shiloh," she snaps. Her voice is warbled, her breathing erratic. She can't seem to catch her breath, no matter how hard she tries.

"Hey, look at me," he says, kneeling down in front of her. Her eyes are red-rimmed, although no tears seem to have leaked down her cheeks. "Look at me and try to breathe."

"What the fuck do you think I'm trying to do!?" she exclaims, her voice coming out as a shriek. Her chest rises and falls frantically, as she tries to keep her breathing steady. It's not working.

"Breathe with me," he says, taking her hands in his. He doesn't care if she's mad at him. He doesn't care if she said she didn't want to see him again. She is his family. "Look at me and breathe as I do." He takes a deep breath, and she tries to mimic him. She stares at him, her green eyes intense even in the dim light. He takes deep, steadying breaths, trying to help Ashtyn calm down.

"You're okay," he says. In a way, he was telling himself the words as well. "You are okay. Just breathe." Ashtyn grips his hands tightly, slowly getting her breathing back to normal as she takes deep breaths of air.

It takes a few minutes, but it works, looking at each other and breathing together. Ashtyn's breath comes back to her, and she sighs deeply, closing her eyes and resting her head on Shiloh's shoulder.

"You're okay," he says.

Ashtyn nods, and then pulls back, "Thank you."

"Of course. I'm always here for you, no matter what."

They're silent for a moment. There's so much he wants to tell her, but he doesn't know how to say any of it. He opens his mouth, but

Ashtyn speaks first. "I really fucking hate weddings."

"Yeah, me too." He doesn't pry, doesn't expect her to offer up any information, but she surprises him.

"His name's Brandon. My ex. He's the reason I hate weddings."

Shiloh stills at her words. She grips his arm in her hand, as if she needs to hold onto him before saying anything further. She takes a very deep breath. "He was my high school sweetheart." She says it with contempt, like she hates admitting it. "We'd been together since freshman year, and we'd planned on going to college together, but we didn't get accepted to the same school. So, we did long distance, because all stupid teenagers think they can survive long distance. Five hours didn't seem like the end of the world, until he kept making excuses not to come see me on the weekends. I just figured he was busy, you know?" Shiloh doesn't say anything. He lets her continue at her own pace.

"One day, he calls me. Tells me it's over, and that he's found someone else. Just like that. Two months later, I get an invitation to their wedding. I got a fucking invitation to their wedding!" She yells it, letting the night air absorb her voice. "Two months after we broke up. Two fucking months."

"And you know what I did? I went. I went to their stupid, fucking wedding. I sat in the audience, and I watched this beautiful woman walk down the aisle toward him. And when the minister asked if anyone had any objections...I stood up."

Shiloh actually feels his head snap toward her, and she laughs bitterly. "I fucking stood up. Everyone in that church looked at me, horrified. Do you know what it feels like to have a hundred people looking at you, all at once?"

She pauses, and Shiloh breathes out, "No, I don't." He'd barely had fifty people at his own wedding.

"All I could see was Brandon. I didn't look at anyone else. I just stared at him, and when he looked at me...he just shook his head, so slowly that I thought I was imagining it. It was like I didn't even recognize him. I'd known him almost my whole life, loved him for so long, and I couldn't even recognize him anymore. I ran out of there as fast as I could, and for one crazy, insane moment, I thought he was coming after me. But he didn't. He stayed up there, and he got married. I mean, what did I expect him to do?"

"Ashtyn," Shiloh starts, but she glares at him.

"I don't want your pity." Her voice is pained. "I'm telling you this so you know why I push people away, because all they ever do is hurt you. And I don't want anyone to ever feel the pain that I felt when I stood up at that stupid wedding. When the person who I thought loved me most looked right through me, like I didn't even exist. That's—that's why I worry about Ava so much. Because she loves so loudly, and I'm scared she's going to get hurt. I don't want anyone to ever look at her like Brandon looked at me. I'm scared she wouldn't survive it." She sniffles and wipes her nose on her dress.

Shiloh decides to be truthful with Ashtyn, since she shared something so personal with him. He clears his throat. "I saw Scarlett tonight."

Ashtyn's head snaps up. "You saw her?"

Shiloh nods. "And apparently, so did Ava."

At her name, Ashtyn frowns. "What do you mean?"

"I think they met in the bathroom. And you know Ava, she befriends everyone. I just don't think she knew who she befriended until it was too late."

"Is she okay?"

"I don't know. I was on my way to find her." Shiloh feels Ashtyn tense and pull away. "Ashtyn, I'm so sorry. I–I didn't mean to keep this from you. And after everything you just told me—"

Ashtyn puts her hand up to stop him. "I know. I didn't tell you to make you feel bad."

Shiloh shakes his head. "I didn't think you did. But, still, we shouldn't have hidden it from you. I'm just so scared of ruining things like I always do. I'm scared of not only hurting Ava, but hurting you too. And that's the last thing I want to do."

Ashtyn looks at him intensely. "Do you..." she lets her words dangle, waiting for him to interpret them.

"I love her," he breathes. "I love her so much, I feel like I can't breathe until I tell her. And I know I don't deserve her. I know she deserves only the best in the world, but I love her, selfishly and wholeheartedly. And I will spend my life trying to prove to her, and you, how much I love her."

He's about to continue when Ashtyn crushes him into a hug. Her tiny body is surprisingly strong as she wraps her arms around him. It was worth the wait for one of Ashtyn's hugs. She holds him to her so fiercely, he thinks she might never let go. He brings his arms around her, holding her close, reveling in the feeling.

"Looks like I finally earned my hug," he says into her hair.

Ashtyn pulls back, tears in her eyes. "You are the best for her." She pulls him into another hug, and Shiloh melts at her embrace. "You always have been."

"I love you, too, you know?" He says, squeezing her.

"Yeah, yeah, I know. I love you too." Shiloh laughs, and Ashtyn stands, holding her hand out to him. "Come on, let's go get our girl."

Chapter 34

Ava's sitting in the gazebo, where the wedding party took pictures just a few hours ago, when she hears a branch crack. Her head snaps up, and she tries to wipe away her tears. The twinkle lights strung upon the pillars illuminate a small figure heading toward her.

"You could have picked a closer hiding spot," Ashtyn says, making her way up to the gazebo. "Took me forever to find you."

"Ashtyn?" Ava questions, her brows furrowing. "What are you doing?"

"Looking for you, obviously." She plops down next to Ava and puts her arm around her. "We've got some things to talk about."

"Ashtyn, I'm so sorry. I should've never kept a secret like that from you. I never meant to hurt you. I'm so, so, so sorry." She's starting to babble, words spilling from her mouth before she even has time to process them.

Ashtyn squeezes Ava to her, tightly. "I'm sorry, too."

"You don't have anything to apologize for."

"Actually, I do," Ashtyn says. "I didn't realize how much you two actually mean to each other."

"Ash—"

"Let me finish," she says, looking at Ava. "You are my best friend in the entire world. I love you more than pretty much everyone. And so, sometimes, when I think I am protecting you, I'm actually hindering you. I can't put my own bad experiences onto you. Or onto Shiloh. That's not fair to either of you. It's not fair to project my own fears onto your decisions. You—you deserve better than that."

Ava holds her friend close. "Still, I shouldn't have kept it a secret."

"But I understand why you did. And for that, I am sorry."

"Never again," Ava whispers, and Ashtyn nods against her shoulder. "I promise."

They sit like that, arms wrapped around each other, as the cool night air swirls around them.

"I, uh, talked to Shiloh. I told him about Brandon."

Ava gasps. "What?"

"He found me mid panic attack and helped me calm down. It just all came out after that. I figured he deserved to know, since he's pretty much family now. Then, he told me about you running into Scarlett."

Ava's cheeks burn. "What are the fucking chances?"

Ashtyn laughs. "Of you making a random friend in the bathroom? Pretty high, I would guess."

"Yeah, I don't think I would say I made a friend. Besides, you probably don't have to worry about...me and Shiloh. I fucked everything up."

Ashtyn sighs dramatically. "Yeah, I don't think you did."

Ava looks at her friend quizzically. And then she sees, over Ashtyn's shoulder, Shiloh striding toward the gazebo.

"What is he doing here?"

"I think he has something he wants to tell you," Ashtyn says. She pats Ava's shoulder and kisses her cheek. "Listen to him. And know that I love you no matter what. Always." And then she's gone, making her way back toward the reception hall.

Shiloh stands a few feet from Ava, hands in his pockets. She stands and takes a tentative step toward him.

"Hi," she says, shyly.

"Hi," he replies.

Anxiety shoots through her system, and she doesn't know what she wants to say. "Shiloh," she breathes.

"I'm sorry," he says. He stays a few paces away from her, giving her space. "I'm sorry...for a lot of things."

"Shiloh, you don't have anything to apologize for. I'm the one that ran away. I'm the one that wanted to keep us a secret." She almost stumbles on the word "us."

"And you had every right to. I understand why."

Ava takes a deep breath, closing her eyes. "She's beautiful."

She hears Shiloh take a step forward. "Ava, look at me."

She shuts her eyes harder, shaking her head furiously. "I—I can't."

"Ava."

The way he says her name... she opens her eyes, taking in every inch of him as he stands in front of her. His hand caresses her cheek. He swallows and takes a deep breath. "I thought that when I saw Scarlett again, I would feel...something. But, I didn't. All I could think about was you, and how I needed to...

"Ava, I love you." His words stop any other thoughts that were bubbling to her lips. He continues, "I love you. I love you so much, and every day when I wake up, all I want to do is tell you that I love you." Her eyes travel up toward his face until they settle on his eyes. They stare back at her intently.

"I thought I was never allowed to love again," he says. His voice wavers, but he continues. "After everything that happened the first time, I figured love was just not in the cards for me again. That I didn't deserve to love again. And then I met you. And every day I woke up and got to see you, I felt myself becoming whole again. Every day I spent with you, I fell deeper and harder than I ever could have imagined. I finally felt what it was like to love again. Every time I touch you feels like a privilege. A privilege that I cannot believe you give me. And every day I want to work so that I may keep that privilege. I know that you deserve someone better than me. I know that. But I selfishly want you. I—I want you. I choose you. I choose to feel it all with you, Ava. The good, the bad, all of it. I want all of it with you even if I might feel pain again. Because you are worth it. You are worth feeling every emotion on this earth a thousand times over. I lo—I love you."

She looks at him with tears in her eyes, her heart thudding in her chest. "You're wrong," she says, quietly and Shiloh winces, face falling.

"No—"

She holds up a hand to stop him. "There is no one better than you. You sell yourself short, Shiloh Brooks. You say I don't deserve someone like you, but how on earth can that be true when you are the best person I have ever met? You say touching me is a privilege, but the real privilege is being loved by you and getting to love you in return. You deserve love, Shiloh, and I hope to be worthy enough to love you. Because I do. You are the only person that has ever made me feel like this. Like my heart might burst out of my chest just by looking at you. Like I want to kiss you and never stop. Like—like I love you more than I ever thought possible."

The look that crosses his face is the most beautiful thing Ava has ever seen. He takes her face in his hands, and he kisses her like nothing else matters.

"I love you," she breathes, and she lets those words wash over her body and settle in her bones.

"I love you," he replies, kissing every freckle on her face. "I want to spend every day telling you how much I love you. How much I adore every aspect of you, Ava Marshall."

"You're going to get sick of me," she teases between kisses.

He silences her with a kiss so long and deep, she thinks she might drown in it. "I could never be sick of you, even if I tried."

Ava smiles as she wraps her arms around his neck. "So, Shiloh Brooks, you really want to do this with me?"

"Yes, Ava, I do. I really do." He picks her up and kisses her like he never wants to let her go. Ava feels, for the first time in her entire life, what a true happily ever after feels like.

DECEMBER

Epilogue

The house is alive with laughter. It's New Years Eve, and all of their friends have come over to celebrate with them. Brooke and Jordan, with matching wedding bands adorning their fingers. Parker and Damien, supplying an exorbitant number of desserts. Derek and Daisy, permanent smiles etched on their faces every time they look at each other. Drew, who can't keep his eyes off Ashtyn. Ashtyn, who is pointedly ignoring him. Mattie, who's taking every moment of Christmas Break to drink as much as he possibly can. And finally, Shiloh and Ava, who are currently killing it in Blockbuster.

Ava holds Jess up over her head, and Shiloh shouts, "*The Lion King*!"

"Yes!" she shrieks, and Jess meows as if she's happy they got the point. Ava puts the almost one year old cat back on the ground, and then looks at the final card. "Okay, this movie made you and Ashtyn debate the ethics of robots for like two hours."

"Easy. *Terminator*."

"We win!" Ava exclaims, throwing her cards up and launching herself into Shiloh's arms, kissing him. The entire room groans. They've become an unstoppable team the last two months, the undefeated champions of the game. A major improvement from their first time being teammates.

"You've got to be kidding me," Drew says. "I swear, you have to be cheating."

"Watch more movies, loser," Ava jests, and Drew flips her off playfully. She giggles, and Shiloh feels it reverberate through his whole body. He still can't believe he gets to love her.

"I'm about to ban this game from our household," Ashtyn says, as she packs up the cards.

"What about that new game I got you for your birthday, Ash?" Daisy asks.

"Also, not allowed. Those two," Ashtyn points between Shiloh and Ava, "have become the absolute worst people to play games with. They always win."

"What can I say?" Ava starts. "We make an incredible team." Shiloh presses a kiss to her temple, and Ava radiates with happiness. She still can't believe she gets to love him.

"Gosh, you two are so cute," Daisy says, smiling.

"It's disgusting, actually," Ashtyn teases, though her voice is filled with fondness, and Ava sticks her tongue out at her. Jess winds herself happily between their feet, purring.

"At least Jess is happy for us."

The TV plays softly in the background, music wafting from the speakers, as the world celebrates the coming of a new year. The countdown to midnight is imminent, and everyone mingles, sipping drinks and chatting amongst themselves now that the game has finished.

"Any hopes and dreams for the new year, Ave?" Shiloh asks, wrapping an arm around her waist. They've retreated away from everyone against the back wall.

She looks up at him wistfully. "I don't know. I feel like I achieved a lot of them this year."

He smiles down at her. "Yeah, I know the feeling."

"But, if I had to pick...I hope you and the girls make District. I hope Derek and Daisy get engaged next. And I hope..." she narrows her eyes toward Ashtyn and Drew, who are laughing together. "I hope Ashtyn sees what is right in front of her."

"Those are hopes for other people, you goof. What about you?"

"I hope to wake up next to you every morning."

"Well, *that,* I think we can do," Shiloh says as he picks her up and spins her around playfully. She giggles as he kisses her, letting her know that he's not going anywhere. "I love you."

"I love you," she says, truly meaning it.

"Ugh, save the kissing for midnight," Ashtyn says, sidling up to the couple.

"And who are you going to kiss?" Ava asks, coyly.

Ash narrows her eyes at her friend. "You, if you don't knock it off." Ava puckers her lips out, and Ashtyn shoves her away playfully.

"Don't worry, Ash," Mattie says, slightly slurring as he slumps next to them on the wall. "I'm not kissing anyone either."

"No one said I was sad about it!" she exclaims, throwing her arms up. "Geez, you'd think I was miserable being single."

"It's almost midnight!" Jordan exclaims, and the group gathers around the TV to watch the countdown.

"Ten...nine...eight..."

Shiloh looks down at Ava whose eyes are sparkling, surrounded by her friends and loved ones. He doesn't even look at the countdown, only at her, as she cheers when the clock strikes midnight. She turns to him, her face alight with happiness, and he presses his lips to hers. This is all he could have ever hoped for.

When Ava pulls back from her kiss with Shiloh, she sees the most shocking sight of her entire life. Ashtyn and Drew, their lips pressed together so lightly, his hand caressing her cheek. They pull apart slowly, and Ava averts her gaze, hoping to give them privacy in a room full of people. It's not like they were trying to hide it, anyway. She buries her face in Shiloh's shirt and whispers, "You are never going to believe what just happened."

But before she can say anything, Mattie is pulling them into a joint hug, screaming, "Happy New Year!"

Ava embraces him and kisses his cheek. "Happy New Year, Mattie."

He leans down, so only she hears him say, "Thank you for being there for him. He's lucky to have you." Ava squeezes him hard, trying not to cry at his words.

Shiloh holds them each under one of his arms, his fingers interlaced with Ava's. "We gonna see you graduate this year, little brother?"

Mattie chuckles. "God, I can only hope. I'm so fucking ready to be done with school."

"What are you going to do after?" Ava asks.

"I have no fucking clue. I just know I'll be free from the shackles of school, my father, and everything else."

Ava doesn't pry, but she feels Shiloh tense slightly. He hasn't talked to his parents since the day he cut them off. He spent Thanksgiving and Christmas with Ava, Ashtyn, and their families. Mattie had been invited, but he spent both holidays with the Brooks family. Ava has a feeling it was a tense couple of months, because Mattie immediately opened and chugged a beer when he arrived at the house tonight. Shiloh told her not to worry about it, but she can't help it. She loves Mattie so much, and she doesn't like that he's still ensnared in the clutches of Mr. Brooks. She knows Shiloh shares the feeling.

"Well, whatever you end up doing, I know you're going to be amazing," Ava says.

Mattie lifts his beer up to her in appreciation and smiles. Before it reaches his lips, Ashtyn snatches it out of his hands and chugs it. She drains it to the last drop.

"I would have gotten you one if you'd asked," Mattie teases, but Ashtyn just shoves the bottle back in his hands and heads toward the kitchen, probably in search of more alcohol.

"What was that about?" Shiloh asks, and Ava just shakes her head.

"I'll be right back," she says, and follows after Ashtyn. She finds her friend frantically filling her champagne glass all the way to the top.

"Don't even say it," Ashtyn warns, not looking up from her glass.

"I wasn't going to."

Ashtyn slumps to the floor, back to the kitchen counter. She gulps her drink hurriedly. Ava sits next to her, placing a comforting hand on her leg. Ashtyn drains the drink and exhales dramatically. "I'm guessing you saw."

"I did," Ava replies, truthfully. "But we don't have to talk about it if you don't want to."

"I don't. I want to drink."

"Then drink we shall." Ava pulls the bottle of champagne down from the island and fills Ashtyn's glass back up. She takes a swig herself, straight from the bottle. They sit in silence for a moment, the chatter from the living room the only sound. Drew's boisterous laugh echoes throughout the room, and Ashtyn closes her eyes, finishing her second drink. A figure enters the kitchen, and Ava looks up to see Shiloh heading toward them. He plops down next to Ashtyn, so she's in-between them.

"We're drinking, not talking," Ashtyn says, and Shiloh smiles.

"Sounds like my kind of party." He takes the bottle from Ava and takes a swig. To her surprise, Ashtyn actually leans her head against Shiloh's shoulder. He presses his cheek to her hair, smiling at Ava over her head. Jess joins the party, coming to sit on Ashtyn's lap with a small meow. She scratches her under the chin, and Jess purrs happily in response.

"It's almost the one-year anniversary of you moving in," Ashtyn says, quietly.

"And what a year it's been," Shiloh replies. 'I—I don't know where I would be if I hadn't met you two."

"Don't tell me you two are the ones being sentimental," Ava teases.

"It's New Years," Ashtyn says. "We're allowed. Besides, I should tell you both that I love you at least once a year."

Ava laughs, "You tell me every day."

"Yeah, but now I have competition."

This makes Shiloh laugh, and he wraps his arm around Ashtyn. "I love you both very much." Ava puts her own arm around Ashtyn, so they squeeze her between them, Jess napping on her lap. It's perfect.

Shiloh, Ashtyn, and Ava sit like that, arms around each other, laughing and smiling together, long into the New Year.

ACKNOWLEDGMENTS

I actually cannot believe I am writing the acknowledgments to my second novel. The idea for this story came to me in high school, where my best friend and I wrote roughly one hundred pages for these characters. Needless to say, it's come a long way since then.

First, as always, thank you to my family. My parents, for instilling in me the need to always be reading. My sisters, for being pretty cool. My grandparents, German and Texan, I love you guys.

My incredible husband, Isaac, who has helped me achieve my dreams time and time again. Loving you is a privilege I will cherish for the rest of my life.

Grace, this book is dedicated to you for a reason. Sometimes, I think the universe made you especially for me. Thank you for inspiring me, believing in me, and for helping me nurture these characters to their full potential. Thank you for being my best friend in the whole world.

Emily, wow. Who would have thought we'd end up here? I feel incredibly grateful to call you my friend. Thank you for helping me shape this novel into the best version it can be, as well as designing the cover. You inspire me every day, and I will forever be in awe of your greatness.

My bananas, as always. Forever my anchors in this world. I love you so much.

Sumer, thank you for beta reading once again! I love sharing my ideas with you. You are such a special friend that I appreciate so much.

My friends, Jenna, Mel, Clarisa, Brenna, and Danielle. You are each so special to me. Thank you for the endless book club discussions, and the love you show me everyday.

Finally, to the readers, old and new! Thank you for picking up this book and giving it a chance. You are the reason my dreams come true every day.

About the Author

A.J. Woods is a native Texan where she participated in Girl Scouts, AYSO soccer, and German Club when she was a teenager. After high school, she attended Angelo State University where she majored in English with a specialization in Creative Writing and double minored in German and Gender Studies. She spent one semester studying abroad in Hannover, Germany. After graduation, she pursued her master's degree in English Literature and graduated December of 2020. She has dreamed of being a writer since the fourth grade. This is her second novel.

You can connect with me on:

- https://ajwoodsauthor.com
- https://x.com/ajwoodsauthor
- https://www.facebook.com/profile.php?id=61563303127340
- https://open.spotify.com/user/31mxwvmdvartl6nl23lvdcbhb62i

Also by A.J. Woods

The Foreign Exchange

Marlee Adams is not looking for love. All she wants to do is not think about the fact that her mother is dead, hang out with her friends at the local diner, and drop out of school forever. She's definitely not looking to fall in love with the new, very hot, and very unavailable German exchange student, Maximilian Hoffman. But, love has a funny way of sneaking up on you when you least expect it. Spanning years and continents, Marlee finds herself inexplicably drawn toward Max for reasons she can't explain, all while dealing with grief, managing friendships, and most importantly, falling in love.